THE
PRAIRIE
CHICKEN
DANCE
TOUR

the
prairie
chicken
dance
tour

dawn
dumont

Freehand Books acknowledges the financial support for its publishing program provided by the Canada Council for the Arts and the Alberta Media Fund, and by the Government of Canada through the Canada Book Fund.

Freehand Books
515 – 815 1st Street SW   Calgary, Alberta   T2P 1N3
www.freehand-books.com

Book orders: UTP Distribution
5201 Dufferin Street   Toronto, Ontario   M3H 5T8
Telephone: 1-800-565-9523 Fax: 1-800-221-9985
utpbooks@utpress.utoronto.ca utpdistribution.com

Library and Archives Canada Cataloguing in Publication
Title: The Prairie Chicken dance tour / Dawn Dumont.
Names: Dumont, Dawn, 1978– author.
Identifiers: Canadiana (print) 20210241950 | Canadiana (ebook) 20210241969 | ISBN 9781988298870 (softcover) | ISBN 9781988298887 (EPUB) | ISBN 9781988298894 (PDF)
Classification: LCC PS8607.U445 P73 2021 | DDC C813/.6—dc23

Edited by Deborah Willis
Book design by Natalie Olsen
Printed on FSC® recycled paper and bound in Canada by Rapido Books

For my two greatest teachers, Vincent and Alicia,
and all the little ones who never made it home.

CHAPTER 1

Day 1

Sunday, June 11, 1972
Saskatoon, Saskatchewan

JOHN

It was John Greyeyes's first time flying. And he wasn't exactly nervous. More curious than anything, at this airport with so many people coming and going, shooting him curious looks as they passed. All monias. Not even a single brown, black, red, or yellow shade to draw the eye, which meant that he stood out like a donkey at a horse track with his long braids snaking out from under his cowboy hat down the sides of his chambray shirt. John hadn't put too much thought into his attire. Someone could choke on the dust from his boots and, from the draft he was feeling, he was pretty sure his faded jeans had more than one hole and maybe one more wash left in them.

His clothes were clean, though; his mom had made sure of that. She'd come over last night, convinced that a bachelor like him had forgotten the important things in his packing. She was right. "Never even packed any gitch," she scolded him.

"Europe's been around a long time, pretty sure they have underwear figured out," he said.

"People over there are different," she told him. "Crazy. Smaller. Loud."

"Yes, Mom, they're all leprechauns."

She didn't find that too funny. 'Course Lenore Greyeyes was the type who couldn't laugh when she was nervous, and she was nervous about sending her "baby" all the way to "that Europe" even though he was a grown man of thirty.

"Hey, ratface!"

John turned and saw his brother stroll through the front doors. When they were younger they'd almost looked like twins. But Amos had taken another path since then. While John had become a rancher, Amos had elbowed his way into becoming the Chief of the Fineday Reserve. His hair was cut into a neat brush cut, his pants were slacks, and he wore a suit jacket. No tie, which meant he wasn't on his way to a white-guy meeting.

"As if, bear-gut." John looked pointedly at Amos's midsection. Amos was getting quite the pot-belly, evidence that he spent too much time sitting around in boardrooms making decisions about problems on the reserve and then having no money to turn the decisions into actions. That kind of life would slowly drive John insane. But Amos thrived on it — a bit too much, it appeared.

Amos stopped a foot in front of him and looked his younger brother in the right eye. He examined people's eyes at length; John had told him a million times that it was annoying as hell. But Amos said he needed to "see a man," before he could talk to him. After a moment of communing with John's reluctant spirit, Amos said, "Thank you for doing this."

John would have blushed if he weren't so dark. "Yeah, well, it's Europe. I should be thanking you."

Amos laughed. "No need to lie, bro!"

John smiled. They both knew John was full of shit. Amos had called him three days before with the ask. "I'm in trouble, little bro. You have to help me."

John had been breathless after running in to answer the phone —

he'd been cleaning saddles on the front porch when he heard the phone; it almost never rang unless someone was having a baby, getting hitched, or dead.

John's first instinct when he heard his brother's taut voice was to hang up. But then his brother twisted the knife and his voice dropped to the volume of a summer breeze: "You owe me."

Seemed like the whole world had gone silent in that moment as John's thoughts raced backwards, back to when they were kids standing in a moonlit bathroom making promises. John took a deep breath; rent always comes due. 'Course it would have to be something that involved all of his least favourite things: travel, dealing with people, and money.

"The dance troupe got some food poisoning," said Amos. "Damn near shitting themselves to death. Doctors say they can't even leave their beds, never mind the country — can you believe it?"

John had no idea what dance troupe Amos was talking about and his silence probably communicated that because Amos went on. "The Prairie Chicken troupe organized by that Redcloud woman — remember her?"

John had a vague memory of a small woman with long, curly black hair. "Kind of."

"She lives across the road from you! Jesus, do you ever pull your head out of your ass?" This was a constant bone of contention between the brothers. Amos thought his brother acted too stuck up and John thought he should mind his own business.

"I'm gonna hang up —"

"Sorry, you lead a very fully and exciting life. All by yourself." Amos's voice was picking up speed. "Anyways, her troupe was supposed to go to a bunch of festivals in Europe, starting off with that Swedish festival for all these Indian people from all over the world — a goodwill tour kind of thing — then they were supposed to head to Germany. Apparently, the Nazis love Indians."

"They're not Nazis anymore, Amos, that was more than twenty-five years ago."

Amos grunted. "Always be Nazis to me."

Their dad had gone to Germany to fight and was buried over there in a field. "Glad you're not in charge of foreign relations."

"Listen to me. I don't have anyone else or I would've went to anyone else. You can drum, you can dance, play any damned instrument — and I trust you."

"I haven't danced in over ten years." John had stopped after his late Kokum Yellow Belly had been laid in the ground. She'd been the reason he started dancing and when she passed, he didn't feel like doing it without her. And by that time, he was needed at the ranch.

"Don't give me that," Amos said. "Dancing is like riding a horse."

"When was the last time you rode a horse?"

"Who cares? I hate the damned things."

John clucked his tongue. "Why not chuck it all?"

A pause. John knew his brother was choosing his words carefully, which meant a big sell was coming. He was taking all his ten-dollar words and making them simple for his little brother to understand.

"You know the National Indian Brotherhood?"

"Sounds like a bunch of guys who go camping together and sing kumbaya around a campfire."

"They're damned powerful here and in Ottawa. Even down in the States they got pull."

John laughed at the annoyance in his brother's voice.

"Anyway — I promised them I would make this happen. I was put in charge and you know I have . . . aspirations, beyond the reserve."

"Aspirations coming out of your ass." John also knew that his brother had a pretty wife and five children and this made his decisions more loaded than John's ever could be.

"Diarrhoea or no diarrhoea, this shit needs to happen. And you are the only person I trust —"

"You said that —"

"I meant it. I know I'm asking a lot — fifteen days with three people you've never met. Travelling through all these foreign countries with a bunch of strangers." Amos paused. "But you know, this could be good for you. You never leave your farm anymore." Trust Amos to turn John doing a favour into Amos doing a favour for him.

"It's a ranch."

"You live out there, all alone. Never even hear about you running around with anyone. You don't go to any parties, don't go on any drunks. It's not normal. You're thirty, not eighty."

John laughed because they were on the phone and his brother couldn't see his face or the way John's eyes scraped the horizon outside. Always searching for something and he didn't even know what it was. *So then how would I know it — even if I found it?*

But in person all exposed in the middle of this pristine airport, John kept a handle on his face. He could even fake enthusiasm and make his brother feel a little better about throwing him into this tornado.

Amos took some tickets out of his pocket. "Here's all of them. You got your passport?"

John patted his front jean-jacket pocket.

"Good."

"What about money? Unless you want a bunch of starving Indians calling you from Europe."

"Oh, right." Amos pulled a well-worn cheque from his front pocket and handed it over with no small bit of reluctance. "Careful with that now. Don't spend it all in one place!"

John looked down at the cheque. "What the hell?"

"You're gonna have to be frugal —"

"$500 for fifteen days? We're gonna be chewing off our damned arms like coyotes when we get hungry."

Amos clucked his tongue. "It's a lot of money to some people. 'Sides the festivals are supposed to be providing most of your food."

John saw that the cheque was made out to cash. "Where am I supposed to cash this?"

"The bigger airports will have banks and stuff. They have concierges that look after travellers."

John looked at him, one eyebrow raised. John folded up the

11

paper and put it in his chest pocket. "You better stay near a phone, just in case."

"Oh! That's another thing. In Chicago, the Chief of the National Indian Brotherhood is gonna meet up with you. Ernest Standing Bull. He's a great guy. You'll love him."

John was sure he wouldn't give a shit either way.

"You know, tell him how excited you are to be on the tour. And that you're planning to spread our culture far and wide, stuff like that."

"Lay it on thick, eh?"

"As thick as shit in a crowded henhouse."

John glanced at the clock. "Where are the rest of these folks? Two dancers, wasn't it?"

"Three. Two women and some shit-hot dancer from the U.S. He's probably driving his ass off to get here. Danielle only got a hold of him yesterday." Amos always smiled when he said his wife's name.

"You're kidding?"

"His name is Lucas Pretends Eagle, from the Hunkpapa people. Championship grass dancer, fancy dancer, traditional dancer — apparently he even does hoop."

John was impressed but skeptical — how would a dancer that good be available on short notice? "And the women?"

Amos paused again.

"Aw shit, Amos, what is it?"

"You see the Thunderchild Chief, Devon Shield. Y'know them, they've got oil money up the wazoo. The damned Chief has always been gunning for me. One time in a tribal council meeting, he called me insincere — can you believe that?"

"It boggles the mind. And?"

"He's got this nineteen-year-old and she's a nice kid — smart, beautiful —"

"And?"

"Bit wild, I hear. But they all are at that age, aren't they?" Amos attempted a knowing laugh. "So being a good dad, he wants her off the reserve for a bit. Y'know, get her away from the boys —"

"I'm not a goddamn babysitter!"

"He practically shoved her down my throat —"

"What the hell do I know about teenage girls?"

"Calm down. She's got a chaperone. Her elderly aunt or something. She'll watch the kid." Amos looked around for eavesdroppers. "But it would be really, really, *really* good if the kid came home without a little papoose in her baby-carrier."

"Are you serious? What do you want me to do, force-feed her the pill?" John had never seen "the pill" himself but had heard that it existed.

"I don't care how you do it — make sure she comes home virginal or at least un-knocked up."

"Are they dancers at least?"

Amos paused again.

If John didn't love his hat so much, he'd be beating his brother with it. "They can't dance?"

"Didn't you use to teach our cousins about dancing? I was pretty sure it was you who taught Muriel and Ernestine in the barn that time before the powwow."

"This is a goddamn professional dance tour, not a traditional powwow in the middle of nowhere."

"But you're going to Europe and what the hell do they know about female powwow dancing? If the girls aren't any good, who's gonna know?"

John shook his head at his brother. "Always the hustler."

"They were available. Okay? And I got them outfits — so you should be thanking me."

"Regalia."

"What?"

"Regalia. Not outfits, not costumes. Regalia."

Before his brother could make some smartass remark, a high-pitched wail reverberated through the airport. It sounded like a cross between a fire alarm and a kettle boiling. As the sound continued, John determined that the owner of the voice was young, clearly upset, and the words were obscured by some bossy bitching. To John it sounded something like, "Quit-hurrying-me-I'm-so-tired-why-did-you-have-to-come!-I-don't-even-want-to-go!"

John could feel stress settling into his bones as he watched the loud voice turn the corner. The owner of the bellowing lungs was much as he expected. Pouty, round faced, too pretty for her own good, long dark hair swishing side to side as she took turns castigating the man beside her and the short-haired woman on the other side. The older woman's right hip dipped a bit as she struggled to keep up.

He elbowed Amos and pointed at the older woman with his lips.

"A touch of arthritis," Amos said as dismissively as one might say "there's a smidge of moose-meat in your teeth."

John gave his brother a pissed-off look, which Amos ignored, preferring to smile warmly at the tall man coming towards him.

John guessed the guy was the devious dad, which would make the woman with the arthritic hips his third dancer. Or not-dancer. She was average height, large glasses hiding much of her face. Her hair was cut into a pixie cut on a face that was more resolute farm-wife than fairy — John sighed.

Amos had his fake smile already plastered across his big stupid face. "Hello there, Chief." Amos strolled up, almost aggressively, his hand in front of him.

"This the guy looking after the troupe?" The Chief's voice was gruff.

"That's right, that's my brother."

"Kind of old."

John bristled. He was one to talk.

"Where's your woman?" said Chief Shield.

"Where I left her, in bed with my cousin five years ago."

Chief Shield chuckled despite his beleaguered state. He pointed at the women beside him. "This is my daughter, Desiree, and my sister, Edna."

Having decided that John was too old to be interesting, Desiree stared past John at the check-in counters. Edna held out her hand. John took her tiny hand in his big calloused one.

"Thank you for taking this on at such short notice," Edna said. "Your brother says that you're a champion dancer across North America."

"My brother says a lot of things," John replied. He hadn't competed in years and even then, he'd never taken top prize money.

"Where's the other dancer?" asked Edna.

John liked this one; she was sharp. He turned that over to his brother. "Amos?"

Amos looked at his watch, a shiny silver one that a crow would be proud to wear. "He'll be here." He added twenty percent more twinkle to his smile. John had seen less bright comets. John glanced at his own well-worn watch, the leather band so beat up, it looked like he had run over it a few times. Ten to seven. Their plane was scheduled for 7:15 p.m. on the dot.

"And what if he doesn't show, is everyone gonna be screwed?" Chief Shield's voice had reacquired its nasty tone.

"Devon, language." Edna was quick too.

Chief Shield waved off his sister. "What kind of show are you running here, Amos?"

Amos stared intently into the right eye of Chief Shield. "As the Creator is my witness, that boy will be here and this tour will be the greatest success that we have ever seen. People all over the world and beyond will be talking about the cultural talent of Saskatchewan for decades to come."

"We should probably get our seats." John scooped his bag off the floor. Watching his brother stack bullshit that high always sucked the energy out of him. "Before we end up sitting at the back or something." He had no idea where the bad seats on a plane were.

Then the girl . . . Desiree? — John had a hard time remembering new names, especially ones that weren't in the Bible — burst into loud, noisy tears. Her father's stoic face immediately fell to pieces and John saw where the problem lay. This little princess had her daddy wrapped around her fingers. The Chief pulled her close and she cried into his nice suit-jacket. "Please, daddy, don't send me away. I promise I'll be a good girl."

"It'll be good for you, Dezi." Her dad patted her back.

Not too good with emotional scenes, fake or otherwise, John turned away and looked at the check-in lines. The airline people were starting to look annoyed.

"C'mon on now, Desiree, it's fifteen days not months." Her aunt's voice was robotic, as though she had a lot of practice tugging her niece out of bad moods.

John turned back and saw the Chief pull out a handful of bills and push them into his daughter's hand. She continued to bawl loudly but he noted that the money found its way safely into her bra.

"Amos, if you see that other dancer, kick his ass and send him on his way," said John. "But I gotta get these ones on the plane."

"See this guy — always focused. He's the one I trust!" Amos patted his brother on the shoulder as he smiled broadly at the Chief. But Chief Shield was too focused on his daughter, whose crying jag had progressed to feral yelps.

Amos looked intently at John. John looked wryly back. Then Amos pulled him close in a fierce hug. "Have a great trip, nicimis." Then quieter, in almost a whisper: "Sohkitehewin."

Then Amos pushed back, his face a mask as if he had not said anything, making John wonder if he had imagined it.

John grabbed his knapsack. He grabbed Desiree's suitcases and a combination of her aunt, her dad, and momentum drove the sobbing teenager forward.

~

Once they were on the plane, Desiree's tears dried up like a slough in a July heat wave. The two women were seated to his left, one row behind. There was a spare seat beside him, mocking him. Had Amos hired another male dancer? Or was that a lie to get John on the plane? Where the hell would he get another dancer in Europe? He went over logistics in his mind — he could play the drum while the ladies danced but then who would play the drum while he danced? He glanced back at the women. Desiree's face was hidden behind a fashion magazine, while Edna had a rosary moving swiftly between her fingers as her lips moved. She had the stern face and ramrod posture of a career-nun.

No drum players there, he guessed.

Another second passed and John decided that he would kill Amos. It was time to take another liar out of the world, try to even things up for the honest and simple people who only wanted a coffee in the morning and a frying pan of beans and wieners at night. He already missed his horses. Their reserve had some damn fine horse-people and there'd been no shortage of men and women willing to look in on his horses but there was nothing like being there.

"It's only fifteen days," he reminded himself. Then he'd be home and he'd have the rest of his life to watch over the horses and kill his older brother. His brother's comment still irked him. "Don't be afraid." Afraid of what? John rode bulls, broke in wild horses, and once chased a black bear away from a newborn foal. Not that his brother would understand that kind of guts.

That was the problem with reserve life: everyone felt like they had a stake in his personal life. He didn't have a wife, yes. Or kids. But he didn't need those things. Those things closed you in and lessened your choices — he had all the choice in the world. 'Course if he had those things, his brother wouldn't have called him in the first place for this fool's errand.

A stewardess with yellow hair teased seven inches off her head leaned close to make sure his seat belt was buckled. Her hair had the texture of cotton candy but John figured the kid who ate it would be in serious trouble. "We're getting ready for takeoff," she said and John noted a sultry tone in her voice. He hadn't heard that in a while and a smile overtook him. Maybe he should stop hanging out with four-legged mammals once in a while.

His attention was torn away from the hairspray-scented stewardess to the front of the plane where a ruckus was brewing.

"I have a ticket!" a voice proclaimed. Then more voices raised, then the same voice, at powwow announcer volume and level of gravitas: "I am Lucas Pretends Eagle!"

John sighed. Another dramatic Indian was on his way down the aisle. Short and shoulders heavy with muscle, his sin-black hair in two thick braids and a snarl on his face: this was his dancer and that was that. No take-backs now. The dancer winked at one of the stewardesses and John saw a flash of eyes as green as algae. On both his cheeks, he had red patches of pimples that told John that Mr. Pretends Eagle wasn't a day over twenty-one — but he could have figured that out from his walk alone. Only young men and goddamned fools walked that cocky.

"Hey brother, you John?"

John nodded.

A smile swept over the young face, revealing a dimple and a missing incisor. "I'm Lucas."

John offered his hand and Lucas grabbed it the way the African-Americans did on TV.

"You want to push over? I pee a lot. Got kicked in the bladder by a one-eyed guy in Minot one night."

That was a new one. John unbuckled and moved over.

Lucas threw himself into his seat and swivelled his hips so that he was facing John. "So how long before we're in Europe?"

"About a day."

"That long?" Lucas's expression suggested that someone had told him vaginas had gone extinct.

This young pup was in a hurry to get somewhere when he'd barely made the plane? "We're flying over an ocean. That takes some time. We have to make stops for fuel and pilots."

"'Course, I knew that. Was jes' hoping this was one of them Concordes — you know the ones that fly about a thousand miles an hour? Heard you leave in the morning and get to Europe for lunch. Sounds groovy to me." Lucas looked at one of the stewardesses hungrily. "There are some perks to long flights though."

John closed his eyes. A second later, Lucas tapped him on the leg. John opened one eye.

"It's free drinks once you're in the sky, right? That's, like, some flying law?"

This fool thought flying was like hanging out in a Vegas casino. "You shouldn't be drinking." John put his hat over his face.

Behind his Stetson, John heard Lucas make a face. "What kind of dancer are you?"

John sighed and moved his hat to his lap. "Chicken dancer, traditional. I can fancy dance if need be but I'd rather not."

"Yeah, creaky knees, I dig it. Leave it to me, old man."

John thought about whipping off his belt and giving the young'un a beating that would last the entire flight but decided that might impede the bonding of the tour group. "I'm thirty."

"Whoa." The sound left the young man's lips before he could call it back. "I mean, that's not that old . . . like I see older guys dancing at powwows back home . . . mostly the specials . . . but yeah, that's not that old."

John returned his hat to the resting position and whispered "Fifteen days," before falling into a sleep more coma than rest.

Day 2

Monday, June 12, 1972
Chicago, Illinois

EDNA

The tour manager, Mr. John Greyeyes, asked me to keep a journal of the trip. I wished that he had asked me to perform this duty honour the day before as I would have started immediately. Irregardless, I am starting this journal on Day 2 of our grand journey but I will talk about Day 1 as well.

On Day 1 we flew from Saskatoon to Chicago. It was my first time on a plane as well as the first time for Desiree, my niece. I am not sure if it was John's first time or the Hunkpapa dancer, Mr. Lucas Pretends Eagle, as neither of them spoke to us on the flight.

The flight lasted a long time. I went through four rosaries before I felt the plane descending into the Chicago airport. I do not know a lot about Chicago except that it used to be a place where old-time gangsters sold illegal liquor that they brought in from Canada. Also, a lot of people got shot there. I am glad that we have no reason to leave the airport. Before the plane landed, I asked the stewardess (her name was Lori — my favourite female name!) if there were any Catholic chapels in the airport and she said that there was one chapel but that it was for all denominations. I suppose any chapel is better than none!

NADINE

Nadine always heard people talking about karma. As in, *that asshole got the karma coming to him or her.* Karma was always a punishment for some wrongdoing like cheating on your boyfriend or stealing someone's last five bucks. Karma wasn't Cree, it came from those East Indians on the other side of the world. Those Indians were the ones that Columbus had been looking for when he showed up on western shores and then he murdered a bunch of people. Did he ever get karma for that?

Nadine did not subscribe to this belief. Because the Cree version of bad luck stemmed from pimatisowin, the good life, which went far deeper than karma. You could be held responsible for stuff that your kokum did, or your great kokum or your great-great kokum. Nadine kept thinking about all those kokums and their sins, all the way back through history. She had a lot of time to think as she sat on the toilet and her insides ran through her body like a chain-gang on the run from the law. What the hell did great-great-great-great kokum do for Nadine to deserve this torture as she was about to embark on the greatest adventure of her life? It better have been something bigger than stealing someone's bannock recipe.

Only a few days before she had finished packing for the trip. How quickly life could change. A few days before she was a successful dance teacher and tour organizer — the first tour to ever leave the continent (that Nadine knew of anyway) and now she was a few squares of toilet paper away from ruining her furry bathmat.

From her perch on the toilet, Nadine could see her suitcase next to her bed. If she had the energy to spare, she would have sighed. At some point, in the distant future, she had to start calling the destinations and let them know that the Prairie Chicken Dance Troupe would not be attending their festivals and events. She would have to take back all of her promises and justify that American phrase she hated so much, "Indian giver." Ugh. Then she had to get their plane tickets refunded, store that money away and start organizing the next tour. Another round of rancid chicken fried rice passed through her and she gripped the toilet. Baby steps, she reminded herself. Baby steps.

Across the room on her nightstand, the phone began to ring. "As if!" Nadine called out to the phone. "As if you have to be all the way over there!" One time she had stayed in a fancy hotel in the city that had a phone in the bathroom — at the time, she could not have imagined why anyone would need to talk on the phone while pooping. But now, she could see the charm of having a phone less than a foot away so that she could pick it up and then ask the nice person on the phone to please put her out of her misery.

By the third ring, Nadine had this feeling. Like a lightning bolt moment, that she ought to get up. She ought to cross that room because that phone call was critical. It was only a feeling because Nadine didn't have room in her head for thoughts, only feelings. Nadine gingerly rose from the toilet, clenching like her heart depended upon it. She held onto the wall and then the bed, until she finally reached the blasted phone. "Hello?" Her voice was faint.

"Nadine!" It was Amos, the Chief.

"Hi."

"You sound better! That's great. I've got some great news for you."

They had discovered a cure for stomach troubles?

"Uh-huh." Nadine only had the strength for noises, not words.

"The tour is going ahead! I found some —"

"What — you're sending my dance troupe?" Nadine was standing. She didn't know how she got to standing, but she was. They were taking her tour without her? How the hell was it going to operate without her, the leader of the dance troupe?

"Not your troupe, exactly."

"The Prairie Chicken Dance Troupe is not going on the Prairie Chicken Dance Tour? How do you figure that?"

"Hey — why did you name the group that? I've never really heard of prairie chickens being dancers — or even graceful —"

"What's going on?"

"Right. You see, I have this brother —"

"John! Yes, he lives across the road." John!

"He's going to lead the tour. I found three dancers and —"

"No."

"What?"

"We reschedule."

"I'm sorry, Nadine. We must have got our smoke signals crossed but when you called me, all heaving and such, I thought you wanted me to make sure it happened and it is happening. They all left today. On a plane," he added. Though how else would Nadine think they were getting to Europe, on the Greyhound bus? "Kind of funny though, the Prairie Chicken Dance Tour is flying across the ocean — and prairie chickens can't even fly. That really is the strangest name. How did you —"

Nadine placed the phone on the cradle without replying. Not only because she had nothing nice to say but also because she had an urgent errand to run in the bathroom. But then — she'd be out the door. Nobody was taking her tour away from her. She headed for the bathroom as she made a mental note to pack some extra pants.

John had found the Saskatoon airport a mite busy, so the airport in Chicago nearly made him crap himself. They got off the plane in a clump and watched their fellow passengers billow out into all four directions with ferocious intent. Crowds rushed past them on every side and John was afraid to stick his arm out for fear of losing it.

"This is a lot of fucking people," murmured his male fancy dancer. It was under his breath but clearly not under enough, as the next second he received a swat from Edna.

"How dare you use language like that? Did you not have a mother?" She held her hand up again, daring something else rude to come out of his mouth.

"No ma'am, I did not." Lucas glared at Edna. Edna glared back.

Desiree held out her hand. "Hello, I'm Desiree and this . . . person . . . is my aunt Edna. She's not a thousand years old, although she probably seems it."

Edna frowned and gave Desiree a look, which the young gal ignored with practised ease.

Lucas stared at Desiree a few beats. Long, embarrassing, glaciers-moving-across-the-plains beats. The acne on his cheeks grew redder. Then he took her hand and shook it like a dog that had only learned the trick the day before and was eager to show it off.

"And you are?" Desiree prompted, her eyes sparkling. John silently kicked himself again for answering Amos's phone call.

"Lucas Pretends Eagle."

"Cool name. I dig it." She scrunched her face like she was concentrating. "You sure have nice eyes."

Lucas blushed, then replied, "You have nice everything."

Desiree giggled and damned if it didn't sound like bells jingling. John had to give it to her — this girl had some strong medicine.

Edna stepped through them, her narrow hips forcing the young people's clasped hands apart. "Mr. Greyeyes, what are we doing about food?"

John patted his chest pocket. "I have to find someone to cash this cheque for me. I suppose I'll have to find one of those concierge people."

"How much is the cheque for?" Lucas's eyes lit up like the Christmas star — and John was sure it wasn't because he was giving birth to some holy thoughts.

"None of your business." John glanced at the large clock on the wall set to Chicago time. "We have four hours to our next flight so let's say I meet you at those seats over there in two hours."

"What if you don't come back?" Edna asked.

"Why wouldn't I come back?"

"Car accident," Desiree offered.

"Stroke," suggested Lucas.

"There's a million things that a man your age can get into," Edna sniffed.

"Well, then I guess youse will have to hope for the best."

Edna frowned. "And what if the plane is called and you're not here — do we leave without you?"

"I'll be here." John took a few steps and then stopped and turned back. "There's going to be a Chief coming. One of the National Brotherhood men — I forget his damned name —"

"Language — does anyone on this tour have any man —"

"Ernest Standing Bull — he's my dad's friend," said Desiree.

"Right. You may hear him page us. So, go get him, all right? He has the details of the trip with him." And likely more expense money but John didn't need them to be focusing on that, especially with that hungry-eyed Hunkpapa in hearing distance.

Before turning the corner, John glanced back at them. They seemed to be separating right before his eyes, the two young people wandering in different directions as Edna stood rooted to the spot staring up at the airport's glass ceiling. He wished he had his blue heeler Ricky here to round them up.

Edna looked into the sunshine coursing through the airport's sky-light and said a silent prayer for patience and protection. She did not trust the lean man in the cowboy hat. As a rule, she didn't trust any man in any type of hat unless it was a bishop or a cardinal. People with hats were hiding something, usually only a bald spot, but deeper stuff as well. She finished her prayer, crossed herself, and looked around for that nineteen-year-old ball of energy that was her cross to bear.

"Desiree, not so far," Edna called as Desiree stretched the distance between them. Desiree looked back and rolled her eyes. That girl. Would serve her right to get lost in this big airport. But, of course, Edna could not let that happen. Edna moved a few steps towards Desiree even though her feet were already swollen. She had known air travel wouldn't agree with her but it was a necessary evil. Edna stopped suddenly and pinched her own arm. Hard. "Nothing on earth makes evil necessary," she murmured.

An airport was an ungodly place and she had to be more vigilant of all of the ideas floating around in all of these heads that were not her own. Edna liked to think of her normal train of thought as a passenger locomotive chugging along with white-robed angels, Moses, and the saints as the passengers and, of course, Jesus Christ as the engineer. Jesus was the reason she was here, after all.

Six months ago she'd been praying in her bedroom in her brother's house — really, an alcove in the basement that during the day was a rumpus room for his children — when a book fell off the bookcase and landed right in front of her. The book read, "European Cooking," a book her brother had probably bought his kids. He was a frequent attendee of flea markets where he bought books by the pound. It was Edna's job to curate the books to ensure that nothing of a sexual, violent, or supernatural nature made it into the house. (It was a self-appointed position.) To her best recollection she had thrown out over a hundred Harlequin novels, at least fifteen westerns that featured a scantily clad woman on the cover, and anything that had the word "desperate" in the title.

When the book fell, Edna stared at it a few seconds before daring to touch it. She knew it was a sign because less than twenty seconds before she had implored Jesus, "Please send me a sign."

That was the first sacred message and would have been forgotten or dismissed as a reason to learn how to cook a European dish like meatballs or cabbage rolls. But then the second one happened. Her church choir had been on their way to sing at a funeral when their bus broke down. They were then picked up by a farmer of Hungarian origins. The man gaped at Edna, saying she looked exactly like a woman he knew in the old country. Normally Edna would have dismissed this as the drunken ramblings of a dirty old man — he smelled like he had pre-soaked his overalls in gin — but he was adamant and even kept asking her if she was in Budapest in 1968 and did she ever dance — sensually — with a pitchfork?

And then finally there was the third sign — Chief Amos of the Fineday Reserve calling at the ungodly hour of 11:00 p.m. Edna had answered the phone; sometimes she waited until the house was sleeping before padding upstairs in her socks and housecoat to cook herself something to eat. It's not that she didn't love her brother and his family; it was that sometimes a person likes their privacy. Also, his wife . . . was not a Godly woman and looked at Edna as another mouth to feed even though Edna had practically raised her children and worked as an unpaid babysitter day in and day out. She also helped out on her brother's ranch now that his Chief's duties kept him in the office all day. It was like working two full-time jobs but did anyone thank her? Not once. Edna would have moved out years ago if it wasn't for the fact that she worried about who would look after her nieces and nephews when she was gone.

Except now she was gone — Edna stopped (two harried stewardesses nearly tripped over her), bowed her head, and said a brief prayer for her nieces and nephews back home on the reserve.

"Oh dear Lord, I pray that woman finally gets off her butt and acts like a good mother." Between her pressed lips, her voice was barely a whisper.

But when she looked up, Edna saw a few raised eyebrows and travellers veering around her. She paid them no attention.

On that phone call, Chief Amos had told her, in an excited, whispery voice, that Sweden was first on the agenda. Edna knew the country; she had looked it up in an encyclopedia to show the kids where small meatballs came from. They liked fish there and that sounded like something Jesus would like. The second country on the tour was Germany, which was not exactly Edna's cup of tea. They'd had some difficulties with Bible interpretation in that neck of the woods and she wasn't sure she wanted to be exposed to their type of Christianity. And she'd attended masses when she was younger in which names of all the young men from the reserve who had died there were recited. It was like watching grief tornado across the church, random and cruelly destructive.

But the third country on the agenda was Italy, specifically Rome. When she heard the Chief say that, she made him repeat it so that she could be sure. "Rome," he reiterated.

Her jaw had dropped: "Where the Vatican is?"

"Is it in Rome? I guess so."

The Chief was not a Godly man.

If she went, Edna would be closer to Jesus than she'd ever been before or would ever be again. It wasn't the Holy Land but was as close as she would ever get in this lifetime and besides there was a chance she'd meet the Pope, who was the head of the church — that was the closest person to Jesus on earth. And if there was a better place than the Vatican for a miracle, she didn't know of one.

Though how dare she ask Jesus for a miracle? He had given her an affliction and she had borne it, as a good soldier of the Lord, for the past five years. She had watched as her once-slim hands became swollen, her knees had grown red and painful, and her hips had tightened like a vise. Sometimes she couldn't even fix a button on the kids' clothes or bend over to pick up a stray toy. There were moments when she felt more a burden than a soldier.

Hadn't she suffered enough? Edna crossed herself again. Such a question should not even be asked! Did Job ask the Lord to leave him alone? Well, yes, but God didn't listen. That was the point.

But still, people asked for miracles all the time; there was no harm in asking, was there?

Edna followed the flowing black hair that was her niece. It didn't escape Edna's notice that her niece made eyes at every man that passed as though testing out her powers on newfound victims. Edna sighed: where had she gone wrong with her?

"Desiree!" Edna made her voice louder and bossier than it needed to be. All heads turned towards her. There were curious looks moving up and down her body and big smiles at her long skirt and two men's jackets worn layered over one another. Edna kept her spine straight and met their glances with her own annoyed look. She wasn't one to care about fashion; she had more important things to worry about, like . . . God, for one, and other Godly concerns of a Godly nature. Besides, people who judged others by appearance were as empty as a politician's promises.

Edna stopped. Desiree had slipped out of her view. It was like her niece was two years old again, running off at the town fair. "Calm down," Edna whispered. "She's a big girl." Rows of people walked past — mostly surly singles, a few doubles rushing to keep up with one another, and groups of stewardesses and pilots flirting furiously.

It was an ungodly place.

Edna planted herself in the centre of the space. She glanced to her right. There was a restaurant, a family establishment. A cheeky-looking boy sat backwards in his chair and grinned at her, his freckles standing out brightly on his chubby face. She smelled the fried potatoes and hamburgers grilling and her stomach growled. She had some money squirrelled away in her right sock but this wasn't the time or place to pull it out.

She glanced to her left, at a dark place of wood and low lights.

There was the low sound of heathen music coming from it. Edna glanced at the sign by the door: "Licensed." She sighed again, all of her disappointment in humanity expressed in a single exhale, and headed in that direction.

NADINE

Nadine was the kind of person who got what she wanted when she wanted it, how she wanted it, and where she wanted it. And what she wanted right now was for this diarrhoea to end so that she could get her sore ass onto a plane to Europe tout de sweet.

In another lifetime she'd have been that ace reporter who always gets the interview. But growing up on her rez with a powwow family and shuttled from one to another since she was an infant, her place to shine was the dance circuit. After twenty years of winning prizes and spending prize money to help out the dancers who wanted to travel and dance but could not, Nadine decided to do something different.

Her dream had taken shape one night at a band meeting. The Chief and council sat at their end of the room and the band members at theirs. People would stand up and go through their usual litany of complaints: the water truck never came on time, someone shot someone else's dog, and there was nothing for their kids to do. That night Nadine's powwow-strong legs pushed her to standing. "I can teach them to dance!" she announced. "I will teach all of your kids how to dance."

People had clapped and cheered and she felt like she was a superhero. And so, the next week, she put down ten bucks to rent the band hall and waited for the kids to show up and for lives to change. Nobody showed up the first week, or the second. Or the third, no matter how loud she played the powwow music. Realizing that she needed to take the initiative, she drove directly to people's yards and beeped her horn long and hard. Just really leaned on it. They sent their kids out, one by one, recalcitrant and jonesing for comic books and

TV shows that never featured anyone who looked like them or lived in tiny houses with friendly rez dogs bouncing through their yards.

At first the kids hated the music, hated the intricate steps, and hated Nadine's drill-sergeant demeanour. (They complained to their parents that her voice gave them headaches. Like she hadn't heard that before!) They wanted her to teach them how to disco. She made a deal with them, one hour of powwow lessons, and a half hour of disco, which Nadine knew was a type of dance that people were doing in big cities. The kids had seen it in movies with that good-looking white guy with the feathered hair. She was a fan herself — disco let you strut around by yourself like a peacock or you could twirl in circles with a partner. Nadine practised the partner-free version and the partner version because one day she hoped to have a partner — the world's most perfect man: John Greyeyes.

John lived less than two miles from her. On his ranch, all alone. She didn't watch his yard or anything but she knew that he hardly ever got visitors and especially no visitors of the female variety. Nadine went over there about once a year to drop off oatmeal raisin cookies before Christmas and they would share a cup of coffee and talk about the gossip on the reserve (or at least she talked and he listened because he never knew anything that was going on). She'd ask about his cows and horses and he'd talk but with a skeptical look in his eye as if questioning her interest.

She did care, of course, because he cared. Nadine knew that the path to a man's heart was through lies, all the lies that you could stomach telling. There had been a time long ago when she believed he was going to be her John. But he went on the road to do the rodeos and he was gone so long that she married Allan, who turned out to be a son-of-a-bitch. That mistake had lasted two years less a day — she got out before it turned into hard time, she joked to her friends. When John came back and started his ranch, she wanted to tell him that she was sorry she hadn't waited for him. But how do you say such a thing? Especially since they hadn't shared any more than a single dance at a cowboy party when they were fifteen years old.

All the women on the reserve wanted John, despite the grey at his temples or the pockmarks on his cheeks. It was something they whispered to each other at fall suppers when he would walk in with his cowboy boots on and his jeans resting on his slim hips. And they would all try (even the married ones!) and fail. Their smiles and flirtatious looks rolled over him like water off a duck's back. He had this way of smiling that warmed you even as it dismissed you, like you were a much older female relative. Women would fawn over him from the beginning of the meal until the moment when he was standing over the dessert table, selecting a single oatmeal raisin cookie. None of them got more than a few moments of his time before he slipped out the door.

Over the last few years, people had started to whisper about him, about what maybe actually got his fires burning — goats, cattle, sheep . . . but Nadine refused to listen to the rumours. He was holding out for a real woman and he would make his move when he was ready.

She wondered if he ever thought about that night over fifteen years ago, dancing on a packed-earth dance-floor to a Willie Nelson song attempted by a drunk cowboy band.

And now, he'd gone and stolen her tour. She'd slaved over it for two years. She'd trained the dancers, connected with the festivals (few people realize how hard it is to make overseas phone calls at the right time to nail down the right person — it must have taken her at least two months to find the contact person for the Swedish festival alone). But once one location had been confirmed, the other two fell into place. The Germans had actually contacted her directly (Germans were very good at getting a hold of people, it turned out) and invited the dance troupe to the Karl May Western Festival. Then, they were off to Italy to dance at some type of International Cultural Festival in Rome. The booker there had said that someone from the Vatican might even attend. Nadine wasn't Catholic and wasn't even a fan of religion in general, but she knew how damned important the Vatican was. She figured that by doing a good job, she'd be able to secure more jobs for her dance troupe, like maybe even make it an annual thing. Then that crew of little bored dancers would finally understand how important all those practices that went long into the night actually were.

As it was, most of her dancers were still lying in bed or huddled near the toilet. It had been a bon voyage dinner at the local Asian restaurant run by a Ukrainian couple that had done them all in. Nadine would be tempted to burn the location down to the ground if the owner hadn't apologized profusely and offered her a lifetime supply of chicken fried cabbage rolls. Not that she wanted to eat any of it at the moment but she knew the importance of free food and the importance of forgiving people for things they didn't mean to do. Not like Chief Amos who had meant to screw her out of the tour. She replayed her second conversation with him as she pleaded with him to call back his brother.

"No way, Jose, that tour is going ahead."

No way, Jose?

After all she'd done for the reserve, after all the training and the planning and fundraising — no way, Jose? She deserved to be on that damned tour — her dancers deserved to be on the tour. She'd argued with the Chief, only to have him shoot down her concerns. "The tour has to go now, especially with the funding tied to the Native Indian Brotherhood."

Nadine hadn't even wanted them as sponsors in the first place but the Chief had pushed them on her. She didn't like the idea of her little tour of goodwill and friendship becoming some kind of political machination. Especially now, when political shenanigans meant that she got left behind.

Why did I vote for this bonehead?

And where did John fall on that blame scale? On the one hand, he must have known that taking the job would be screwing over Nadine's dance troupe — and that hurt (especially considering their romantic past). But then on the other hand, maybe this too was another sign he was giving her? The man never went anywhere, but then, when asked to go to Europe to participate in a dance tour — the tour that Nadine organized — he agreed. Maybe he thought that he was doing her a favour? Maybe he thought that he was saving the entire tour from disrepute?

It would have been a public relations nightmare to have pulled out at the last minute. Those Europeans would have accused the Indians of not keeping their word — and Indians always keep their word! It was the Europeans who forgot to honour their promises.

So then, even a ragtag band of dancers was better than nothing (and Nadine knew that Chief Amos was sending a ragtag group). When she'd heard about the Thunderchild Chief's sister Edna (Edna!) and her niece being sent — the niece was rumoured to be a hot little piece and useless as tits on a boar — Nadine had rolled her eyes in disgust.

Nadine knew that John was an all right dancer. Plus he was fit and handsome and sexy and women from around the world would fall in love with him — he was actually kind of perfect for the tour. If she'd known that he was interested in attending, she would have asked him herself and they would have been in Europe together right now seeing the sights and walking hand-in-hand over cobblestone streets and then snuggling up together on those cold European nights (if it was cold, Nadine had no idea what the weather was like over there). It would have been so much easier if he had picked up the phone and asked her, "Would you like me to go?" But men were like that, they never liked asking for permission; you had to do all the talking and convincing.

Nadine drove through a deep pothole and felt her tummy roll. "Oh hush." She hadn't eaten anything solid in four days. Her theory was that she would keep her stomach empty because as long as nothing went in, nothing could come out.

She thought back to the phone calls she'd made the night before about the fourth member of the ragtag group — the Hunkpapa dancer. She never got a name but rumour was the Hunkpapas were good powwow people.

Nadine clutched her stomach as it rolled again. Clearly her

theory was not working. She saw a gas station and pulled in. She rushed in and said in a strangled voice, "Bathroom key." The man looked frightened as he held it up, and she snatched it and turned in a single swift motion.

She rushed to the back of the building even as her body told her that time was too short already. She opened the door with shaking hands and threw herself in — and landed directly in the arms of a man so tall her boobs were pushing against his belly. "What the hell?"

"I'm free!" he exclaimed.

"Good for you!" Nadine yelled back and pushed him out.

Nadine slammed the door, locked it, and stumbled backwards onto the toilet with barely enough time to pull her pants down. Oh, thank god for the toilet — her old friend and lover these past few days.

After spending a long time on the throne, probably much longer than was necessary but one liked to be absolutely certain under circumstances such as these, Nadine washed and rewashed her hands. She fixed her braids, which though ornate and tight when she left the house had grown a bit loose and messy under her straining and heaving. She tut-tutted the circles under her eyes — dehydration was no one's friend — and decided that a nice ginger ale was what the doctor would have ordered. Except that was a lie, what the doctor had actually ordered was another three days bed rest. But she didn't have three days, if she was going to make it to Europe. She had a ticket in her pocket with a takeoff at 9:00 p.m. — a result of an hour of begging and pleading with the airline after she missed the takeoff the day before.

Nadine opened the bathroom door directly into the man she had tossed out of the same bathroom. "Hello?" She pushed the door all the way open and he moved aside.

"Sorry," said a voice so deep, Nadine felt like she had crawled inside a velvet sweater.

She stared up at the deliverer of the fulsome tones. "You always stand outside bathrooms?"

"Not sure where to go, ma'am," answered the man who Nadine

36

could see was probably the tallest, handsomest Indian man she'd ever seen in her life.

"I see. Would you like a ginger ale?" Nadine had no idea why she was offering one except that he did seem under the weather and she was under the weather and that seemed like the best plan for both of them.

"I would," he answered. Then as if just remembering, "I was robbed."

Nadine looked him over. He didn't look like one of those sad Indian brothers you saw outside of bars asking for change so that they could head back inside and try their luck again at the spin of the beer bottle. "I could take you to the police."

He looked down the road for a long bit, his eyes searching the flat expanse of wheat on both sides of the road undulating under the wind, before replying. "I suppose we'll have to."

JOHN

After asking at a few different counters, John came to the realization quite independently of anyone pointing it out to him that an airport concierge did not exist. Instead he found himself taking a taxi to a tiny strip mall about three minutes from the airport, standing in line at a bank, and explaining his predicament for about twenty minutes to a surly twenty-year-old woman who looked like she had never trusted anyone in her life and never would. The cashier looked him up and down and kept saying, "That's a lot of money."

The manager had to be called out and phone calls were made across the border. Finally, the wad of cash was stuffed in John's jeans and he made his way back to the airport. He thought about stopping in the bathroom to disperse the money through his pockets but also knew that time was growing short. He was almost back inside the airport when a sharp tap on his shoulder reminded him that no man is time's master.

"Can you come with me?" The voice told rather than asked.

He was led to a small room by a chubby guy in a black uniform with the grey bushy eyebrows of an older man. The uniform had a tiny American flag on the shoulder. John hoped that they had kept up on their Canadian Indian's history and politics but wasn't going to hold his breath, seeing as he how he'd need it all to explain himself.

The officer showed him a metal chair and John took it, sitting a bit off-balance as one ass-cheek hung about three inches higher than the other. Say what you will about money, it sure can take up space in your pocket.

The officer opened the door and barked out a name and a middle-aged woman with auburn hair neatly pulled back in a bun joined him. She was rancher-lean and John had a good feeling from her. Both the officers stood. This gave John a bit of hope. People who stood had no intention of making anything last a long time.

"I'm Sgt. Marlow and this is Carol . . ." His co-worker shot him a look. "I mean — Officer Carol Dixon."

John tipped his hat at her. "John Greyeyes."

"Passport?"

John handed over his passport and his airline ticket, hoping they'd see the time on it and make this go a lot faster.

"Stockholm? What are you doing there?"

No such luck. "Dancing. It's a tour. A bunch of Cree Indians from Saskatchewan showing the world our type of dancing."

"Indian?"

"Indian, like y'know . . .the kind with tipis and the buffalo. The kind that John Wayne shoots . . ."

Carol smiled. John smiled back.

Sgt. Marlow did not smile. "And this tour goes to Stockholm?"

"And Germany and Italy."

"I see." Marlow looked at Carol with his eyebrow raised. "It seems the Indians are off the reservation."

Carol looked embarrassed. John squelched the desire to boot Marlow in the face.

"It's unusual to see an Indian person — which makes me think you might be up to something."

"You don't see a lot of Indians in general — so that's a clue?" That was a new one to John.

Sgt. Marlow ignored this. He looked over John. "You seem a bit uneven. Can you remove the contents of your pocket, please?"

John used to cowboy around with a lawyer-turned-bronco-rider so he knew that searches weren't supposed to be conducted unless you were under arrest. And before arrest he was supposed to have his rights read to him. This search was definitely of the illegal kind. John thought about asserting this fact but decided that the path of least resistance was best and placed his wad of cash on the table. Sgt. Marlow reached for it and then, remembering that he was the big cheese, pushed it over to Carol. She took the money with a look of apology to John and began to count it. As it turned out, Carol wasn't much of a money counter. As John's mother would say, she was as slow as molasses in a blizzard. Or as he would say, she was slow as shit.

Marlow shifted from foot to foot, indicating that maybe a chair was in his future. John's eyes moved from Carol's slow-handed counting to the clock behind them, imagining a bleak future for his three charges wandering around Chicago's airport. The Hunkpapa would probably get lost and end up on a flight to Antarctica. Desiree would get kidnapped to become part of some sheikh's harem. And Edna would give the wrong person a lesson in manners and get punched out.

"Five hundred dollars." This was Carol's pronouncement after she placed the cash into three separate stacks.

John was still working out her sorting method when Sgt. Marlow slammed the table in front of him.

"What's an Indian doing with so much money?"

John glanced at his watch; fifteen minutes had passed since they'd entered the room so Sgt. Marlow had had a fair amount of time to formulate that question. John guessed that he wasn't dealing with the brightest member of the U.S. Border Patrol, probably just the most racist.

John cleared his throat. "I'm in charge of the dance tour which means I've got to keep everyone fed for fifteen days with all that money. There are four of us, in case you were wondering."

Carol gasped. "That's not enough money."

John grinned at her. "Would you care to donate some funds?"

With a rueful smile, she replied, "They barely pay us."

Sgt. Marlow hushed her with a sharp look and she took a step backwards. Marlow cleared his throat and reasserted control. "A trip to Europe and cash for expenses? How'd you get such a great job?"

"What I've found is if you're willing to put on some feathers and bang on a drum, white people want to see it." John shrugged. "What can I say — I'm an Indian. They pay us for being alive."

Marlow grunted at this. "It's still a lot of money to be carrying around."

"If you think that's a lot of money to feed and house four Indian people for fifteen days, then you should be running this tour instead of me," John replied. "You got any coffee?"

EDNA

Edna had oceans of faith in God, but not a single drop in humans. Though humans were made in the image of God, so one would think that they should also be good? And if God was all-knowing, wouldn't he have known that humans would fall short of goodness and there-fore ought to have made them nicer beings? Also, if you had angels, why would you want humans? Edna made a mental note to discuss these questions with Father Henry the next time she went to confession. (They often ran out of things to talk about as Edna was short of sins to confess.)

Edna pushed open the bar door which swung on its hinges as a proper bar door should. She scanned the room, saw many old men drinking in the company of young women at small tables dispersed throughout the bar. Then in the back, her own young woman, Desiree, looking like she was growing younger by the second. And directly to the left of her, a man who looked old enough to be her father, sitting closer than a man that old should be to a young girl.

She marched over to the table, already upset about how many drinks this reprobate had probably fed her niece.

"You should be ashamed of yourself." Edna wagged a finger in the face of the offensive man who she noticed smelled quite good.

Desiree started at the sight of her aunt and then returned to her normal sulky state. But the man had the gall to look amused.

"Excuse me?" His voice was deep and Edna caught a hint of an Indian accent, though she couldn't place it. With his hair a touch too long for white jobs, his button-down shirt and shiny cowboy boots, he was a typical Indian politician — intoxicated by money and power and now he thought he could prey on the young and ungodly.

Edna stood up straight and said with the cadence of a preacher, "This young woman, my niece, who has recently been confirmed by the Catholic Church of Canada, is only nineteen years of age. She's not even old enough to be in this establishment!"

"I can be here, I just can't drink." Desiree held up her glass. "This is Coke."

The man held out his hand. "And who are you? Other than a follower of Jesus Christ and his cross?" The man had a hint of a smile, which Edna would think was flirtatious if she had any experience with men flirting with her.

"I'm Edna Shield. My brother is Chief Devon Shield." She emphasized *Chief.*

"He knows, Auntie. This is Dad's friend, Chief Ernest Standing Bull."

"I see." Edna didn't have a lot of faith in her brother's friends. They were men after all. "And, why are you in this bar with him?"

Desiree shrugged. "We were talking about the tour."

Edna sighed. "Did you not think that if you run into a man

41

that we all need to talk to that you would bring him to me or to Mr. Greyeyes?"

Desiree rolled her eyes. "I didn't know where either of you were."

Edna turned her attention to the man who was smiling now. "Chief Standing Bull —"

"Ernest —"

"Chief Standing Bull, I must apologize for my niece's lack of manners. I'm afraid she is in the grip of an extended adolescence that appears to be robbing her of good sense." She looked at Desiree. "Tonight I would like you to do two rosaries in atonement."

"Uh, you're not the Pope." Desire laughed and turned her attention back to Ernest. "Are we gonna have any time to sightsee on this tour?"

"It's part of the experience," Ernest answered. "When we thought up this tour, we saw you all spending time with other cultures, making inroads into worldwide unity. You see, it's important that the Indigenous people of this world unite so that we can take a stand politically, as one."

Desiree's eyes were glazing over. "But there'll be time to shop, right? Like, I hear that there's a store that's like so big it covers two city blocks in London."

"We're not going to London," Edna corrected her. "Our destinations are Sweden, Germany, and Italy. That's more than enough to keep us busy and certainly not enough time to engage in frivolity."

Besides, she wanted to remind her niece, *we still have to learn how to dance!*

"We at the — National Indian Brotherhood — believe that this mission . . . I mean tour . . . could have far-reaching consequences . . ."

"What do you mean?" Edna was suddenly suspicious.

He indicated that Edna should sit down. Reluctantly she sat.

Ernest then looked around the room. When he seemed satisfied that there was no risk of being overheard, he leaned in with such commitment that Edna found herself doing the same. He lowered his voice to a whisper. "Were you wondering why I wanted to meet you here, in the Chicago airport?"

"I thought you were in the area," Edna whispered, although she hadn't really thought about it at all.

"I couldn't meet you in Canada because I am carrying . . ." Ernest paused and licked his lips, "a package." Edna and Desiree shifted a few degrees backwards uncomfortably. He pulled out a package about the size of a wallet from his jacket pocket

"It's a politically sensitive item," he placed it on the middle of the table, "that could do a lot of damage if it fell into the wrong hands."

"Cool," Desiree said.

"Like political damage, not like a bomb or anything," Ernest explained.

Heads turned in their direction.

"Don't say that," hissed Edna. "Never say that."

"I said it wasn't a bomb."

"Stop saying it."

Ernest leaned close. "Will you do it?"

Edna frowned. "The way I see it, you're playing with crooked dice, and you want us to take the heat if anything goes down." This was wording taken straight from an episode of *Hawaii Five-o* that she'd seen the week before.

Ernest looked offended. "Nothing like that. None of this could ever have any negative consequences for you. If it were found on you, you tell them that it was given to you by the National Indian Brotherhood. But it would be best not to let that happen. But if it did, I would fully expect you to turn me in personally."

"We would never!" Of course, Desiree was ready to jump into any bad decision with both of her size-six feet. "We'll do it."

Edna held up her hand. "Not so fast. You're gonna answer my questions first: Is this stolen?"

"No."

"Could it hurt anyone?"

Ernest shook his head.

"And how much are you going to pay us?"

"Auntie!" Desiree seemed incensed that her aunt would insult a politician. But Desiree wasn't the only one who had grown up surrounded by politicians. Edna knew that they routinely paid people to do all kinds of small things, so why not a big thing?

Ernest nodded. "Of course." He pulled out a wad of bills and counted out a few of them on the table under Desiree's wide eyes and Edna's deliberately unimpressed ones.

Edna took the money and counted it again (it was always important to show everyone that you didn't trust them). Then while keeping her eyes on Ernest, she swept the box into her bag and the money into her bra. "Who does it go to?"

"When you reach Italy, you must go to the German consulate. My contact is there."

"What's his name?"

"Oscar."

"And this is all legal and legit?" Edna pressed this point again.

Ernest looked off in the distance. "What does legal mean? Is it legal to steal our land, take away our children, and our rights? Is it legal to throw us in jail for dancing to our songs or holding our ceremonies?"

Desiree was nodding her head in agreement but Edna merely pursed her lips and crossed her arms.

"Are we breaking the law as it is currently written?"

Ernest looked into her eyes. "As long as you don't look in the package, you'll be fine."

Edna felt like there was another question she should be asking but the money in her bra was making her a lot less curious. She reached out her hand and Ernest took it. Instead of shaking it, he lifted it towards his mouth. Edna felt his lips warm against her skin.

"You're a strong woman," he said, and though Edna felt her belly doing flip-flops like a two-day-old salmon, she frowned and yanked her hand back.

Ernest smiled then checked his watch and said his plane was leaving soon. Before walking out, he came back to the table and set a piece of paper on the table: "Here's the itinerary. You'll need that.

Oh, and tell Frank or Joe or whatever-his-name-is that I'm sorry I missed him."

"John Greyeyes," Desiree said.

"Yes, that one." Ernest kissed two of his fingers and blew them at Desiree and Edna. As he pushed open the doors of the dark bar, the fake lights of the airport lit his high cheekbones and Edna felt a flash of something she hadn't felt since she was a teenager.

"He's handsome," Desiree cooed.

"He's old enough to be your father," Edna intoned.

"First of all, gross. And two, Dad's voice isn't sexy like that. And finally, I wasn't talking about for me, I was talking about for you."

Edna's voice was strangely high-pitched. "Me?"

"Aren't you ever gonna meet a guy and settle down? Not that you aren't settled down — you're the most settled person I've ever known — you're like a plant." Desiree pressed her soft hand on top of her aunt's to demonstrate her point. "I know you have a heaven family with God and Mary and Joseph and Jesus, but I'm talking about getting your own kids to boss around, your own house to clean, and your own husband to nag."

Edna stared at her niece. Desiree had a smile that could bring a person back from the dead. And Edna knew that Desiree only smiled when she was happy. That quality made Edna hopeful that there was a good girl somewhere inside this wild young woman.

"Don't you worry about me, God will take care of me," Edna said.

Desiree laughed, a melodic sound that quickly drew the eyes of men old enough to know better. Edna waved her hand impatiently. "Finish your pop, we've got to go find the others."

"Should we tell John about . . . ?" Desiree gestured with her lips in the direction of the old Chief.

Edna shook her head. "Ernest trusted *us*. We'll take care of it."

The local RCMP detachment had one car parked out front. There were two cars altogether, which told Nadine that it was a moderately busy day for the cops. On the ride over, the tall man had been mostly silent, every once in a while saying something like, "I should have known," or "Never again . . ." or "goddamn it, I'm an idiot" under his breath.

"I'll come in with you," Nadine announced. "But I can't stay long, okay?"

"You've already done enough," he said, awakening from his regret stupor. "I don't know how to thank you."

Nadine's pale cheeks flushed slightly then she felt her stomach roll again. "Okay, let's go, we don't have much time before I have to find the bathroom again."

They walked up to the front desk where a young officer stood with a flyswatter. He was eyeing a fat fly about three feet from him. On his chest was a badge and directly below it, affixed crookedly, was a nametag: "Cpl. Martin."

"Hello, we're here to report a robbery," Nadine said. "This man here," she rested her hand on the rather firm shoulder of the man next to her, "was robbed."

Cpl. Martin looked at Nadine. "And you are?"

"I'm Nadine Redcloud."

"How are you involved?"

"I found him locked in the gas-station washroom and brought him here."

"I was locked in there by the criminal," the man explained. "I didn't lock myself in there. And nobody came no matter how much I hollered."

Cpl. Martin snapped the flyswatter and missed the fly. "Crap." His gaze flicked back at the two of them. "Sorry." He put his swatter down and started opening and closing drawers in front of him. "I can't find the form for stolen stuff. Can you come back in about an hour? My boss will be in then and he knows where everything is."

"I need you to take this man's statement now. Grab any piece of paper." Nadine looked out the window where she could almost see the plane taking off without her.

Cpl. Martin sighed and grudgingly picked up a yellow pad and wrote the date on it. "Name?"

"I already told you."

"Not you, the victim."

Nadine looked at the man expectantly. How did she neglect that piece of information? This could be her name some day. He cleared his throat. "I'm Lucas Pretends Eagle."

"Hell yeah!" Nadine exclaimed. She clapped her hand over her mouth. "Sorry. But that's a very cool name." She mumbled through her fingers.

Nadine Pretends Eagle, it did have a nice ring to it. Nadine squelched a grin.

The corporal paused and looked at him skeptically. "That's your real name?"

"Yes."

"Yes, that's his name." Nadine patted Lucas on the arm.

"A new one to me . . ." The corporal paused to scratch his head long and hard. Nadine could actually see the detritus collect on his fingernails. "What all was taken?"

"My car, my luggage, my regalia, my identification."

"Whoa . . . slow down a second . . . that's a lot of stuff." Cpl. Martin, with painstaking slowness, attempted the word *Identification*. It took a few tries before he abandoned it and went with *I.D.* "What did the guy look like? No wait, did you get a name?"

"He said his name was Shane but I don't know if that was real or not."

"You get his I.D.?"

"You mean while I was being robbed, did I rob him?" Lucas's brow was wrinkled.

"Yeah?" The officer also looked confused.

"I didn't see his I.D." Lucas spoke slower. "I picked him up on the side of the road near Moose Jaw. We rode together for a few hours and then he pulled out a knife —"

"Wait, wait, wait — you picked this guy up?" Cpl. Martin's mouth dropped. Nadine saw the fly hovering nearby, considering the open invitation. "Was he like a friend of yours? A relative? Or, y'know . . . a friend in the bedroom?" Cpl. Martin's voice dropped to a whisper on the last one.

"I'm assuming he was a hitchhiker." Nadine looked at Lucas for confirmation. Lucas nodded.

Cpl. Martin hit the counter with the swatter, sending a pile of papers flying. "Oh man, you should never pick up hitchhikers. They are all hopped up on speed and PCP and they're mostly hippies. Seriously never do it."

"I'll remember that," Lucas said.

"Okay well, we'll keep an eye for your stuff." Cpl. Martin put his pen down on his pad.

"You haven't even gotten a description of the car!" Nadine's chest was heaving (which was a nice change from her stomach, actually).

"I was gonna." The corporal's voice was pouty. "Hey! I have an idea, do you want to look at some mug shots? We have a book." Cpl. Martin jumped to his feet, fired up suddenly.

"Mug shots sound like a good idea," Nadine said to Lucas, her voice as encouraging as a kindergarten teacher's.

"This seems like it could take a long time," Lucas said to her. "Maybe you should go."

Nadine glanced at the clock. Right now, the troupe would be in Chicago and flying out in a few hours. The only way she'd catch them was with a direct flight. She glanced at Lucas as he watched Cpl. Martin meander around the office opening and closing drawers. It didn't feel right to leave him behind. But Europe! And John! And wandering along cobblestones hand-in-hand! But she couldn't leave a good man behind. Nadine packed the dreams into a safe place and planted herself beside Lucas.

When he arrived back at the gate, his heart leapt like a baby goat when he saw his little herd. Two members anyway. He'd been gone so long, he figured they would have given up on him. Desiree and Edna sat together. Desiree slept against Edna's shoulder as Edna read a magazine, shaking her head even as she continued to turn the pages.

"It's about time," she hissed at John when he stepped in front her.

"Had some unforeseen difficulties," John drawled. "You see where that young man wandered off to?"

"I only had to watch one of them and I did my part." Edna nodded at the sleeping girl. "He was your responsibility, or at least his own. He appeared to be a grown-up male, physically anyway."

John glanced at the large clock on the wall. "He's got an hour. He shaved it pretty close last time so I'm guessing that's probably his style. Did that Native Brotherhood Chief show up?"

Edna nodded. "Chief Ernest stopped by and passed on the itinerary." She pulled it out of her pocket and handed it to John. "It has our hotel rooms on it and the names of contacts. Without this, we would have been —"

"Royally screwed."

"In a lot of trouble. Honestly, the manners with young people these days."

"Even my mom doesn't consider me a young person," John pointed out.

Edna sniffed in reply.

John reached for the document and Edna handed it over reluctantly. It seemed like there might be two chiefs on this trip, which wasn't always the worst thing, considering that the first chief didn't want the damn job in the first place.

John heard a commotion behind him. He turned and saw a crowd and a flurry of movement. Taller than most of the people, John could see what was making everyone so damned excited. The Hunkpapa. The young man flew through a few steps of an impromptu fancy dance. He had torn the sleeves off his T-shirt and was bare-foot. He'd also put war-paint markings on his face. A group of people were watching him jump and weave, his feet a blur. John figured that the young man was eager to get dancing until he saw the hat on the floor next to him.

"Little shit." John stalked over and picked up the hat before more people could throw money in it. "Stop it," he hissed to Lucas who barely slowed his steps. "Lucas!" John called louder and Lucas stopped and arched a brow at him. The audience let out a collective "Aw."

Lucas shrugged at John. "Giving the people what they want!"

"You can't do that in an airport, they have rules," John said. "Now get your ass over here."

Lucas grinned, then began dancing again.

John started over, getting ready to grab the young guy by the scruff of his neck. But before he got close, a crowd of fascinated white people swallowed Lucas. They peppered the Hunkpapa with questions about the dance and where he learned it and what his tribe was and did he have a squaw back home? (This was from a tall blonde lady with a few crow's feet dancing around her eyes and shiny jewellery hanging from her ears.) The young man gobbled up the attention, even to the point of autographing people's plane tickets.

John glared at him until the crowd dissipated. The wealthy lady was the last to linger and, from the way she kept looking back at Lucas, John figured she might miss her plane to continue her "conversation" with the dancer.

John stalked over the moment she had turned the corner. "What the hell was that all about?"

"I was hungry," Lucas said defensively. "I haven't eaten in two days."

"Don't you know how to feed yourself?"

Lucas shrugged as he stuffed cash into his pockets. "You gonna buy us some food with those travel funds?"

～

John chose a family restaurant that specialized in cheap hamburgers and fries. It barely tasted like food but John wanted to keep them on their budget. With the current state of their finances, they were going to cut it pretty damned close. No need to share that information with them, however. He was comfortable sticking that secret under his pillow like a rock. He'd be the only one suffering from the lack of sleep.

"How much longer till we're in Europe?" the Hunkpapa asked through a mouthful of meat and ketchup.

"Plane ride is a few hours," John said. "Close your eyes and you'll be there when you open them."

"And close your mouth too," Desiree added. "We don't need to watch you digest."

Lucas opened his mouth wide at her. "Like this?"

"Gross." Desiree threw a fry at him. He threw it back at her.

"Kids!" John said sharply. They both started laughing.

Desiree cocked her head and studied Lucas's war paint. "Hey, is that my lipstick?"

Lucas only grinned.

"Ass." Another fry went flying.

"We'll be in Europe before dawn," John said more to himself than to them.

"If the good Lord allows," Edna intoned and John could tell from her ominous look that she was still annoyed that they had forgotten to pray before throwing back their food. For himself, he prayed about once a month — if God needed to hear from him more than that, then God maybe had some issues and should look into getting one of those analysts that movie stars were always talking to.

John checked his watch, gathered his tribe, and pointed them in the direction of the plane. He could tell they were feeling a mite tired: feet dragged and tempers were sharp. Desiree snapped at her Auntie for losing her fashion magazine and John watched with growing impatience as she flounced off to grab another one.

"Hurry up, now!" he called after her. Desiree shot him a dirty look and he gave her one right back. If he had to be on each and every one of their asses for the next fifteen days, then he would be. If he could handle 250 head of cattle, he could handle three Indians.

They loaded onto the plane and John took his seat with a bit of relief. Nothing to this tour managing stuff, he smiled to himself, and he drifted off to sleep to thoughts of being surrounded by his horses with a pail full of oats.

C H A P T E R 3

JOHN

John woke to the sound of screaming, high-pitched and fearful. Like a horse that had broken a leg and was done for. His heart jolted. He opened his eyes and was hit in the face with something big and blunt. Blood rushed into his mouth. He threw his arms up and opened his eyes. It took a few seconds to realize that the blunt weapon was the back of Lucas's big head. Lucas was swearing and grunting as he struggled with what looked to be a security guard. Or at least John assumed it was a security guard of some kind, considering Lucas's propensity for causing trouble wherever he went. John swallowed some blood from where his teeth had rubbed against the inside of his mouth and grabbed for Lucas's long braids. "Stop it there!" he ordered and pulled at the same time.

"Ow!" Lucas yelled and slapped John's hand away.

All around John, bodies were moving. It seemed as though the entire plane was engrossed in a life-and-death struggle between black-clad "security guards" and ordinary-people types.

"What . . . the . . . hell . . ." John let go of Lucas's braids and Lucas sprung forward and punched his opponent straight in the kisser. Seeing that Lucas appeared to have his situation in control, John squeezed past to intervene in a wrassling match between a stocky stewardess and a slight black man. John punched and caught the man's throat. Not the best hit but it had its desired effect as the man fell backwards clutching his neck. John was about to deliver another punch, this one aimed at the nose, hoping for that always-good fountain of blood but then he felt an unusual feeling at the crook of his neck: small, cylindrical, and metal. And then a click.

"Hands up!"

John raised his hands as he straightened himself. He used his peripherals to establish indirect eye contact with a tall dark-skinned woman holding an authoritative-looking handgun. He nodded, even though she had not asked a question. He leaned back against the stewardess. He could feel her shivering through his back and his own body began to shiver in response. She slid into a seat behind him, probably grateful for the cover he was providing.

"Back to your seat," the woman ordered. John couldn't place the accent — maybe he'd heard it in the movies — but then again he'd never been anywhere outside of the prairie provinces. And he was regretting his decision to leave them.

John backed up slowly, not wanting to anger the tall woman. He had almost made it to his seat when he felt a hand on his shoulder. "You, forward," a deep male voice ordered and John made his feet do the opposite of what they wanted. The tall woman nodded at the man behind him and allowed John to pass.

John kept his hands up, so that everyone knew that the man with the dark skin and the long braids was not in cahoots with the other people with dark skin and short dark hair. When he slowed even a half-step, he found himself prodded with the metal cylinder again and that kept his speed constant. Who knew how good these young'uns were with their guns? He'd run into enough fools on the rez who didn't know their asshole from their trigger finger and he didn't want his death to be an accident. *So, I'd rather be killed deliberately?* He silently counted the rows as scared faces looked up at him. He reached twenty-two when he realized that he was at the front of the plane.

"Stop."

John stopped so fast his toes hit the end of his boots.

"Sit there."

John saw the two stewardess seats, the ones that were tiny and faced backwards. He slid into one of them. He looked across the plane, feeling self-conscious as everyone's eyes were directed towards him. To avoid making eye contact, he looked for his dancers and spotted the two females: Desiree's face was frozen into a silent scream, and Edna's face was on shutdown, a look familiar from when John attended the St. Joseph's boarding school. He could count on her to hold herself together when shit hit the fan.

The black-clad young people (not a single one looked a day over twenty-five) conferred next to his seat. He glanced behind him and guessed that the tall guy with the jazzy goatee was the leader from the way the others deferred to him. John heard one of his men call him "Jamil." He hoped that wasn't his real name. Jamil was a nice name as far as names go, but if they felt comfortable throwing it around, it meant they had no plans for a regular life after this event. *Please let it be one of those pseudonyms or writing names.* Although in this case, it would be a hijacking name.

Besides Jamil and the scary woman, there were three men standing near him. John could see another three stationed at various places throughout the plane. Eight seemed like a lot. Each of them had a gleaming handgun in their hands, held at attention as if daring someone to make them use it. What happened if a bullet went through the plane's walls? John wished he knew about something other than cattle and dancing.

"You Indian?" Jamil stared at him, his eyes unreadable. Once again, John was reminded of students of St. Joseph's boarding school. But no African-Americans attended from what John remembered. There had been one half-Indian, half-black student who had been there but after a month he got sick and was sent to the hospital. John never saw him again.

Jamil held out a handkerchief. John flinched. "For your face." Jamil gestured and John rubbed his face. He'd forgotten that head-butt to the kisser. Damn hard-headed Indians.

"Indian?"

"Huh?" John replied, fear making him forget his manners.

"Native American Indian?" The man indicated John's braids.

"Not American, Canadian Indian. Not Nixon, Trudeau Indian." John hoped that would make a difference.

"Ahhhh . . . " Jamil's goatee of tight curls waved as he nodded in understanding. "Trudeau — Canada. You're Canadians."

"We call ourselves sovereign people." John felt that his brother Amos would want him to say that. "We have treaties with the government."

Jamil's eyes lit up. "And does your government honour these treaties?"

"Depends on what day it is," John replied.

Jamil threw his head back and laughed. "Same trouble, different country."

The tall woman came up, glared at John — making his intestines all twisty — and announced, "They're ready." John was beginning to get the idea that the enterprise was a well-oiled machine, with different parts moving in the background.

"You — Sovereign Indian, come with me." The laughter had left Jamil's voice.

John got back to his feet. He snuck a glance at Edna. Her eyes had questions floating in them that he couldn't answer. She was probably worried that something would happen to him because he was carrying the expense money on him. He smiled despite himself. John felt the looks of other passengers, all harsh glares accusing him of being a traitor. (Though he was a Canadian, not an American, so technically could betray America and still not be a traitor.) One elderly woman did offer him a watery smile. John nodded at her. At least she got it; the hijackers might like him now but he'd be the first one biting the bullet if things went all to shit, as things often do.

Jamil pushed open the cockpit door and despite his fear, John was excited to see inside. There were two pilots seated there, one grey haired and grouchy looking, the other handsome in a Ken doll way. The older pilot had a radio to his mouth. "The leader of the group is approaching now. Please stand by." He handed the radio to Jamil, who then handed it to John.

"What's this?" John asked. Which was a stupid question — he knew what a radio looked like.

"You speak my words, dig it?"

John nodded. He pressed on the red button and looked expectantly at the young man.

"Go ahead and introduce yourself," Jamil said softly.

"Hello there, this is John Greyeyes. I'm standing in for the . . . uh . . . guy in charge here."

A loud voice crackled through the cockpit, "What do you want?"

John looked questioningly at the leader. Jamil said quietly, "Tell them that we will be landing in twenty minutes and will require a truck for refuelling."

"Sounds simple enough," John murmured.

"And one million dollars in cash and the release of the African goddess of light and truth Angela Davis from federal prison."

That sounded a lot more complicated.

"When these things are provided, we will release all of the hostages except for the pilots." He handed John a piece of paper with numbers. "These are the coordinates of the landing strip."

"Okey-dokey." John caught the older pilot glaring at him from the corner of his eye. John did feel like a brown-noser at that moment.

John cleared his throat and passed on the message through the radio lines. There was a slight pause before they responded in the affirmative. John handed the radio back to the pilot and stood there a few seconds with his hands in his pocket, wishing he knew how to get back to his seat without getting shot.

A guard was posted in the cockpit with the pilots. Jamil sat in the stewardess seats and patted the one next to him. "Do you know the hardest part of being a man?" he asked John. This Jamil did not believe in small talk.

John deliberately kept his life as pared down as he could, but even he made decisions sometimes. "Guess it would be living with the choices you make."

Jamil nodded. This was the answer he was looking for. "First you make decisions, then you make peace with the consequences even if they are nothing like you anticipated."

"Yup, the law of unintended consequences." John felt like they should have pipes and a porch.

"Intended or not, your only choice is to accept and deal — even if one of the consequences may be death," Jamil added.

"Hopefully not today," John said lightly. He surveyed the people in front of him. A few women were weeping; other people were praying, their lips moving silently. Some were glaring at the guards and whispering — it would only take a single wrong move to plunge the plane back into chaos.

"You ever faced death?"

"I spent a few years riding bulls in rodeos. Had some close calls back then."

"The hat's more than a chick magnet, then?"

John touched his brim. It was his favourite hat, stayed on in windstorms and under heavy rain and the colour made him look dangerous. "I thought I broke my neck one time. Got lucky. Ended up with sore back and a creaky neck bone." John cracked his neck to demonstrate.

Jamil smiled again. His teeth were bright against his skin. John hadn't been up this close with a black man in his life; they sure were a good-looking people.

"And every time they open that . . . gate —"

"Chute —"

"You know that your life could be over."

"Yeah."

"And still you did it."

"Yeah."

"You are one crazy fool."

John shrugged. He looked down at his hands, brown and cracked from the weather. He still had a rope callous from when one of his calves showed a lot more strength than he'd been expecting. "I had a friend who was one of the best riders in the business. Never backed down from a bull. Then he met his girl — 'the one that makes you forsake all others' is the way he put it. She hated bull-riding, tells him 'it's either me or the bulls.' So he quits. I'm glad 'cause, for once, I'm the one winning the prize money. And he goes off to live in the sunset with his girl. Then about two months after he quit, he gets hit by a car — crossing the street to the post office."

Jamil nodded. "And you'd prefer to die falling off the backside of a bull."

"I'd prefer not to die at all."

Jamil smiled. "I'll do my best, John Greyeyes. But ol' Nixon may not cooperate with me."

John didn't know much about American politics but he guessed that the young man was probably right.

"Where were you headed?" Jamil asked.

"To Sweden. We have a dance show there."

"You're a dancer."

"Powwow."

"I know. They got Indians where I'm from too." Jamil smiled again. "It's some kind of dance troupe?"

"The Prairie Chicken dancers."

"What's a prairie chicken?"

"It's a bird. Sort of a fat little thing."

"Graceful?"

"They can't fly but they sure can shake."

Jamil laughed. "Y'all shaking those feathers in Europe?"

"We're heading to a big festival with Indians from all over the world. Supposed to share cultures and whatnot."

"I've been to Sweden, you'll like it. Went to a jazz show in Stockholm that lasted until the morning — never met whiter people who loved jazz." Jamil stared out the window as if he could still hear the music. He turned back towards John. "What do Indian people say about death?"

"My grandfather said that it was returning to the land. There would be horses and buffalo and we would eat over an open fire every night. And it would always be nipin, summer." John had been in the

59

room when his mushum died. The family had set him up in the big room so that he could speak to anyone who sat near him. Even as his breathing slowed to a drop of air, he was surrounded by family. John remembered the smile that was on his face.

"That is a good place."

"Got no interest in seeing the happy hunting grounds today, though," John joked.

Jamil took out a thin knife and John immediately regretted his attempt at humour.

Jamil pulled an orange out of his pocket and started peeling it with the knife. He handed a piece to John. "Hungry?"

John sucked out its sweetness and looked out the window. Nothing but white clouds. He figured that meant they were flying pretty high still. Descent would be tricky because that was when everything would come to a head.

NADINE

Nadine realized that her stomach problems were over when she took a few sips of the grainy coffee she took from the coffeemaker and didn't need to motor over to the bathroom immediately afterwards. She put the cup down and said a silent prayer of thanks. She was sitting next to Lucas on a wooden bench, a big rough table in front of them. Each of them had a mug-shot book of photographs in front of them. She wondered absently if she'd happen upon one of her relatives. Lucas flipped slowly through his book, his finger moving underneath each picture.

The officer stood by the window, watering a plant. It seemed to be taking on a lot of water as he had been standing there a long —

"Oh shit." The corporal was backing away from the plant. Nadine could see that his feet were wet from water flowing down the side of the wall. He rushed to a back office.

Nadine leaned over Lucas's book. "Anyone?"

Lucas shook his head and sighed. "You can go. Really, you've done enough."

"But how are you gonna get home? I mean, do your people know you're here?"

"Everyone knew I was coming to Canada. Everyone thinks it's so safe up here — I don't think my family was concerned."

"When you say family . . . ?"

"I mean my mom and my sister and my son, Thomas."

Nadine took a careful breath. "What about your wife?"

"She's dead."

"Sorry." Nadine stifled an excited feeling. *Do not have feelings,* she cautioned herself. *Do not have stupid feelings like how you can feel the exact proximity of his thigh to yours on this bench. Do not feel how warm he is, or how he smells like clean wood — cedar to be precise.*

"Hey!" The corporal was suddenly in front of them. "What did your car look like again?"

Nadine stifled a desire to tell him that it wouldn't be *again* because he had forgotten to ask the first time.

"It was a Chevy Chevelle, 1970, green and white four-door."

The corporal whistled. "Nice car."

"The license plates are registered to North Dakota — 14007."

"All right."

"You should be writing this down." Nadine held up a pen and paper.

"Oh, I'll remember."

"What were the licence plates?"

He glared at her.

Nadine scrawled out the information and handed it to him. "There."

The young cop mumbled "bossy" under his breath as he walked back to his desk. He picked up the phone and dialed a few numbers.

"I wonder why he's running this office himself," Lucas said. "Who would leave him alone?"

"I would leave him alone, preferably on a deserted island."

Lucas smiled and turned the page.

"What do you do back home?"

"I run my own business. Have since I was a teenager. Maybe I should have taken up a trade or joined the army like everyone else, but I've only ever felt like doing one thing and I guess that's why I kept doing it."

"What was that one thing?"

"Dancing. Fancy dancer, crow step, traditional, but my specialty is hoop dancing."

Nadine felt the breath leave her body. Her mind was up on the ceiling looking down at her watching as her skin turned white and her hands shook and damned near dropped the giant photo album in her lap.

"You — you —" Nadine took a second to kick her stammer to the curb. "You're a powwow dancer — and you were coming up here to dance with the —"

"The Prairie Chicken dance group. Heard they're pretty good. Strange name, though."

"We're the best."

"You dance with them?"

"I'm the founder and the manager. And I dance too — mostly jingle dress but some fancy dance."

Lucas smiled. "Isn't that a kick in the head?"

"You are a dancer," Nadine said, a big dumb smile glued to her face. "A dancer."

Lucas frowned suddenly. He tapped on a black-and-white picture. Nadine glanced down and saw a high cheek-boned young guy with a cocksure smile, pimples, and pale eyes. "That's him."

Nadine peered closer. "You sure?"

Lucas nodded. "I've always been good with faces and I'd recognize that smirk anywhere."

Nadine read the name in the caption. "Shane Buffalo."

"Yup, that's the little bastard that stole my car, my regalia, and my ticket to Europe."

Nadine read the description underneath the picture. "Wanted for assault with a deadly weapon? Omigod, what if he's on tour with John?"

"Who's John?"

Only the best man who has ever lived. "He's my friend, he's managing the tour right now."

"Any way we can reach him?"

Nadine thought about the itinerary she'd put together. "We might be able to reach him in Stockholm. If I can get a message to the Canadian embassy."

Lucas stood up. "Officer? I think I found the guy."

"All right!" The corporal had been staring out the window and his transition from slack-jawed repose to all-fired-up was extreme. "I knew he'd be in there."

"Any luck with the car?"

"What car?"

"Lucas's car."

"Right, yes." The corporal hit his pockets as if the car might be shoved into one of them. "Was I supposed to be doing something with it?"

"Putting out an all-points bulletin of the plates and description."

"I'll get to it."

"Why not now?"

He rolled his eyes as if Nadine were asking a stupid question. "'Cause if you must know — the radio is down and only the sergeant knows how to fix it and he's not here. So."

Nadine sighed and put the book down on the counter. She pointed to the small picture. "This is the guy that attacked Lucas."

The officer had no reaction other than a casual "'kay." But he took the picture and walked to the back of the room where he picked up a phone. Nadine presumed to call in the description but then again, he could be calling for a pizza for all she knew.

"Now that we've cracked the case — with the help of that amazing Hardy boy — you have any idea what you want to do next?"

Lucas rubbed the back of his neck. "Call my family. Get one of them to pick me up. Will take at least a day though."

Nadine's next breath was going to be spent telling him that he could stay at her place and don't mind the fact that she cooked non-stop, when the front door clanged open and heavy footsteps announced the arrival of a big man. Nadine looked over, the brightness from outside making her shade her eyes. Silhouetted in the Saskatchewan sunshine was an imposing man. Built like a brick shithouse — his wide shoulders were matched with a pair of wide hips and he walked with his hand resting near his gun, which immediately drew one's eyes to the weapon. Nadine figured that was no accident. He looked her up and down with a sneer that Nadine recognized as the "just-an-Indian" expression that she saw when she ventured into town or the city. Her back stiffened and Nadine forced her eyes away from him. She knew the type and there was no sense in getting him riled up when he was getting ready to be riled up.

"Corporal!" the man bellowed across the room, which seemed unnecessary as the room wasn't that big to begin with. The corporal jumped up and raced to the front like there was a bungee cord attached to his body.

"Hey there, Sergeant Baker. How'd the B and E go? Was it the brother like you figured?"

"Who are these people?"

The corporal looked at Nadine and Lucas like he hadn't noticed them until this particular moment. Then the hamster wheel jolted to life. "They're here for a missing car case. And a passport. The guy is an American. Indian, that is. Native American Indian." The corporal savoured the words as he pronounced them.

The sergeant leaned against the counter and it protested with a squeak. "Your car and identification were stolen?" He said this without looking at Lucas but rather at a point on the counter.

"Yes." Lucas spoke calmly and Nadine figured Indians in the States had the same problems with the men in blue as Indians in

Canada had with the men in red. Normally none of her family went to the police for anything.

"Then you have no identification on you at this time?"

Lucas shook his head.

"Cuff him." Everyone reacted in surprise, the corporal most of all. He even dropped the paperclip he had been using to clean his teeth.

"Sergeant?"

"He has no identification and he's not a Canadian citizen. Did you call the border to report an illegal crossing?"

"No."

"This is ridiculous." Nadine slapped her hand on the counter.

"Ma'am, I would ask that you do not assault police property." The sergeant's voice was guard-dog vicious.

Nadine blinked and withdrew her hand.

The sergeant returned his attention to the corporal. "He could be a fugitive from down there — did you run his name?"

The corporal shook his head like a bad dog.

"We are here to report a crime, we didn't commit one," said Nadine. "Lucas is a victim."

"And who are you?"

Nadine hesitated. There was no reason why she shouldn't give her name — she hadn't done anything wrong (had she?). But she didn't want to; she wanted to get as far away from this redneck as possible. Still, not giving your name was some kind of crime, wasn't it? "Nadine Redcloud."

"And which reserve are you from?"

"Fineday."

"Your Chief know that you're here?"

"Why would he? This isn't the 1950s." Nadine's anger engulfed her fear. "We are free to come and go."

The corporal grabbed Lucas arms. "You want the cuffs in the front or the back?"

"He doesn't need them!" Nadine protested.

"Miss Redcloud — do you want to be arrested for obstruction of police business?"

Nadine pressed her lips together, hearing her mushum's voice in her mind: "Save your breath and use it to start a fire later." Maybe to burn this turkey's house down.

Lucas elected for cuffs in the front and Nadine elected to glare at the Sergeant who ignored her as he escorted Lucas to the cell area.

Nadine picked up her purse and headed out the front door in one fluid motion. Dancers don't waste steps.

EDNA

Edna had liked it better when people had thrown themselves at the hijackers, anger making fear seem foolish. Now it seemed like they had all given up like chickens — and when had that ever helped anyone? Sure as hell hadn't helped the Indians when the white men came — why didn't you attack and destroy instead of being friendly and engaging in trade? What Indian person didn't think that from time to time?

"Jesus be with me," she whispered and her rosary moved in a loop through her fingers. Desiree shot her a scared look as if to say, "Don't be weird around these people." But what better test could there be for a good Catholic woman than maintaining her faith in the face of these beasts? "Jesus be with me," Edna's whisper was louder.

Among the armed people, there were two women, which showed Edna that hard hearts were in women as well as men. Of course, she knew that. She'd seen enough smiles on nuns as they doled out beatings to the kids of St. Joseph's to know that females were as capable of evil as anyone else. She imagined those nuns' woman parts were filled with rocks instead of softness.

And what to make of these strong young women? If Edna was honest with herself, they did look beautiful with their jet-black hair curved around their faces like dark halos. They carried themselves proudly, much like the dancers she saw at powwows. But no, they were evil. They followed the message of the Old Testament, "an eye for an eye," forgetting Jesus's admonition to "turn the other cheek," and this is where it had gotten them. In control of innocent people . . .

Why was no one rising up? When John had passed by, his weak posture told her that he was going to go along with everything they said. Now she knew he wasn't a real man, despite the way he wore his jeans and tilted his cowboy hat.

Where were the real men? She risked a look backwards at that young, wild Hunkpapa. He had been quite loud when the fighting had broken out but now he looked to be sleeping.

"Look at that idiot, sleeping away like a newborn baby," Edna whispered to Desiree.

Desiree looked over her aunt's shoulder. "He's unconscious."

Edna looked back and realized her niece was right. She crossed herself and then said a quick prayer to the Virgin Mary that he wasn't dead or wouldn't wake up even crazier than he was before.

"Where's that John?" she whispered.

"He's sitting with the leader-guy, that good-looking guy with the goatee." Desiree's eyes were very sharp.

"Bite your tongue. You should never admire evil."

The blonde woman next to them whispered, "Shhh . . ."

Edna rolled her eyes. They couldn't pretend to be statues, especially not when she had a pain in her bladder. Animals, that's what they were being reduced to.

Edna was about to raise her hand and demand a bathroom break when she saw a shadow on her lap. She glanced at the window and Desiree's head was blocking it. She tugged on Desiree's hair. Desiree whined but moved a fraction to the right. It was enough for Edna to see the outline of a plane, pointier than their plane, like something you would send into war.

"Holy shit, that's a jet!" Desiree exclaimed in a whisper.

Hallelujah! Someone, likely the President of the United States of these Americas, had decided to fight after all.

Edna whispered a prayer of thanks and then took up her prayer beads and double-timed her prayer, as these warriors in the sky would need her help. She hoped she wouldn't piss herself before they made their move.

JOHN

John saw the shadow first, then the mechanical bird that cast it. At first, he was excited — what man doesn't love a jet? But when he realized the consequences of confrontation, his concern grew like sugary bacteria in a petri dish. He turned towards Jamil, who was staring at the jet as well. Jamil's face was set in a determined scowl but his foot shook like a wet dog with rabies. John stifled a smile; usually, it was the cockiest guys whose legs trembled the worst before their turn at the bull came.

John looked around at the rest of the hijackers as news of the jet passed through the airplane. Generally, when people were shit-scared, they did one of two things: they got quieter or they got louder and bigger and cracked dumb jokes to fill the silence of waiting for the axe to drop. John fell into the former group and pursed his lips together.

Jamil turned his dark eyes on John. Then elbowed him. "Cut it out. You look more nervous than a hippie getting tested for the clap."

"Thought I mastered the stoic Indian look."

"Don't mistake me for a white guy. I'm brown too and I can see right through you." Jamil tapped John on the forehead. "I can't tell you not to worry but I'll tell you this: we knew that plane was coming; we planned for it." He laughed sharply then rubbed his hands together, long straight fingers more suited to piano playing than the trigger of a gun.

"Did that plan involve some of us dying?"

Jamil smiled up to his eyes. "I cannot make any guarantees that John Greyeyes will make it to his next destination safely. But I'll do my best."

Suddenly he leaned close, his breath making John's cheek quiver. His knife was dangerously close to John's neck and the heartbeat there. "Look scared."

John immediately acquiesced.

"Good job, you look inches from filling your jeans. Let the sheep think I'm threatening you and after the fact, you'll have more deniability — get it?"

John nodded.

"Like I would kill an Indian. There's probably only like twelve of you left in the whole damn world."

Jamil leaned back and John's blood pressure ceased its climb up Everest. He flipped the knife closed with a slight wrist movement. "This knife was a gift from my dad. He was a small man, but one of those tough little fuckers who couldn't walk away from a fight. He lived back in a town where you were supposed to hang your head when white men looked your way. My mom said she never knew how he lasted as long as he did. Long enough to make me and my brother and walk us to first grade. Then they strung him up for stealing a chicken or some other made-up nonsense. Guess how old he was? Twenty-five, same age as me."

John figured Jamil wouldn't make it much past twenty-five. But he kept that to himself.

Jamil went on. "But in that little bit of time, he made a difference. I've never hung my head in my life." Jamil stuffed his knife into his pocket. "Duty calls." He moved to speak with his soldiers.

John's eyes were drawn out the window. He could see the jet clearly now, even the white helmet of the pilot. When they got close, they got close. The other passengers on the plane were straining their head to see the jets on either side of the plane and the feeling of hope was palpable in the air.

"You."

John's body already recognized the voice of the tall strong woman and he jumped to his feet without thinking.

She led him to the cockpit, which smelled sharp and hot from the fear wafting off the two pilots. Or maybe it was hot in there with three extra people with guns and now, a sweaty Cree man.

"Good, John." Jamil reached out for John's shoulder and pulled him to the front. John noticed again how the older pilot's eyes narrowed. *I'm not doing this out of the goodness of my heart, I'm clearly a pawn*, John tried to communicate with him but he was sure his telepathic message was not getting through.

"John, we're landing in a few minutes and I want you to reiterate our position and make clear the gravity of the situation."

John nodded and cleared his throat. "Hello — this is John Greyeyes, I'm a passenger on this plane." He snuck that in but Jamil didn't seem to mind.

"Can we speak with the terrorist Jamil Turner?" The voice on the other end was gravelly but calm.

John glanced at Jamil who shook his head slowly, a gentle smile on his face. "He only wants me to speak. Sorry."

Jamil handed him a piece of paper and John read from it.

"We will require the plane to be refuelled at the next stop. We will require one million dollars in cash and we require the release of political prisoner and goddess of truth and strength, Angela Davis, from an illegal prison sentence. Do this and all 220 passengers and all members of the flight crew minus the pilots will be released at the next location." John saw the next part and took a deep breath before continuing. "Failure on even one of these points will result in the death of each and every person on this plane." He tried not to think of how young Desiree and Lucas were or how Edna probably never went anywhere in her life before this or how his dog would run all the way down the approach to greet him every time he came home.

There was a long silence from the other end and then, "Can we speak to the hijacker Jamil Turner?"

John looked at Jamil. "They're asking for you again."

Jamil shook his head. "Nah, I don't negotiate with terrorists." His compatriots guffawed; John managed a half-hearted chuckle and then felt like an asshole when he met eyes with the old pilot again.

"You should tell him that he's a dead man," the voice on the other side said in a voice so cold that John shivered.

John did not repeat this or the other nasty words that followed, feeling that if Jamil didn't already know that, he was a fool. John was a strong believer in not giving people a reason to kill the messenger.

John saw the jet in front of them. It veered into their path. The old pilot struggled with the plane. Alarms and beeps started going off — John didn't know what they meant but they sure as shit sounded scary.

The plane leaned towards the right and John held onto the wall beside him to keep his balance. One of the soldiers wasn't so lucky and he stumbled and John felt a gun brush against his hipbone. He almost screamed.

Don't panic, eat bannock. It was a silly thing his mom said all the time when someone was about to lose it. It didn't fit here but it felt good to have his mom's voice in the cockpit with him.

Jamil grabbed the radio and put it in front of John's face. "Tell them that if they don't move that jet away, I will shoot the pilot."

John's mouth went dry. His eyes went to the back of the pilot's head. The pilot didn't move but John could see his shoulders tense.

"Hello, uh . . . you gotta get that jet away or they are gonna shoot the pilot."

There was no answer on the radio.

"Hello?"

Jamil grabbed a gun from one of his soldiers and held it to the pilot's head.

John was closest to the two of them. He could reach out and shove the gun away from the man's head but could he do it before Jamil pulled the trigger?

"Please don't, I have kids —" the pilot began.

"Shut up," Jamil replied. His voice was cold and John knew that he couldn't be pushed.

John held the radio to his mouth. "He's going to do it."

There was silence on the other end. John wondered if everyone could hear his heart knocking against his chest. He had decided that he would knock the gun away. He'd be shot, of course, but it was better than watching a man die in front of him.

"Okay." The voice came from the radio.

John leaned down and looked out the cockpit window. The jet was moving away from the plane.

"It's leaving," he told Jamil. "It's moving quicker than a dollar bill at an Indian casino."

Jamil pulled back the gun.

"John, you are an interesting man."

John inclined his head.

~

It was only a few minutes later when John felt the plane tilt downwards and saw the ground grow larger. He saw lumps and then green and then forests stretching out on both sides of the tiny runway. The landing was smooth, the pilots admirably keeping their shit together. John was grateful because Jamil hadn't let him go back to his seat and he didn't think it was safe to be clinging to the back of the head pilot's seat during a landing.

The plane hit the brakes hard and everyone jolted forward. John crumpled against a piece of equipment and felt some knob rub against his knob and he grunted. He grabbed onto a door handle and took a few deep breaths. Despite the pain in his gut, he appreciated the killer view from the cockpit. He'd definitely never see that again — the ground rushing towards him, growing larger each second. And growing too were the military vehicles lined up on the runway, plus police cars and ambulances. The red and white whirring lights made John wonder how a bullet would feel. He'd always thought that he had a strong pain tolerance. But bullets were probably sharper than bull hooves.

John spotted a fuel truck and allowed himself to feel some hope that everyone would get out of this alive. Jamil looked at his men and women — "It's time." He walked out of the cockpit and John, as part of his entourage, followed him.

Jamil walked down the rows as he addressed the airplane passengers: "It would appear that your government values your lives more than political rhetoric." His voice was deep and clear and John imagined that he had probably trained as a preacher at some point in his life. John certainly felt more peaceful listening to him. "I apologize for the inconvenience that our actions have caused you today but there are moments in life in which we must take a stand for a cause that is greater than ourselves —"

Jamil looked as though he had a lot more to say but then Edna dive-bombed into his torso and knocked him to the ground. She and the young man became a tumble of limbs and tortoiseshell glasses. John wondered if she had been possessed by the Holy Spirit or some other religious fervour the way that she kept striking at Jamil's handsome face as he attempted to grab her flailing fists. Her fists looked like cashews in his big mitts. John could hear Jamil laughing as he struggled but his people weren't enjoying the show — that scary lady aimed her rifle butt at the grappling bodies — John heard a thwack that made him flinch.

The next second, Jamil was on his feet straightening his turtleneck and Edna was a soft speed bump. Jamil turned and grinned at John. "You Indians are crazy."

The hijackers ordered the passengers to stand in front of the windows as a sharpshooter could make this plane a whole lot more empty in a few seconds. John saw Desiree standing in her window, her body barely covering the space. He couldn't see Lucas and figured he was still down for the count.

Jamil looked at John. "Showtime, Mr. Greyeyes." He pushed John to the front door. "Don't come back empty-handed."

John put his hands up at the front door and watched as dozens of guns simultaneously aimed at his head as he made his way down the stairs. A white guy with a brush cut and muscles bursting out of a tight button-down shirt, looking like a military businessman, greeted him. "John Greyeyes?"

~

John sat in a metal folding chair under a tent and wondered how'd they set things up so fast. He could feel, rather than see, the gun aimed at his head.

In front of him stood the brush cut guy — he told John to call him Bill. John recognized his voice from the phone. Next to him was a slim dude with Beatles hair and a full three-piece suit; he was Mike. Bill leaned close: "How many militants are on the plane?"

John mentally counted. "About twelve."

"Armed?"

John nodded.

They looked at one another. "Do you think he's serious?" Bill asked.

"They had some pretty serious guns."

"Did he seem like a killer?"

John thought about the cool detachment on Jamil's face as he held the gun to the pilot's head.

"Seems like if you corner a wild horse, they'll come out kicking," John replied.

The two men exchanged looks. John watched as they called for the fuel truck and exhaled a breath that seemed to travel the entire length of his body. And yet, he knew that there was still more worrying to do.

~

In a dazed state, the plane's passengers climbed down the stairs. John half-carried Edna down, while Desiree clung to the back of his shirt. Where the Hunkpapa was, John had no idea.

"What happens now?" Desiree asked, a shiver in her voice.

"Now we get interrogated," John said, noting the unfriendly faces of the police officers waiting to "rescue" them.

"I hope they let us eat first."

John's stomach growled in agreement.

John was on a bus when he saw Jamil for the last time. It was a glimpse of his face in a window and then the plane was racing down the runway again.

"Can't believe they let those savages go," an old white guy muttered.

"Didn't hear you talk like that when they were in front of you!" Desiree snorted. The old man took one look at her mocha skin and backed down.

Day 3

EDNA

On our third day, our flight to Stockholm was delayed by a hijacking. The hijackers were a group of young African-American men and women who called themselves the Black Fist. Nobody was killed, thanks be to God. The hijackers were not apprehended. They made their way to Europe and then to Africa where the country of Algeria took them in. I guess hijacking is not as frowned upon there as it is in North America. Being kidnapped on a plane was unpleasant as you cannot go to the bathroom whenever you want and they do not hand out meals. That being said, the flight and landing were both managed well.

We were taken back to Chicago where we spent a day being questioned by police as one person in our troupe had acted suspiciously during the hijacking ordeal (according to the FBI and the majority of the passengers). During this time we drank a lot of coffee and ate some donuts. The dancer, Lucas Pretends Eagle, put on several spontaneous fancy dancing shows. Security guards attempted to stop one of his shows but due to the popularity of his activities and the pleading of his fans (mostly female ones, I noted), his shows continued. I am sure his head has grown at least two sizes in this past day and I do not know if his roach headdress will fit him tomorrow.

I have been informed that we will be on our way to Europe shortly.

JOHN

John was glad to see the border security guards Marlow and Carol again. He had been delivered to their custody after being flown back to Chicago. One step forward, two steps back.

The moment John sat down, Marlow launched at him: "How long have you known the hijacker Jamil Turner?"

"Met him on the plane."

"You never met him during any of your activism?" Marlow paused for effect. "With the American Indian Moment?"

"Who?"

"American Indian Movement," Carol clarified.

"Oh, AIM. I've heard of them. American Indians, right?"

"And Canadian Indians. They run down here and get into our affairs."

"Indian affairs," John whispered at Carol, who giggled.

"I would take this a lot more seriously if I were you. You could be facing treason charges!"

"I'm not an American citizen." John had heard, of course, about how Indians in Canada could travel down to the States and get a social security card because of the Jay Treaty but he'd never been interested. Two of his cousins had followed that route and joined the American army; one of them had died in a tour of duty in a jungle and the other was shooting his veins full of a drug that made him forget about his people waiting for him back home.

"Tell me how it is that the hijacker picked you — of all the people on that plane — to help him out."

"I guess to a black guy on a plane full of white people, the Indian guy seems like a safe bet."

"What about the money you had? Was that for weapons?"

John pulled the wad from his pocket and laid it on the desk. "Five hundred minus ten for hamburgers and fries. You can count it, it's all there. How much does a gun cost these days?"

"Depends on the gun," Carol said with a smile.

"I don't know what else to say," John said.

"Were you helping them?"

John shook his head.

Marlow grunted with frustration. "If you weren't helping them, then how did a bunch of ni —"

John slammed the top of the table before he could finish. Carol jumped and John shot her an apologetic glance. "Look, I ain't fan of that word. In my area, it's preceded with prairie but it don't make it any less ugly." John picked his hat off the table and stood up. "I think I've had enough questioning without a lawyer. So, if you want to continue then I'm gonna need my phone call."

John was bluffing. He didn't have a lawyer.

Marlow grunted and threw himself into a chair with his arms crossed. Then he got up, flounced out of the room, slamming the door behind him.

"Bathroom," Carol said.

"When you gotta go, you gotta go."

Marlow didn't return. Carol brought John a flattened ham sandwich and a hot chocolate and John was grateful to be saving money on food.

By the time they were all released, they had only a few minutes to make it to their gate at the airport. Though dog-tired, John hustled his troupe back through customs, back through the check-in desks and then on to a drug store to pick up some painkillers as both Lucas and Edna had fearsome headaches.

He handed out his purchases near the gate. While washing down her pills with a swig of Fanta, Edna proclaimed: "I have a good mind to sue those black people for battery."

John didn't have the heart to point out that she had attacked first.

Desiree had no such heart. "Go ahead, Auntie. I'm sure the African country they're in now will take your side over theirs."

But John noticed that Desiree was carrying her aunt's purse as Edna was nursing her hip.

And that is my dancer, he sighed and shook his head.

Lucas grabbed John's shoulder. "Can I get some more drugs? My head is still killing me from where that black dude clocked me." John handed him a couple more painkillers though he was sure that the first four should have been more than enough.

Once they got settled on the plane, John took a walk ostensibly to stretch his legs, but more to look for possible hijackers. But everyone looked as normal as people can look and he walked himself back to his seat, satisfied that he would wake up in Europe.

C H A P T E R 4

N A D I N E

Nadine drove directly to Chief Amos's house, woke him up, and pissed off his wife. (Again.) The Chief led her to the porch; he was wearing pajama bottoms and a Coca-Cola T-shirt. His eyes were slanted with sleep. "Nadine, what's this about? If it's about the tour —"

"Your brother is travelling with a violent criminal."

"Edna? She's got a temper but she's not a criminal."

"The Lucas guy. Except he's not really Lucas — he's some punk named Shane Buffalo who rolled the real Lucas, who's locked up in the RCMP cells right now."

Amos blinked. "Huh?"

"It's okay. I'm breaking him out."

"What?"

Nadine wished she'd left that part out. "The sergeant is on some kind of power trip. You know how he is."

Amos nodded. As the Chief, he was familiar with complaints against the sergeant: like how he threw Indian guys in jail for shits and giggles, and how he had a tendency to break heads when talking would do as well, and how he insisted on wearing his Redskins T-shirt all over town on days off. "But to break in? That's a jailable offense, Nadine."

"I can't leave an innocent man locked up!" Nadine exclaimed. 'Specially not one with shoulders that square and thighs that muscled. "Besides, when we find that criminal, we'll need another dancer to take his place."

"You're going to Europe?"

"I've got my ticket rescheduled — and my emergency funds." Nadine patted her front pocket.

Amos turned abruptly and Nadine followed him into the house. "Where are you going, Amos? Are you calling the police on me?"

"Hush." He pointed upstairs with his lips, reminding her of his sleeping kids and grumpy spouse. "I'm helping you out." He reached above the fridge and pulled out a black passport and a wad of cash. "You find my brother and you make sure he gets home safe."

"Of course," Nadine said, although she had no idea how she was going to complete even step one of her plan.

He whispered. "My mother would literally kill me if she found out that I sent her favourite son on the road with a dangerous criminal. Murdered in one blow. And then crucified on top of that."

Nadine checked the passport pic. "This is yours."

The Chief smiled. "Yeah, no stamps so far. Always dreamed of one day flying to England and spitting on a royal person — but life hasn't happened that way so far."

Nadine studied the picture. If Lucas could fake a double chin, duck down a couple inches and lighten his skin a couple shades . . . "You think this will work?"

"You think they can tell the difference between two Indians? It'll be fine. You bring my brother home safe."

Nadine nodded at Amos and waited for him to do his searching eye thing and once he seemed assured of her good intentions, he nodded as well.

~

Breaking in turned out to be easier than expected. The RCMP detachment was staffed with officers during the day. But at night they hired a security guard from the local town who came in and checked on prisoners to ensure that they weren't trying to off themselves and then slept in his truck.

Nadine parked on the main road and walked down the approach.

She passed the security guard's truck, where he slept peacefully as a Johnny Cash song played over the radio. She quietly climbed the steps to the detachment and tried the door. It was open.

The keys to the cells were sitting on the counter as the security guard had probably just checked on the prisoners. Nadine grabbed them and walked to the back. She wrestled with the keys a bit at the first door and then once it opened, craned her neck for Lucas. There were four cells and Lucas was in the last one. He was sitting on the edge of a bunk when she walked in.

"Hey there," she whispered.

"Nadine?"

She liked the way her name sounded on his lips. "Yeah. I came to break you out."

"You think that's a good idea?"

"Probably not, but we don't have a lot of time to think about it."

Nadine fiddled with the keys, going through them one at a time.

"I'll be a wanted criminal."

"Better wanted than unwanted is what I always say." Nadine laughed.

Lucas looked at her as though he was questioning her intelligence or sanity. "I don't think you've thought this through."

"Logically, they had nothing to charge you with in the first place. And who knows how long you'll be stuck here before you get in front of a judge and he throws this case out? We only have court once every two weeks in this area — we're expediting the legal process." The key in her hand turned to the right and clicked as the lock opened. "You are free to go," she announced with more confidence than she felt.

They walked out the door and down to her car without incident. As they walked past the security guard, Lucas remarked, "Worst guard ever."

"If he's smart he'll make up a story about a jailbreak with ten armed thugs. That's what I would do."

Lucas raised an eyebrow.

"Just thinking logically."

Day 4

Stockholm, Sweden

EDNA

We arrived in Stockholm at 11:00 at night, our time in Saskatchewan. But it was 6:00 a.m. for the Swedish people. While we were craving our pillows, they were already serving breakfast, which, from what I can see, is mostly fish. The Swedish people are blonde and blue eyed. As one of my fellow dancers noted, it's almost like this is where God got the idea for the monias.

We went to pick up our bags and were disappointed to find out that the men's bustles were not on the luggage carousel. We went to the airline and they tracked them down to Buffalo, New York. Who knew they had Buffalo in New York?

That is a joke.

The airline says that the bustles and other parts of our costumes regalia are on their way now but we have to wait for them to fly over the Atlantic Ocean. Fortunately, we have a lot of time to wait for our flight to Kiruna, a town in northern Sweden. John, the tour leader and suspected FBI criminal, says that if we had to fly without them, then we'd have no way for them to reach us once we got into northern Sweden. Which would mean that myself and my niece, Desiree, would be the only two dancers. That would not be worth the price of admission in my opinion.

Kiruna is supposed to be a barren, unpopulated area. Much like Saskatchewan. Let's hope there are fewer mosquitoes.

John has decided that instead of wasting time, we will now be practising as a dance troupe. I'm looking forward to learning new dance steps although I am surprised that a man knows more about dancing women-dances than most women.

JOHN

John's kokum was a well-known eccentric. Or if you were truly impolite (or if you were John's mother, who had never gotten along with her mother-in-law), a kook. Her name was Yellow Belly, although most people called her Belly for short. She married John's grandfather when she was forty-five years old and had her only son nine months later, defying all the people in the village who said she was too old for babies. She lost that same son to a war for white people twenty-eight years later.

Yellow Belly wasn't much of a talker. And when she did bother to speak, she only spoke to people that she liked (she had only spoken a few words to John's mother, for instance). When she did speak, her words were pinchy weeds.

Yellow Belly was a short, wide woman with muscles on top of muscles. She'd grown up on the plains, following the hunt all the way from the prairies to the Rockies. But she told John that it was dancing that made her legs strong. "Look at me, I'm as old as dirt and not a single vein in my legs." She'd pull her skirt aside to show him smooth thighs and calves.

Yellow Belly watched her grandsons every afternoon as John's mom went about her chores. Kokum Belly's role was to teach the boys what they needed to know to grow up to be good men. Her only rule was that she wouldn't teach them what they did not want to learn.

At his first powwow when he was a toddler, John spent the entire day dancing on the sidelines until he screwed up the courage to run into the grand entry and join the dancers. John remembered seeing his grandmother's eyes on him. After that day, John's instruction turned to footwork, regalia, and stories surrounding the dances. Yellow Belly taught him the men's dances first and when he mastered those, she taught him the women's. It was a bit perverse of her to do it because most of the elders coming out of the residential schools were insisting on keeping the genders separate. But she explained to John that it was his mom's fault for not giving her a granddaughter to pass her teachings onto.

Yellow Belly invited John's older brother to their dance practices but Amos was more interested in listening in on old men's conversations. "That one will become fat with talk," Yellow Belly would sigh.

When John was nine, she presented him with his regalia. His colours were his grandfather's colours, gold and green. His beadwork was a geometric design like most Plains Cree but his was based on the north star. "Like your mushum, you will lead the way," his kokum told him, even though John never felt the desire to lead anyone anywhere.

When he was fifteen, his grandmother passed away. His mother brought him a big bag. "She wanted you to have this." When John opened it, he saw female regalia: a fancy dancer outfit, a jingle dress and a traditional shawl. Yellow Belly had apparently hoped that someone would have daughters and had put her fingers to work in pursuit of that dream. When his brother started having kids, John had approached his sister-in-law and the regalia had been put to good use.

During his powwow years (which had preceded his rodeo years), John had been a favourite. This was due to his kokum's perfectionism. She'd made him practise hours a day. Each movement of his feet and hands had a meaning that must be clear. Only after he mastered one part of the dance would she allow him to move to the next. He hadn't minded; those afternoons in the barn while she played the drum were the happiest he'd ever spent.

Surveying his students now in a seating area at the Stockholm airport, John murmured to himself, "But that kind of perfectionism ain't gonna work here."

Desiree had already plopped herself onto a chair and was buffing her nails with a pink emery board. Edna was leaning against the wall and rubbing her hip with her free hand as if trying to start a fire. Lucas leaned against a wall, looking lazy and mischievous at the same time.

"Can you close your mouth when you chew your gum?" John asked Lucas. "They can hear you back in Canada."

Lucas laughed.

"What's going on with your skin?" Desiree peered close at Lucas's cheeks.

Lucas shook his head. "Nothing."

"It's like it got redder," she added. "From my lipstick, probably."

"He might have an allergy, is all," Edna pointed out. "You put some Noxzema on that and it'll disappear right quick."

"It's nothing." Lucas's left hand was on his cheek now and he was half-turned away from them.

John signed. He redirected their attention. "We'll start with shawl dancing." John tossed a fringed shawl in Desiree's direction and it hit her full-on in the face.

"Hey!" She tossed it to the floor. "What the hell!"

"Sorry, but when I said shawl dancer, I assumed that you would know that I meant you."

She glared at him. "I wasn't listening."

Lucas guffawed. "Great start."

"Shut up." John walked forward and picked up the shawl. He held it out for Desiree. "It's the dance where the girls use their fringes — you're supposed to look like a butterfly. There's spins and hops and it takes an athletic woman to pull it off."

"Good luck with that, princess," Lucas said.

"Screw you, PretendsIdiot!"

John was glad to see Desiree's glare directed at someone else.

"Sorry to have offended the princess." Lucas bowed.

"Redskin!" she hissed back.

"That's enough." Edna spoke up from the corner. "You know the dance, Desiree. Your friend Nicky is a shawl dancer or what we call a fancy dancer. Remember when we watched her compete down at the Standing Buffalo powwow? You said then that you wanted to learn how to do it."

"Oh yeah, I remember." Desiree's pout shifted into a lopsided smile. "Lots of one-foot stuff and then there's that hop-running you can do."

"That's right," John said.

"Yeah, I can do that. Nicky's like twice my size 'cause she had a baby at sixteen and never lost all the weight."

John didn't know what to do with that information. "Let's start with the spins."

Desiree wasn't the most graceful young woman in the world but she was a fast learner. Before long she had the basics down and was able to get through most of them while John beat on his hand-drum. He wished that their practise would stop attracting onlookers but there was little he could do about that. He was proud of his student for ignoring their stares. More likely though, John figured Desiree was a born ham. He could tell from her body language that she was leaning into their attention like a plant into sunshine.

"Lucas," John called. "You take over the drum for a bit."

Lucas jogged over. "Getting tired, old guy?"

John could feel his blood pressure rising. "No. You need to practise the drum."

John walked over to Edna, who had moved to a seat near the window. Her eyes were still on Desiree, now engaged in an argument with Lucas.

"She's going to be good," she said quietly.

John nodded. "She'll be all right." He sat down next to Edna on the windowsill. "How's your hip?"

"Fine, both fine."

John straightened his legs and lifted them both off the ground. "Can you do this?"

Edna hesitated a second before attempting the move. She winced as her legs raised only a few inches off the floor before gravity reclaimed them.

"Arthritis?"

She nodded.

"My mother has it too," John said. And God knows, he'd never try to teach her to dance. "You've seen traditional women's?"

"It's my favourite."

"The movements are subtle. Sometimes it's tough to teach young people because they have so much hurry-up-and-go in them."

Edna laughed. "No worries about that here."

"It's mostly in the knees."

"That's good because they bother me the least these days."

But there would be pain, John could tell from looking in her eyes. He stood up and offered his hand to Edna and pulled her to standing.

The traditional woman's regalia was somewhere in transit with the men's bustles so a sweater draped over the shoulders stood in for long fringes, a hairbrush for an Eagle fan and bare feet for soft moccasins. Edna followed John's movements, her back straight and regal. If her joints were bothering her, she didn't let it show.

"When do I raise the Eagle feather?" asked Edna.

"Can you hear the honour beats?" He paused so that they could listen to Lucas's drum. A good drummer would make them clearer, but beggars can't be choosers. "When Lucas hits hard, that's when you raise up the fan. It's to honour a son or husband who has fallen in battle." John paused, not sure if she'd ever had one of those things. "Or you know, someone you care about."

Edna nodded as if she had someone in mind. John didn't ask for details; a woman her age had her secrets.

John kept the practice short, not wanting to tax her and also because Lucas kept speeding up the drum like a moron. After a couple songs, John told her to take a break.

Edna sat down and Lucas walked over to her.

"Edna, you should do this stretch." Lucas sat next to her and then crossed his right leg over his left and pushed on the knee. "That'll loosen up those hips. Before you know it, you'll be jumping around like a lady goat making all the male goats excited."

John had spent his entire life on a ranch and had never seen that behaviour.

"Oh, go on, you." Edna gave Lucas a pinch.

Lucas jumped up away from her fingers, still laughing. John was about to thank the young man for helping out, when he saw Lucas take gum out of his mouth and stick it to the underside of the hand-drum, while leering at a group of stewardesses.

~

An airport employee woke John when the last of their bags arrived. He nodded his thanks. He rubbed the sleep from his eyes and stretched out his back, which cracked in half a dozen places. He was too old to be sleeping in chairs.

Desiree and Edna were stretched out on benches they'd made out of plastic chairs, their jackets and scarves arranged over them like blankets. Lucas was curled up on a stretch of floor (had he rolled off the carpet?) looking for all the world like an abandoned puppy.

John got up and checked the board. They had an hour until the Kiruna flight; once they reached their destination, he hoped that food and beds would be plentiful. He thought about calling his brother, maybe to explain why they were a day behind but couldn't do the time conversion in his head. And to be honest, his brother's remarks still stung. "Sohkitehewin." Him — the guy who hung out with a hijacker and lived to tell about it? The guy who got questioned by FBI and border patrol agents twice — was a chicken? The guy who had to defuse daily blow-ups between three tired, jet-lagged Indians? He was a goddamned hero. Amos didn't know anything about him. John busied himself packing and unpacking the bags before waking up the rest of the group.

"What's the name of the guide again?" Edna craned her neck to search through the airport for a sufficiently trustworthy person.

"His name is Per Ollman." John checked the itinerary to make sure he'd remembered that right.

"Pear like the fruit? I hope he's sweet as one too." Desiree's bawdy comment drew Lucas to her like a fly. He had nothing to add other than an eager smile so he just hovered near her.

"P-e-r," John spelled out. "Not a fruit."

"And no one is getting sweet with anyone." Edna sniffed. "Good girls don't even think about things like that."

Desiree rolled her eyes. And Lucas leaned close enough to smell her hair.

They sat on their suitcases and chewed some dried fish that John had purchased from one of the airport kiosks. He was looking forward to being out of an airport, that was for damned sure. This airport was the smallest one yet, although they tried to make up for that lack of space with large glass windows. He'd stood there after they arrived, staring out at this new world. The land was bare, with few trees dotting the landscape but the buildings were brightly coloured and cheery-looking.

"Prairie Chickens, welcome to Kiruna!" a strangely accented voice called out to them. As though bound by a single mind, their heads all turned in the same direction simultaneously. The owner of the voice was a slim man wearing jeans and a jacket trimmed with what looked like rabbit fur. He had a long straight nose and full lips and the light hair of a Métis but the brown skin of a Cree.

"Wow," Desiree said.

"I'm Per and you must be . . . Nadine?" Per held his hand out to Edna.

Edna shook her head, and to John's surprise, seemed too shy to say anything else.

John took the lead and held out his hand. "I'm John Greyeyes. There's been a change in the . . . uh . . . lineup. Nadine and the rest of the troupe got sick at the last minute with . . . well, you don't need the details, and so we're here to replace them."

Per took John's hand in his and winked. "Yes, adapting to change quickly, that's what we Indigenous people do."

John didn't know how to take the wink — he couldn't remember ever having a man wink at him. But he was relieved that this Per fella seemed to be a go-with-the-flow kind of guy.

Per helped them gather up their luggage and took them outside to where a small vw van waited. Per and two other men loaded the luggage. Per hefted their bags with ease. John noticed and was impressed; Per didn't look like he was much more than a buck forty. Per and John jumped into the front seats.

"I'll have you at the camp in less than an hour — in time for lunch," Per announced.

"What kind of foods do you eat around here?" Edna asked.

"Lunch will be fish but we have a special treat for tonight — some reindeer."

"You're joking?" Edna looked at John. "He's joking, right?"

John shrugged.

"Like Santa Claus reindeer?" Lucas joked.

"We shot them out of the sky like ducks," Per said agreeably.

~

On the way out of Kiruna, Per drove through the city centre, pointing out places of interest. There were more colourful buildings and even a pretty church that impressed Edna. She declared that the Swedish must be a very Godly people. She asked Per what denomination attended the church but he didn't know.

"How could you not know the city's history? Haven't you lived here your entire life?"

Per laughed. "Kiruna is where the Sami people settled over six thousand years before the people who founded this city were even lumps in their father's balls. That is history to me."

Edna was shocked into silence. John directed a grin out the window.

On the drive to the camp, Per explained that over four thousand people were attending the Indigenous World Gathering, which had been the brainchild of a local Sami tribe.

"Four thousand?" Desiree asked. "I didn't even know there were that many Indians left in the world."

"That's a lot of chicks," Lucas said.

"We were expecting about five hundred," Per explained. "We've had to make some adjustments. Things are coming together," he added with a grin.

John swallowed a lump of fear. He'd never danced for that many people. He hoped his troupe wouldn't choke.

Per explained that their Chief had decided that they needed to gather people from around the world "to share experiences and gather energy and strategies for combatting ongoing imperialism and colonialism." He finished with a smile.

"Imperio-what-ism?" Lucas said, exposing himself as someone who does not worry about looking stupid.

"Most Indigenous societies have been exposed to imperialist policies and by working together, we can throw off the chains that hold us down," Per explained.

"Like what?" Desiree asked.

"Like racism. Many Sami people can't find jobs or get apartments in cities."

"We get that in Canada too!" Desiree said.

"And people calling you dirty Indians or Chief — even though you're not a Chief," Lucas added.

"Name-calling, people being thrown out of stores or thrown in jail because they were in the wrong place at the wrong time."

"My uncle got arrested for acting drunk in public," said Desiree. "He wasn't even drunk — only acting drunk and the police still put him in cuffs. He was trying to explain and everything."

"Sounds like a lot of complaining to me," Edna said. "Complaining never got anyone anywhere."

"What about the civil rights movement?" asked Desiree.

"They could have gone a lot further, if they'd been nicer."

Desiree had a horrified look on her face. "You don't mean that. You're only being stubborn."

"I do mean that. People act like they have no manners these days."

Lucas stood up in the back of the bus. "Hey guy, why don't you let this nice white man hang you in this tree. Hey now, you settle down and let him put that noose around your neck. After all, he did say pretty please." He mimicked a noose around his neck and gave what John thought was a funny hanging-man face with his tongue sticking out to the right.

"That's morbid to talk like that," Edna warned him.

"Those who do not speak, cannot be heard," Per replied.

Edna crossed her arms.

Per went on. "We're also talking about sharing political strategies, like getting the right to vote, fighting for access to our traditional lands and resources, ensuring the survival of our stories, culture and languages — do you know how many languages have died already?"

"A lot, I bet." Desiree nodded. If Per suddenly announced a run for office, he had a candidate for campaign manager.

"There are many things we need to work on together. Unfortunately we only have a few days together."

"We came here to be a dance troupe," Edna said.

And we are barely that, thought John.

"I didn't know we'd be getting all political," she added, looking at the other occupants for support. Although John figured she'd have a better chance of finding a space alien.

"To be born Indigenous is to be born political," Per said mildly.

"I did not sign up for any of that," Edna said. "I am here to dance and that is all."

"The expression of culture is a form of resistance," Per said.

Before Edna could deny even that, John interrupted. "I'm looking forward to hearing more of this . . . uh, stuff, but hopefully after we eat."

"Of course," Per grinned. "No politics on an empty belly."

The camp was in the shadow of a large hill, and was a hodgepodge of brightly painted buildings and tents, sod homes, and tipis spread out in all four directions as far as John's eyes could see.

"Those tipis look groovy," Lucas said. "That where we're camping out?"

"If you'd like," Per said.

"I am not sleeping in a tipi," said Edna. "I want a bed surrounded by four walls and a floor and a roof. And a bathroom with running water."

"Oh go on, Auntie, we don't even have running water at home," Desiree said.

"I am a guest here and I expect to be treated like one."

"Of course, we can make those arrangements as well. The bunkhouses are fully equipped and the best part is that your roomies are from all over the world," Per assured her.

"Co-ed?" Desiree asked innocently.

"Absolutely not!" Edna roared. "Your father did not send me five thousand miles to watch you hang out with strange Indian men from around the world."

"Technically he did," Lucas said from the furthest seat in the back.

"This is none of your business!" Edna stamped her foot for good measure.

John chuckled. If Edna were a horse, John would be stabling her for the winter.

Per glanced in the rear-view mirror before answering Desiree. "There are options for everyone, including all-women cabins."

"I suppose it's too much to ask for them to be Christian." Edna's voice had a shrill whine to it.

"We're here!" Per parked the vehicle next to a group of busses, cars, and trucks. He risked a raised eyebrow at John as if to say, "How have you survived this far?"

John smiled. "So, where's this Sami food you were talking about?"

It was more than Sami food. The women around the camp had

tried to outdo each other with their traditional dishes. The troupe gorged themselves on dried, smoked, and fresh fish, berries from around the world, and at least five types of flatbreads (including a fried bannock that the Navaho had whipped up). After lunch, Desiree and Edna headed off to a women's cabin area to wash up and John hoped, in Edna's case, to take a nap. Lucas disappeared into thin air but John had no inclination to worry about him, confident that the camp's isolation would keep him out of trouble.

John patted his stomach at the end of the meal; he hadn't been full since the trip started. He looked up and saw Per watching him.

"Would you like to see something interesting?" Per asked.

It wasn't the kind of question John liked answering but he nodded anyway. He felt tired but also like he couldn't stop moving — this travelling was making his body strange.

Per and John walked through the camp. Per said hi to pretty much everyone and even introduced John to many of them. John had never seen so many different shades and shapes of Indians in his life. They were curious about his origins and he stated, "Nehewin, from the prairies." He got some compliments on his cowboy boots. Turned out the guys from Peru were big fans of horses as well.

Per kept walking past the crowds and huts and tents. They hit a small dirt path that led around the hill. The hill itself was about the size of the hills in Fort Qu'Appelle, near John's reserve. Not mountains to be sure, but big enough that they got you huffing.

John was breathing hard (and noting that Per was not) by the time they reached a wooden hut with square shoulders. Steam rose off the building.

"I heard you guys liked your saunas," John commented.

"Like the sweat lodge you Crees like."

"Not much of a fan myself. Got too much work to do to spend hanging out sweating all day."

"You have work to do right now?"

Per peeled off his shirt. His slight body was pure muscle and John was envious as thirty was making him softer than he'd like.

Per's pants came next and John looked away and busied himself removing his own clothes.

Per opened the door and slipped inside. John saw a glimpse of bare ass as Per slipped inside but decided to keep his gitch on, not sure what he'd be sitting on.

John took a deep breath of the cold air — liking how it made his lungs feel open and free — before heading inside. It was hot but not the hottest he'd ever been inside. There some lodges out on his reserve that felt like your skin was on fire. He could handle this.

Once his eyes adjusted to the smoke in the air, he saw Per across from him. Per smiled. Another bearded man sat in the corner and John couldn't figure out his origins. The beard threw him, for one thing, but his eyes were almond-shaped so John figured somewhere out east.

In the last few hours, he'd met more kinds of people than in his entire life. Wasn't that something? Back where he from, there was Indians and there were whites, and then an Asian café in town. You had to go all the way to the city to see anyone more exotic.

A wave of heat wafted through the room and John shut his eyes. Let it run over him. He wasn't much of a sweater so he wasn't sure how long he'd last. A voice started a song in a language John had never heard before. John opened an eye; the bearded man was singing with his eyes closed. John let the music wash over him too. *Hot music*, he mused.

It seemed that with his eyes closed that he could understand what the old man was singing about. He saw animals moving on a plain as one giant body, the dust rising to obscure their size and only the sound of their hooves assuring you that they were many. The song changed and he saw children sitting around a fire; the children stared at the fire as if it contained the answers to the world. And then it was only sky as if he were on his back, the clouds flowing in one direction, more quickly than he'd ever seen them back home. He wasn't sure when the singing stopped but suddenly he knew that the bearded man was gone and Per wasn't across from him anymore. Per was next to him, breathing heavier than John would have expected from an athletic person. John wanted to ask him what was wrong but words seemed too difficult. He felt warm instead of hot as if the heat inside the sauna had become the same temperature as his blood. He felt the brush of fingers on his arms, tracing out his muscles and then on to his shoulder. He felt the fingers move up to his neck and dance across until they reached his lips. He nipped at them and heard Per laugh softly. Then lips replaced fingers and John told himself that he was asleep

dreaming. He'd had dreams like this before. And when he'd wake up, he'd pretend it was something that happened to everyone when they spent too much time by themselves. He reached out with his right and touched the hair that lay against Per's neck. It was soft and he let his finger twirl into it. Per sighed and John became aware of where his lips were, where his tongue was pressing, where his chest was leaning and the dream was too real. He pushed Per away. Roughly. Noting even as he did how firm Per's body was and that there were places that John wanted to bite —

he pushed away and then he was alone again on his side of the sauna. *My side,* John thought to himself. *This is the right side.*

The cold bit at his face when they left the sauna. Even though the sun was still bright in the sky, there was no warmth too it. John kept his eyes in front of him down the hill, moving faster than his knees wanted. He stumbled a few times and caught himself.

He heard Per behind him, not his footsteps which were hidden in Per's soft-skinned boots. He heard the Swede take in long breaths, the kind you take when you're about to say something and then stop yourself. Every time John heard one of those heavy sighs, his feet moved faster down the path.

Let sleeping dogs lie was one of his mother's favourite sayings; he wished more people stuck to that.

Once they reached the camp, John slowed because he didn't know where he was supposed to go. Per caught him then. "Most of the men are staying in the tents," he observed. John could barely hear him because sociable fires had cropped up throughout the area, people telling jokes that were more laughter than words, others yelling over one another. "But we can find room for you in one of the buildings if that suits you better."

"I'm fine wherever. Tired enough to fall asleep where I'm standing." John awkwardly held out his hand. "Keys to the van? I need to pick up my bag."

Per pointed to the west. "If you squint, you can make out the colour." Per handed him the keys.

"Won't you need them?"

Per shrugged. "I'll find you or you'll find me." Then he strolled up to one of the campfires, his hands in his pockets.

John watched as the people greeted Per and he merged with the circle as if he had always been there.

John trudged to the van alone, hoping that he wouldn't run into anyone. People tried to make eye contact but he kept his eyes above them. *I want to sleep.*

He stuck his head in a few tents before he found a small one, big enough for him and his bag. He shoved his belongings with his foot and then crawled in after them.

But, of course now that he'd finally found a place to lie his head, he couldn't sleep. Too damned many people's faces dancing around.

He propped himself up on his elbow, resting against his duffle bag. He set himself to thinking about the dances that he and the troupe would be doing. He played the choreography in his mind, step by step, over and over, until he fell asleep sitting up.

~

Their first show was at 9:00 p.m. and John had to keep an eye on his watch because the sky remained unchanged. He rounded up the members of the troupe in record time. The ladies were the easiest because they had stayed close to their bunkhouse. Lucas was a hell of a lot tougher to locate. John must have described him to at least fifty people before a finger pointed in the direction of a sod house or a wigwam as some of the people said. The wigwam was located on the edge of the camp. John jumped down the steps of the sod house before crawling through a rounded door into a low room that was as cool as the sauna had been hot. Lucas sat close to the doorway and John almost tripped over him. "Lucas," he hissed like a kokum giving her grandchild shit at a bingo for missing numbers. (He sure had taken on the sound of an old woman since he'd met this young guy.)

Lucas turned to him, a lopsided grin on his face. "John! You came at the best time."

John looked around the room. Five men sat around the circle. John saw a bag pass from one man to another. The second man slipped his hand in and ate a handful of whatever was inside. Next a drink was passed to him and he took a long swallow.

"Is that peyote?" John asked. No one paid him any attention. Those who had taken the medicine were turning into themselves and those that had not yet were focused on the movement of the bag around the circle. John took a page out of his brother's book and looked at Lucas, really looked at him, deep into the depths of his eyes. Lucas's eyes switched in and out of focus like a five-dollar TV. "Did you take some?"

Lucas stared at him.

"Did you take some?" John repeated.

Lucas shook his head as if to clear it. "Oh, that's weird, I thought you could read my mind. I said yes like four times."

John stifled the urge to cuff him. "Why would you do that? We have a show tonight."

Lucas shrugged.

"I don't give a damn if you're stoned out of your head. You need to come with me now."

Lucas stared at him intently, probably attempting more telepathic communication. John grabbed Lucas's arm and tugged him to standing, using his own direct form of kinetic communication. Lucas came along willingly enough though John had no idea how his peyote-laden charge was going to dance two solos and take turns at the hand-drum without making a fool of himself, the Prairie Chicken dance troupe, and all the Crees in Saskatchewan. (Lucas wasn't a Cree but they did hire him so they'd still have to take the blame.)

John pulled Lucas behind him as he charged through the crowd. Outside in the sunshine, people moved more slowly as their bodies wound down, even though the light had not. John felt no fatigue himself, figuring once they got through this first show, he'd have a better chance of being claimed by sleep. Though he wondered about that too — did he want to be asleep? A snippet of poetry jumped into his sleep-deprived mind: "To sleep, perchance to dream . . ." John didn't want to know what secrets his dreams wanted to reveal to him. Maybe he'd stay up for the rest of his life.

"I heard that," Lucas said.

"I didn't say anything."

"I meant that guy." Lucas pointed at a man whose size could only be measured with reference to wildlife like moose or bears. He had an expanse of tattoos on his chin and he was staring at the two of them with a menacing look — or maybe that was his natural expression. Neither option made John feel better. "He's thinking I'm an idiot — you think I'm an idiot, don't you?" Lucas yelled at the giant man.

"He wouldn't be wrong," John said. The man, thankfully, had already dismissed Lucas.

"Why don't you like me?" Lucas asked.

"We have a job to do and that's what I'm trying to do right now. It's nothing to do with whether I like you. This is a job."

"So, you do like me?"

John saw the dance stage straight ahead. It was an open-air platform. There were two guys with flutes, playing that music that ranged from wind haunting a desolate house to shimmering sunshine dancing across a lake. They played and two women danced with effortless grace. John had no idea where the hell they were from.

John reached a clearing in the crowd and looked for the two women. He spotted them leaning against Per's van, clad in their full regalia. Desiree had on a pair of sunglasses that were jarring against her colourful fancy dance outfit. Edna's arms were crossed and her face was even crosser. But they were dressed. Desiree's hair was neatly braided. Edna had an elegant braided barrette holding back her bangs. They looked professional but, at this point, John didn't care if they ate ice-cream cones while pedalling bikes — as long as they did it on stage.

"He's not ready," Edna scolded and stated the obvious at the same time (a speciality of hers, John figured).

"What's with his eyes?" Desiree asked. "Those are some spinny green eyes."

"You're an angel from the heavenly skies," Lucas half-sang to her as he kneeled in front of her.

"Holy crap-cakes." Desiree's mouth went into an "o."

"What on God's green earth —"

John could hear Edna's judgement motor picking up speed and he put his hand up. "I'm on it." He pulled open the door to the van and pushed the Hunkpapa inside. For the next five minutes, John did things to the young man that he would rather not remember. There was tugging, pushing, hair-braiding, and a lot of giggling from Lucas. John got himself through remembering something his kokum used to say. "When all is said and done, someone's still gotta dump the slop-pail."

EDNA

As John headed into the van with the wild Indian they were pretending was one of them, she felt her old heart beating wildly. Edna had never expected to be a dancer at her age and she wasn't crazy about the idea of being in front of people doing something she wasn't sure she even knew how to do.

For the last three hours (after their two-hour nap), Desiree had shown her the steps again, even talked a woman in the cabin into using her hand-drum while they practised. The other women in the cabin had oohed and aahed as they practised, which had helped quell her fears somewhat. But looking out at the stage — it was at least six feet in the air — a fist of fear clenched around her heart. What if she fell off it or froze or started crying or fainted and hit her head and went to the bathroom involuntarily . . . ?

"Auntie, your face is white."

"What? I'm as brown as you are. Come here, I want to fix your braids."

Desiree dutifully walked over and turned her back to her aunt. Edna reached up; Desiree was nearly a foot taller than her. Edna's hands shook as she rebraided Desiree's already tight hair. She tied the hide tightly around the braid and made sure the muskrat fur on the end was straight. These were nice outfits her brother had located for them. Of course, he was the Chief and when the Chief wanted something, people generally found it for him quick.

"I can't believe we're going to be in front of all of these people!" Desiree exclaimed. "Do you think someone will film it?"

"Why would they? Doesn't the government have enough pictures of Indians?"

"Maybe ours, but not this government. Besides, this isn't a government thing, this is an Indians thing. You heard what that Per guy said."

Edna felt her belly churn with bad feelings. She hadn't signed up for being some kind of radical. She was a law-abiding, Christian woman and would be until the day she died. Let the others find reasons to be angry; she was done with that herself.

"It's tight." She patted Desiree's braid.

"It was tight before." Desiree craned her head to see the stage. "It looks like they're finishing up."

Edna looked at the stage and saw the dancers lining up, their heads bowed as their flute-player held onto a note. The crowd around them seemed to stop talking all at once and the note moved through them, filling them with melancholy for something that they could barely remember.

The note ended and the dancers began to file offstage.

"Now it's us." The brightness of Desiree's smile nearly knocked her aunt on her ass. What it must be like to be young and fearless.

Edna knocked on the van door. "Mr. Greyeyes, John, time's up."

The van door opened a second later and Lucas fell out in one motion, a collection of limbs, braids, and bustles at Edna's feet. John stepped out behind him and pulled him to standing with one hand.

"Use your legs," John ordered.

Edna stared at the sleepy-eyed young man staring up at the sky and turned to John. "What's your plan?"

"We're going to start with the men's fancy dance as planned."

"You're sure?"

John strode ahead dragging the Hunkpapa behind him, not even dignifying her question with an answer.

"Well, then," Edna said with more than a few ruffled feathers, "let's go knock their socks off."

Would it kill that man to offer some words of support once in a while? Some leader he was turning out to be! Her brother would certainly hear about his surliness once they landed back in prairie territory. She caught a glimpse of herself in the van mirror and stopped. With her hair pulled back, a long feather affixed to her head with a beaded barrette, she looked more Indian than she'd ever looked in her life. Not that she wasn't proud of course — but it was clearer now. She shook off the thought but snuck one final look in the mirror.

JOHN

When John began the hand-drum, it seemed to him that every damn Indian within four square miles stopped moving, talking, smoking, joking around — and turned towards the stage. There were moments in your life when you had the complete attention of the world — and he would certainly share his with anyone else. He wished that they had a different time, closer to 3:00 a.m. when everyone would be no longer held hostage to this unnatural sun and would fall asleep wherever they stood, like the magical kingdom in the story about that lazy princess.

After twelve beats on his drum, John could feel the attention creeping into his spine and it made him want to stomp a hole into the stage and fall through it like a dying Cree star. But a stage collapse was only a short-term solution to his fear. And then the truly miraculous happened: the stoned bones of Lucas Pretends Eagle moved up the stairs (he actually danced up the stairs!) onto the stage and he leapt a full foot into the air with his first jump. John kept his ear on his drum and his eyes on the dancer. Lucas's feet flew and kicked. He cartwheeled, flipped, and nearly danced off the edge of the stage. Though even if he had, the crowd would have caught him and threw him back on — they loved him that much. He spun so fast, it looked his bustles might fly off into space.

Three-quarters through the song, John's fears changed course — *How would he get this fool to stop dancing?* He held his breath as he closed the song off as the dancer did not slow even a second, seemed to pick up pace actually, as if he was getting paid every time his foot hit the stage and bounced away from the earth. John hit the drum one last time, hard as hell, so that it reverberated through the dark hills. When he looked up, Lucas was frozen in place, one hand pointed at the sky, his eyes craned in the same direction with such conviction that a few people turned their heads to see what he was looking at. John held the drum silent as Lucas bowed. The crowd burst into applause like a sudden downburst.

Lucas walked soundlessly off the stage like nothing had happened. John looked down at his two female dancers standing off to the side, their mouths open, Desiree's sunglasses halfway down her nose. John nodded at them and began to drum again.

Desiree and Edna were more tentative in their approach to fancy dancing and traditional respectively. They made it on stage — which John was grateful for. They were in beat with the music, most of the time. And Desiree did attempt some jumps, which many would describe as brave rather than graceful. Edna kept her body frozen in one direction and moved her knees so imperceptibly that John would require a microscope to measure it. At one point, Edna did show some life — but just because Desiree had lost control during one of her spins and her aunt had to scuttle out of her way, lest they both fall to the ground in a heap.

It took every ounce of John's self-control not to laugh.

When the song was finished, both women bowed and hurried offstage. They were supposed to do another song but John felt that they had cheated death enough for one day.

NADINE

Nadine woke up suddenly on the plane. Her mouth twisted into a scream. Fortunately for the other passengers, only a tiny "No!" squeaked out.

Her eyes snapped open. Lucas was looking at her. "Bad dream?"

"Hell yes." She rubbed her eyes. "Something about being buried alive and then someone dancing on my grave."

"Hope it was a good dancer at least."

"Sounded off beat to me." Nadine yawned and looked around. "They come around with food yet?"

"I would have woken you up for that."

Nadine glanced at the drink next to him. "Whatcha drinking?"

"Iced tea."

"Sip?"

He handed it over. His finger brushed against her finger and Nadine's body glowed like a full moon. Think about dirty toilets, she said to herself. Stinky, dirty toilets.

She took a short, ladylike sip of the drink and then before she could stop herself, gulped more down. She handed it back reluctantly.

"When I first saw your drink, I was thinking to myself, hey, I should have asked this guy if he was a drinker."

"I'm not."

"Me neither. I used to drink but I had to get clean. It caused me to make some bad decisions." Nadine took another sip of the drink. "Miss it though."

"I make enough bad decisions without it."

"Picking up hitchhikers."

Lucas laughed. "Among others. When did you quit?"

"About five years ago, after I got off the powwow circuit. Actually, those two things happened at the same time. I drank and danced. And then I stopped dancing and stopped drinking. Funny." Had the powwow trail driven her to drinking or vice versa? "You know, when I was a powwow dancer, everyone thought I was this straightlaced traditional lady and here I was a big drunk."

Lucas signalled the stewardess; he held up the empty glass and held up two fingers.

"There's always a bigger drunk."

"My parents were pretty good drinkers. Still are. Not that I'm judging. I mean, I know they went through some crazy bad stuff. From the old days when Indian agents and cops were dragging kids off to those schools," Nadine added.

"My grandparents went to one called 'The Rosemount School for Indians.' Sounds fancy but kids almost went bald from lice, everyone had scabies and were half their weight when they got home. Only good thing was the school ended at grade five." A stewardess brought two iced teas. Lucas thanked her and handed one to Nadine.

"Thank you, Judith," Nadine read off her nametag. "This juice looks like an abyss in a desert," Nadine joked.

"An oasis," Lucas said.

"I knew what you meant." The stewardess winked and headed back down the aisle to deal with a drunk guy who kept flicking his smoke on the floor.

"Isn't that interesting? Your school sounds exactly like the one we had on our reserve. It was located right in the middle of the reserve. All roads led to it. My grandparents went, my parents went, aunties, uncles, pretty much everyone went — until someone burnt it down. Good for them." She remembered driving by the brick wreckage with her parents. She'd always wanted to explore the ruins, poke through and see if she could find money or toys or other treasure, but they never went near it.

"Good place to leave the past. In the past."

Nadine had a flash of her pretty mom: her face red from drinking and her nose swollen until she wasn't pretty anymore. "I left home at fourteen."

Lucas whistled. "Young."

"Yeah."

"How does a fourteen-year-old make it on her own?"

Nadine thought about that fourteen-year-old girl packing up her clothes, shoes, and magazines while listening to Elvis Presley on the radio. The last second before she left the room, remembering her regalia hanging on the back of the door and hesitating before plucking it off. "Sometimes I wake up in the middle of the night and I hear them in the kitchen, talking, laughing, and yelling at each other. I can hear the chairs scraping the floor when someone would get up to fight."

Lucas cleared his throat. "Where'd you go?"

"I had a cousin, Danita, who lived in town so I hitchhiked there. She was a powwow dancer who travelled half the year and worked as a motel room cleaner the other half. Seemed like she was having all the fun in the world so I joined her."

"You landed on your feet."

"Wasn't no happily-ever-after. It turned out that she was also hooking along with her motel cleaning business — more hooking than cleaning really. And that was never something I wanted to get into. Too dangerous, y'know?" Nadine hated seeing Danita with those guys, the way her cousin had to pretend to be whatever the men wanted. Packaging herself up nightly, Nadine wondered if she'd forget who she was.

Lucas nodded. "Most dangerous job in the world. She okay?"

"I haven't heard from her in two years."

"Oh . . . I'm sorry."

"Yeah, well." Why had she gone down this road?

"You danced full-time? Tough way to make a living, prize money being what it is. I've only been able to do it in the last few years."

"Not exactly," Nadine said. "I mean, I tried to be frugal and save money but there's only so much you can make on the powwow trail. There's transportation, food, entry fees and after a while, people started looking up to me to help out other dancers — or maybe that was just me — I couldn't stand by while elders weren't doing well or going hungry. I mean there's rations for everyone but sometimes that doesn't cut it, y'know?"

Lucas nodded.

"Maybe if I'd fallen in love with another someone with a job, instead of singers — which was kind of my kryptonite back then — then maybe I wouldn't have had to look to other forms of . . . fund-raising." She took a long sip of her juice. "I could get used to this. Well, no, not really — wouldn't it be weird to be rich?"

"What makes you think I've never been rich?"

"'Cause you're an Indian?" Nadine put her glass down. "Plus I'm kind of an expert in sizing people up. That's how I ended up paying for my powwow days. I became a thief."

"What kind?"

"House kind. I liked breaking into people's houses. And I mean that, I really liked it."

"Kind of dangerous."

"They weren't home, of course. What I liked best was going through people's junk drawers. Like, it's junk to them but I'd get glimpses of what people — white people's — lives were like. Postcards from vacation spots, 'Lois and I nearly missed our plane!'; credit card bills that showed balances being paid on time; invitations to weddings and baby showers; requests for donations to alma maters. Lots of pictures lying free . . . I'd leaf through them and imagine these were my people and give them background stories, this here was Grey who loved hockey but who would never make it far but that was okay because he was taking pre-law classes anyway. Or this was Nicole — she was growing so fast and the boys were coming around but she always ended up making up with the neighbour's boy, Cole. *We can practically hear those wedding bells!*" Nadine laughed. "Can you imagine?"

"You ever get caught?"

Nadine shook her head. "I had rules. No dogs, no houses with people in them — it's not hard to figure out who's on vacation — and only houses that were twice the size of a reserve house. I was into size back then."

"You feel bad about taking from them?"

"I didn't at the time. 'Course I didn't think too much at all. I did stuff to get to the next day. Like my cousin and those hotel rooms, I guess."

Lucas frowned. "My house was broken into, one time. A few times, now that I've moved back to the reserve. There's nothing more annoying."

Nadine laughed sharply. "It wasn't me." Then slapped him on the leg. "Don't worry, karma got me good. My car's stereo has been stolen so many times, I've learned to enjoy the sound of my own singing. And my house — every second window is boarded up to save me the expense. Plus it keeps the bugs out. So where did you grow up?"

Lucas allowed a smile. "I used to live in one of those houses you were talking about. One of those rich folks."

"A rich Indian, well la dee dah!" Nadine was embarrassed but damned if she was going to show it.

"My dad had a concrete business. He started on the rez, built the casino, and then moved on to residential."

"An Indian guy running his own business? How'd he get white people to hire him?"

"It helped that he didn't look exactly Indian. Most people figured he was Italian and he didn't enlighten them. Kept cashing those cheques. I had a pretty good childhood."

"Like a nice bike?"

"A new bike every year."

"Did you go to a regular school? Or like one of those places with uniforms?" Nadine grinned, enjoying the thought of Lucas in pastel colours and knee socks.

"Regular."

"Aw well."

"I guess I would have ended up like those guys you see on the golf course talking about their investments and their last vacation. But life had a different path for me."

"The big stock market crash?"

Lucas laughed. "How old do you think I am?"

Nadine shrugged. "I don't know how you rich people lose money."

"My dad couldn't leave behind that feeling that he wasn't good enough, that he was just another dirty Indian. My mom found him in bed with another woman." He lifted his iced tea to his mouth, then remembered that it was empty and bit on the straw absently. "Mom didn't mean to kill him. And the court believed her. She only got manslaughter but eight years is eight years. By the time she walked free, I was eighteen years old."

"So not the stock market."

"Boring old legal bills."

"Lawyers."

"Yup."

Day 5

Kiruna, Sweden

EDNA

Our first performance at the Indigenous World Gathering went better than expected. We did not expect to be dancing for thousands of people. And we did not expect to be invited to dance the next day in the town of Kiruna and then at noon back at the Gathering and then again at 2:00 and 4:00 p.m. By the end of the day, our legs were aching but it felt good to be sharing the Plains Cree culture. We also watched the other people engage in their dances and traditions. We also ate more fish, courtesy of the Sami people. They do not seem to ever tire of fish. (Reindeer was also available but I turned it down — felt too much like eating Rudolph. That is a joke.)

There are so many people from all over the world and so many languages that I have never heard before. I am reminded of the story of the Tower of Babel when God punished the people for attempting to build a tower. There is no tower here but perhaps this camp is so big that it will bring down God's punishment. In any event, I am glad that I have my rosary with me.

From what I see everyone in the troupe is doing well. Those that I see regularly anyway.

JOHN

There were at least thousands of souls in the camp but it seemed to John that he only ever saw one person. That face was open and friendly and often laughing and the eyes were smiling, except when they were searching his own. John would turn his attention back to his tasks, repairing regalia, carrying firewood, watching over fires, whatever chores needed doing. He talked with a few people. He had a too-long conversation with a large Samoan man about the quality of women's lady-parts in Canada versus Samoa. John did not have any set views on the topic but tried to answer the Samoan man's questions as best he could. He avoided fires with people seated around solemnly as they tended to turn to serious talk.

After their first show went okay, he called his brother in Kiruna and got his nephew Bryce on the phone instead. The boy was bright but only six years old. Bryce asked John if he could bring a reindeer home for him. John promised to try.

He was heading back to his tent when a small hand reached out of a crowd of people and grasped his. John looked into Desiree's worried face. "John? You need to come."

He followed her to a small fire where a group of people were milling about and voices were growing in volume, like a bar crowd spoiling for a fight. You could have knocked him over with a piece of straw when he saw Edna standing in the centre of the circle. She was too close to the fire but the look on her face suggested she wasn't paying attention to practical concerns. Next to her a dark-skinned woman with thick grey hair held a book over her head and Edna lunged at the book. The two women were on the verge of grappling, their chests heaving, their hands curling into claws.

John rushed in and pushed them apart. "What's going on here, Edna?"

"This woman," Edna jabbed her finger at the woman, "is trying to burn the Bible. The word of the Lord!"

John looked at the woman, who nodded with zero repentance and even a certain amount of pride.

He took his charge by the shoulders. "Edna, we're visitors here."

"It's God's book!" Edna's scream reverberated around the valley. He could see people fall back in the crowd, cringing at the passion in her voice.

The other woman stood strong. She held the Bible over the fire and looked in Edna's direction and then dropped it into the flames. John could see that the fire wasn't hot enough and that it was going take a long time to eat through the hard cover. Women, he thought, could never build a decent fire.

In his arms, Edna yelled and struggled to get at the book but John held firm; she would have burned her hands if he'd allowed her to go.

"Edna Shield!" He hoped to remind her of herself.

"You let her!" Edna slapped his arm.

John had no words to explain that people had a right to their views even if those views disagreed with yours. He had no real love for religion though he took his mom to church on Easter and Christmas Eve. When he went inside, his mind turned off and he heard nothing. He heard nothing that could remind him of that school. That school was locked behind solid doors.

"People have a right to be angry," he said finally.

The crowd broke into applause.

Edna glared at them. "You're all so damned negative! Got no idea how to say anything positive. All this complaining won't get us anywhere!" Her face was mottled with pink and John worried that she might give herself a heart attack.

John looked at Desiree; she was staring at her aunt, her own face pale. John didn't think she'd be much help. He stayed close to Edna, ready to restrain her if she lunged at the burning book — or another person.

"Jesus is our saviour and I feel sorry for you!" Edna yelled.

"I feel sorry for you. You're so steeped in denial, you stink of it!" This was from the woman who had burned the Bible. She had long hair, down to her ass. Her voice was deep and smooth. A singer's voice, no doubt. John stayed between her and Edna.

The woman went on. "When I think about all the terrible things those priests and nuns did to the kids in the schools — did to me — then I know that this Jesus" — she pointed at the fire — "is evil and so are all the things done in his name."

"Then I'm evil too!" Edna roared.

John would have to admit that her red face and her dark hair sticking straight up did give her a look of demonic possession.

John looked around the circle to see if someone was going to take control. Maybe one of the organizers could poke their head into this business. But John didn't see any reassuring faces. He looked at the crowd. Some of the people looked confused, some were getting riled up; one elderly woman was weeping.

John cleared his throat. "Edna, you are upsetting some of the folk here."

From the way Edna's posture softened, John knew he'd hit a weak spot on her. But she quickly straightened herself. "Someone must defend the Lord."

John figured the lord should be able to do that himself if he was so powerful. "Say your piece then."

Edna took a deep breath, then crossed herself. There were some shocked sighs at the motion and John wondered how hand gestures took on such meaning. Unless you were using your hands to punch someone in the face, then who cared what other things were done with them?

"I went to a residential school at the age of seven. I was sent there by my mother who wanted me to learn how to read and write. I learned how to cook, sew, and look after a home. The day I left that school, I wept. And it sickens me that so many people talk about these schools as if there were no good to them. I am a good person and I went to them. If you were good, then you were left alone. If you were bad, then yes, you would be punished. Is beating a child bad for them? I think it's good for the soul."

John remembered strappings that had come out of nowhere and slaps to the head so hard that he thought about killing the person who inflicted them, so he disagreed with her on those points.

"It seems like everyone wants to focus on that abuse and the other kind . . ." Edna's voice caught. "There are evil people every-where. But it was during the darkest nights that I knew I could trust the Lord and baby Jesus more than anyone else. It was during those times that I prayed the hardest and Jesus took me. He took me far away. I was safe."

John could still hear the squeak of the floors, the opening and closing of doors, and feel his heart rate speed up as he wondered if this would be his night. Hoping, praying, that the darkness would pass over him to someone else. *You were a kid,* John reminded him-self when one of his dreams took him back to that place and he would wake up hating himself. *You were a kid.* But so was the sacrifice who died each night for their sins, just another kid. He remembered walking into the bathroom one night and hearing a boy weep. He did not want to look, did not want to see. But humans, their bodies don't listen. He kept walking, each footstep bringing him closer to a truth he did not want to know.

John sunk his nails into his palms; it brought him back to Sweden, to this bright valley, to the sweet smell of the fire work-ing its way through the pages of the "Good Book." He took a deep breath — wasn't that supposed to calm you down? — and the smell reminded him of the stink of the Church and his mind —

— flashed back. His footsteps bringing him to the doorway and pushing it open, hearing it squeak on its metal hinges. And there, crouched between the toilet and the wall, his older brother. The cries coming out of him — like a coyote with its foot in a trap. And his brother's eyes on him. "Don't tell, don't tell, don't tell . . ."

Edna shouted, bringing him back. She had slipped into some sort of trance; she was now speaking in tongues, her eyes squeezed shut, her body vibrating with her Jesus and his power. She sunk to her knees and John had to drop her. Gently as he could.

She stayed like that for a few minutes; the camp was quiet as people shook their heads or bowed them. Finally, she slumped into the dirt, her talking done. John helped her up. She did not struggle. Behind him, he heard a hand-drum and voices raised in a healing song. This was enough to bring tears to his eyes — man, he wished these people had been there to save those kids back in the day. Seeing some doe-skinned boots, he looked up and met Per's eyes.

Per stepped forward. He put his hand on John's arm.

"She was . . ." John gestured at the woman in his arms.

Per shook his head. "It's okay."

But it wasn't. None of it was. This valley seemed to be filling with the sadness of those kids; their screams echoed off the hills.

"Focus on the music," Per said.

John thought he would rather focus on the way the breeze lifted Per's brown hair.

"Do you want to walk with me?"

"I have to take her to her cabin."

"Later then."

John walked away feeling like he had made a promise that he wasn't sure he could keep.

~

It was cold later, sitting by the vehicle with Desiree. John was glad he had taken the time to grab his jean jacket from his tiny tent.

"She never talks about anything like that."

"Most people don't."

"It was really bad, huh?"

John's head felt heavy. He'd like to leave this conversation behind, like he had his entire life. "It was." He took a deep breath and looked at her. "What do you know?"

Desiree shrugged. "Nothing. They've never told me anything. Just shush each other when the topic comes up. What happened there? What did they do to those children?"

She was not his child. Not even his relation. He owed her nothing. But she was awful bright and it must be so confusing for her walking among all the wounded.

"There were beatings. Especially if you cried. And there was never enough food — kids would sneak off to the dump and eat garbage. Man, you would celebrate if you found some old bread. We'd even cook potato peels over a fire." He thought about those kids smiling across the low fire. Daring everything for a couple bites of warm food. "And there was all this prayer, like we did something wrong and needed to beg for forgiveness. Whatever happened to us — it was because the devil was in us. It was so . . . I don't know . . ." He took a deep breath. "And there was . . . other things . . . the kind of things that people can't talk about, maybe not their whole lives." He thought about his brother and how he talked about everything else in the world.

John heard Desiree sniffle and looked over at her. She had tears and snot running down her pretty face.

"Aw, Desiree." He put his arm around her.

Tears slipped from her eyes and she did not wipe them away. He patted her shoulder and made himself think of horses in the fields, pulling at the hay with their teeth and pushing one another out of the way in their hunger.

She sat up and gave him a watery smile. "Thank you, John."

Someone was whistling behind them. John turned and saw Per coming towards them. He fought the urge to run away.

"He's really cute," Desiree commented but the flirt was gone from her voice as she wiped at her face with the back of her sleeve. "I hear he's two-spirited."

117

John looked at her in confusion.

"A homosexual." Desiree grinned, pleased to have shocked him. "That's what one of the Sami ladies said. They said he had a lover for a long time but he died. They say Per howled like a wolf. Do wolves sound different from coyotes? I've only heard coyotes."

"Maybe you shouldn't believe everything you hear."

Desiree looked at him with one eyebrow cocked.

Per stopped a few feet from them. "How is Edna?" Her name sounded strange in his mouth. Like a whole different word, prettier somehow.

"She's less crazy," Desiree said. "Like she stopped calling people godless spawns of the devil."

Per nodded. "It was something we should have anticipated. Not everyone is ready to move forward."

John was about to nod and then stopped himself, not sure exactly what he was agreeing with.

"Do you guys have wolves around here?" Desiree asked.

John didn't have to look at her to know there was a mischievous twinkle in her eyes.

"There are many," Per said. "Remember the vest I wore the first day I met you? That was wolf fur."

"Oh right. The one that brings out the grey in your eyes," Desiree teased.

"Some of us have to use tricks. Not all of us sparkle naturally like you, Desiree." Her name was drawn out purposefully.

Desiree blushed and unfolded her legs. "My aunt probably needs water or a blanket or something." She hurried inside.

"The boldest ones are usually the shyest," Per said.

"I don't know much about nineteen-year-old girls."

Per said nothing, just smiled and John felt stupid for no reason that he could fathom.

"You see Lucas around?" John asked.

"He was with the Peruvians, then the Apaches. He seems to go wherever he hears there might be mind-altering substances."

"Doesn't surprise me. We've had six shows and I'm sure he was on something for all of them."

"It's not healthy. It is one thing to use the medicines to go deeper into yourself and another to get high."

"He's not my kid."

"No. You have no children, John." Per sat next to John. "You have no wife. No girlfriend. No lover."

Now John was the one who wanted to fly up the stairs of the cabin and hide with the women. His heart rate jumped twenty points, he was sure. He put his hand over his heart trying to will it to slow down. He said into the ground: "I can't do this, Per."

Per stopped talking. And then after a half-dozen breaths, he said, "The sun will stay out for another month."

"I don't know how you get used to it."

"I miss the sun when it's gone. Until then, there is no dark to hide in."

No shadows. What Per didn't know was that John didn't need a dark place to hide. If you tried hard enough, you could hide right in front of someone, in front of a whole damn reserve.

John kept his eyes on the horizon line. If he searched hard enough, he could see his horses waiting back for him at the ranch.

"Can you tell me why?" Per said.

"Because it's wrong. It's . . . against God. It says so in the Bible."

"And you are a follower of Jesus and his disciples —"

"I don't have to be to know what's wrong is wrong —"

"It's not wrong!" It was the loudest John had ever heard Per raise his voice. A couple walking by glanced at them. "It is not wrong," Per said.

"I've said my piece." John meant to sound stoic but his voice came out whiny. Why did this man make him feel like a dumb teenager?

"I need you to tell me why."

"I've said my piece."

But Per was a patient person and probably could have sat next to John until John's spine crumbled (and Per's would still be straight).

Per hummed low and it was a song that John had never heard. People kept calling out to Per about this and that. He was their chief for this event and only the chief could fix most problems. John knew this and still he said nothing. Finally, Per rose to answer someone's query about firewood supplies. And John felt like he had won nothing.

EDNA

There were few times in Edna's life when she wanted to lie in bed all day. When her mother died (at least twenty years ago now), she huddled underneath the covers for most of the morning, making strange promises to God if he would turn back time. Or trading places. That was one of her deals: for one more day of her mother on Earth, Edna would spend ten in hell. That sort of thing. Finally, by noon, one of her aunties had stuck her head in the room and told her to come help cook. There was no time to rest in her family; that was not how they grieved.

Even now her body wanted her to rise and walk outside, start preparing supper like she'd been doing every night since she had arrived. The women near the cooking fires spoke different languages and had different dishes to prepare but the hands were calloused in the same places and the exasperated looks and sweaty brows were identical.

She had liked those women. Knew instinctively that they valued the same things — community, family, and tradition. But now she wasn't sure. She hadn't realized that while she was becoming the organist and first assistant to Father Henry at her church, others were pulling away from their collared priests. They were building cases against them. Learning to resent them.

Then what did they do when they were sad? When the death and drinking built their cares so high that they threatened to totter over — where did they go then? Edna worried for them even as she resented them. Every time one of them left the fold, the church became weaker.

She knew that. She saw the look on Father Henry's face when another church pew went empty. Edṇa thought that people were getting lazier (because people were getting lazier) but now . . . could it be that they hated the church? Despised. Condemned. Cursed. The church, the priests, the nuns, the message, and even Jesus.

"No," she whispered. Not Him.

She wanted to get up. She wanted to walk out to the firewood pile. It was a long walk but Edna had always loved walking. There was enough firewood to last months. After a tense moment on the first day when the organizers had run out, not having expected as many people to attend, a big group of men collected this stockpile. She would walk out there and collect firewood and deliver it to a campfire where she would listen to people sing in languages she didn't understand. But now, she didn't know if there was a place she could go where people would not stare. She had condemned them all.

"Auntie, do you want some water?" Desiree's voice was soft.

Edna wanted to say no, wanted to not be a bother, but her throat was bone dry. Desiree handed her a cup and Edna half sat up and drank it down. Beads of water fell onto her chin and she wiped them with the back of her hand.

"Are you tired?"

Edna shook her head.

"John's outside talking to that Per guy. He's so handsome, Auntie, I can't stand to be around him. Even though I heard that he's . . . too old for me."

"Are there any boys your age here?" Edna asked.

Desiree shrugged. "The Navaho have this one young guy but he's vain. I saw him staring at himself in the reflection of my sunglasses. What does my mom always say? Never date a man prettier than you."

"There's no one prettier than you."

"Ha, you're my aunt, you have to say that."

"Do you miss them?"

Desiree bit her lip. "I didn't at first but after today, I kind of do."

"Because I scared you."

Desiree nodded. "I thought you were going crazy or something."

Edna rolled her eyes. "What Cree woman gets to go crazy? There's too much work to do."

"Yeah." Edna could tell from her voice that her niece didn't know what she meant at all. But she was trying to be agreeable.

Edna wanted to ask what people were saying about her. She wanted to ask if people were going to stare if she went outside. She wanted to ask if she could steal that handsome Swede's funny-looking van and run away before she had to face anyone. But she was the auntie and Desiree was the child and questions like that scared her more than anything.

Get your big girl panties on. Edna sat up and curled her knees over the edge of the bed. "Do you want to help me make some bannock?"

"You're not tired?"

"If I don't make the bannock, then everyone will be stuck with only fried bread and who the hell wants that? Not this savage."

"Let's put raisins in it!"

Edna laughed. "That'll blow their minds."

NADINE

Her first thought when they got into Stockholm was that it had the look of a nice reserve. The houses were painted all different colours and were close together and there were people walking all over — like a friendly reserve on a hot Saturday night. She half-expected to see a rez dog come loping out from between the narrow buildings.

But she wasn't here to have a look around. Nadine directed the cab driver. "Canadian embassy," Nadine said with more confidence than she felt since she didn't even know the address. *Did they even speak English here?* Fortunately, the cab driver did. He took off without a second glance. Before long, the cab was screeching along city streets over bridges (so many bridges). Nadine glanced down and saw fast-moving, roiling waters. He stopped short in front of their destination. It was a tall skinny house in a row of other tall skinny houses — wasn't even a Canadian flag or anything to tell you that you had found it. On the door was one of those brass knocker things.

Nadine looked at Lucas.

He shrugged. "It's your embassy."

Nadine picked up the big knocker and let it fall. There was no response. She flipped the knocker a few times, hard. "How the hell do you get this thing to work?" she asked.

Lucas tapped her arm and indicated the buzzer. "Ahhh . . ." Feeling a bit stupid, Nadine gave it a good long press.

This time she could hear doors opening and closing — three sets? What kind of mansion was this? — until a short man with white-blonde hair and a prominent nose appeared in the window. He peered at them curiously, his mannerisms much like a chipmunk. Finally, he opened the door. "Yes?" It sounded like "yas?"

"We need to use your phone," Nadine said. "I have to report a criminal hanging out with some Indians."

The man blinked. "What kind of Indians?"

"Canadian Indians in your country."

"In Sweden? They're in Sweden right now?"

"Yes."

There was a pause and Nadine looked at Lucas with a swirling in her gut. Lucas flashed a smile back at her. He had confidence that the door would be opened, but he was from the States and even though he was an Indian, that American confidence had rubbed off on him some.

The door opened and Nadine slipped through before anyone could change their mind.

The man was a good deal shorter than Nadine and she felt gigantic standing next to him. She wondered how Lucas felt; although Lucas was taller than most people so maybe it didn't matter to him anymore.

"I'm Rolf Meyer, the Canadian diplomat for Sweden."

"I'm Nadine Redcloud, the manager of the Prairie Chicken Dance Troupe."

"I remember you!"

Nadine had written to the consulate to ask for funding and a possible night of lodging. They'd responded with an invite to dinner, which she'd been looking forward to. At the time she thought that anyone who offered to feed twelve hungry Indians was a brave man. "Right, that's me. And this is one of my dancers, Lucas Pretends Eagle. He's an American."

"American Indian. Very impressive." Lucas held out his hand to Rolf. Rolf's slender hand looked fragile in Lucas's grip. "You said something about a criminal?"

"Right, well, we're going to need to sit down for this one."

Rolf nodded. "Let's get some tea then." He stepped backwards gracefully and motioned with a nod for them to walk ahead. Nadine had to give it to these Swedes; they had some style.

EDNA

People were definitely looking. But Edna told herself that they were looking at Desiree who was bouncing beside her, long hair and arms akimbo, her legs stuffed into a pair of shorts so small that Edna could see her bum-cheeks peeking out. She normally would have told her to go change (and Desiree would have whined and Edna would have pushed and finally Edna would have given in. But not without reminding her of what happened to girls who showed too much skin — they left the protection of Jesus our Lord and Saviour). But Edna hadn't wanted to discourage her niece from joining her in the walk across the campgrounds towards the cooking area. The kitchen, as usual, was packed with women. Hands were moving quickly, meat was being cut, fried, and boiled. And, of course, there was fish.

There was a familiar cacophony as people complained about a

lack of this and that. As in the days before, there wasn't enough water to go around and a young man was being sent to get more.

Edna pulled out a huge pail out from under the counter. It held a large sack of flour and Edna pointed with her lips for her niece to grab the lard. Desiree found some and then handed it to her aunt. She chattered on about how she had learned a new braiding technique from a Sami girl.

Edna got to work quickly. She could feel eyes on her but she kept her back straight. As she reached for some baking powder, her hand touched another woman's much meatier hand. Edna's eyes met the other woman's. She lowered her eyes as she saw the anger there. Edna let go of the container. A few minutes later, the container was placed next to her workspace.

"Wow, Auntie, you work so fast," Desiree said brightly. "My mom would still be mixing in the water."

"Your mom has other talents," Edna said. Mostly watching television and gossiping on the phone with her friends, but Edna left that out.

Edna was halfway through kneading the life out of her bannock when she saw a handsome face in her peripheral vision. It was that Per man, the organizer. "Hello." Edna noted that her voice was a bit stiff and tried to soften it with a tight smile. "You here to eat some bannock?"

"Let me tell you a secret." Per leaned in close so that his breath tickled her neck. "It's my favourite dish."

Edna blushed. "Oh, go on." He was certainly a charmer, this young man. She hoped that her niece wouldn't pick up any of his moves.

Per leaned against the counter. "I wanted to talk to you about an idea."

"Okay." Edna wiped one of her floured hands on her apron to scratch an itch on the top of her nose.

"I have heard of a tradition among the Cree people, I believe they call it the round dance."

Edna had been to hundreds of those when she was younger. It was a fun way to spend an evening. She'd had her hand squeezed by more than a few cute boys. And she had boldly squeezed back, excited to be flirting right under the elders' noses (of course the elders had probably once done exactly the same thing when they were young). Edna wondered whatever happened to those boys? Probably jail or have a hundred kids, or jail *and* a hundred kids. But since she'd reached a certain age, she'd felt the difference when she walked into the hall during a round dance. Women her age either had a passel of kids following them or they were the target of sad looks and innuendos of "bad eggs" and "rotten wombs."

"You're having a round dance?"

"I wouldn't know where to begin. But if you could show me how, we could organize one. It is a friendship dance, yes?"

Edna nodded. "Though the young people, they see it as something a little different." Seeing the frown on Per's face, she hurried on. "It's a great idea. Did John suggest it?"

Per shook his head. Edna saw a faint blush come and go from his cheeks.

Edna went on. "John will have to be the drummer, unless he can teach one of the songs to the other drummers. He probably could, the man could teach a hippo to dance if he wanted to. Do you want me to ask him?"

Per hesitated and then shook his head. "No, I will. I know where he is."

"All right then. Tomorrow?"

Per smiled and walked away. He had a graceful walk. Wonder why I haven't seen him dance yet, wondered Edna.

Desiree tapped her on the arm. "What did Mr. Hot-pants want?"

"He wanted to talk about a round dance."

Desiree sniffed. "I guess that could be good."

"You should head back to the cabin and go change those shorts; they're too short. I can see the coins in your pockets."

"Coins, right." Desiree looked away, but not before Edna saw a grin on her face. Edna shook her head; she spent one afternoon in bed and her girl had already run wild. Never a time to rest.

"Okay, time for you to knead." Edna pushed Desiree's hands into the dough. "Did I ever tell you the story about my friend Martha who got hit by a pickup truck because some man was looking at her outfit?"

JOHN

"This is some loud music," John said to no one in particular. He wasn't talking to Per, who bopped his head in time with the raucous sounds. He wasn't saying it to Desiree, who was jumping and waving her arms like those hippies he'd seen in the summer of love (on TV, of course.)

They were standing in front of a band of young guys who had taken over the stage at midnight. It was an impromptu performance of what was, John surmised, rock covers by Indigenous guys.

"Dance, cowboy!" Per yelled into John's ear, his hot breath making John pull away.

"If this was music, I would dance."

Per gave him an annoyed look.

"I like country," John said. "You'd think you'd know that from the cowboy hat," he added under his breath.

Desiree was being swallowed up by the crowd so John grabbed for a braid and caught her.

"Ow!"

"Stay close," John waved his hand at her. It had been Edna's last order before she limped off to bed: "Watch her like a hawk."

"Why don't you get handcuffs?" This time Per's breath was on John's neck.

"Are you going to come to Canada and explain to her dad why his kid is knocked up?"

"Are you asking me to come to Canada?" Per smiled at John.

"You need to stop that."

Per smiled and patted his arm. "I will think about it."

John had this feeling that the more he told Per to stop the worse it would get, like complaining about having a sore throat.

John glanced over at Desiree. She had a couple of guys on either side of her now. One was the idiot Lucas, his tongue half-hanging out of his mouth. The other was a taller sort wearing those big Indian Affairs goggles.

"Jesus, Mary, and Joseph," he sighed. "Keep some distance, boys."

"Uh, I'm nineteen," Desiree announced.

"Uh, I don't care," John replied. Then felt stupid because he sounded like an old man in front of Per.

Desiree ignored him and continued to dance provocatively, inviting warm stares. But the boys kept an eye on John and a respectful distance. John stayed close and Per stayed close to him and John had never been to a less relaxing concert.

The young man with the coke-bottle glasses pushed his way towards John. "My name is Clark." He pushed his glasses back on his face. "Clark Rockthunder. I'm from the Peguis band."

John nodded. "Okay then."

"I'm here representing the band and people from the Manitoba area. We are a diverse group of people interested in improving our lives." John stared at him. Clark went on. "And, I know that you are also here from the prairie provinces. Are you part of the Prairie Alliance?"

"The Prairie-what?" Behind Clark, John could see Desiree catching the eye of a tall guy with a tattoo under his eye. One of those Maori guys. Where were they from? New Zealand? That was definitely too far away, if she ran away to go shack up. He grabbed the back of her shirt.

"Let go," she hissed and slapped his hand away.

Clark leaned in. "It's a political movement of like-minded Chiefs who are interested in enforcing Treaty rights."

John's ears struggled to swallow all those words. "Not involved in any movements, political or otherwise. I'm here to dance." Desiree was now tracing her finger along the Maori man's tattooed arm.

Per pretended a questioning look. "And yet you refused to dance with me a few moments ago?"

"I dance on stage when I am paid to do so."

"That's very corporate of you," Per countered. A brunette with hair down to her ass held out her hand to Per, he grabbed it, and she pulled him away.

John glared at the back of his head.

Clark seized the opportunity to get closer. "Sir, I would like to speak further with you. I am interested in setting up alliances with you and other like-minded leaders. And Chiefs."

"You're sniffing up the wrong tree," John replied. "I'm not a Chief and got no plans to ever be one."

"But surely you understand the importance of alliances especially when the government is not respecting the Treaties or our Treaty rights, when thousands of veterans have been disenfranchised from their rights, it's a human rights travesty — it's not right."

The young man was using the word *right* so much that it was losing meaning. "Look, Chuck —"

"Clark —"

"Right. I come from a political family, my brother is a Chief and my grandfather was a councillor — but it's just words to me — I'm no more useful to you than tits on a boar."

"My dad is a Chief." Desiree's head butted between them. Clark's eyes lit up. Desiree started chatting with him in earnest. The Maori guy must have displeased her in some way.

John was no more happy about Clark than anyone else but if she was flirting with Clark, the bespectacled young man wasn't talking to him and John was a-okay with that. Was that what it was like for his brother? Having all kinds of strange conversations with all kinds of strange people at strange times? Seemed like a helluva way to make a buck.

And as long as he kept his eye on them it shouldn't matter who she took up with, right?

But what about the Hunkpapa — where had he gotten to? There were a lot of young people gyrating together in small groups but he didn't see his dancer among them.

The music was so loud, John felt like it was boring a hole in his head. How had he become the sole caretaker of the young ones — couldn't Edna lend a hand? John sighed. At least Desiree . . .

Desiree was gone. And so was the Clark kid.

Per had not gone anywhere though. Neither had his smile.

~

"She is nineteen."

"Yes, but she's a young nineteen." John glanced at a fire they were walking past. He listened for her twinkling laugh.

"And there is this thing called the pill."

John grunted. "Do not talk to me about stuff like that."

Per grinned. "Prude. You would have made a great dad. Why are you not a dad?"

"Why not you?"

"I am a dad. I raise my brother's son."

"And where's that kid?"

"In the north with his grandparents."

John looked around the mostly bare field. "I'm not going to find her."

Per nodded in agreement. "Why don't we go grab something to eat?"

They found paper plates and some kind of meat in the kitchen area. Per grabbed some bannock and broke it off and handed a piece to John. They found a fire to themselves that was burning low and sat on a couple of stumps near the fire.

"What time is it?" John asked in between bites.

"Do you really want to know?"

John shook his head.

A couple walked past, arms around each other's waists.

John took a bite of the bannock. He wished for strawberry jam, like the kind his mom made every second summer.

"Do you want some water?"

"Nah, I'll be okay."

"It's not a problem." Per held out a canteen.

John took a swig. "Kinanâskomitin."

"I like your language."

"I only know a few words."

"Have you ever been with a man?"

John dropped his plate. His bannock and dried meat flew across the dirt. "For fucks sakes."

Per smirked. He offered his plate. John waved him off. "I don't know how you could ask me that."

"I tried subtle. You ignored me."

"Maybe that's the answer."

Per nodded. "Perhaps. But I feel something around you. And I don't want to go through life feeling something and pretending that I don't." Per waved his hand at the campsites. "There are over a thousand people here and I've met all of them and you're the only one that I'm eating dry bannock with after midnight when I'm tired off my feet and have to wake up at dawn. And I don't know why — if it was my choice, I sure as hell wouldn't have chosen some shy Cree guy from Canada."

"Nehewin."

"A Nehewin man." Per sighed. He put down his plate and studied John. "You're so different than him."

John looked up at him. "I'm sorry. Desiree said something."

"The Moccasin telegraph." Per chuckled. "You should have seen him. He had big dark eyes that seemed endless. And this laugh that everyone could hear for miles. And he could sing too. I don't think we ever fought because we knew that it doesn't happen very often. We were grateful. Kinanâskomitin."

John liked the way Cree words sounded when Per said them.

"Did you ever feel that?" Per was looking at him.

"I had this horse once . . ."

Per threw his head back and laughed. He stopped and smiled at John. "You don't know love."

John stood up. "Not all of us need that kind of thing."

John pointed himself in the direction of his tent and dreaded the walk back. He could feel every bad decision of his thirty years weighing him down. Thirty years of having nothing — he only had to get through another thirty more.

For the best, thought John. Nothing good comes of playing with fire. What I don't know, I won't miss. John turned down a well-worn path. You can't teach an old dog new tricks, everyone knows that. And then he stopped. He looked back at the low fire and the man standing there.

And then he heard his brother's voice wafting through the low grasses. *Sohkitehewin.*

Day 6

EDNA

Every day, there are sharing circles that people participate in. Sometimes whether you want to or not. They are intended to discuss issues of sovereignty and rights. Rights to this and rights to that. It reminds me of an old joke my dad used to tell. "A Métis man was complaining that he didn't have any rights so I gave him two rights and a left." My father was a silly man.

Talk of politics turned to talk of religion. I am sorry to say that people became blasphemous. I am proud that I stood up for my Christian beliefs. Also, I do not know if I mentioned this before but the sun never goes down here and I think it makes people grumpy.

I must confess that despite the honour of being part of the Prairie Chicken dance troupe, I am missing my bed. I am missing the feeling of different clothes — or even clean clothes. We are still in a camp and there is no laundromat for miles. A man definitely designed this camp. I miss confession with our dear Priest back at home. There is something peaceful about ridding yourself of sinful thoughts and receiving absolution from a good pious man. In its absence, I will assign myself some rosaries. It would be good for everyone to see how a Christian comports themselves.

"Something has changed," Desiree said at the tables set out for breakfast. Women were moving around the tables putting out platters of food. Edna glanced at her niece. She noticed dark circles around her eyes and the wan skin of vampires who refused to sleep at night.

"We are in a different country," Edna replied, curious about the Peruvian breakfast that a Quechua woman had been cooking up. So far, so good.

"Things are changing. People here are different, they don't walk around with their heads hanging down. There's a mission in them."

"Bunch of fools." Definitely some good eggs. Edna would have to track down the lady for the recipe.

"People with a mission can accomplish a lot."

Edna shrugged. She hadn't had enough coffee to take on that statement.

"Good morning, ladies." Edna squinted up at the young man standing in front of her.

"Who are you?" she asked.

"This is Clark," Desiree gushed. "We met at the concert last night."

"I am from the Peguis Band, which is in Manitoba." Clark held out his hand.

Edna didn't take it. "I am from a place which is none of your business."

"Auntie!" Desiree held out a hand to Clark. "Please sit down."

Edna sized up this Clark. "What do you want?"

"I apologize for my aunt. She's not sleeping well here. Different sun and all."

"Yes, I understand. I haven't been sleeping much either." Clark replied, with a look that Edna could only describe as *dirty* aimed in her niece's direction. Desiree giggled.

Instead of smacking his face like he so deserved, Edna smiled politely. "How did you end up here?"

"My Chief contacted me. His name is Harold Thomas and he asked me to attend on behalf of our nation and I was very grateful to get the call because I want to represent my people on a bigger stage. I am hoping that I can attend more such events."

"You don't really talk like someone who grew up on a reserve . . ."

"I grew up with my mother in Winnipeg. She's white — which is where I got my blue eyes. But even though I was raised in the city, I went home a lot. To visit my dad and learn our ways."

Edna arched an eyebrow. "That's very good." She paused. "Can you go grab me some water?"

"Yes, of course. I was raised to respect my elders."

The young man got up and hurried away. As soon as he turned his back, Edna lunged at his jacket on the table and started rifling through his pockets.

"Auntie! What are you doing?" Desiree hissed.

Edna ignored her as she pulled out a wallet. She went through the folds: there was a small amount of cash, some I.D., and a card. On the card was emblazoned "Department of Indian Affairs." She showed it to Desiree.

Desiree's eyes narrowed and she shot daggers at the young man's back. "He didn't mention that."

"An Indian agent spying on all the Indians, making sure we aren't up to no good."

Desiree got up and pushed back her sleeves. "I think it's time his face met my fist."

Edna waved her hand. "I will handle it."

John felt that he was walking around in a daze. Or a haze. Or a fog. He had crawled out of the tent that morning while Per still slept.

Maybe there was a way to go back in time, to when he was sitting on his porch and heard the phone ring. That was the last time he had felt like himself. Back when life made sense. Wake up early, feed and water the animals. Spend the afternoon checking on the cattle. Eat supper. Think about plain things until he fell asleep. And now, he couldn't even remember what his thoughts were before they had been invaded by soft words.

He wandered through the camps, each footstep a choice between forward or right or left (backwards was out of the question). He stumbled along and people gave him looks, probably thinking he had partaken in some homebrew or whatever else people were sharing around their fires.

He wanted to talk to his brother more than anything. So much so that he was thinking about hotwiring a car and driving to town to find a phone. But then he thought about what he would say. "Bring me home." Which would require explaining and what was there to explain? And where to begin? And what words to express feelings that were feathers floating through his mind? Be brave, yes, but what steps came after you jumped off of the cliff?

And so, he walked.

"John!" The voice came from behind him and he stopped without turning. The voice caught up with him. "John, where you been?"

It was Lucas, looking rough.

"You look weird," Lucas pronounced, "like someone died. Did someone die?" He scratched his head. "I would have heard if someone died. Right?"

"Nobody died, you damned fool." John looked him over. His clothes looked like he had slept in them. "You all packed up? We're leaving tomorrow, y'know."

Lucas nodded. "I'm always ready. Where're the girls?"

John figured Edna wouldn't be happy to hear herself referred to as a girl. "They're around."

"Did that Per guy pay us yet?"

"This isn't a paying gig."

A worried look passed over Lucas's face.

"What's wrong?" John asked.

"Nothing, nothing. Running low on food-money."

"The food is free."

"Yeah." Lucas looked over John's shoulder, then took off. "Okay then, see you later."

What was that little shit up to?

There was some banging around on the mainstage and John glanced over, thinking that another impromptu concert was starting up. He sighed, not sure he could survive another one.

It was a group of women, solid-looking sorts. The grey-haired woman who had tangled with Edna adjusted the microphone. "Aiinin! Welcome everyone. As we all get ready to say goodbye it is important to offer thanks to our hosts."

There was a loud whoop from the audience. John glanced around him, sure that Per had to be in the vicinity. The crowd began to thicken as people approached the stage. John saw Edna in the group now; she was shorter than the rest but looked like she fit in fine.

"As we say thanks it is also important to acknowledge some of our visitors." A young man was pushed on stage. John recognized him as the talkative fellow, Clark, from the night before. He looked darn near ready to shit himself. Clark tried to jump off the stage and a solid arm caught him and pulled him back. Two women stepped forward and held his arms.

"This young man who calls himself Clark is actually a spy sent by the Canadian government. Let us welcome him," bellowed Edna.

There were general boos from the audience.

The young man shook his head and yelled but couldn't be heard over the crowd.

"Holy hell." John was concerned for the young man. Like any good Cree man, John knew not to cross a group of women elders.

The grey-haired woman cut in. "We aren't going to hurt him. Although he probably deserves it but I do think he needs to learn some manners, real tradish-like."

Desiree stepped forward. There were general hoots and cheers. Desiree, of course, received the adulation with her usual level of comfort and flashed the crowd a bright smile and flicked her dark hair. No false modesty in that one.

Desiree approached the young man who shrank back. Two women approached him from behind and wrestled him to his knees and then further down to his back, where he flailed like a turtle.

Desiree laid down next to him and raised her leg.

John knew the next steps; he had seen a thousand Indian leg-wrestling matches at the band office, the band hall, in the grass beside the church. Always a hell of a thing to witness. The young man clearly hadn't. That much was clear as Desiree hooked his leg with hers and flipped him over, ass over teakettle. One of his shoes and his glasses went flying across the stage.

The crowd laughed and hooted. "Good for him!" "Get out of here, Indian Agent," and other jeers of "apple" and the like.

Clark scrambled across the stage and picked up his glasses. He got himself to his feet and looked out at the audience.

John wondered what Clark saw. Did he see the rejection that he had always feared because he was different? Did he see a bunch of people who he thought were beneath him because of the colour of his eyes?

John would never find out because before he finished the thought, Clark leapt off the stage. He fought his way through the crowd like a bingo winner at the end of the night.

Desiree stood up and received her applause. John joined in as heartily as anyone else.

Rolf sipped his tea thoughtfully with his eyes focused on the shelf of tiny figurines behind Nadine's head. Nadine had given them a look over when she walked in, lots of shepherds guarding their flocks. It seemed like a strange thing to waste your money on, but then Nadine had never been a fan of knickknacks. Hadn't even stolen any back in her thieving days.

"The police must be notified. Interpol, as well." Rolf placed his teacup delicately in the middle of his saucer.

Nadine glanced at Lucas, who shook his head.

"Unfortunately, that's not an option," Nadine explained. "You see, before we left Canada, we had an altercation with the RCMP and now they want to arrest the real Lucas Pretends Eagle." She waved in Lucas's general direction. "And me too probably. As I'm the one who broke him out of jail." Nadine saw a fearful look cross Rolf's face. Honestly, the man had some serious trust issues. "But as you can see, we're not dangerous. We're actually both dancers."

"Really?" Rolf looked skeptically at Lucas, who was as big as a house.

"Traditional, fancy and some hoop," Lucas offered.

"Hoop!" Rolf's eyes went bright. "What is that?"

"Only the most exciting thing since sliced bread," Nadine gushed. And she wasn't exaggerating. It generally was the big money-maker for most dancers. "We don't want the police involved, but we do need to find the guy who's running around pretending to be Lucas Pretends Eagle —" Nadine laughed. "I realized how strange that sounds — someone pretending to be Pretends Eagle."

Lucas gave her an annoyed look. "Like I haven't heard that before."

"I'm not sure how I can help you then," Rolf said.

"The next stop for the tour is in Germany — Hamburg area. Maybe you can get on the phone and give the diplomat there a heads up. Like, hey, there's some Indians coming by and one of them is pretty dangerous."

"That exact wording?"

"Maybe don't scare them," Lucas said. "Ask them to hold him at the airport. Then I can grab my passport and other I.D. from him."

Rolf nodded and then looked at them curiously, "Wait, how did you get here?"

Nadine opened her mouth and then closed it, not wanting to implicate anyone else. "That's not important, is it? The real important thing is saving this group of innocent Indians from a violent criminal."

Rolf reluctantly nodded. Nadine hoped he found his post boring as shit and appreciated the excitement that they were bringing. Otherwise she and Lucas were going to find themselves sharing a cell in a Swedish prison — not that that sounded too bad. She'd read somewhere that prisoners got to have intimate relations in Swedish jails — the Swedes were some progressive people, that's for sure.

Nadine stretched her arms over her head and yawned. "That was a long trip."

"Yes, yes," Rolf replied.

Nadine went on. "Thank you for your help — I appreciate the kindness and — letting us into your home — this sure is a big place. Probably has a lot of bedrooms."

"Of course, you should stay," Rolf said. "Let me get the housekeeper." Rolf padded down the hallway.

"Subtle," Lucas said.

"Subtle is for farts and people who have credit cards. I am sleeping in a bed tonight."

~

Their host attempted to engage them in political talk after they had a rest in their respective guest rooms. Nadine had encountered linens so white, she felt like she was sleeping in a snowbank.

"What do you think of your prime minister? Europeans are quite enamoured of him."

Nadine only knew a few things about the current prime minister — "handsome," "brilliant," "interesting dresser."

Rolf asked the same of Lucas's leader. Lucas was as closed-mouthed as usual, mumbling something about the president not really impressing him.

Rolf turned the conversation around to Indian politics. Nadine stiffened a bit, knowing that it could go two ways — either Rolf would believe that Indian politicians were shining examples of humanity (the pure Indian) or that they were corrupt, sneaky bastards (the dirty Indian). Nadine voted in band elections but never paid much attention to the Chief and council, knowing from the way wrinkles were forming on their faces that they were facing off with the government on a regular basis. Government officials gave you special wrinkles — this was why she'd never got into a fight with one herself. She liked her face.

Nadine described the Chief and council system, briefly explaining that it was nice to be able to walk over to your leader's house and give him shit personally if the roads weren't great. Rolf nodded. "So then your political systems are local and not national?"

Nadine thought about that. She remembered hearing about the Indian Brotherhood that was made up of Indian war veterans, guys with brush cuts who walked around with straight backs. They came back from the wars and refused to take any shit from anyone. She mentioned that she heard they had been talking to the government on a face-to-face basis. "Seems like bullets make you impervious to government bullshit," she said. "And I guess that's a good thing."

Rolf asked her questions about the Brotherhood excitedly but she had no information about them — except that they had donated most of the money for the trip. After that the conversation turned back into them silently smiling at one another in the big living room, the clock behind them ticking.

Nadine was starting to get the feeling that their host had been looking forward to an evening of wit and exciting repartee and even though he was trying to be brave, his eyes showed his disappointment. When he looked at his watch and suggested a trip to the local disco, Nadine jumped to her tired feet and said dancing sounded perfect.

Nadine had been to a few nightclubs in her day. Her cousin, the powwow-dancing, hotel-cleaning sex worker, had dragged her out, telling her that it was a way to practise her dance moves but it was really a way for her cousin to meet more clients. But once Nadine got used to the blaring music and drunk people bumping into her, she started to enjoy the glamour of dressing up in heels and a pretty dress. She noticed people were less judgemental in nightclubs, there was more race-mingling, and she didn't feel like she stood out like a big rez Indian — she felt like a pretty girl. Once she moved back to the rez, she hung up her heels and retired her moves. Nobody, except crazy people, wore heels on the reserve.

~

The nightclub was filled with the same type of people you'd see back in Canada, except thinner, taller, and better-looking. Everyone looked like they were straight out of a cigarette ad, except that no one was smoking. Nadine smiled at a couple of men with cheekbones so sharp they could cut glass. They looked at her curiously. She figured they were trying to figure her out — she was strange-looking after all with her black hair, brown skin, and "Rez Wolverines" T-shirt commemorating the perfect record of her slow-pitch team the year before.

Women stared at Lucas like rez dogs standing in the front window on Thanksgiving Day. Nadine watched as a woman caressed his upper arm. She stifled her jealousy; he wasn't hers. Yet.

Rolf led them up some stairs and then up some more stairs until they were in a private area. "This the swingers sex area?" Nadine joked.

"That's one floor up," Rolf replied and then introduced them to a few people lounging on the soft velvety chairs. It seemed like a lot of people knew him and he took the time to introduce Nadine and Lucas to all of them. She liked how people's eyes lit up when they heard her name, "Redcloud." Yup, she sounded like a real old-timey Indian. Of course, Pretends Eagle was a thousand times better. Not that it was a competition or anything.

Rolf ordered a round of drinks. Nadine sipped what tasted like a vodka and orange and put it down carefully. She noticed that Lucas didn't touch his. Rolf greedily drank his down as he stared out at the dance floor and tapped his feet. Nadine knew a hint when she saw one and tapped him on the shoulder. "Let's get our butts down there." She pointed at the colourful dance floor (with coloured blocks of light, that is; it was pretty much all white people.) She led him out to the dance floor, determined to put him out of his misery and maybe shake off the jet lag she was still feeling.

They were probably about five songs in when she noticed that Rolf seemed to be more focused on a tall drink of water to her right than on her. She was familiar with gay men, having known more than a few two-spirited people on the powwow trail. Even though two-spirited was supposed to be respected by the culture, she'd seen some of them come limping into camp with a broken nose or black eyes because someone hadn't liked their way of being.

Impulsively she pulled the tall guy closer to them. Rolf and the young man smiled shyly at one another. Nadine was congratulating herself on her modern attitudes when she suddenly got shoved from behind. Then another shove to the right and she almost bit it on the dance floor. She turned towards the offenders and saw two large men with shaved heads facing off against Rolf and his pretty friend. They reminded her of some men she'd seen back home proclaiming "white power" at a parade a few years back. The parade had featured a group of Cree veterans riding horses and Nadine had wondered if those guys yelling their nonsense knew what it was like to stare down the barrel of a machine gun when you were barely out of high school.

"What the hell is your problem?" Nadine inserted herself between the two groups of men, deciding that her novelty might be enough to distract them. Instead she found herself pushed out of the way again and one of the men grabbed for Rolf's collar. She grabbed the arm and tugged on it — to no avail. Apparently Swedish assholes were stronger than sin. She was deliberating taking off one of her heeled boots and clobbering him with it when Lucas popped up beside her.

Rolf had already taken at least one hit to the face and the crowd around them was opening up as if to give the bullies more room for their beating ways (honestly, were crowds ever helpful?). Lucas used this space to his advantage and delivered two kicks in quick succession to the side of the skinhead's face and body respectively. The bald guy turned his attention to Lucas and ran straight at him. This was a mistake. Lucas gathered his momentum and sent him flying off the dance floor like a mechanical bull losing a rider. The music came to a stop then as everyone, including the DJ, watched to see if he would get up. He laid there for a few seconds and then finally rolled to sitting. Bouncers descended on him and dragged him and his buddy out the door.

Nadine nudged Lucas and pointed with her lips at the sign above the door. "Look at that — utfart." She grinned. "Just like at home, you fart and you gotta go."

Lucas grunted, not in the mood for her foolishness.

The DJ took the mic and announced, "Time for a new song by a band that's going to be huge." Nadine missed the name of the band as she went to check on Rolf. She heard the catchy phrase, "honey, honey," filling the room as she watched Rolf touch his face tentatively. "Wasn't expecting that," she said finally.

Rolf shook his head sadly. "There's all kinds."

The music was catchy and made Nadine's hips twitch. She tugged on Rolf's arm in the direction of the dance floor.

He looked concerned.

"Enough of that," Nadine said. "We'll worry when we're dead."

Rolf laughed and followed behind her.

Nadine looked over at Lucas. He was staring out at the crowd with a snarl on his face. She went over to him and grabbed his arm as well. "Hey Hercules, dance-time."

She led him behind her like a pony or an extremely dangerous male that both frightened and intrigued her. As for the questions of how he became such an ass-kicking Indian — she left those in her throat. Ideally you wanted to know everything about your travel companion before you left but if you couldn't have that, it was probably best to keep their secrets under wraps if you were only halfway through your journey.

EDNA

After the supper meal, Per announced the round dance. The crowd turned in the direction of the dance stage area but Edna could quickly see that there would not be enough room. She hurried over to Per where he stood next to John.

"We can't do this here," she said breathlessly.

"I was telling him the same thing," John said.

Per looked disappointed. "Everyone wants to do this. Many people have heard of the round dance but nobody has seen it."

Edna looked at John. John looked at Edna and shrugged. Finally, Edna gave out an exasperated sigh. Why did all ideas have to come from the women?

She pointed at the peak behind the campsite. "Up that mountain there, we'll assemble around the top of it."

"Technically that's a hill," John said.

"Whatever it is. Let's start moving people up there."

It was about thirty minutes later before Edna found herself at the top of the mountain. Through a series of cars, busses, trucks, and on foot, people were arriving by the dozens. Edna looked down the side of the hill and saw an ant-like line of people climbing upwards. The mountaintop was mostly flat, kind of sloping towards the west, but there was no chance of anyone falling off. She glanced to the centre of the flat and saw that two drums had already assembled, along with John and his hand-drum.

John took his time explaining the song to the other drummers. Edna knew that John was one of those people that a tornado couldn't rush — but couldn't he feel the expectations of hundreds of people weighing on him? Strange man. Strange, slow-moving, stupid man.

Finally, he went to the edge of the mountain, lit a cigarette, and mumbled a prayer to himself. Then he laid down the cigarette. He walked back to the centre and before he reached it, he hit his drum. The drum echoed through the air. He opened his mouth and began his song. Without thinking, Edna plucked up the hands of the people next to her, a woman who had one side of her head shaved and another woman who had tiny, red, straight lines tattooed from under her lips down to her chin.

Edna moved her left foot in beat to the music and the right one followed. The women beside her followed along and then more were added to the chain. Edna could see the line stretching to at least a hundred and even more were joining. She stepped outwards making the loop larger to fit the rest. The circle grew until Edna could not see the beginning or the end. And then she noticed that the chain had encircled the mountain. Edna looked behind her; her feet were a few steps away from the cliff. She could see down the side and her heart gave a start. Then she reminded herself that she was holding hands with a hundred people who would pull her up if she stumbled.

What would this look like from space, she wondered? A group of Indians from everywhere holding hands around a mountain — would it appear to be the miracle that it felt like?

The dancers moved clockwise as Edna had always remembered and then when the entire body of people was included, Edna wound the group inwards, curling and curling until there was no space left.

When the music ended, hands broke free and clapped (even though Edna didn't think that was exactly appropriate). Edna rubbed her hips, which had already started to protest the dancing. Slow as it was, even the round dance was offending her joints.

A few minutes later, a new song began. This time, one of the other drums took over. With the strength of six hands, it felt like the beat was coming from inside of them. It reverberated off the rocks and mountain and you could not stand still even if you wanted to. Edna looked for Desiree, who was standing between two handsome long-haired fellows (damned if Edna knew where they were from.)

Lucas was near Desiree and he was glancing over the shoulder of the people next to him like he wanted to be a lot closer. On either side of him was a flirtatious woman on the dark side of her thirties shooting him a toothy smile, who ought to have known better. And John? Edna had to look for him a long time. Bachelor like him, she expected him to be stuck in a crowd of eligible females. But he stood between two female elders, helping them through the dance. On the other side of one of the women was Per. Funny how those two always found each other.

But that's how it always was back home; the men that every woman wanted always seemed to be busy hanging out with each other. Such was the way of nature. Fortunately, less attractive men knew how to make themselves available. Edna felt a 'specially sharp twinge in her hip and had to break one of her holds with an apologetic look to rub it.

Edna switched hands and joined with a small one. She looked down and saw a crooked smile looking up at her. Long braids and shiny skin, the little boy could not be more than ten years old. With the tiny warm hand in hers, she felt more energy creeping into her cold bones.

Day 7

EDNA

The final full day of our stay in Kiruna was spent visiting with the other tribes. We had a giveaway ceremony where we gave away a collection of blankets and hair barrettes that my niece Desiree and I had brought with us. We explained that the giveaway had been out-lawed for decades in our country because the government did not want large groups of Indians to meet. As a result, our ceremonies were practised in secret. I saw many people nodding as I told my story because this happened around the world. In order to make us like them, the government tried to take away the things that made us a people. But considering how many people were sharing in our ceremony, they didn't do a very good job!

Now we're off to Germany where we are dancing in a festival. I wish that I had more information about the upcoming festival but our tour director, John, has been too busy to fill us in.

John packed up his backpack (it took him about ten seconds), did a quick survey of the tent, and then backed out. He checked his watch. It was ten minutes to the time that he and Per had decided on the night before. It was a quick decision seconds before Per had left the tent. In a quiet voice, Per had asked, "What time?" John mumbled "Ten?" and Per nodded.

John could say that both he and Per were busy: John with the drum and showing steps to people who kept coming up to him. Plus pictures — he must have posed for at least two dozen. His body was sore; he must have danced too hard because every limb felt heavy. "You're getting old, John Greyeyes," he reminded himself for the thousandth time. He wasn't looking forward to the next leg of the journey. But at least the plane ride was short.

He went to the tent next to him and hit one of the poles. It made a dull clang. "Lucas, git your ass out here."

There was no response, which didn't surprise John in the least. The kid was a late riser, another one of John's least favourite qualities. If you weren't up by 7:00 a.m., then you might as well be dead, was John's belief. Whole damned day was wasted.

"Lucas!" He used his calling-the-horses-in-from-the-field volume. Everyone in the vicinity turned and gave him a dirty look. But there was no movement from the tent.

John squatted and opened the tent. It was empty.

"Well." John slapped his hat on the ground. He started downhill towards where breakfast was served. The camp was quite a few people lighter. Many had left for home after the round dance the night before and others had left earlier in the morning. He hoped that his male fancy dancer hadn't jumped in with the wrong crew, deciding that he might find a path better than the one that led to Germany or to some other godforsaken place. John wasn't too excited about heading to Germany but when he had a job, he damned well did it.

John slung his backpack over his shoulder and hurried down the hill. He said passing goodbyes to a few Navaho men who he'd had breakfast with a couple days before. Funny how you could meet so many people in such a short period of time and get used to their voices and faces. This crew had even invited him to come down to their reservation and ride their horses sometime. John was definitely tempted to take them up on that.

A Sami woman stopped him halfway down the hill. She was soft-shouldered and had the weariness of middle age on her body. She was sitting outside a tent that looked a lot like a tipi but stood as she saw him approach. She reached into her pocket and handed him a necklace with a reindeer tooth on it. John pulled out a beaded hair barrette. His mom had given him about a dozen of these in preparation for moments like these. Of course, his mom had hoped that he'd be handing them out to potential daughters-in-law. That plan had certainly gone awry, he thought.

The woman's face lit up as her hands explored the intricate beadwork. She slipped it into her hair, clipping back her greying bangs.

John saw Per's vw van parked near the breakfast area; John opened the door and dropped his bag inside. Desiree and Edna weren't there yet. He glanced at the tables around the cooking area, but didn't hear Lucas's fool lips flapping or see his hands moving wildly as he told some cocky collection of lies.

He turned in a circle, looking at each camp, each fire, each bunkhouse. The view was pretty clear as most tents and tipis had been pulled down.

"Hey Mr. John." Desiree popped up beside him. "You look worried."

"Can't find Lucas. You see him?"

She had circles around her eyes and a tiny hickey high up on her neck. "When I left the dance, he was still there, hitting on some Maori girls, I think."

"Where's your aunt?"

Desiree pointed at the kitchen. "She's scrubbing away by the sink. I swear she's trying to prove that Crees are the cleanest Indians in the world. Probably lost half the skin off her hands by now. And like, who cares anyway?"

If John hadn't been so annoyed with Lucas, he might have chuckled at the frustration and embarrassment in Desiree's tone. "It's something women care about. Older women."

"I don't think he's here," Desiree said. "Because we would have heard him by now. He's not exactly quiet."

"No, he's not." Then where did he go? John hadn't seen Lucas stick with a single group for more than a day, he hadn't been sweet on a specific girl (he threw out moves at every single woman in the camp), and he hadn't been interested in talking to any of the elders. (This was a quality John found to be a serious failure in a young person. He'd spent most of his early twenties sitting next to elders at campfires learning something new every day.)

Per ambled up to them. "Hello John."

"Morning."

Per leaned close to Desiree. "Rumour is that many men were sobbing last night because a Cree princess broke their hearts."

Desiree giggled. "How are you doing, handsome?"

Per looked at John before answering. "I don't think I slept a wink last night."

"All the work you did bringing all these people and all the phone calls and, uh, whatnot." Desiree had clearly not organized anything in her life. "And now you're gonna miss everyone, huh?"

Per winked. "Some more than others."

Desiree's face was turning a new shade of red.

"People got to go home sometime," John said sharply.

Per turned his attention to John. "I don't need to ask how you are doing. Lucas, right?"

"The little shit pulled a disappearing act on us."

"I've got news."

"Good or bad?" Desiree asked brightly.

Per hesitated. "It's not . . . all bad."

John took his hat off and fanned himself with it. "Bad, huh. Well, give it to me."

"I've heard there was a card game last night and things did not go well for your young man."

"He's not my young man." John sighed. "Where is he?"

"I'll take you to him but you should know, he owes a lot of money to the Navaho."

Desiree rolled her eyes. "That jackass."

Per cleared his throat. "That was also something else that my friend mentioned. Some people believe that your young dancer was stealing."

John closed his eyes and sighed. Not only did he have to find this idiot, now he had to beat him too.

Desiree let out a low whistle. "Wow, he is one seriously screwed up little Indigenous person." Desiree looked at John. "Let's keep that part from my aunt."

John glanced over at her aunt, who appeared to be explaining the proper way to clean a pot to another woman.

John had no intention of filling Edna in. She would spend the rest of the tour lecturing Lucas if she found out. Not that John was against that, but he'd have to listen to it as well.

He couldn't kick the dancer out because he only had three and truth be told, Lucas was the best. "I know we've outstayed our welcome, Per, and you're probably busy as all hell — but can you take me to him?"

～

It was a long walk to the Navaho camp. And a quiet one. John felt a smile tugging at his lips — that kind of smile that comes when you don't know what else to do with your face. He distracted himself by thinking of all the things that he'd like to do to Lucas, but his mind wouldn't focus. It kept shifting and moving; now it was focused on the brightness of the sun and the next second he could only smell the hide vest that Per was wearing.

"This land, right here, reminds me of Saskatchewan." He interrupted the silence. "Like the way it looks like it got picked clean, there's land like that off the reserve. The reserve itself is full of trees because we never burnt out our trees for farming. We farmed around them."

Desiree looked at him with undisguised boredom and then darted away to speak to a group of young people.

Per was not bored. "Do you farm back in Canada?"

"I've never been one for machinery and seems like farming, you spend a lot of time fixing it. I like horses, simple and their engines don't need tinkering. You get on them and go. I handle the cattle for the reserve."

"But animals get sick, no? They get old. They need attention too."

John chuckled. "Well yeah, I've been known to do some doctoring. Bringing colts inside on cold days, tending to mares with infected teats, sewing closed coyote bites. You never know what you're in for. I remember this one time, I had this horse — Ebony was her name — I didn't name her that. Her owner before me was a twelve-year-old girl and they always give names like that."

"Sure, sure."

"But Ebony was a good quarter horse, fast but a smooth gait. I had this dugout in the field where I would break the ice and the horses would drink. I must have slept in or something 'cause when I was heading out the door, I saw Ebony standing on the dugout ice already, hitting it with her hooves. Damn smart horse, that girl. And she'd broken some of it when I heard this crack. Like a gunshot. It was the ice underneath her caving in and when I heard the sound — I wasn't even sure what it meant but I started running full speed. I heard her whinny when her front legs went in, then more of a scream as the rest of the ice cracked around her."

"Horses scream?" Per asked.

"Worst sound in the world. I ran as fast as I could but the dugout was so deep, I could see her head dip below and then come back up. I was close by then and I grabbed my axe and ran across the ice.

Didn't think or nothing. One of my strong points, my brother always says." John gave an angry laugh. "I ran towards her, and hit the ice right near her front hoof. Ice shattered and made a hole bigger than a dining room table. That's when I went in. But the horse had more room to move then. Then I hit again towards the shallow end and the ice broke again. But still not near enough. I kept striking it — which was hard because I had to use one arm to keep afloat, plus steer clear of her hooves. I kept on hitting and swimming, hitting and swimming and then — thank God or whoever is out there — my feet reached land. We walked out of there then. I looked Ebony over, she was fine except for some scratches on her legs. I was so damned tired, I had to sit myself down until my arms stopped shaking. And the horses walked around me to get to the water. I remember thinking how lucky I was that none of them had followed Ebony in. 'Cause I only had one horse-saving in me that day."

"Well, now I don't mind being compared to a horse so much," Per said softly. "Knowing what you did for one."

"Good story," Desiree broke in. She had wandered back to catch the end of John's story.

"That's the most I've heard you speak," Per added.

"Not all of us are big storytellers, y'know." John hadn't had a whole of time to speak growing up with Amos flapping his lips all the time.

"And, some people can't help but share their lives with others."

"And, some of us like our peace and quiet."

Per fell silent. John looked at the road ahead of them, a mix of brown and black dirt, and wondered what Per did with his time when he wasn't organizing international festivals.

"See," Per let out the word like it was a breath he was holding. "I can be silent."

Desiree giggled.

"You save horses, you dance, and you spend time with your mother . . . everything is good back there in Canada?"

It's just a life, John wanted to say. *Get up, work, go to bed.*

Nothing less, nothing more. But that was only lately. When he was younger, there were rodeos and drinking and fighting and poker games in the back of pickup trucks. There was camping underneath the stars, next to the horse trailer. There were injuries and recovery from injuries and being dragged to the doctor by his mom for second opinions; each time she hoped that the opinion would be "no more rodeo-ing." There were dinners with his brother and family, watching his nieces and nephews go from being dirty little shitters to gap-toothed toddlers with bewitching smiles to talkative youngsters who liked to wrassle with their uncle. And there was this feeling underneath all of that, like doors were closing.

"You like horses?" he asked finally.

"I don't mind them," Per answered.

"Then you'd like it jes fine." John felt like there was something in the air that was sucking his sanity out of him.

"I like horses," Desiree offered. "My dad owns a bunch."

Per slowed as they approached a small camp of tents. There were people milling about, packing up their camp.

"Ya'at'eeh shi'kis!" he said loudly and a young woman returned the greeting. She was nearly as tall as John and had narrow dark eyes like the Indians from up north.

John raised his hat in greeting and the young woman nodded. "Sarah," she said.

"John," he replied.

Per said, "We are here for the Hunkpapa."

"Brown hair, green eyes, kind of looks like he's always up to no good."

"The thief." Sarah spit. "He owes us a lot."

John gulped. "How much?"

"Six hundred. American."

"Keep him." John turned on his heel and stalked away from the camp. He didn't pay attention to the shock on the faces of the people around him. If they knew how much trouble this little shit had been since the tour's beginning, they would understand completely.

Per jogged to catch up with him. "Interesting negotiation technique."

John grunted.

"I understand that he is frustrating but he is young and he is your dancer."

"He is not my dancer. I would never have chosen him."

Per pulled on his sleeve to stop him. "How much money do you have?"

John stared at him.

"If it's a matter of money, I can front you some of it. Then you can — or he can — pay me back when you get back to Canada."

John knew who would be sending that money order. "I have expense money for the entire group, not to pay for one fool who can't help getting himself in trouble every five minutes. Who is definitely a gambler and drug user. Who it now turns out is a thief as well!"

"I know you're frustrated. But you can't leave him with them."

John wasn't convinced of that. Lucas's relatives were probably wishing that someone would keep him for a few years.

Per leaned close. "I don't think they would kill him but they would definitely think up something interesting."

John smiled, liking the sound of that. He looked back up at the sky. So damned bright all the time. He grunted. "I have a second offer."

~

During one of his few travels, John had headed up north and visited with the Dene. Most Cree spoke bad about the Dene, said they were wild as hell. But John found them to be Indians like the rest of them, more into hunting and fishing than most because of their proximity to some of the lushest woods he'd ever seen. Another big difference — they loved their hand games. John figured that since the Dene and the Navaho were long-lost cousins that they would appreciate playing the game of their ancestors. Or at least that is what he tried to sell Sarah. Sarah's eyes narrowed at his explanation but when he showed her a couple of hundred-dollar bills (his only American ones), she nodded tersely.

John explained the basics of the game: "So we line up in two lines here, and you have four team members, I got four."

Sarah pointed at a couple of guys who jumped into line.

John looked at Per. "I'll need you."

Per stepped into line beside him.

"And next we will have Desiree," John pointed at her and she smiled and stood on the other side of Per. John searched for Lucas. He was sitting around the fire, his head hanging. A formidable looking woman was standing next to him. "And . . ." He sighed. "That guy." He pointed at Lucas, whose eyes lit up like a puppy dog.

Sarah frowned. Then yelled and Lucas was brought over.

Lucas smiled as he got closer to John. "I knew you'd come for me!" He gave John a hard hug.

John pushed him away. "What the hell did you get yourself into?"

"Nothing. I was hanging out, having fun — I think this is a racial thing."

This little shit was never going to take responsibility for anything. "Get your ass in line."

Lucas smiled warmly at Per, who pulled him into a hug.

Sarah was standing across from John. Beside her was the same large lady that had been guarding Lucas and a younger slim guy who had the tight body of a boxer. "We have our team. Who will keep score?"

"I will." All eyes turned to Edna. Where the hell did she come from?

Edna's chest was heaving so John figured she had hurried over quick. Desiree patted her on the shoulder. "Wow, you really get around, Auntie."

"Oh, go on now." Edna pushed away Desiree's hand. "I know your tricks."

"Not fair," Sarah said. "She's from your area."

"But she's as straight as a nun. You all know that," Desiree explained. "She won't even pick up a deck of cards at home."

Sarah looked around the grounds. It was getting sparse as people were packing up their camps. She eyed up Per and then glanced at John. John saw the glimpse of a smirk on her face.

"All right then. Let's get started."

Sarah and her team knew the basics. John explained the game to his team. Per and Desiree caught on quick.

Lucas was a harder sell. "I take this rock and hide it in my hand and they guess which hand. But I can't throw it or hide it in my mouth?"

"What are you, five?" Desiree asked. "Who puts a rock in their mouth?"

John pushed them apart. "No. It's in your hand. It's about moving it around or distracting the other side. First team that reaches six points wins."

"Are you sure you wouldn't like to scrap it out? You're a big guy, you could take like two guys or that big woman?"

John glared at him. "We're not fighting for you. This is how we settle this."

"And if we lose?" Per asked.

John shook his head. "We get there if we get there."

The two teams squatted down in two lines facing one another. Sarah lined up against John, Per was up against a strong-looking young Navaho man and Lucas's favourite Navaho woman was across from him. Desiree held up the line against a handsome middle-aged man.

Someone brought out a hand-drum and they started to play. The beat was addictive. Being selected to go first, John brought out some moves he remembered from the Dene games he'd watched. He shifted his hands deftly back and forth and squinted and made faces that he'd seen a Dene elder do. Sarah looked at him like he was the biggest ass in the world. She pointed at his right hand. He showed them the smooth stone in his left.

Edna tossed a stick in the middle of everyone. First point.

Only five more to go.

Unlike the rest of him, Per had big hands. Mitts is what John's mom would have called them. The rock looked like a pebble in his palm. He stared out dispassionately at the people in front of him, his eyes cold and aloof. John had to squelch a laugh. Per was trying so hard to have a poker face as he moved his hands. His opponent saw through him and pointed at his right. Per opened his hand. Point Navaho.

Desiree looked confident but her hands were shaking. She dropped the stone as she juggled it in her slim hands. She picked it up with an apologetic look to the older man in front of her who smiled encouragingly.

"Sucker," thought John.

She moved the stone back and forth, picking up some speed until her hands were a blur. Then she moved them once behind her and then held them out, her smile bright.

She won her point.

When the crowd — and there was a crowd by now — turned to Lucas, he was ready to go. He bounced on his knees, moving to the beat of the music. His hands snaked back and forth. The big Navaho lady guessed — she was wrong. Another point for them.

It was the Navaho's turn. Sarah lost her point and snarled afterwards. But her team members won theirs.

John did the math quickly in his head. Four to four. He felt a bead of sweat making tracks down his forehead.

"Tugay," John said under his breath.

Per nodded. "Agreed."

John moved the stone between his hand and looked up at the Navaho. Sarah stared into his eyes, didn't even glance at the stone. She pointed at his left. John opened his hand. The stone wasn't there.

This time, Per made a big show of it. His attempt at poker face all gone, he threw his energy into smiles and fast movements. As John's mom would say, "it was all for naught." The boxer in front of him guessed easily and correctly.

"Last point wins!" Lucas announced with the confidence of youth (and stupidity, John added. Never underestimate the confidence of stupidity).

Desiree raised her hand. "Can I change my position? The sun is in my eyes."

John felt like the sun was always in everyone's eyes but Desiree wasn't addressing him. She was addressing the very accommodating smile on her opponent's face. He nodded and changed position with her. Sarah looked like she might want to raise a fuss but didn't. John figured Sarah was trying to work out the angle Desiree was playing — but the only pertinent angle was that Desiree wanted this guy to be able to see down her shirt. She switched to her knees and bobbed along. She switched her stone back and forth a couple times and smiled up at her opponent. He smiled at her and the woman next to him elbowed him hard in the side. He focused again.

Lucas started cheering loudly.

"Shut up," John yelled at him. And then added an "atimachisk," for good measure.

Lucas made a face at him.

"Stop that, you jackass!"

Lucas made a worse face. John lunged at him, knocking Per over into Lucas.

"Watch your old ass," Lucas shot back. "Before I come over there and kick it back into the 1800s."

John started to get up. Lucas shot up. (Before John had even gotten to his feet. God, young'uns.) Per held his arms between them. "Men," he said. "This is not good."

"I've had it up to here with him," John said. "He's a lying, no good, stealing son of a bitch."

"And he's a sour-faced old kokum."

John reached past Per and pulled Lucas by his collar. Lucas looked shocked that John had reached him and then laughed. "You got some moves, hey, old man?"

Desiree slapped at John's arm. "John, that's not cool."

John let go of Lucas.

He sat back down. His heart was beating hard.

"Can we finish the game now?" Desiree did not sound impressed at all.

"Yeah, grow up," Edna said. "Let's get on with it."

Desiree threw her stone between her hands. Sarah growled something Navaho to the man; John didn't know Navaho but he was sure it had something to do about looking with his eyes and not with his man-parts.

Desiree started the bouncing-dancing technique that Lucas had been using. The man was lost. He pointed at her right hand.

Desiree looked askance. She frowned.

John's mouth went dry.

Then she opened her other hand. She had won her point.

John smiled.

Later as they rode in the van to the airport, Lucas bragged about his performance, including his fight with John.

"We thought that up, like, way before," Lucas said. "We knew what we were doing."

In the front seat next to Per, John said. "I wasn't faking."

"'Course you were." Lucas patted him on his shoulder. "Good one."

Day 8

E D N A

Before we left, we ate with the Sami people. People had many questions for us about Canada and how it was for Indian people there. I tried to explain as much as I could but as we have so many tribes in Canada, I'm sure people were confused by the end.

The Sami people described how they were treated in their country and much of it was not good. Like us in Canada, many Sami fill the jails and live in bad homes. They don't have a lot of money and not many of them get good jobs. It's sad that things have turned out for us like this.

We also played a game with the Navaho. They were good sports when we won the hand games. And I exchanged more hair wraps. Perhaps it is time to think of growing out my hair again. I saw so many women my age with long hair; it did not look foolish on them.

After a morning of hijinks, I wasn't exactly looking forward to the flight but the sleep would have been nice. There's been too much walking, too much dancing, too much sleeping in strange beds.

When we pulled up to the airport, it looked like those oases that you see in desert movies. But once we got there, we saw that the Lord wasn't finished testing us. We had missed our flight.

CHAPTER 7

JOHN

Per took them as far as Stockholm in his van. They tore along the roads at a breakneck pace, past muskeg, open waters, and reindeer. There was a ferry that crossed once a day and they were in danger of missing it. They unpacked their bags and Per left them to get their tickets. He stood at the entrance to the ferry and handed them their tickets one by one. John felt the pressure of so many words and as he neared Per, in his mind, John lined them up, "Goodbye, thank you, take care . . ." but when he reached Per all he could manage was a pat on the arm.

John left Per standing at the dock as they got settled on the boat. John stood on the boat away from the edge, as though he was scared of a wave plucking him over the edge. Desiree and Edna waved. John kept his eyes on Per. As long as I can see him, John thought. He could trace him even now with his eyes and he did so until the island was gone.

John could still conjure up Per's shape and hear his voice, musical and strong and soft and all things that John needed to hear. He could even remember his scent . . .

John forced his thoughts on to the steps of the grass dance. He forced himself to remember how to hide in the grass, shaking and quivering and rising at the right moment to move and stalk and then hide again. The sneak-up dance, some people called it.

John looked at his fellow passengers, trying to gauge their level of comfort. Though he'd failed as a leader — this was an assessment he was sure he shared with Edna — he still felt responsible for their well-being. His male dancer was sleeping off his guilt. Each mile they passed, Lucas seemed to rest even more easily. Edna had torn a strip off of him, stating in no uncertain terms that Lucas was ruining the tour and possibly their lives and that the good Lord would make him pay for his wickedness. There was more but John had to go make sure the gear was packed correctly and didn't have time to hear the entire rant. Lucas hung his head during the lecture. John did realize later that the rant coincided with the heaviest of the lifting and next time he'd ask Edna to let Lucas help stow the gear before launching into her discipline.

When John got back to their seats, Edna was asleep in the centre of the bench seat, quite close to Lucas actually, as close as two people could get without touching.

Every so often, she moaned. Her arthritis was acting up and John felt guilty as hell. He reached down and tucked her blanket between her bones and the edges of the bench she was sleeping on. John had his own twinges of pain, thanks to some wild horses back in his youth, but they could be managed with a couple aspirin.

The problem was the trip wasn't going to get shorter. The long ferry ride would not be easy on anyone.

There was an itinerary in his pocket but it was crossed with red so many times that he was sure that only a World War II codebreaker could decipher it.

NADINE

"You're kind of a tough guy, hey?" Nadine punched Lucas's arm. They were standing in line to get off the plane. "Like, you took down that big guy and barely broke a sweat. You're kind of Indian Hercules." Nadine could not stop herself from bringing it up over and over, replaying the fight for anyone who would listen. It had something to do with how seeing Lucas use those big muscles to clock someone made Nadine tingle. It was also because she saw someone who stood up for others — she hadn't seen that in a long time. Back home, it seemed like people had been beaten down to the point that they never wanted to stand up again.

"Anyone would have done the same," Lucas replied.

"The hell they would," Nadine scoffed. "Whole room full of people and you were the only one who stood up." Nadine slipped her hand into her purse and grabbed some gum. This flying was murder on her ears. "Papa was a rolling stone," she sang. It was the last song she had heard before they left the disco.

"You're in high spirits," Lucas observed.

"Today we meet up with them."

Lucas narrowed his eyes.

"This is it. You ready?"

"I'm more than ready." Lucas rubbed his jaw. "Definitely owe that little shit a parting gift."

Still giddy, Nadine punched him in the arm again. "Their plane is scheduled to arrive in a few minutes. We stake out the gate they're flying into and soon you'll have your name and your life back."

"How long, you think?"

Nadine glanced at a watch on someone else's wrist. "About an hour." She wanted to rub her hands together — she was that gleeful. What was she so happy about, though? Was it seizing control of her tour? Was it helping Lucas get reacquainted with his stuff? Or, was it seeing John? She jumped to the image of the couple walking on cobblestone streets, except maybe that wasn't John's hand in hers.

Lucas. John. Lucas. It was good that they would finally be able to stay still for a while — and then she could figure out if her feelings about Lucas were real. And if they were like the real thing — like Richard Burton and Liz Taylor real — how did he feel? She glanced at him . . . he was stoically moving through the crowd. He was a tough one to read. She would have to make out with him and see what his feelings were. Then she had to figure out how she would move all her stuff to the States and all the paperwork involved with that. *Research the Jay Treaty*, she mentally added to her to-do list. Nadine stole another look at his perfect profile and silently prayed to whatever god controlled lust and chemistry and love — *please, please let this be the one.*

They grabbed a quick lunch and then Nadine hurried them over to the gate for the plane from Stockholm. She had a grin pasted on her face as the passengers got off. Wouldn't John be surprised to see her smiling there? He thought he ditched her but Nadine wasn't that easy to shake off. "I'm a woodtick," she murmured.

"What was that?" Lucas asked.

"Nothing," Nadine replied. "Thinking out loud."

People streamed past them, mostly blondes, and Nadine's eyes searched for a dark head among them. The stream slowed to a trickle until finally it was only a couple stewardesses. Nadine went up to the front. "Is that all the folks on the plane?"

The stewardess nodded.

"What happened to all the Indians?" Nadine asked.

"They were killed by smallpox?" said the stewardess.

"There was a group of Indians on the plane or supposed to be on the plane — did you see them?"

The stewardess's eyes moved to where Lucas stood and slowly she raised her arm and pointed at him.

"I came with that one," Nadine replied.

JOHN

The ferry crossing was smooth except for one choppy part that woke up John up. He looked around for his other tour members and saw that they were safe. Desiree was leaning against the railing and smiling out at the water. Edna was sitting up, her hand clutching her stomach. Lucas was sleeping curled up on the floor again.

John had heard about an island in Canada where these little

shaggy ponies ran free. He imagined Lucas running with them.

John crossed over and sat next to Edna. He looked to the shore and saw city lights flickering ahead. "Hang in there. We're almost there."

"It's almost over," Edna replied.

"Hasn't been all bad."

Edna hooted.

"We gotta keep it together for a few more days. And this stop is an easy one. It's a big music festival, I think, and no outdoor tents —"

"Thank God," Edna sniffed.

"And there's less shows. We will have more time to rest and relax and . . . uh . . . think." Thinking sounded like the worst thing in the world so John stood up and busiest himself with packing up their things.

Day 9

Hamburg, Germany

EDNA

We arrived in Hamburg at dawn. It is a port city so we got treated to the sight of sailors throwing up on the side of the docks, after spending the night drinking and committing God-knows-what-other sins. The light from the water was pretty though and I would recommend it to anyone. Because we were late, our host was not there to receive us. Instead he sent his driver. The driver explained that the mayor had showed up at the airport for our arrival time, along with other dignitaries. Not to mention, there was a parade planned. You cannot imagine my embarrassment that we arrived too late for our welcome. They must think us the rudest of Indians.

Reportedly our host was not pleased but he understood that many things can go wrong when many people of different person-alities are travelling together. Especially when some personalities

are not very responsible and make everything difficult for every-
one else because they are selfish and could have benefitted from
having their bottom warmed a few times.

The driver is to take us to our new accommodations. Someone
mentioned something about a castle but I'm sure they were exag-
gerating. Nobody really lives in castles anymore.

NADINE

"A castle, hey? I wonder if there will be a moat," Nadine mused. She
was in the back seat of a small car being driven by Andre, the driver
for the castle. He had picked them up at the airport and let them
know that he worked for their host.

Lucas sat in the passenger seat. "I don't think such things exist
anymore, if they ever did."

"They did," Andre replied. "Back in 1050. Bit before my day."

"Wasn't there a famous German guy who lived in a castle and
drank people's blood?" Nadine asked.

"Romania," the driver spit out.

"There was a German royal family that interbred until they
couldn't chew their food anymore."

"Soup eaters then." Nadine smiled, enjoying Lucas's historical
tidbits.

"The rich do many stupid things," Andre added.

"But not your boss?"

"He is not rich."

"The castle though?"

"Castles cost money." The driver's shoulders rose in a shrug.

"It's why I prefer small houses," Nadine said.

"Except in your stealing days."

The driver looked at Nadine in the rear-view mirror.

"When I was very young. Many years ago." Nadine slapped

the back of Lucas's neck. "Go on now making this man worry for nothing."

The road changed and they were heading uphill.

"What's all this then? This road is starting to look a bit lonely, like it misses having a shoulder," Nadine observed. She could see a far drop below.

"We are almost to the castle."

"Holee hell," Nadine slapped Lucas's arm again. "Like I said, stick with me and great things will happen."

"You didn't actually say that. But okay," Lucas replied.

Nadine sat back in the back seat and assessed her "relationship" with Lucas. So far, she had progressed from grabbing Lucas's arm to affectionately hitting him. Her next goal was to find a way to get close to his firm, supple lips.

She jumped forward again. "Do you need some chapstick?"

"Chapstick?" Lucas glanced back at her. Nadine was applying a thick layer to her lips. It was glossy pink. He shook his head.

"If you're offering, Miss, my lips are very dry," Andre said.

Nadine handed it forward, mentally cursing herself for not learning how to seduce men earlier in life.

EDNA

It was a real castle. It burst out of the mountains and cascaded down the side of the hill. It was one of the most impressive things Edna had ever seen (she hadn't seen the Vatican yet so she felt okay saying that). They all stared open-mouthed at the thing as they travelled by bus (again) up the mountain that led to it.

"Dear Jesus, I never thought I'd live to see the day that four Indians would be spending the night in so grand a place," Edna exclaimed.

"I hope it's haunted," Desiree said. "Like with a maiden who didn't get married to the man that she loved and so she threw herself

171

off one of the walls. Those walls are high," she added, peering out the window.

"Don't be morbid," Edna murmured, but there was no real force in her voice. She didn't want to discourage Desiree from talking; she'd been quiet for a few hours and Edna was worried that she'd gotten homesick. "Maybe it's a ghost who loved her home and she wants to watch over everyone who lives there."

Desiree laughed. "That would be a good horror movie: the ghost who wants you to be comfortable."

"I saw a ghost once," said Lucas. "It was missing an arm."

"Did you steal it?" Edna asked. It was petty but she still didn't like the little cuss.

Lucas gave her a wounded look.

The castle did look like the kind of place where ghosts lived and Edna was fine with that. There was more than enough room for them and the living.

"How do you keep out thieves?" Desiree wondered aloud. "'Cause there's so many nooks and crannies, seems like anyone could sneak in there."

Lucas nodded. "You couldn't keep me out. I bet we could sneak in a whole family. Live in one part of the castle, rent-free. Probably no one would figure it out for weeks."

Edna refused to acknowledge their nonsense.

"I heard that the castle is over five hundred years old," Edna said. "I heard one of the sailors on the dock mention that when we got picked up. The one who was vomiting, remember him, John?"

John shrugged.

"Over five hundred years old — that's older than Canada!" Edna remarked.

"Groovy," Desiree murmured, not very excited by the history lesson.

Edna craned her neck to see more of the delicious bits of the castle. In places the stone was covered with ivy that must have been thirty feet in length. Real people lived there too, she could tell, because the stone looked freshly repaired and mortared, none of these ancient ruins they'd passed a ways back, only grey rocks left behind to tell the tale of a grand manor and a grander time. She'd felt a bit dismayed when they'd left Hamburg, feeling like they hadn't had a chance to really enjoy the city or even look it over, but this clearly made up for all of that.

"How many bedrooms in a place like that?" Edna directed her question at the driver. He was about twenty and shy. Or at least had become shy when Desiree turned her gaze on him.

He cleared his throat. "I have no idea, thirty? I know that there's two libraries, two kitchens, three great rooms —"

Desiree jumped in. "What are great rooms? Like a room that's better than good?"

"Um . . . sort of a cross between a dining room and a ballroom."

Edna had immediately liked the way these German people handled themselves. Even the drunk sailors had been polite as they pointed out where they would meet their bus. Then the driver was there — on time, waiting for them with the name of their troupe neatly written on a sign. He'd broken the bad news but in such a formal, direct, no-nonsense way that Edna hadn't felt the sting of disappointment for long. They'd missed the mayor of Hamburg and the mayor of a neighbouring village, all the councilmen, two owners of the finest hotels in the city, and an assorted collection of artists and musicians, including one marching band. (Okay, that one had still stung.) Then the driver had escorted them to the bus (another vehicle was following with all their luggage. Edna had watched as two young blonde men packed it in with an efficiency that made her understand why the world had feared these people). And now they were on the road to the largest home she'd ever seen. "Who owns this place again?"

"His name is Robert Adlerflügel. Here's an interesting fact — Mr. Adlerflügel lived in Canada for part of his life. In a place called Sassa-Sask-Saki . . ."

"Saskatchewan," Desiree said, putting the driver out of his misery. "It's where we're from too!"

Edna wondered about this Robert Adlerflügel. She hadn't met too many non-Indian people in Saskatchewan herself who were eager to host a big group of Indians. Other than the police, that is. She smiled at her own joke.

Edna glanced over at John who had been quiet for a long time, even for him. His head was turned and his eyes were out the window but he hadn't reacted to anything. If Edna didn't know better, she would have said that he was sad. But why would he be sad? They were halfway through the tour now and still together! There were challenges to come — like how many shows exactly did they have this week? And what about the Italian shows — what did they expect? And, would she be able to make her meeting with the spy-guy? And more importantly, would she end up getting arrested and forced to spend the rest of her miserable life in prison? She remembered reading about an Italian criminal whose punishment was to be holed up in a wall and forgotten — did they still do that? She shook that idea out of her head; no sense in borrowing trouble.

"Check that out, Auntie." Desiree pointed at the window to Edna's right. "Look at those giant horses."

Edna saw a group of black horses marching up the side of the road, their riders clad in similar-looking outfits and tiny black hats on the top of their heads. The lead rider tipped his hat as the bus passed them.

"Those horses are huge!" Desiree gushed. "What kind are they?"

"Percherons," John said and then closed his mouth again and didn't open it up again until they were inside the castle's gates. Edna hoped he wasn't coming down with some kind of flu. That would be the last thing they needed, the whole group ending up with sore tummies and loose stools.

Nadine had settled her bags in her room and was heading to the kitchen to grab some food when she heard them. She recognized their voices before she saw them; the Cree accent from her area gave her a misty-eyed feeling. Strange how you could recognize your people from only a couple of sentences. John was the first around the corner, looking as contemplative as he did standing out in his pasture at dusk. She felt that same jolt when she saw him. God, would that ever wear off?

Next was Edna, that nunnish lady. Nadine had seen her around at powwows but had never met her — mostly because she was never much of a Jesus-proclaimer herself. She found those types a mite boring. Next was a vision of loveliness with a spoiled expression on her face, and then the fake-Lucas. He looked a lot younger and more wide-eyed than he did in his police mug-shot photo. Those green eyes were unmistakeable, though.

"Stop!" she ordered and all of them stopped in unison (a good instinct for a group). The criminal, of course, put his hands up and then lowered them. And then he laughed as though his life up to this point had been one big joke.

"What are you laughing at? Ain't nothing funny," Nadine said.

Lucas appeared behind him and grabbed fake-Lucas's arms in a kind of hold that Nadine had seen on TV. The criminal started struggling and hollering for help. John ran to his side.

"No, John!" Nadine scrambled to stop John before he got involved. She was too late and he was already trying to pry the fake Lucas from the real Lucas's grasp. "He's with me." She launched herself onto John's back.

John struggled to get her off. "Who the hell is this now?"

"It's me, John. It's your Nadine."

"My who?"

"Nadine, your neighbour."

John stopped and craned his head to look at her. "Nadine Redcloud?"

"Yeah, I'm here. You got on this tour with a criminal." She pointed with one hand and lost her grip on John and felt her feet touch the smooth stone surface. She stood up straight and smoothed out her clothes. "This young man," she pointed a finger at the fake Lucas, "is not who you think he is."

"He stole my passport," Lucas said.

"That's the real Lucas Pretends Eagle." Nadine moved to stand next to him. "This one is the fake." Nadine pushed the young man with her other hand.

"What?" protested the fake Lucas. "They're lying!"

"Oh hush," John said. "Let's see some I.D."

"Hold his arms," Nadine ordered Lucas, who did so with relish. Fake Lucas struggled but the real Lucas outweighed him by a good thirty pounds. Nadine dug through the young man's pockets. She found: a pocket knife, a fancier Swiss Army knife, a chocolate bar, a postcard that was bent in half, a polaroid photo of a stripper sitting on the young guy's lap, half a croissant, a bus ticket, a length of wire, and then finally a passport, bent in half as well.

He protested. "This is an illegal search!"

Nadine unbent the passport and opened it up. There was Lucas Pretends Eagle. The real one. She showed the picture to John.

"Who the hell are you?" John demanded.

The fake Lucas struggled against Lucas's arms. Then gave up. "I'm a dancer," he said finally.

"I can help you out there, John," said Nadine. "That there is Shane Buffalo and he is from Saskatchewan, although he's wanted in Manitoba and Alberta and when I say 'wanted' I mean, like, police wanted."

"We assumed that," Desiree interjected.

"Shane, huh?" John looked the young man in the eye.

Nadine pointed at Lucas. "You took this man's wallet, his I.D., his plane ticket, his car, and his suitcase — you're nothing but a nasty little criminal." Nadine peered at him. "And you can't even apologize for all that you put him through?"

The little thief's eyes flicked from person to person looking for a friendly face. Nadine glanced around; nobody seemed disposed to help him, which spoke volumes. He hadn't ingratiated himself with this group of people, and these were all a bunch of softies. She saw some white people standing a distance from the group, watching. Nadine felt herself blushing but it couldn't be helped. They had to confront him.

"What are you going to do with him?" Desiree asked.

"Probably jail," Nadine said. She hadn't thought that far ahead.

The young man started struggling in Lucas's arms again. Nadine was wondering if she should go find some rope when someone interrupted her thoughts.

"You should let him go."

Nadine turned towards Edna.

"He can't go anywhere now and this is throwing our host off. We'll decide later what we will do with him."

Shane jumped forward like he was going to run and then stopped. "Nobody has the right to hold me," he said. "None of you are the police."

"Oh, shut up," John said. "You think the RCMP don't like little weasels? Trust me, the Germans aren't any more understanding. And you should know, torture is legal in Europe."

Nadine knew that wasn't true (didn't the Geneva Convention start here in Europe?) but was glad Shane didn't.

"Now that we know who everyone is — we should — well, I will introduce you to our host." Nadine waved to a man standing by the front door. "Robert!"

Robert strolled over. She was glad that she had asked him to hang back until she got reacquainted with her troupe.

"Hello there." He held out his hand to John, who shook it warmly.

"Thank you for inviting us to share your wonderful home with you. It's very impressive."

Nadine looked back to ensure that the rest of the troupe was similarly ready to meet their host. By showing some good manners, perhaps they could make up for missing the parade and arriving like a ragtag crew. Then out of the corner of her eye, she saw Edna dropping like a sack of flour to the ground.

Nadine sighed. That's what you get for hiring a bunch of amateurs.

EDNA

When she opened her eyes, Edna was looking into the eyes of a man she thought she would never see again. "Bobby," she said.

She was on the ground but someone had propped her up with a jacket under her head. Desiree was crouched down peering at her. A man was crouched next to her.

"It's Robert, actually," Nadine broke in. "Our host."

"Do you need a doctor?" Bobby asked. "I can call one."

Desiree had her aunt's wrist in her hand. "She has a good pulse and she didn't bump her head. Thanks to Luc — I mean Shane." To her aunt she added, "He caught your head."

Shane nodded.

"Fast hands come in handy," Edna replied.

Desiree giggled. "I think you're okay."

"This is Edna," Nadine said to Robert. "She's one of the older dancers in the group. We tried to reflect all age groups in our troupe. From youth to elders."

Edna did not know this Nadine woman all that well but she was not a fan.

"Let me up," Edna said. "Let me help you —" Desiree broke in and they rose together in a clumsy clump of limbs.

Nadine made a face. "Let's get our stuff inside, then I can do an inventory of the regalia. Afterwards, let's convene and do a quick rehearsal —"

"Hell no," said Desiree. "I'm not doing a single damned —"

"We've been travelling for a day and night," John said. "These people need to get their bearings."

178

"Of course," Robert replied. "My staff will show you to your rooms."

"Where's your crapper at?" Shane blurted out.

Although Edna wasn't one for crass talk, she did enjoy Nadine's offended look.

JOHN

Seeing Nadine had shocked him out of his stupor. He'd felt like a condemned inmate destined to walk down the hallway to his certain death and then he was suddenly free. He didn't have to put up with that Lucas Pretends Eagle anymore because it turns out that the real Lucas was a giant guy with meaty arms and a solemn face that promised no bullshit. That was the kind of guy John needed from the beginning. Not some scrawny troublemaker with more cock in his walk than cock in his pants. John had so easily dismissed the former Lucas that he nearly walked through him on his way to the castle dining room.

He was stopped by an uncertain, "John?"

John saw Shane, as it turns out, standing near a fireplace that was nearly as tall as him. He looked like he was a cord of wood about to be thrown in the fire. His face was pale, and damned if John didn't feel sympathetic for a second. Like you would feel for any pitiful pup that lost its way. So, he stopped. "What?"

"Nothing," Shane said.

If he wants to talk, then let's talk. "How could you rob a man of his identity?"

"I didn't mean to. He attacked me —"

"Lie."

"Okay, I took his stuff but he hit on —"

"Lie."

"Okay, we pulled over for gas and when he went into the bathroom, I knocked him out with a rock and robbed him. Does that make you feel better?"

"No! It doesn't." John wanted to punch a wall but noting that the walls were basically stone — instead, he paced in a circle. He stopped and looked the young one in the eye. "Do you understand how the stuff you do hurts other people?"

Shane shrugged. "Couldn't he get other I.D.? I've done it a few times."

"You could have killed him."

"I checked his breath — he was okay when I —"

"Do you hear yourself? Would you want someone knocking out your dad like that?"

Shane shrugged.

"Your mom?"

Shane shrugged again.

John paused. "You got any people?"

Shane stared back at him.

"I see." John left the room. How could you reason with someone who didn't care about anyone?

The stone floor gave off little sound but voices carried far. John could hear everyone in the dining room long before he reached it. He could hear the voices of the tour group, along with their new tour leader and their new Lucas. John felt nothing but relief to have everything in Nadine's capable hands.

He was turning into the large room when a little body coming out launched itself into him.

"Sorry there, John." Edna looked a bit red-faced.

"You okay?"

She burped and turned red. "I've never been a fan of wine. Not that I've had a lot. Do I seem drunk?"

If you have to ask. "You seem fine."

She was walking upright. Edna leaned close to him and John felt warm wine breath on his upper arm. He also sensed a revelation coming and wished he could still her lips.

"John, I know him! I know him, know him. I know him from the Bible."

John thought about the men assembled in the next room. "Lucas?"

Edna shook her head. Shame and booze were making her movements thick. "I know Robert, our host." She gestured at the house. "He wasn't Robert back then. He was Bobby, the farmhand, and I was very young and . . . now he's here and I didn't think I'd ever see him again."

"Sometimes people turn up like old burrs and you got to pick them off and flick them away again."

She gave him a teary smile. "I take this burr wherever I go."

"Do you want to go back to your room? I'll tell them you were feeling sick." Although he did question the wisdom of leaving her by herself in this cold dark place.

"Yes." She paused and shook her head. "No. I'm gonna sit back down and watch him and know that I made the right decision and that he's a bad man and we're in his castle but only bad people own castles, right?"

John agreed — the Queen of England had done some terrible shit or at least crap had been done in her name. But he didn't believe that Edna was going to sit back. Whenever someone made an excuse to be in the same room with an ex, that generally meant that the drama was not over. One of the benefits of avoiding romance his entire life was that he had a lot of experience watching other people's go down.

Tried to avoid. A face floated in John's mind. He could even hear his voice saying his name. *Like I'm being bloody haunted.* Unfinished, undone, so much longing that he wanted to take a sledgehammer to these stone walls and hit until all he could do was sleep. John considered going Edna's red-wine route but figured two drunk, foolish Indians was more than one castle could handle.

John followed Edna back into the dining room. She swayed before she plopped back into her seat and John noted her niece's concerned smile at her aunt's condition.

Edna's remarks had made him curious about their host so John's eyes were drawn to the head of the table, where a salt-and-pepper-haired man wearing a fur collar was holding court. The fur collar gave the optical illusion that he had a beard growing out of his neck.

His rapidly blinking eyes, tight smile and loud, nervous laugh gave John the impression that maybe he regretted inviting all these Indians to his house. Or maybe he was always weird. Time would tell.

"Sorry, I'm late," John directed at him. "Robert, right?" John offered his hand. Robert stood up and shook it. A good handshake — firm, albeit a bit long. "We didn't get a chance to meet, what with people fainting."

Edna grunted. John couldn't tell if it was with annoyance or agreement.

"You're very tall. I remember the people from your area being smaller." His voice reminded John of the white farmers around the reserve. A touch of residual accent?

"Some of that was lack of nutrition. I ate well," John replied. "Sorry I'm late," he added, looking at the plates of food on the table.

"No, no, don't be. I only hope you got some rest."

"I should have slept but I spent most of the time exploring this castle of yours. How old is it?"

"It was originally built in 1035 and then burnt down and then rebuilt. Burnt. Rebuilt. It's quite a phoenix actually."

"We'll try to leave it intact." John sat to Robert's left as it was the only seat free. Damn shy Indians took all the seats away from the host.

"We were talking about the event tomorrow night," Nadine broke in. "We're going to begin with a performance from the dancers, then Lucas will play a song on his flute for everyone."

John looked at Lucas. "You're a man of many talents."

"Oh, he definitely is!" Nadine exclaimed. Her voice echoed around the room and she blushed. "I mean in terms of dancing and music and whatnot."

"Whatnot, huh?" Desiree snickered. This earned her a glare from Nadine.

"When are the fancy folk arriving?" John broke in. "I wore my best jean jacket for them."

Robert looked at his jean jacket more closely.

"I was joking," John explained.

"Of course!" Robert's loud, nervous laugh rang through the room. John attempted a smile. He felt about as comfortable as that time a mother and her twenty-year-old daughter hit on him at the same reserve fowl supper.

"The guests were arriving tonight. Unfortunately, there was a rain and part of the road was closed," Nadine explained.

"Like a reserve road," John offered.

Everyone laughed except Nadine, who made a face.

"What's on the agenda tonight?" Edna asked. "The world's largest game of hide and go seek?"

"Holee crap, that would be fun," Desiree said.

"The castle is haunted," Robert said. "I would advise not too much exploring in the dark. Particularly the battlements; they seem to be where most visitations occur."

"Oh go on," Edna roared.

"It's what I've been told," Robert replied. "The staff has taken to locking the doors — though I doubt that would stop spirits."

"You believe everything you're told?" Edna countered.

John cringed for both of them. It's beginning. He stabbed his food and held it up. "Is this sauerkraut? Never had it before."

"You're right, it's important to have a critical mind," Robert replied to Edna, in a softer voice.

"Exactly! Can't be narrow-minded your entire life." Edna took a long sip of wine while John wondered how drunk you had to be to become the biggest hypocrite in the room.

"This sauerkraut is pretty delicious," John added.

"Let's get back to the ghosts," Desiree suggested. She was pulling a wineglass closer to her. John moved it out of her reach.

"Why is it that at any gathering, Indians have to bring up ghosts? Why is that?" Nadine tittered nervously.

Desiree ignored this. "Are these ghosts of knights and princesses?"

"I don't know," Robert said. "I'm afraid the ghosts don't favour me with their presence. I seem to be immune."

"That's convenient." Edna didn't seem to care what she stabbed with as long as the comment was made.

Desiree prodded. "Like you don't hear doors opening or creaking floors or anything? How long have you lived here?"

"I've been here for nineteen years. And it's the type of place where the noises never stop." He paused and they listened. It was true, you could hear footsteps a long ways away, the sound of a door opening and shutting. John even heard what sounded like a woman laughing.

"I've seen lots of ghosts." Edna's voice was now twice as loud as anyone else's. She sounded like that guy in the bar that everyone avoided because they knew he was looking for a reason to punch someone in the throat. "I've always seen them, even as a girl. That's why I take my rosary with me wherever I go."

Not because you're the most pious woman placed on this earth? John thought.

Edna had one hand on her wineglass as though it were an anchor. "I saw my first ghost when I was ten years old. It was a horse."

"Of course," Robert joked. Nadine laughed like Robert was Johnny Carson.

"It was my horse, his name was Peter, and he was standing in the front yard, exactly where he'd been standing when he got struck by lightning the year before."

"Your horse got struck by lightning?" Nadine was incredulous.

"Why's that so hard to believe? Lightning can kill anyone."

"A horse, though? John, you ever seen that?"

Edna was the last person in the world that John wanted to disagree with. "I guess anything could be hit if it was standing out in the open. Most animals got sense enough to move."

"This horse had sense!" Edna protested. "But he got struck so fast that he didn't have time to hide. One of those out-of-nowhere Saskatchewan storms. Dead before he hit the ground. I think that's why he kept showing up in the yard, because he was confused."

"Is that all he did? Just show up?" Robert seemed genuinely curious.

"What else is he supposed to do? Sing 'Oh Canada'?"

"Is that your only ghost story? Because that's not very scary." Desiree frowned. "And you never told me you had a horse. You never ride at home; you never come out riding with me and the other kids."

"When I was a young woman, I rode all the time. I even had the reserve's only Arabian horse — my dad bought it at an auction. People used to come from miles to see it."

"I never heard of an Arabian on our ranch."

"It would have been long before your time. Your grandpa was a very wealthy man — for an Indian."

"Yes, there are rich Indians," Nadine said a bit loudly. "Mostly from the States, I hear."

John glanced at the Lucas fella. Seems like Nadine wanted them to know he was more than the regular reserve Indian. For his part, Lucas seemed more interested in his bratwurst than the conversation.

"You had Arabians and ghost horses? What else did you have?" Desiree was enjoying this too much.

"They had peacocks." Robert said this suddenly and everyone's eyes turned to him. "Two males, two females. Nobody had ever heard of them before on the reserve."

"We'd heard about them, but never saw the need," Nadine said.

"They're beautiful, what other need is there?" Robert asked.

"She's right," Edna interrupted. "When you live in a place where people's babies die because they're hungry, you need a reason."

Robert inclined his head.

"Then why did you have them, Auntie?"

"They were a gift." Edna picked up the large glass decanter of wine. All eyes were on her shaking hands and John wished someone close to her would take it from her. But the wine made its way into the glass.

Desiree laughed. "I'm sure learning a lot tonight — what other secrets are you keeping?"

Trying to ensure that that question wouldn't be answered here at this table while Edna was three sheets to the wind, John broke his own rule about not opening his mouth in groups and leapt in with his boots on: "I got a story about a ghost."

Five sets of eyes turned to him.

"Or I guess I should say ghosts," he added. "'Cause there were a lot of them. A herd, sort of. They all came down to the reserve. During the Second World War against the goddamn — well, Germans —"

Robert shrugged, in a way that was far more French than German.

"All right, all right, keep going," Desiree prodded.

"A lot of Indian boys went over to fight for the Canadians and the world is what they were saying back then. We were gonna save the world from Hitler and his Nazis. Even though we didn't have anything to do with how the war started, once it started, well, we had to go. So off they went, all these young guys, some of them even lying about their age to get overseas. And they fought and worked as translators. Some of them, they came home and they started up businesses and even got politics started for Native people and got lots of stuff done, still doing it, in fact. But then others — they didn't make it home. A lot from my reserve, in fact, twenty-three in all. Twenty-three mommas sent their boys away with a kiss and twenty-three boys never came home. By the time the war ended, there were a lot of sad families out there on the rez. You could feel the sadness, taste it in the air. The animals could feel it, chickens stopped laying, pigs didn't fatten up, dogs jes up and stopped barking. Farmers said that crops were dying in the fields. The Chief at the time — old George Lucien — went down to see the Medicine Man. And he and the Medicine Man used to work together all the time back then because lot of times problems need a spiritual solution. The Medicine Man, his name was Manyhands, he decided to do a homecoming ceremony. And nobody really knew what that was. Manyhands remembered it from the Indian Wars, hundreds of years ago, before white-man times." John took a sip of water.

"Holee John, you tell a story like an old woman," Desiree pouted.

"I'll take that as a compliment." John winked. "So, Manyhands goes into the woods for four days and four nights. Seems like every day that he's there, the skies get darker. By the time he comes out, it looks like we'd never see the sun again. He didn't look too good after all that time in the woods. The colour had been drained out of him, like he was a ghost or a monias. He comes out and gathers together the families with the boys overseas and he tells them to go to bed early that night and to leave the doors unlocked. All of them. Everyone listens to him because they know he has powerful medicine. Even the people who say they follow the Catholic or the Christian ways know to listen to Manyhands. They all go to bed after sundown or what would have been sundown if they could have seen the sun. And they sleep or more likely they wait. If you were near a window, you could see the mist pouring out of the woods and filling all the fields, moving up and down the roads. Then by the time most of them start to doubt Manyhands, they hear their front doors opening and the sound of boots in the doorway."

"Who was it?" Desiree asked.

John smiled. "If you knew Manyhands, you'd know better than to ask. The soldiers had come home. They sat at the table and talked to their families, they hung out by the fire and drank tea. They hugged their children and their wives, their mothers and their fathers. Then, in the morning, they left through the back door."

"If that was my dad . . . I would lock the door and never let him go," Desiree said.

"One little boy tried that." John smiled. "He was little enough that he still thought he could trick the spirits. But even if humans are weak, spirits aren't. His daddy opened the door and left as they promised old Manyhands they would. When the sun came up the next morning, the soldiers were all gone."

"And things got better?" Nadine prodded.

John nodded. "As good as they could get." He thought of his brother and that hole that he kept feeding in his quest for more and more power. He thought about all the times he and his brother could have used a father's shoulder to lean on.

"Every good thing must come to an end," Edna mumbled from her end of the table. She stood up unsteadily, rocked a bit on one foot, then caught herself. "This is boring," she proclaimed. "Let's get some dancing started." She glared at Robert. "You must have music somewhere in this ghost-town."

Robert grinned. "That I do."

~

While the rest of them collected themselves, John tramped down the loud stone hallway to the room with the big fireplace. Shane was still in the corner of the room, though by now he'd found a place to sit and had his hand in his mouth as he worked over his fingernails. He looked young and sad and John could feel something niggling in the back of his mind.

"You been taking care of this fire?" John asked.

Shane shook his head. "They have a guy who does that."

"I see," John said. "You eat?"

Shane shook his head. John pointed in the direction of the kitchen. "Head down there and go get yourself something."

Shane nodded and wandered down the hall.

The rest of the group joined them and in a short time, the furniture and rug were cleared away, instruments were found — a guitar, a fiddle, and a piano. John grabbed the fiddle. Nadine strummed the guitar and tuned it up. Robert was on the piano.

The biggest question was, what music? Nadine, being in possession of the loudest voice and anxious to get back her manager status, suggested some Métis jigging music. As she was the only person in the group with a Métis background, this did not go well at first. But John remembered a few tunes from travelling with his dad and with her encouragement and frequent criticism, was able to churn out a decent jig-worthy song.

Surrounded by everyone, Edna felt a rising panic that kept expanding in her chest. Before long it would be bigger than the Great Room that they were in. She felt it in her toes, climbing up her legs into her hip bones; she felt it in her back and into her neck.

She took a sip of wine, remembering someone tell her that it was a "depressant." That ought to slow her down, she figured. It didn't. The nervous feeling climbed up her throat and found its way to her cheeks, which began to quiver. Then up higher, her eyes began to twitch and she knew she was in a bad way. She glanced at her niece, who was staring up at the handsome American. The American had his eyes on John. John had his eyes on his instrument. That bossy woman, Nadine, was looking from John to the American. The fake Pretends Eagle was staring at the fire. And then, finally, the last place she allowed her eyes to search, there was Robert and his eyes were on her.

She moved.

Backwards, through the doorway, slipping a bit as she did, though her wine did not spill. She moved slowly, hoping that it looked as though she was fading, rather than running away. Once out of their sightlines, she moved quicker then, around the corner, down another hallway. Then up a few steps. Then into a room that was round and had four doorways leading off it. Two of the doorways were closed, the other two led to staircases. She chose the left staircase. The stairs wound in a circle and she felt she was in a dream. What is life, other than a dream? Wasn't that something Walt Disney told everyone? And everyone believed it as there are many different kinds of dreams. She kept climbing and the anxiety in her cheeks ebbed. It moved lower, into her belly, and she paused for a second to heave a few times. There was nothing in her belly but wine. And wine soaks into stone in a beautiful way so she felt no guilt when two spit-fulls found their way onto the steps and the wall. She put down her wineglass and continued to climb.

There was a door at the top of the stairs. Heavy, brown oak, with a star shape cut into it so the light from outside shone through. She opened it and saw a walkway. Edna paused. She'd always been afraid of heights. Even as a child, she refused to climb trees. She would rather tell the other children which branches were beneath their feet or run to tell the parents when the child missed their footing, than be one of the adventurers herself. But she could still hear the music from downstairs and decided that "out there" could only be better than "in here."

She stepped outside, the big door creaking closed behind her. The first thing Edna noticed was that battlements only came up to her waist and if she leaned a little to the left or to the right, her body weight would carry her to the ground. People in the olden days were shorter. Edna kept walking, seeing another tower on the other side of the walkway. Make it over there and this is an adventure, she told herself. Only over there. But her feet began to slow and she looked down to see why and caught a glimpse of the view over the left side. It was far. She could see their van in the courtyard. She could see a range of outbuildings, she could see the moonlight reflecting off a puddle that looked only drops deep. Edna swallowed a gulp. "Move," she whispered. Instead she froze into place, her limbs trembling and she wondered how long it would take for her to shake herself to death.

It was in this pose, with one foot in front of the other, hands clasped in front of her, that Edna saw a ghost. It was a woman, much younger than herself, wearing a pair of jeans and blue top. She was smiling and laughing. The ghost stared past Edna and strode towards her as if there were someone calling to her on the other side. Manners meant that Edna should step aside but she couldn't move. The young woman kept coming, not seeing Edna but Edna still whispered, "I'm sorry" as the young woman ran through her. Edna kept her eyes closed and felt a cool breeze. She heard the young woman laugh sweetly. Edna opened her eyes and craned her neck to look behind her. Nothing but the door and battlements and cold air that was beginning to crawl into Edna's clothes. Edna wanted to turn around or at least take the requisite steps to make it to the other side but she was frozen.

There would be more ghosts.

Nadine's heart kept beating fast as she moved between the two men. Sometimes she danced with Lucas and then other times with John. Once she danced with Robert and tried to give him her full attention but her eyes tugged to the other men. John was watching her and this worried her — would he feel hurt that she had moved on? And then the second thought: had she moved on? John's face still had the ability to make her heart stir. But when they spoke, she slipped into the conversation like old shoes.

"Good to see you," she said. "Can I give you a hug?" Without waiting for his answer, she wrapped her arms around him. They had never hugged before but they were in Europe. She let him go. "Hope it wasn't too stressful being on the road."

"Had its moments," John replied. "I am glad you're here now."

John looked into her eyes in his steady way and Nadine felt herself melting into the ground. He was saying other things about travel mix-ups and hijackers but her mind couldn't process his words. She could only feel the heat that had started in her feet and was working its way up her body.

"I'm glad too," Nadine said. But it was more of a whisper than a declaration and she hastily sipped some water and pretended that she had a cricket in her throat.

Nadine found that she could think better when she danced but not on this night. It's all that talk of ghosts, she said to herself, it's gotten my blood up. For one thing, she kept thinking she saw glimpses of people in the shadows. And then too she didn't want to leave the room even though she was tired as a waitress after a fourteen-hour shift. Still, choice was a foreign concept to Nadine. John had been her first love and Lucas . . . he was something special but how could she throw away all those years with John? And John had come this far for her, didn't she owe him something? She wanted to run to her bed and throw the covers over her head.

When refreshments were brought out, she sidled up to Desiree.

This is how desperate she was. And she muttered under her breath, "What would you choose?"

Desiree blinked at her. "It's cake. I think you can have all of them."

"I mean of the men, which would you choose?"

"Who are you again?" Desiree's eyes narrowed, which made her even prettier as her big eyes squished together suspiciously.

"I'm Nadine Redcloud, the tour manager. The person that John was filling in for."

"The woman with the shits."

Nadine smiled wryly. "Yes, the woman with that . . . problem."

Desiree half-smiled, then surveyed the two men. "You want my opinion on these guys as dancers? I've never even seen the big one dance. John's okay but sort of slow. The older women really like him though. They cheer like crazy when he dances."

"Oh, and did any of the women . . . did he hang around with one of them . . . y'know?

Desiree moved her cake around on her plate with her fork. "Are you asking me if John got laid?"

"No! Of course not. He's a man in control of himself and that would be — I mean for us to care — for me to care, that would be . . . silly. It's not like he's married or . . . or . . . in a relationship and how would we know? I mean, would we know that?"

Desiree cocked an eyebrow.

Nadine forced a laugh. "I was asking as a fellow woman — y'know, girls being girls — what if you had to choose between John and Lucas, the real one, which would you find more handsome, is what I mean."

Desiree made a face. "They're both older than dirt."

Nadine looked at the two men, fortunately standing next to one another as they were locked in conversation. John was lean and Lucas was taller and broader. Their dark hair was the same though and they both looked serious as if they expected the world to turn on them any second, but they were ready for it. Their mouths had the same stubborn set.

Desiree said again, "They both have grey hair. My dad doesn't even have grey hair."

Although you're probably gonna give him some soon. "But if you had to choose between them," Nadine persisted.

Desiree turned her attention to her cake. She took a bite and chewed. "Y'know, I've found that whenever I thought I had a choice to make and I couldn't choose, it always turned out that I didn't have a choice at all."

Desiree's deep doe eyes sized up Nadine, making her feel like she was having one of those naked dreams where everyone else had clothes on and she'd forgotten her pants and panties at home.

"Yes, yes," Nadine said quickly. "It's a game that I was playing. Asking silly questions, that's all."

Nadine quickly found a cool corner where she could regret blabbing her feelings and fret in peace.

Her body moved to a normal temperature and she had time to feel embarrassed about her behaviour. *I'm too old to be acting like a teenager*, she warned herself. *I don't want any man. I'm a feminist.* She didn't know what that word meant exactly but she saw it on the news as the white women burned their bras. She only had one bra so she didn't understand the point of doing something so destructive but she liked that all the women were sticking together.

Women on the rez never stuck together for anything, except to turn on a woman who deserved it. Nadine hadn't had a lot of women friends over the years. She knew the mothers of the kids she taught, some she liked, some she wanted to beat with the business end of a rake for the lack of interest they had in their children. Residential school killed the mother in them, her kokum had told her once. She'd been referring to Nadine's own mother, who had given birth and then left the hospital without her infant. It had been her kokum who had finally brought her home and shoved her into Nadine's mother's arms.

Be sad, Nadine told herself. It's damn sight better than being hopeful or confused. *Who are you to think that you could have either one of these men?* Opportunity, she whispered to herself. Opportunity.

"Who are you whispering to?"

Nadine jumped. "Where did you come from?" She was looking at the young criminal — Shane. He was short and good-looking in an ornery sort of way. Pretty green eyes. Nice smile. Although her kokum had said to never trust anyone who smiled for more than a second.

"I've been standing here all night. This place has weird light. Like you kind of disappear into the walls, you notice that?"

Nadine shook her head. "I don't skulk around like a criminal. Which you are," she added in case he thought he could charm her.

"Yeah, I know. But that's in Canada. Here I'm just a guy. This rich dude gave me a room, even."

"You can thank me for that. I told him that we would deal with you back in Canada. Enjoy it while it lasts. You're gonna get your own room when we get back as well. With bars."

He went silent. Nadine glanced at him to make sure he wasn't crying or anything. He was smiling. "I danced real good for your group."

"Yeah, I heard." Nadine couldn't help herself. "I've never seen you on the circuit though."

"I never did powwows. This old guy taught me and a bunch of other kids at the Friendship Centre when I was young. He was hoping it would keep us out of trouble. Guess it didn't work on me."

Nadine knew to tread lightly. "Everything is choices."

"What's my choice now?"

Nadine glanced at him. He looked younger than his age even as he curled a lip at her.

"You could stay with the group. And do a good job and — maybe — that will make a difference when we get back."

"You mean like even that Lucas guy? Like he won't kick my ass?"

"I didn't say that. You did rob him and lock him in a garage bathroom. And take his I.D. And he got arrested for that."

"He did?'

"Yeah."

"Shee-it."

The music switched to a two-stepper. Lucas beckoned for her from the dance floor. There were only two women after all. Two? She wondered even as she hurried across the room. Where was Edna?

JOHN

John played until his fingers cramped. He remembered songs he'd heard when he was a boy and his father invited over all the families on the reserve to their two-room house. Everything was pushed aside to make room for all the guests and the inside was filled with people, talking, smoking, dancing and yes, some even drinking, but that usually outside around a fire. The dance would last over a day. In the morning people would eat or go hunting and then return to dance again that night. So hard to leave once you got somewhere on the reserve. It took about five hours to get from one side of the reserve to the other via wagon, much longer on foot, which many of his neighbours were. "I invite, so that they don't have to," his father would say. His father, because of his farm and his work, was better off than most of the other people and he didn't want others to feel like they had to return the favour.

"Also," Kokum Yellow Belly would add, "we don't have to travel all the way across this goddamn reserve." Yellow Belly was a complainer when it came to travelling, even though she had travelled further than all of them. Until her son left to fight the Nazis, that is.

John remembered jigs from when the Métis visited. They'd gotten stuck on the reserve, some by choice, some not. One Métis father had explained to his dad, "The government took our children." And so they had followed them across the province. He'd been asking for permission to transfer to the reserve so that they could visit their children at the residential school. And John's dad had agreed, of course. The government had taken the reserve's children as well. Taken even the Chief's sons.

John remembered the day he was taken to school. His dad was about to head overseas. That goodbye at the end of the road was loaded up with tough feelings. Nobody could even talk. John kept swallowing over and over, not able to blink enough to see his dad clearly. The last time he saw his dad alive and he was a blur. "I'll see you on summer break," his dad had called out to the wagon of kids.

John pressed his fingers into the metal strings, the cool pain bringing him back to this strange castle. He remembered the Métis well. As dark as Indians, their bodies as strong and frail from the peaks and valleys of starvation, they carried themselves apart from the Indians. They did not want to lose themselves into the reserve but they would never be able to live on their land again, John's dad explained.

"And whose land is this?" Yellow Belly laughed at him. "Our land is the mountains, the hills stretching in front of them, the blueberry bushes in the north, the plains to the south where the horse traders always knew my name . . . whose land is this? I shit on that hill over there once when I was seven and now this is our land? This?"

John's dad and mother would shake their heads at her argumentative tone but John knew she was right.

Yellow Belly was the first Indian woman to try the jig. She'd laughed at herself when her feet wouldn't move fast enough but she kept moving and in a matter of minutes, she was as good as many of the Métis dancers. John had to learn how to play the music then. Because after they left she would ask him, "Grandson, play that half-breed music." On this night he played snippets and then improvised from there. He'd forgotten a lot. Nobody seemed to notice.

On a break, he was applying more rosin to his strings when their host joined him. Robert was sweaty and had removed his fur collar. "Do you know a song called the Red River Jig?" he said, his breath heavy with meat and wine.

John nodded. (He'd already played two versions of it.)

"Okay, give me some time, I have to track down that stubborn woman."

John didn't have to ask her name.

She was frozen, in all ways. Her veins were icy, though red-hot where the cold touched her arthritis. Her legs were shaking but she could not will herself to move. Another ghost had entered the rampart. This was a soldier holding a bow, a pack of arrows on his back. Like her, he was cold and kept blowing into his hands. Then he would stare down at the ground, spot someone, aim, and fire. Then, almost immediately he fell back, his eye exploding. Then it would start all over again. He must not have known he died, Edna realized and made the sign of the cross, like she had five other times this night.

"Bless them, oh Lord, they do not know they are your children. They do not know that they have been called home. Please bring an angel to guide him." Edna wondered if she too was dead, if she had fallen as the door opened or an aneurysm had burst in her head (this was how one of her aunts had gone — blown her nose and boom, she was dead) or a heart attack, like all the men in her family. What if she was dead and now she was one of these confused ghosts? She might have believed it, except that she was in so much pain.

The door behind her creaked and she craned her neck, expecting to see another soldier emerge, or a young woman or a child. It was Robert. His face red and sweaty, looking out of place on this cold night.

"Edna," he whispered. "Is that you?"

She sighed, glad to be found, not glad that it was him. "Yes."

He came closer. "What are you doing up here?"

"I think . . . or at least I've come to think . . . that some spirits led me here." It was difficult to talk through her chattering lips.

"What?"

"I got lost," she said.

"Are you okay? You look pale."

"Cold."

Robert laid his hand on her cheek. It felt like a hot brand and Edna winced. "You've made yourself sick," he said. Edna leaned against him with a groan.

"Easy there." He sounded like he was talking to a horse.

"It's arthritis," she replied. "You get used to it."

They limped down the stone path together.

"Did you know I was coming?" she asked.

"No," he said. "But I'm glad."

~

When Edna was twenty-two years old, she had figured out that some people had good luck and some people had bad and the best thing to do was accept which was yours. Her younger brother (he was two years younger and six inches taller) met the love of his life when he was seventeen, got married at twenty, became the Chief of the reserve the same year and from there on laurels (and more importantly, cash) were strewn across his path. In the same time frame, Edna had been pulled out of school to nurse her ailing mother, then her ailing father, then an ailing cousin. When she had finished her duties and was ready to head back to school (she wanted to be a nurse), she was waylaid with a particularly virulent pneumonia and spent three months in the hospital. She wasn't even able to attend her younger brother's wedding and for some strange reason, his wife always held this against her. When she finally left the hospital, the only place she had to go was with her brother. "For the summer only," she assured his wife, when Edna showed up on their front steps.

"Of course, you'll stay here," her brother told her. She set up in one of the bedrooms but moved to the basement when her sister-in-law made hints about it being needed as a nursery.

Her brother had inherited their father's ranch operations and while he had a foreman to run it, there was always something that needed doing. The foreman got tired of waiting for the Chief to make decisions, realized the wife was useless, and went straight to Edna.

Edna, unwelcome in the house, and so pasty that she needed the sun, found herself outside more and more. It was a large operation and the foreman kept the bunkhouse full of guys from the rez. "Indian guys work the hardest," he said (he was Métis himself), "and on the least amount of food." They also responded well to the routine he set with whistles and dinner bells. Edna understood this; it was their training from the residential schools that made the men so disciplined and amenable to routines — she had the same qualities herself. She noticed that on their days off, the Indian cowboys got anxious looks as if feeling guilty for having time off. They spent those days drinking in the shade. She and her sister-in-law would keep themselves busy inside.

Edna visited the horses and even looked after them. She enjoyed carrying the water from the well, not noticing how it slopped over the sides, splashing her clothes. She wouldn't ride the horses (a bit too scary for her after being thrown a few times as a girl) but liked being around them. She'd stroke their velvet noses and stare into one of their large brown eyes and know that they understood what loneliness was and didn't judge her for it.

Edna's health was improving and she began planning her next steps. She contacted a girlfriend who had moved to the city and made plans to move in with her. There were great jobs in the city for Indian girls, if they could type and keep their mouths shut and not party. "Geraldine, that's my friend, she lives right downtown, so she says we can go to dinner every night if we want," she told her brother and his wife over dinner.

"That sounds expensive," her brother said.

"It's me and Geraldine," Edna replied, "not like I have any expenses."

"When are you going?" asked the wife who never beat around the bush (she was also pregnant and any ability to pretend that she liked Edna had long ago left her swollen body).

"Three weeks," said Edna.

It was a busy time at the ranch; they were getting the herd ready for sales. Some of the cows belonged to the band and those also had to be separated and sent out for butchering. The meat would be dispersed among the band members and would keep the families fed for most of the winter. The foreman hired on a few guys, and to everyone's surprise, some of them were white.

There was Tim, a Swedish guy from a few farms over; Edgar, an old man who had lost his farm a few years before and wasn't bitter about it because his wife left him at the same time; and then there was Bobby, who was exploring Canada. He had a strange accent.

"What's that accent?" the foreman asked.

"French," Bobby answered.

Many of the nuns in the boarding school had been French, so Edna knew that was bullshit. His accent reminded her of the Doukhobor farmers that they saw in town sometimes. She didn't say anything; war was terrible and people didn't need any reminders of people they were supposed to hate. Besides he worked hard and kept a smile on his face.

That smile. Edna found it directed at her more often than not and didn't understand it. She would turn and look behind her, expecting to see the object of the smile. When Edna went for a walk after dinner, she would run into him, coming from a different direction. Bobby would insist on walking her back to the house even though she explained that there was nothing in Saskatchewan that could injure her. He told her how he had hoped to visit all of Canada but it was bigger than he expected.

"It would take a lifetime," he said.

"If only we got two," she agreed.

He asked her about her time in hospital and she told him about the books she'd read and how she'd learned how to knit. "I made hats for the kids. The nurses said that the kids loved them but I don't know for sure. I couldn't visit them."

"I'm sure they liked them. Hospitals can be cold."

He told her that he had polio as a child and spent many months in bed. He promised himself that when he got out, he would see everything.

The weeks flew by.

"Where are you going next?" Edna asked.

"There is a farmer in the valley who needs help threshing," Bobby replied. "I don't know what that is but he seems to like me."

The valley was less than ten miles away from the city and Edna felt optimistic. It felt like being tickled by fate.

She and Bobby took a long walk that evening until they found a soft place to watch the sun go down. There is no place in the world with sunsets like Saskatchewan. Edna had never travelled but even she knew that there was something special about them. She could see in the way people were transfixed by the dance of red, pinks, and yellows. Always different, like a snowflake. The sunshine slowly turned into moonlight and Edna didn't feel like going home. Bobby came closer and they made promises with their bodies in the way that young people do.

~

For the next week, she smiled at the breakfast table, and her brother smiled because she was smiling, and her sister-in-law rolled her eyes.

Edna left for the city, she got a job, and her roommate took her out for dinner. She had Bobby's address and wrote him a letter, as they had agreed.

A week later, she received his reply.

"Dear Edna, my father is ill and I must return to Germany. I am sorry. I will always treasure the time we spent together."

Edna would have mourned but she was faced with other news. She was what the old people called "with child," and what the young people called "knocked up," and what everyone agreed meant "ruined."

She left her job and her apartment and showed up on her brother's doorstep again. He could not muster a smile that everything would be okay. He turned away from her on the doorstep but left the door open. Edna thought about walking from the steps to the dugout that was over eight feet deep this time of year. Its slippery sides eased you in but would not let you out. But one thing the nuns had drummed into her head: it was a sin to escape the punishment that God had set for you. And being so full of sin already, Edna chose to step inside and close the door quietly behind her.

As it turned out, even lucky people have bad days. Her brother's child, her nephew, was stillborn. Edna's sister-in-law crawled into bed and refused to come out. Her brother lost weight and Edna kept the house and ranch going even as her feet swelled and belly grew large. Out there on the reserve, she knew there was no shame in raising a child alone. But a child without a father would know and feel it.

The next decision was easy. Her sister-in-law had a baby to hold, her brother had a child to spoil, and Edna had a place to stay forever — in the basement, if she behaved.

She didn't get to pick the name, however. Desiree? What were they thinking?

CHAPTER 9

JOHN

John woke early the next morning. They had a short trip from the castle to the grounds where the Karl May Festival was being held. He remembered Robert's words about the festival the day before and wished that he'd read one of May's novels. Then again, it was best to be yourself; it was easier and there were fewer lies to remember.

He got dressed quickly and opened his door as Lucas was exiting his room.

"You ready for today?" John asked. He didn't know much about the guy despite all of Nadine's bragging about him the night before.

Lucas held up his duffle bag about the size of a hockey bag. "I brought my hoops. You don't have a hoop dancer, right?"

"Always wanted to learn."

"I could teach you."

John shook his head. "I don't need to add to the list of things I do badly. Best to focus on the things I know already and try not to fuck them up. Pardon my French."

Lucas grinned. "I heard you're a cowboy."

John nodded. "I raise some cows and walk around in cowshit all day long."

"How does a cowboy become a dancer?"

They walked companionably down the hallway. "Was a dancer before I was a cowboy."

They fell silent as they passed some giant paintings. John watched Lucas's eyes flicker up and down the artwork. "You into art?"

"I can't believe how big this place is. How does anyone get this rich?"

John had no idea. His idea of rich was having enough food for himself and his animals. "White people," he answered simply. They seemed to have an unlimited stream of opportunities to better themselves.

They turned a corner and almost banged into Shane, who was again standing in the hallway.

"You," Lucas said.

"Oh hey," Shane commented affably. "I wanted to say again how sorry I —"

Lucas shoved Shane aside and kept walking.

"That guy can keep a grudge," Shane said, rubbing his arm.

"You sure are some kind of stupid," John replied. "What are you doing anyway? Hanging out here by yourself? You find something to steal?"

"No!" Shane said. "'Sides, if I was gonna steal something, why would I do it on the first day? You always got to wait until you're leaving."

"I hope you're kidding."

"There are some strange sounds in these hallways," Shane said. "Have you stopped and listened?"

"Do I have time to stand in hallways and listen?" John asked. "Are you coming today?"

Shane nodded. "Yeah, that bossy lady, er —"

"Nadine."

"Yeah, her, she told me I should go, do my best, and then she'd see if she could help me when we get back to Canada."

John wanted to admire the optimism of the criminal mind but it interfered with his ideas about justice and not being a shithead so he raised an eyebrow and kept walking.

"There is breakfast," he said as Shane fell in beside him. "I can smell it." He had high hopes for breakfast in a castle.

"Do you know anything about this Karl May guy?" Shane asked.

"I hear he's a big hero here in Germany, like they worship him, and he's a writer. Like that is crazy. Worshipping a writer!"

"I've never heard of him," John said. "But if he's anything like Louis L'Amour, I guess I can understand the draw. He writes about cowboy life, right?"

"He writes about Indians. Indians like us, so I'm guessing these people must really love Indians."

"Not all of them," John replied. "Lot of Indian vets, y'know."

"Right, right," Shane said quickly. "But let's not bring that up right away." Because that would interfere with being lauded, John figured. He was never the type to work out angles but people like Shane could see all the angles in a kaleidoscope. Survival could be an ugly thing.

They ate in the kitchen, Lucas, Shane, and John, surrounded by a round woman who stared at them as they ate. "Eat, eat," she repeated as this was the only English word she knew. Her hands kept grasping and ungrasping her apron as if she wished to reach out and touch them. To see if they were real, to feel if their skin was hot as it was so red. To feel their hair and see if it was as slick as it looked. John liked her and would have allowed her petting if he was alone. He felt the need to look stoic and manly in front of the other two. Whenever they finished a food, she would cook another batch. She was learning their appetites and John wished he could pack her into his suitcase.

He had a full belly by the time they found themselves by the bus. Nadine stood by the vehicle's door; she seemed already busy with something. She'd found herself a clipboard and was writing on it. She wore the skirt of her regalia and her top was covered with a shawl. Her hair was neatly braided. John felt the lumps in his hair and knew he should have braided it fresh this morning. He glanced at the two beside him — they were both good-looking enough that nobody would notice if they were unkempt. The joys of being of young.

He looked for Desiree and heard her sunny chattering before he saw her. The castle's butler, one of the stable boys, and another random guy were standing around her with adoring smiles.

205

Now where was Edna? John looked around and didn't see her trim self anywhere. Normally she was within scolding distance of her niece. "Where's Edna?" he asked Nadine.

Nadine looked at him without comprehension. "Who?"

"Short hair, traditional dancer . . ."

"The Bible lady?"

"Yes," John said. "Where is she?"

"Haven't seen her. And we don't need her really if she wants to rest or recover or something. Doesn't she have arthritis or something?"

John headed for Desiree. "Where's your aunt?"

Desiree looked flummoxed. "She went to bed early last night. I thought she'd be the first one here."

"Did you see her go to bed?" John asked.

"Well, no, but she wasn't dancing and she was pretty drunk and she's no night owl, so I assumed . . . you don't know where she is?"

John was growing anxious but he had no desire to search an old, probably haunted castle.

Then there she was, standing on the front steps of the castle with their host, Robert. Edna looked tired and more spindly than usual. John walked up. "Where you been?"

"Got lost last night," Robert said for her. "She's not feeling too well this morning."

John could see that from the way she was leaning on him. Edna never leaned on anyone. She would stand upright during a hurricane.

"You staying here then?" John pointed with his lips at the giant stone building behind them.

"You're not getting rid of me that easy. I'm coming; I'll take it easy, if that's all right with everyone? Which it should be since none of you have to deal with arthritis." She glanced at Shane and sniffed. "Hope you haven't stolen anything this morning."

John smiled. Edna may have been feeling under the weather but her balls were still firmly attached.

Day 10

EDNA

Germany is an old country with old castles, old memories, old wars, old wrongs and ghosts. The Bible tells us that there are no ghosts, only lost spirits that need to be led home, perhaps through an exorcism. I do not know any priests here and besides people look at you like you're crazy if you tell them that you see and hear spirits. In an old country like this, maybe they even throw you into the water to see if you can float. And I don't know how to swim.

It's the first day of the festival for a writer that loved Indians so much he wrote a whole bunch of books about them. We are excited to show our culture in this old place and remind them that we don't live in books, we live in real places. We are not ghosts.

Edna felt like she was walking around inside a fog; one of those thick ones that made driving impossible or at least poorly advised. She'd run into a mist like that once near Wadena, coming home from a powwow. She had two sleeping kids in the back seat and a sleeping friend in the passenger seat. It enveloped the car and looked orange under the headlights. Edna could barely see the road underneath her and the white line was a hint to her right. She kept driving though, feeling that pulling over would guarantee getting rear-ended by a drunk on his way home from the bar. Her friend, Josephine Kay (who loved powwows and church too), woke up when they were nearly through the mist and half-screamed when she saw it. "Jesus,

Mary, and Joseph, you drove through this!" she exclaimed to Edna. Don't panic, eat bannock.

The wine from the night before had removed all sense of urgency from her body. Less anxious, she was able to survey the people around her. Even the man at her side with whom she both shared secrets with and kept secrets from was fine with her.

More wine, she wanted to yell, knowing that this feeling would wear off eventually. But there was no more room in her body for alcohol. Maybe grease.

She turned to Bobby, who was wearing a strange costume (what had happened to him over these years that made him wear these outfits?). He wore a baby-blue jacket and pants made from what seemed to be soft buckskin and then the fur collar was back in place. Perhaps it was from not having a wife. Men started to go slightly insane from spending too much time on their "projects," Edna had noticed on the reserve. She'd see old bachelors come into town and their gitch would be sticking out of their zippers. They would eat strange things and their manners were atrocious. "Got your pick," her brother would tease, her sister-in-law would laugh, and Edna would shudder.

"What is this Karl May festival?" she asked.

"It's where all the worshippers of the author gather," Bobby replied. "And tend to their hobbies."

"And what are those?"

"Being Indian, of course."

Edna cocked a brow at him. "Indian like us?"

"Not anything like you." Bobby led her to the bus doorway. It felt good to lean on someone, though she'd be burned alive before she'd admit it. "Their own imagining of what an Indian is. If I had not been to western Canada, maybe I would have thought it was real."

Edna stopped him. "Are we here to prove a point? Did you invite us to show them up? I won't be a part of something like that." It would be cruel to shame people in their home.

"I did not invite you. The festival invited you," Bobby corrected. "I invited you to stay in my home only because I knew you were from

Saskatchewan and I'll always have a fondness for that province." He added, "I do think it would be good for people to see the real thing. I think that they have become arrogant in their imaginings."

John laughed.

Once they were all loaded onto the bus, Nadine went up and down the aisles, asking everyone questions about their regalia. She even pushed Desiree over in her seat and started braiding her hair. Desiree looked at her aunt and made a face but Edna nodded at her. Desiree couldn't make a fuss about that; she couldn't braid her own hair tightly enough and Edna's fingers were a bit too gnarled this morning to do a good job.

"We should pay someone to do it once," Desiree had suggested when they were in Sweden, "and then we'll spray it in place for the next ten days." If Edna wasn't too afraid of a bunch of spiders moving into her niece's hair, she would have said yes.

Bobby sat next to John and Lucas and they talked quietly amongst themselves. Desiree stared out the window and Shane stared at her. He had a crackling energy running through his body that Edna could almost see. If he were her son, she would sit beside him and ask him what the hell he was thinking because she could practically see him planning shenanigans.

$$\sim$$

It was a half-hour trip from the castle to the festival ground. Edna was drifting in and out of sleep but she woke up when the bus slowed to a stop. She opened her eyes and saw people walking alongside the road in large groups. They were predominantly blonde-haired and she felt like she was back in Sweden. It was a few minutes before their outfits began to register with her. Many of the women wore white dresses; the men wore a lot of brown. She peered closer at their costumes, the men appeared to be wearing buckskin — but where would they have gotten this much? She glanced at the women; they were wearing mini-dresses made from hide but they had a Hollywood Indian flair with fringes cut into the fabric and low bodices. She shuddered.

Edna looked around at the other passengers. They were also staring out the windows with stunned looks on their faces.

"Holee shit," Shane said, expressing the opinions of most of the passengers.

The bus jolted as everyone got up and Edna felt a wave of nausea. She closed her eyes.

When she opened them again, the others had disembarked and Desiree stared at her from the seat in front. "Are you getting off, Auntie?"

Edna nodded. "If I lose you guys now, I'll never find you again."

"Ha. You would find us."

Edna doubted that. Her pace was limited and there looked to be too many people to push past. She placed her purse over her shoulder and stood up on her sore legs. She'd have to ask someone for a painkiller — that Shane kid probably had drugs.

She moved down the bus, Desiree following behind her. Desiree was dressed in her full fancy dance regalia. "You look pretty," Edna said over her shoulder. Desiree said nothing, as compliments were ordinary occurrences.

The sunshine was startling when Edna stepped off the bus. It took a while for her eyes to adapt and then suddenly she realized that they were surrounded by gawking Indians. Edna blinked again and then recognized the costumes. "What is this?" she said under her breath.

"That's how they dress here," Desiree explained. "This is a white people's powwow ground."

Edna looked for another of their group. "Where do I go?"

Desiree pushed her from behind. "Keep moving."

Edna forged ahead. The gawkers moved for her to pass. She felt hands reach around her.

"Ow!" Desiree protested behind her. "Hands off the merchandise!"

The crowd moved back a bit at her roar. But they were still inching forward.

"If I hadn't waited for you to wake up," Desiree complained, "I could have walked with everyone else."

"Why are they staring at us?"

"Because we're real Indians and they're kind of obsessed or something."

Edna didn't see too many people staring at her, truth be told. Perhaps her blouse, slacks, and short hair made the onlookers think that she wasn't an Indian. Just a short brown lady travelling with the Indians. Though she'd never been mistaken as anything else in her life.

She stared back at the people; they chattered in what she assumed was German. The women's short buckskin dresses moved dangerously high as they walked. Is that how they thought Indian people used to dress? How on earth would you start a fire with all that fringe? And what about bugs? You'd be eaten alive in the Saskatchewan grasses. And berry picking — you can't pick berries in a dress up to your thighs; you'd get scratched to death and mosquitoes would feast on what was left.

Edna guessed that the difference was in the details between playing an Indian and being one.

Desiree, to her word, led her directly to the tent where everyone else was gathered. Lucas and John stood at the entryway staring out like guards. They were attracting a lot of attention, as they looked like movie-star Indians. They ducked inside the tent. Edna saw Nadine in the middle of the tent, focused on her paperwork. She looked up and her natural crab-apple face got even more sour.

"You're late! We're only fifteen minutes from our first performance." Nadine ushered Desiree through the tent. "You're up first."

"I don't want to be first," Desiree said.

"It's not a choice, that's how I scheduled it."

"Then change it."

Edna recognized that tone in Desiree's voice.

"Do I need to remind you —" Nadine's tone was taking a turn for the much worse as well.

Edna stood between them. "Desiree was late getting here because of me. She needs more time to get me settled."

Nadine scowled. "I'll put her on later." Under her breath she mumbled, "Goddammit, no respect."

"I hate her," Desiree said to Nadine's retreating back.

"It's wrong to hate anyone. She's only trying to do her job besides." Edna wished for a cup of tea. Where would you get tea in Germany? Did they drink it there?

"But she's so bossy and she's old and she's hot for John. And Lucas."

Edna smiled at Desiree's gossipy-ness. "She's not that old. And, it's good that she's still trying."

"Yeah, but talk about barking up the wrong trees . . ." Desiree started and then stopped herself. "But whatever, it's her life."

"You're here to dance, not be nosy," Edna reminded her.

"God, don't remind me, I'm so nervous! This is a huge crowd," Desiree said but her face lit up.

John sidled up to Edna. "She ready?"

"Nearly," Edna said. "You going up first?"

John shook his head. "Putting Shane up first. Probably for the best, let him burn off some of his energy. Then I'll be up. Lucas is taking care of the drum for now. Although . . ." he leaned close to Edna, "I heard that the Germans want to play their own music, like they know drum songs."

Nothing would surprise Edna now.

"Can that be done even?" John asked.

"Ask the boss over there, she must know all the protocol," Edna said, grateful to pass the buck. John looked like he'd rather not broach the topic with the dragon lady but he headed over nonetheless.

"Where's Shane?" Desiree asked.

Edna glanced around the tent. "Is that him helping Lucas with the drum? Looks like we're switching to a big one." Once again, she marvelled at how good Shane looked in his regalia. It was as though it made him come alive. His sneaky demeanour was washed away and replaced with a noble glow; he had painted on face paint that made him look powerful and fierce. Edna wondered what kind of parenting he had. Seemed like someone had tried to pull him in the right direction at some point.

Desiree whistled. "The new Lucas is hot."

"So," Edna said, unsure of how to begin. "You're nineteen years old."

"You'd rather I went for Shane?"

"I'd rather you focused on something other than men or boys."

Desiree sat down on the grass. "I was asking Shane which reserve he was from. Said he doesn't know. Police found him abandoned at a hospital back door — can you believe that?"

Edna nodded. "Somebody tried to do right by him."

"And then some white couple adopted him but they didn't want him to be Indian so he ran away when he was young and ended up living with an Indian family in the same city. The city's where he learned how to dance. And how to steal."

"I see." Edna supposed the Indian family had tried to instill some survival skills in their young charge.

"It's kind of sad but at least someone wanted him. Maybe if the right person took care of him, he'd be a better man."

"Right." Edna studied her niece, thinking again about how stubborn Desiree had been as a baby. She held her own bottle when she was only five weeks; she'd thrown it away altogether when she was less than a year. She practically demanded to be toilet trained after eleven months. When she wanted a pony at four, family members had driven across the province looking for a Shetland. Her whole life she'd gotten what she wanted, when she wanted it, even how and where . . . she was an Indian girl who never heard the word "no" and now that scared Edna. The world had never been kind to Indian people, least of all to the girls.

Edna looked past the round-faced young woman in front of her at a tiny crack in the tent, through which she could see a bright blue sky and said, "I don't want you to get your heart broken."

She didn't actually say it out loud. She said it in her heart and meant it for the spirits that watched over her baby girl. Let them not fail now, after all this time.

"So, Auntie." Desiree woke her from her reverie. "This Robert guy . . . he was in Saskatchewan once upon a time, huh?"

Edna flinched. "Who told you that?"

"He did, last night at dinner. You were there . . . well, you were sort of there, in body. Not so much in spirit or mind —"

Edna snapped her head towards Desiree and her neck cracked. "Ow."

"Relax! It's not like I'm gonna snitch on you to my dad. I've never seen you drink before but god knows, if anyone deserves to drink, it's you. You must have like a thousand beers saved up in rosaries."

Sacrilege. The mouth on this girl.

"It's no big deal. I'm glad you're loosening up — was it the castle? Did that freak you out?"

Edna nodded. "It's a very strange place."

"It is intimidating," Desiree agreed. "And the owner's kind of creepy too . . ."

Edna steeled herself. "Yes, he's a strange man."

"Kind of handsome though . . . if you're into monias."

Edna busied herself with the ribbons on Desiree's dress; she smoothed them down.

"I should hook him up with that Nadine lady. She's sure hot to trot."

"That sounds like a good idea," Edna said quietly.

"'Cept he doesn't seem interested in her. He never said boo to her all night. Seemed like he was distracted by someone else. Or by the someone else not being around —"

"I have to find the ladies' room," Edna said.

"Good luck with that." Desiree smiled. "Who knows what these savages are using for a toilet."

John studied the drum. It was the right size, same depth and circumference as the ones he'd grown up with. The drum was covered with skin and had a deep sound in the middle. He hit the sides and the same notes from his youth escaped. It was a perfect Cree drum. Except that it wasn't. It had been made by Germans. A tall imposing man stood on John's right. He had crafted the drum, Robert explained, based on pictures he'd seen in books.

"That must have taken some time," John said.

Robert shrugged. "German ingenuity knows no bounds."

"Certainly not borders," John said agreeably. He held up one of the drumsticks; it had an ornately beaded covering at the bottom.

The craftsman spoke and Robert translated. "He says that was from Montana, it was a gift. From an elder who visited here last summer. The Festival attracts people from all over the world."

"I see." John wondered if the Germans understood how much rebuilding the Cree were doing back on the reservations. How they were relearning songs that had been forgotten when the ceremonies had to be taken underground. He wondered if they knew that elders had died before passing on their knowledge of dances and ceremonies and protocols and how the surviving elders, whether they wanted it or not, were consulted for every aspect of everything. What if I was the last, John wondered? What would I remember and pass on? What mistakes would I make? Yellow Belly only taught those who came to her young; she would not teach anyone over the age of twelve. That was her way and she would not explain why. John figured she liked kids and wasn't a fan of adults but who knows, maybe she had her own teachings about teaching.

"Our culture was interrupted," John said more to himself than to Robert. "We're still taking inventory of what we've lost."

"Yes, well, we've rebuilt a time or two," Robert said. "The Phoenix from the ashes, that is European, that is German, that is life."

John nodded and wondered how that bird remembered how to remake itself the same way each time.

Lucas walked up. He stood quietly beside John until John handed him a drumstick. Lucas tested the drum immediately as if John were not even there. Lucas was all business, a bit like Nadine, actually.

John heard the jingle of bells and knew that Shane was there. "Can I do some drumming?" he asked. "I know a few songs."

John shook his head. "You're dancing." Shane, then the ladies, then John, then Lucas to end the show.

"I could drum too," Shane said. He wanted to be indispensable, likely so that they wouldn't get rid of him. Not that John had any say in that. Lucas was the only person who could help him now. John glanced at Lucas; his face was rigid. Forgiveness wasn't in the cards today.

"Nah, you got bad energy . . . not good for the drum," John said finally.

Shane's face fell, making John wish he could yank back those words. John heard his jingles receding.

Two tall men in dark braids walked into the tent. Their skin looked mottled, the sun had done something strange to their . . . makeup? He could see that their cheekbones had been darkened so that they stood out from the rest of their faces and if you squinted, they did look exactly like those Hollywood Indians.

They looked around the tent, almost shyly, and then spoke to Robert.

"This is Karl and Michael, they are the drum leaders . . . here . . . they want to know if they can join in your group."

John looked at Lucas, who shrugged. "It's not like these are ceremonial songs."

John nodded. Exclusion was not his way.

Nadine entered at a run, her clipboard flapping beside her. Her brow was furrowed and she had a frown on her face. John was beginning to regret turning control over to her. "Are you ready?" she asked — demanded, actually.

"Yes," John said. "Drum's still being set up though."

Nadine swallowed a swear. "Why is everyone moving so slowly? You do realize there is over a thousand people waiting for you to begin. This is not some for-peanuts performance; this is a big show. Do you know the size of the shows they do here? They re-enact the Battle of Little Bighorn. Like the real battle, with a Custer and Sioux and real Crow Indians and there's trick riders . . ."

"They have trick riders?" John hadn't seen any of those since his rodeo days.

"That's the stage part. God, what you don't know about presentation," Nadine mumbled under her breath. And then, remembering that she needed John's goodwill to keep this tour going, she paused: "You've done a great job so far, though."

His "thanks" was as sincere as her compliment.

Nadine started pacing. "All this waiting makes me crazy."

John wondered what didn't.

"And, I don't want to disappoint anyone. And we're already at such a disadvantage, we're missing half our dancers. I'm dancing the traditional portions plus I'm stage managing, I wouldn't normally do both. I actually have a very good stage manager. I've been training him since he was twelve years old —"

"He'll come next time, then."

Nadine flung up her hand. "What if there isn't a next time? What if we goof it up so much this time that they never want us back? What if we're barred from ever coming back — that can happen, you know!"

Edna broke in. "You think this is the only place obsessed with Indians? You'll always find a place that's cuckoo for neechees. Don't you worry about that."

John was beginning to like this hungover Edna.

Nadine faked a smile and then went to stand near the stage. John headed over to the drum.

Shane opened with a fancy dance. He prowled across the stage, filling it with jumps and backflips like his life depended on making this dance impressive. (Maybe it did?) He'd powered through half

217

the dance when Desiree joined him on stage with her shawl flowing behind her. She was moving faster than usual to keep up with the young criminal. The two made eye contact as they danced around each other, her fringes grazing his brown skin. Their youth and beauty made them seem like young lovers, flirting through their steps, and the crowd loved it. John had to give it to her; Nadine sure knew how to choreograph a dance.

The boss herself was up next. She danced a traditional song and John noted that she managed a look of humility and grace as she blessed the four directions with her fan.

John was up next and did a passable grass dance. Shane was on stage with him, also wearing a bustle but dancing twice as hard as John, without even breaking a sweat. Whenever John looked over at him (difficult not to do considering how flashy Shane was), John would move faster. Then he'd notice that he was out of beat and move slower.

After that one, John rushed over to the drum and they finished the performances with a hoop dance from Lucas. Shane stood near John's shoulder so he heard him mutter, "That's the one I have to learn." John smiled at that.

CHAPTER 10

JOHN

John had not heard Lucas talk much, so was surprised when he turned up with some heated opinions about people that he had not even met.

"The Crow are goddamn betrayers," Lucas said.

"Everyone has done wrong sometime in history," John said. "The Cree used to attack every other tribe for hundreds of miles."

"The Crow fought for the white soldiers, they fought against the Sioux."

"They had their reasons, I'm sure. I've met a few Sioux I wouldn't mind betraying," John said, kind of liking the colour in Lucas's face when he was angry.

"Don't expect me to speak to them," Lucas said.

"But don't go punching in them in the face. They work with the festival and we haven't been paid yet."

"Not yet. But we will be!" Nadine exclaimed.

They were sitting in a circle around a fire, eating their very traditional lunches of dried buffalo and berries (where the Germans got buffalo was beyond John). Lucas had taken to calling them the "May Indians." The May Indians didn't believe in chairs or tables so the ground was the only place to sit. Edna hadn't bothered trying and had taken her lunch back to the bus.

"When are we being paid?" asked Lucas.

"They didn't say," Nadine said. "I went up after the performance to speak to Hans, one of the organizers. He's the guy over there in the buckskin leggings."

"The brown buckskin leggings?"

"No. The other one."

"White buckskin?"

"No, the other one."

"Oh, the guy in the black leggings."

"Yes, that's the one. His English isn't too good."

John sighed. That would make things difficult.

Nadine continued, "Anyway, I went up to him and he said that he loves us. Like he used the word 'love' twice and then he said that we had to ceremony with him and that he looked forward to our next performances."

"Sounds like his English is pretty good," John observed.

"Yes, but he still didn't answer my question so . . . it was starting to piss me off talking to him," Nadine said. "I'll talk to him before we get to the next shows."

"Next shows?" prodded Lucas. "How many are we talking here?"

"He said something about us finishing the Festival," Nadine squeaked out. She hunched her shoulders as if she was trying to shrink under everyone's eyes. "The whole damned thing."

"How long does this Festival last?" John directed this at Robert.

"Another week," said Robert.

"We can't stay here that long!" Desiree started but then was distracted by three young braves with abdominal muscles that would have made a washboard weep. "I mean, we have airplane . . . tickets or something . . ."

"I'm sure he didn't mean that long," Nadine said. "I mean, that's ridiculous."

"What does the contract say?" asked John.

"It was in German," Nadine said.

"Do you have the contract?" Robert asked. "I could review it for you."

"I left it at home," Nadine said. "I never thought we'd be haggling once we got here."

Rookie mistake. Even John knew to carry contracts with him

until the deal was done. He'd been ripped off one too many times by ranchers in his younger, greener days. "We'll find Hans and with Robert translating, we'll explain our predicament. They'd like us to stay but we have to get on with the tour and we'll ask for the payment for this performance."

Nadine nodded but did not rise.

John got up to his feet. After a certain age, chairs were absolutely necessary and his knees cracked to remind him of this.

"What the hell was that?" Shane said, the sound waking him from his nap.

"That was John's knees," explained Desiree.

"Jesus, thought it was a gunshot," Shane muttered and laid his head back down.

John noticed that Nadine and Robert took more circuitous roots to standing. Cowards.

NADINE

Nadine, John, and Robert trudged across the beautiful grass to the organizer's tent. Nadine was starting to feel like she was under attack. Nothing was going the way she had expected. So many people! So much complaining! And so little money!

And it was all on her shoulders. Why couldn't John take over? But Nadine knew that wasn't fair; John had done his part. He had handed over his stack of American dollars the night before. He explained the twists and turns of their travels — but it was still startling to Nadine how little cash was left.

Why did she have to do everything herself? "Stop it," she told herself. Blaming and whining got you nowhere. Nadine was no whiner. She was a woman in a man's world and she fought to stay there.

"We have to get paid," she said under her breath. "We must get paid. We need our money now. Now." She punched into her hand for emphasis.

Nadine looked around the valley. It was hard to believe that a war was held here not that long ago. War was such a male act; no woman would want to mess up land this beautiful.

Then Nadine thought about what it would feel like to run out of money halfway through the tour and thought about how satisfying a bazooka would feel in her arms right now.

Hans stood with his back to her and Nadine tapped his shoulder gently. He turned and his profile looked magnificent. He looked like he had stepped from a John Wayne movie, with his flowing black hair, one side neatly braided and his cheekbones looking like they could crush a diamond.

"Ah . . . the Indians," he said, his mouth loving each syllable.

"Yes. That's us. I have a question for you —" *Not a question, a demand!* "It's about payment."

Hans scratched his ear and waved his other hand to indicate that she should go on.

"We expected to be paid today, after the show, because we cannot stay long. We have other shows to do. In other countries," she added for emphasis. They were international and he should know that.

"We agreed that you would do shows here, for the festival. That is, for the entire festival."

"That was not what I agreed to. Two shows, then we have to go." Nadine made little walking motions with her hand.

"This was one day. Six more days. Six more shows. It was all in the contract. Would you like another copy?"

John laughed. "Only if it's in English."

Nadine had a sinking feeling. "That won't be necessary." She looked to Robert for help. "Can you explain to him?"

The language barrier wasn't the problem; Nadine knew that. But she would not be able to wriggle out of this on her own.

Robert spoke rapidly in German; Hans replied as rapidly. This continued for at least three song lengths. (Nadine was humming a song under her breath; she did this when she was nervous.) They finished talking and shook hands.

"Is it settled?" Nadine asked.

"Oh yes, you're released from the contract," Robert explained.

"And the money?" prompted John.

"There will be none," Robert added agreeably. "Shall we head home? My cook is preparing a selection of German game birds for tonight." He rubbed his hands together, a move that Nadine had only seen done by kokums at bingo.

Nadine felt faint. "I feel faint."

John put out an arm to steady her. "Nadine, how much did we need this gig?"

"It was our highest paying performance," she whispered. "It was going to pay for our next accommodations."

"You were in a delicate balance," Robert said. "That is unfortunate. It is not wise to travel so far, with so little."

Nadine wanted to run after Hans and beg for the money but the crowd had already swallowed him up. Nadine saw John sizing up Robert — how much could he afford to give them? He already had the castle of a rich benefactor — now why not the spending habits?

EDNA

"This is a terrible idea!" Edna protested. "He's already given us so much."

The tour group had assembled a quick meeting after Bobby was sent to find some pop or whatever the German equivalent might be.

"A meal, some beds, and a ride, that's not a lot to a guy who owns a castle," said Nadine. "He could probably afford to send us back to Canada first-class."

"We're not asking for that much from Robert," Desiree added. "Enough money to get us to the next stop and maybe a new dress for me . . . nothing fancy. That's peanuts to him."

"And the two of you seem to be . . . friends," Nadine added. "Doesn't everyone want to help their friends?"

Edna didn't think it was fair to assume anything. "It doesn't matter if he's rich as Midas, it isn't right for me to hit him up for money."

"Right. Okay then, I'll hit him up when he comes back," Nadine said.

Edna waved her hand in Nadine's face. "Atimachisk, I won't stand by and watch you put this man on the spot like that. Hasn't he already opened his home to us? What kind of ungrateful Indians would we look like to be trying to get some cash out of him?"

"We would pay him back!"

"Or we could say that we would pay him back and then not pay him back," Shane offered.

John stepped up. "Let's keep it as an option. I'm thinking there's a chance this Hans fella might change his mind."

Edna pointed in John's direction. "He's making sense." The thought of approaching Bobby about money made her cheeks burn. Could you imagine? Asking the man who jilted her to save them? The thought was too much. They had to find another solution.

Nadine signed. "Fine, let's meet back here at 2:00 p.m. They wanted another show — I'll talk to them about paying us before we start. And this time, Desiree, a little more energy — Lucas, maybe some more acrobatics, your hoop dance was a bit on the dry side — John, there's another speed other than slow and Shane . . . try to make some eye contact. You were moving like a whirling dervish out there. You can't always rely on more energy — you gotta have some showmanship."

And with that, the whirling dervish of criticism stalked away.

Shane broke the silence with a sharp laugh. "Goddamn, never had a complaint yet about my moves."

Lucas shook his head. "I do the dance the way I was taught."

"I'm old, not changing now." John rubbed his forehead as if searching for a cowboy hat.

Edna was sure as hell glad she hadn't danced.

Robert stuck his head into the tent. "The re-enactment is happening over the hill. We should make our way over there before

Custer gets his throat slit. They use lots of blood!"

The dancers picked up their feet and made their way out of the tent.

"John," Edna called before he strolled out of the tent. She sidled up next to him. "You . . . understand, right?"

John touched Edna's shoulder. "I'm sorry they asked you to do that. I won't let it come to that."

Still though, Edna decided to make herself scarce for the rest of the afternoon.

NADINE

Nadine found Lucas wandering near the food tents. There was a variety of wild meats hanging and he seemed to be sizing up every option.

"Did you hear that? Edna won't even think of approaching Robert for the money. And after everyone heard me beg the booker for more cash. It's like they don't even want to solve this problem."

Lucas touched a piece of wild boar. He pulled back his hand, appearing not to like its texture.

"I'm not afraid to ask for shit. Never be too proud to beg, that's what my mom used to always say. Or maybe it was Tina Turner? I always get them confused. What do you think?"

Lucas looked down at his watch. "What time was this show supposed to start? I thought Germans were known for their punctuality."

Nadine sighed. The complaints of leaders were rarely important to followers. She spotted two brown-skinned men a few feet away. "You see those guys?" she elbowed Lucas. "I think they're real."

"They're definitely real, I see them too."

"I mean real Indians. Look at their skin — it's not peeling or sweating off." Nadine waved to them. "Hey! Hey!"

The men turned and walked closer. They were young, not even drinking age in the States. "Where'd you come from?" Nadine asked.

"North Dakota," said one. "Wyoming," said the other. Which was strange because they looked like twins.

Nadine looked from one to the other. "How's that possible?"

"Ain't you twins?" Lucas asked the obvious question.

"Well, yeah," said the slightly taller one. "But we were separated at birth and adopted to different families. Luckily it was kind of close so we were able to find each other on the rodeo circuit."

"We have a rodeo rider — his name is John Greyeyes," Nadine said.

The twins nodded politely.

"He's a lot older than you two," Lucas explained.

"What are you doing here?" Nadine tapped the earth with her foot.

"We're trick riders." "We do all the stunts." The twins spoke over one another. "We started on the Indian relay race circuit. Then we got invited to come be in this show."

"Oh, so then we'll be seeing you later," Nadine said. "In the show."

The twins nodded.

"You're the Crow Indians," Lucas announced.

"Yeah," said the older one. "But we don't get to spend a lot of time on the rez. We've only been once, to meet our dad. That was, what — three years ago?"

The other twin nodded.

"Then, you don't know what the Crow did to the Sioux."

Nadine glared at Lucas. "I told you not to bring that up."

"I have an idea of what went down," said the slightly bigger twin, "but I'm not a historical scholar."

"If you have a problem with us — then we can settle it right now." The younger one pushed his chest out to show he meant business.

Lucas stuck out his formidable pecs. "You should have a problem with it; the Crow were traitors."

"They were loyal to their people!" shouted the smaller twin.

Lucas pushed closer to the twins. Nadine leapt between everyone. "Oh, c'mon. These two are no more guilty of the crimes their people committed than these German people are of the Holocaust."

"Well," said Lucas. "That is probably wrong."

"It was less than thirty years ago," said the older twin.

Lucas nodded. "Lot of people killed — millions — would take a helluva lot of people to do that. I mean even if one person killed like a thousand . . . I'm not even including the people who were like, 'I don't care what happens to them Jews.' Those people are guilty too and I'm sure a lot fall into that category."

Nadine was exasperated. "There is a lot of guilt to go around. Canada could have entered the war a lot earlier for one thing. America too." Nadine glanced at Lucas. "But apparently, these people" — she indicated the deerskin-clad white people — "were busy learning to sew buckskin skirts and shirts. I saw a dog wearing a buckskin outfit, which doesn't even make sense — 'cause that's an animal skin on another skin." Nadine took a breath. "But let's think about us, right here, right now. We're all Indians in a strange place and we have to stick together."

The boys slowly nodded. It was though they were mesmerized by her intensity — Nadine knew young folk were generally looking for a direction for their energy; she had to give them one. She put her arms around them. "Now let's walk you over to your show. I want to hear how much money these neechee Germans are paying you."

Lucas stomped behind them. It was hard for him to shed his anger. That was a pretty big flaw. Maybe it was time to downgrade him from potential husband to potential shack-up.

EDNA

She was following the crowd, not really by choice — she had intended to make her way back to the bus. But the hordes of people had got her turned around and now they were pushing her along with them. She could hear cheering and whooping and the sounds of hooves. The crowd deposited her at the top of a hill from which she could look down and see a valley.

On one side, dressed in white and khaki, were a group of riders, their horses mainly white. On the other side, some on horseback, some on foot, were the braves. Their skin was darkened to a deep brown and others to a mahogany. Some had only reached a dark yellow colour but that was okay; it was clear which side they were on. The armies met in the middle and though they fought valiantly, it was patently clear that the white khakis were going to lose.

A few began to run in the opposite direction — "Cowards," mumbled Edna — and others faced their probable deaths bravely. They were run through with spears generally (it would be hard to fake a death via arrow as it would mean catching the arrow, Edna figured). Men fell one by one until only one man stood. He wore a white hat, white pants, and a light brown-fringed jacket. He had a beard that was long and full and Edna guessed this was Custer. He stood still and began to recite a speech. "I stand here defending my country . . ." and he couldn't get any more words out because the crowd booed him so loudly.

A tall "Native American" man came from the group and stabbed him through the heart and held a knife to his throat. He beckoned the crowd like a gladiator and they gave Custer "a thumbs down." *I wonder if they ever give him a thumbs up?* And down he went, into the ground, still dusty from the battle. The grass worn to nothing.

From nowhere, two riders began to circle the valley. They were small and lithe and from where she stood, they looked female. But then one stood on the back of his horse and Edna could see that he was a small man. The other acrobat did a handstand on the back of his horse. Then one jumped off the horse, sent his horse running with a slap to the ass. The other one rode close to him — there was a quick jump — and then both were on the same horse. The crowd was, of course, off their butts cheering.

Edna was less impressed, having grown up on a ranch with a bunch of crazy drunk cowboys and her own horse-crazy nieces and nephews. These young men were good but she'd seen as good in her day.

Nadine had never seen anything so impressive in her life, standing backstage at the show with the rest of her crew. These Crow boys can ride, she crowed to the dancers behind her: Desiree seemed suitably impressed, Lucas looked skeptical, and John looked focused. Shane, of course, appeared to be staring off in the wrong direction. There was no pleasing some people, Nadine figured.

The boys rode back towards them and jumped off their horses before they stopped moving. They dusted each other off. Nadine strode towards them, her jingle dress announcing her walk. "You two are the best damn riders I've ever seen," she declared. "Like a couple of squirrels or something. Come meet my dancers." She hit the "my" hard, wanting these boys to know that she was somebody important, that she commanded a group of people. "What are your names again?" she asked, not sure if she had bothered to ask them before.

"I'm Samuel," said the taller twin, "this is Ed." He indicated his slightly smaller, slightly younger-looking brother. Both had their eyes on Desiree, which was no great surprise to anyone, least of all Desiree. Shane took a half step closer to her.

"You're Crow, huh?" Desiree asked.

"Traitors," Lucas said under his breath.

"A matter of opinion," said Nadine, elbowing him. "Now they work here for the Germans. How is that?"

"They're paying us," Samuel said brightly.

"Not much!" said Ed.

"But we get to ride all the time, so who cares," finished Samuel.

"You're young," Nadine grunted. "You'll change your mind on that someday."

"What kind of horse you got there?" John stroked the slender neck of the bay.

"That's Cherry, she's half thoroughbred, half Arabian. Not sure where the Germans got her but she's been here longer than both of us. 'Bout eight years old, I guess. When we got here she was only half-broke, had kicked the shit out of a bunch of riders but turns out she needed a Crow touch." Ed said all this as he stared at Desiree.

"She's a good horse," Desiree said.

"It's really the rider —" Ed announced.

"Rider makes all the difference," Samuel added.

"Can I ride her?" asked Shane.

"Nah," said Samuel. "We don't know you. She don't know you."

"So what, it's just a stupid horse," Shane replied.

There was an awkward silence as the twins stared down Shane who stared back. Frankly, Nadine thought they all looked like triplets at that point. She broke the pregnant pause. "Let's go find something to eat. We found a place that has wild meat — but like, weird, German meat."

She headed in the direction of the stalls and felt the crowd follow behind her. Lucas moved to walk beside her. "You see, Lucas, the secret to making friends is to ignore differences —" She broke off as she heard hoof-beats, hard and fast across the ground. She turned and saw the pretty little bay jumping a fence that looked much too high for her and on her back . . . at first, she thought it was Shane but then she realized it was Desiree.

"Holy shit," Lucas said.

"Goddamn," John echoed.

"Fuck me," said Shane.

The twins ran wordlessly after their horse.

"That is a Cree girl," Nadine said. "Ride first, ask questions later."

It turned out that the sight of a long-haired, pretty, round-faced Native American Indian girl giving hell across the field had a special effect on the German audience. Nadine was hearing "Indian Princess" more times than she would have liked. She had never been a fan of that part of powwow culture. No need for hierarchies in a community when everyone has to get their hands dirty.

By the time they made it back to their bus at the end of the day (after another gruelling performance under the hot sun), Hans was waiting. He held out a wad of cash and nodded in Desiree's direction. "For the girl."

Desiree looked horrified.

"She's not for sale," John said bluntly.

"For two performances, tomorrow and the day after." Hans pushed the money at Nadine. (He must have figured, rightfully so, that she was the money-hungry one.)

Nadine looked sideways. "And for today too."

Hans nodded and reached into his pocket for more cash.

Day 11

Munich, Germany

EDNA

The Karl May Festival was one of the largest festivals I have ever been to — and I've been to the Regina Exhibition. There were many people dressed up like Indians. They wore a lot of headbands which I read in Hollywood were used to hold down wigs. I do not know if these people were wearing wigs as I wasn't cheeky enough to tug on them. It seemed like a strange way to spend a few days, playing dress-up, but I suppose it's better than other hobbies you might have.

The group danced their shows but the best part was seeing my niece Desiree participate in the re-enactment of Custer's Last Stand with two young Crow men. The performance required a certain amount of trick riding. There was one move in which the two Crow horseback riders — Samuel and Edward — switched riders on horseback. This is called the Indian relay. Desiree became the third rider in this feat. By the time the horse reached her, it was at its top speed. Desiree did not hesitate however and swung up on the horse like it was standing still. One inch too far and she would have gone over the other side but our girl has the balance of a gymnast and put on a show that would make any parent proud.

I do not recall there being a beautiful Indian Princess in the historical story but as they say history is the story told by the victors. And we certainly told an interesting story today.

JOHN

John didn't mind that they extended the stay in Germany for a couple days. Castle life was growing on him, especially when he discovered the stables where the big Percheron horses were fed and groomed. He was happier than a pig in shit, hanging out there making a pest of himself with the stable hands. They bent over backwards to explain the care of the horses in their limited English. A couple times Lucas joined him but he didn't come close to the horses and hung back by the stable doors. John wondered why he even bothered.

One morning, John even took a spin on one of the biggest Percherons, a gelding named Otto. The horse had a smooth trot and a gallop that felt like they were flying across the country.

In the evenings, the meals were generous and gregarious as Robert opened his wine cellar even more widely and told them about his adventures in Saskatchewan. Seemed like that tiny province had a big impact on the guy. He kept going on about the skies, the people he met, and the work he'd done. He mentioned that he once slept in an abandoned church for a week and woke up to mice eating his hair.

"You're darn lucky you didn't die from inhaling mouse shit," John told him. "It's a well-known poison."

"I was young." Robert laughed.

John noticed something else: with every meal, Edna seemed to be sitting closer and closer to Robert. One night when John left the table, they were the last two sitting there even though both looked like they needed a good night's sleep.

John knew of something that could keep people up when they should be sleeping. And when his mind touched on that thought, his heart exploded with Per's face and John had to walk briskly for half an hour before he could clear his head. He didn't envy their lovesick gazes; the aftermath hurt too much.

As for the young people, Shane still showed off for Desiree but she didn't seem very impressed. She also flirted with every young male within flirting distance. Must almost drive that young man insane, John thought. He spotted Shane in the stalls one day. His face was redder than usual. John figured he was reacting to the makeup he'd been putting on his face to look extra fierce during dances. He struck up a conversation. "How does your skin feel?"

"S'okay." Shane replied. He raised his hand to his cheek defensively.

"When I was younger, I had some bad skin," John said. "Tried near everything, then my kokum brought me something that worked good."

"Like some kind of special medicine?"

"Horse piss."

Lucas made a face. "For real?"

John nodded. "Worked better than anything else."

Lucas looked down at the stalls. "Jesus."

"You ready to head back?"

Shane nodded as he reached through a stall to pet a black horse. "Yep."

"How are you gonna handle that warrant waiting for you?"

"Back to jail, I guess." Shane shrugged. "Not the first time."

They watched as a mare invited her colt to suckle. The colt looked confused at first and then figured it out quick and started sucking like crazy at the teat.

"Would . . . could you leave your reserve?" Shane's voice was faint.

John sighed. "Everyone leaves eventually. Some of us come back and some never do . . . Y'know, my dad's buried somewhere in this country."

"But he would have gone back?"

"Of course. He had two kids and my mom." John remembered how his mom had collapsed when she found out Adelarde would not be coming home. Her legs had lost strength, like a newborn colt. He remembered wondering what would happen if she never got up again. She got back up. But John never forgot that moment.

"Plus," John added, "he loved the reserve. He had a big farm and a garden and he was the reserve's best fiddle player."

"I don't have any kids," Shane said. "And my last girlfriend tried to stab me."

"Single, no kids, guess the world is your oyster — sow your wild oats — be all you can be." These were things people had told John when he was young and he'd never found them very comforting, more like a challenge he could never meet.

"What about you? You ready to go home?"

John nodded. "Miss my horses, miss my dog. Miss the quiet."

"Like, you have a house and everything?"

"Yeah."

Shane nodded and turned his attention back to the young colt, now drinking so enthusiastically that milk flowed down his neck.

EDNA

"Will I get to see you dance?" Bobby asked. Then a day later, "When will I get to see you dance?" and then later that day, "I want to see you dance." His voice had a hint of a command in it and that was almost enough to convince Edna to dance. But her hips, tired and aching, had better arguments.

"You're not missing anything," she said. "Truth be told, I make everyone look bad. I only came to keep an eye on Desiree, you know. Now that Nadine is here, I'm not needed." Although Nadine had been glaring at her lately during the performances and saying pointed things like, "It would be nice to have a new thing to throw at the audience," or "Would be nice to give someone a break."

There was a part of her that was secretly glad her body was acting up; she didn't want to dance for Bobby.

"You used to dance," Bobby reminded her. "The barn dances, the square dances . . . out in the fields."

"I was young then and my body wasn't full of complaints," she replied.

"Has it been that long?"

"A whole lifetime, some would say."

He would tease her about not having aged a day and Edna would laugh but stick to her guns. Men only missed you when they saw you. He'd probably not even thought about her once he stepped off Saskatchewan soil. She knew enough about men to know that. "I'll love you forever" really meant "I'll love you as long as we are within convenient proximity to one another." There was no such thing as love that moved mountains. She'd seen her brother move furniture around the house for his wife, but he'd complained the whole time.

Edna drank a glass of wine at dinner, but only one. She wasn't trying to hide anymore and she couldn't explain where this strength was coming from. Maybe from the night with the ghosts. She'd hinted to Desiree that she'd seen something on the battlements but when she tried to show her the staircase, they couldn't find it.

"Weird," said Desiree.

The spirits had no interest in Desiree, Edna realized.

On their last night, Bobby invited her for a walk. Normally she would have said no but it was the last night and risks could be taken.

Were she to do something . . . shameful . . . she'd be in a bus heading down the mountain a few hours later.

"Where are we going?" she asked, glad she'd brought a sweater with her. It was a siwash sweater that had been in her family for at least a generation, made by her grandmother for her mother. Four deer were on the sweater: an animal special to her grandmother's clan. Edna didn't know anything more than that. Her grandmother had died while she was at residential school. Even before she died there had been a distance between them. When Edna came home to visit, she'd forgotten all the Cree she'd once known and Grandmother had only spoken Cree her entire life.

"There's an orchard on the south side of the castle. I've done nothing with it but I should take a look at it. I might get to it this year." Robert had been restoring the castle bit by bit. He figured it would take him at least another five years to reach all the corners.

And you'll never be able to get rid of the ghosts.

The orchard was full of weeds of varying heights. Edna kicked aside the thigh-high ones and trod down the calf-length grass.

"Time to hire a gardener." Bobby seemed embarrassed.

"Always good to let a garden go wild for a few years. Lets the soil rest."

"Do you still run the ranch?"

"We have a foreman who does that. He's been there so long he could do it with his eyes closed."

"What do you do now?"

Edna thought back — it was only the month before, but she had difficulty remembering what she did with her days. "I help out," she said finally. "I go where I'm needed."

They kicked down more weeds. Bobby stopped in front of a tree; it was old and moss grew along the bottom. Edna could not put her arms all the way around it.

"This tree is dying," Robert said.

Edna shook her head. "Cut off the top branches, those big ones, she's still got some life in her yet."

236

"I married once, you know," Bobby said.

Edna felt a pang, so sudden it took her by surprise. Of course, he had. "And?"

"She died. Pneumonia."

"Castles are drafty."

"It was so sudden. Who dies at twenty-nine from pneumonia?"

Edna patted his shoulder.

He smiled. "You and I — did we talk about marriage?"

Edna shook her head. "It never came up," she said carefully. *We talked about the rest of the summer, which I thought was the rest of our lives.* Edna laughed sharply; she'd been such a silly girl.

"What was the joke?"

"I was remembering something John said."

Bobby looked at her expectantly.

"You wouldn't get it. It's a Cree thing."

They walked some more. Bobby spoke of his wife and the travelling they'd done together. He talked about how he inherited the castle. Edna talked about her brother's children and how they had almost turned her hair white with their adventures. It was late when they made it back to the front door.

"Will you dance tomorrow?" he asked.

"No," Edna replied and went inside.

Day 12

EDNA

Our time in Germany is done. It is not a place that I ever wanted to visit but I am glad that I did. We were able to put some spirits to rest. John's dad is buried in this country and he put some tobacco down before we left the castle ground. It is not my belief — being a Christian woman — but I know that it means that his prayers are carried to God. As he prayed for his father, I thought of my own dad who wanted good things for my brother and I. Most of all that we looked out for one another and we did.

Our host invited us to come back. I cannot speak for my other companions but I think one trip to Germany is enough for me. Too many ghosts.

Our next stop is Rome, Italy, where we may visit the Vatican where His Holiness the Pope lives. He is the living embodiment of the Catholic Church and the holiest person on earth. Of course, everyone is nervous about being so close to someone so sacred but I have been preparing them by conducting multiple rounds of the rosary.

Nadine leaned over John's seat and whispered in his ear. "If she doesn't stop praying, I'm going to throw her off this fucking train."

"Tune her out." John tilted his hat over his face.

Nadine wanted someone to confront Edna about her behaviour but everyone was chicken. Edna wasn't dancing, she'd flirted outrageously with their castle host, and she was barely watching her niece. How much more would this woman get away with?

Edna's voice rose in volume as she started another round of Hail Mary's.

"Oh, for God's sake!" Nadine flounced out of the train car, slamming the door behind her. The next car was also a passenger car with at least four newly woken people shooting her angry looks. Nadine avoided eye contact. Normally she was a nice person, a calm person, a sweet person, even. Wherever she went, she made new contacts. That was how you built a business.

"Hey boss lady." Desiree waved her over. "My aunt still praying?"

Nadine nodded.

"Ugh." Desiree took a sip of her Coke. "Did you notice anything when we were loading up the train?"

"All the bags were there, all the regalia, the bustles, the shawls. Everything but the kitchen sink, yeah."

"Not everything. Shane is gone."

Nadine sat up straight. "Are you sure?"

Desiree nodded. "I wasn't sure at first but I've walked this entire train, checking all the seats and cars, and he isn't in any of them . . . plus I saw him talking to those twins a lot."

Nadine had noticed that too. But she hadn't found it suspicious. They were all about the same age, with the same frenetic energy.

"He stayed with them?"

"Must have. I think maybe he was trying to say goodbye to me last night."

"What did he say?"

"That he was in love with me and could I ever love him? And I was all like, nah, you're not really in love with me . . . plus you're a criminal . . ." Desiree paused. "Maybe I shouldn't have said that part? I don't think he's a criminal really. Just a thief."

"Well . . ." Nadine was at a loss. Would she get in trouble for losing one of the dancers? Was he even technically a dancer? What about bringing him to justice? "Does he even have a passport?"

Desiree shook her head. "The police are looking for him, hey?"

"Yeah, the RCMP are looking for him."

"But they ain't looking in Germany, right?"

"Nope."

"Guess he made the right call then. Gonna miss him though — he does the best impressions of John and my aunt and you — y'know, people in general."

Nadine sighed. She wasn't happy to lose one of them, especially the best dancer. She suddenly regretted not taking him aside sooner and asking him what his plans were. "How is he going to survive?"

Desiree shrugged. "How has he survived until now? Guts and bullshittin'."

Nadine nodded, not sure that would be enough. 'Course, it had been enough for her.

"Do you ever think of doing that? Running away?" Desiree asked.

"I left home when I was younger than you."

"Oh." Desiree hadn't been expecting that. "I thought about it — like what if I went with Shane — stayed here in Europe. It's nice here. I like all the history and stuff, the buildings . . . mostly I like how people look at you with curiosity instead of . . . disgust." Desiree made a face. "People follow me around here and people follow me around at home too, but only to make sure I'm not stealing. I could stay here and be a 'special Indian' or I can go home and be a 'dirty Indian.'" She laughed.

Nadine remembered a fight outside of a small-town bar in which she had taken on three white women who had called her that name. She remembered how the last person who had hit her in that fight was a man who had come to the defence of the women. She remembered how she laid on the ground pretending to be dead so they'd leave her alone, listening to the women cry, thinking, *What the hell are they crying about? I'm the one who is bleeding.*

Nadine rested her head on the window and let the train lull her to sleep. Hopefully she would dream of young colts running wild through the long grasses.

JOHN

John did not want to remember his dreams. He'd wake himself suddenly and be left with the image of a long pair of legs walking away from him. And him with "don't go" stuck in his throat. He never could talk in his dreams. One time he woke and thought, "There are phones . . ." but he couldn't imagine that Swede waiting beside a phone for a call. No moss on that stone. One weekend in Stockholm and John would be forgotten for sure.

John could hear the prayers behind him. Unlike Nadine, he found them soothing. Every time he heard the rosary begin again, he dedicated the prayer to another person. He'd started with his mother, then Per, then his brother, then his dad, his nieces and nephews, his horses, and now he was on that green-eyed devil.

"I'm not going home," Shane had announced to John in the doorway of his room. He'd had an impish look on his face that John hadn't seen in days. His skin was looking clearer too.

"Do you even have a home?" John asked.

Shane smiled at that. "Not for a long time. But you know what I mean."

"You sure about this? You don't speak the language and you ain't got any money . . . that I know of."

Shane's smile turned sly. "I'm okay for money."

"Y'know, young people always say that but they never know how much money it takes to stay alive and then they never think about how long it takes to make new money." John remembered being

242

stuck a time or two when he was in his twenties. But he had a big brother to bail him out. (Even though it came with a head-splitting lecture every time.)

"I got a job. The festival goes on tour and they hired me to dance and help out with the horses. The twins helped me get it." Shane looked so excited, John almost felt excited himself. For a second he wished he could change places with the bright eyes in front of him. Travelling through Europe, working with horses, hanging out with a couple of other wild guys — younger John would have leapt at the chance. But now he had a ranch, horses, and a dog with big sad eyes. Strange, John always thought he was free of encumbrances and now here he was with encumbrances up the ass.

"You take care of yourself then. And don't steal or lie or cheat at cards."

Shane grinned. "Better not, without you to save my ass."

Shane held out his hand. John shook it, catching a faint whiff of horse piss. "Be careful, young man."

"You know, it's been a long time since I was young," Shane replied. And when John looked at his eyes, they didn't look young.

In those seconds, it was like Shane's life flashed before John's eyes. 'Course that was impossible. But it was a life, or lives that John had seen in his peripheral vision: teenagers standing in clumps outside the liquor store, girls too young to be mommas pushing strollers, kids sitting in the back of social service cars being shipped off the reserve and never to be seen again. Hell, he'd seen that look on his classmates: a flash of pain so sharp that it made your heart cramp. He reached into his wallet and fumbled around until he found a twenty-dollar bill (the only one) and handed it to Shane.

"You call the Fineday band office if you need help."

"And ask for you?"

"Ask for the Chief and tell him I said so." These were John's last words before the green eyes swept out the door.

John hadn't been expecting that goodbye although logically he knew the kid was going to ditch them eventually. Lucas was too dangerous-looking and being around him was like asking for a lickin'. Still, John was going to miss the little shit.

He pulled the worn itinerary out of his pocket. Three shows tomorrow in Rome. Then one more show the next day and then home. He got up, thinking it was time to check in with his brother. But as quickly as he stood, he sat back down. He'd have to wait for the train to stop before he could find a phone. Besides, what was he going to tell his brother? We've been late for every show, we're barely breaking even, we lost our youngest member, and the Chief's daughter has fallen in love at every stop . . . it could all wait. Edna's voice rose again as she blasted her way through another version of the rosaries. John fell asleep before he gave the prayer to someone.

Day 13

Rome, Italy

EDNA

The City of Rome is home to thousands of people. In the olden days it was the place where they sacrificed Christians to lions and the Romans crucified Jesus. Basically if you're a Christian, don't turn your back on Romans is what I say.

However, the Vatican is also located in the heart of Rome and the Vatican is where Pope Paul VI lives. Now he hasn't requested that the Prairie Chickens dance for His Holiness but once he finds out that Indians are around — especially CHRISTIAN Indians — he'll probably send a personal invitation for us to join him. I believe this will happen with every fibre of my being.

They pulled into the station around 3:00 a.m. and walked through the huge station with its smooth floors and high ceilings. Their voices echoed around the room even when they spoke softly. They seemed to have more bags than hands and John wished fervently for a cart of some kind. Nadine reached the street before any of them and found the cab stand. She began to haggle in broken Italian that she was reading out of a guidebook for a couple of cabs to take them to the hotel. Hotel Roma was on the itinerary and John had marked it with a star. Because it was the last place they'd be staying in, not because he thought it would be special or anything. A young cab driver exited his cab and hurried towards them. "I'm Paolo!" he exclaimed with more energy than anyone ought to have at 3 a.m. "Welcome Prairie Chicken Dance Tour!" he announced. John lifted his hat politely. The others just gaped.

"I work for Hotel Roma!" Paolo pointed at another cab. "That is my friend, Marco, he will take the other half."

Nadine walked over to Paolo. "I'm glad that you all are so professional."

"Your hair is so pretty," he replied and combed the side of her head with his hand.

"Thank you." Nadine pushed his hand away.

Paolo began loading her bags. Nadine gestured to the rest of them to follow. John and Lucas dutifully followed her demands. John had been tired when they got to the station but he was starting to perk up now that they were outside in the warm air. John jumped into the cab with Lucas and Nadine. Marco, their driver, was an older man with sleepy eyes. He nodded when Nadine mentioned their destination. They drove past buildings that were young and modern-looking and others that were older than Jesus. John glimpsed the Coliseum and joked, "It'd be nice if they ever got around to finishing it?"

Lucas chuckled and Nadine rolled her eyes.

It was a heady feeling, being in a place that he'd only seen in movies. Sometimes movies made you feel like places weren't real.

After a long drive, they pulled up at their hotel. It was good that he'd kept his expectations low because it was literally the worst hotel he'd ever seen. (Or maybe he'd gotten used to fancy castle life.) But even the tiny licensed hotels that you found in small-town Saskatchewan had more class than this one and those hotels were only around to make sure people had a place to pass out. If John had one word to describe Hotel Roma he would have to say "sweaty." It leaked moisture and looked like it was only getting hotter. There were no cool breezes off the water. And it was surrounded by what looked to be nearly a hundred people milling around on three sides.

As the cabs pulled up, the crowds of dark, unruly people shifted in their direction. Nadine said, "This does not bode well." John felt for his wallet and moved it to his front pocket.

"Why are all these people here?" Lucas asked.

"To kill us?" John offered.

"Probably expecting someone important," Nadine offered. They stared at the people now pounding on the windows of the cab. "Well, it isn't gonna get any easier." She pushed the door open.

John followed her out. "It's definitely about us," John said as someone yanked on his braid. He slapped their hand away.

"Times like these, I wish I'd learned more lang — goddamn, someone grabbed my ass!" Lucas spun and glared at the people behind him.

John had both hands full of bags and started moving forward and his progress was immediately hampered. "Ex-cuzi," he said. The crowd laughed. He tried again, "Get the fuck out of my way." More laughter.

"I feel like a zoo animal," Lucas said.

"I can't move," Nadine said.

"Shit." Lucas had a bag in one hand and his other held out to stave off more butt-grabs.

There was a beep behind them and John turned and saw the other cab. "Oh hell." He didn't have any control over this situation.

The doors opened as Desiree and Edna emerged. The crowd surged towards them, giving Lucas and John some wiggle room. John wanted to seize the moment and race into the hotel but he couldn't leave the ladies behind. He pushed himself through the crowd.

"Bit of a problem!" he shouted.

"What?" Edna yelled.

"Problem!"

"What?!"

John pushed through the crowd; the woman was deaf as hell. "I said — this crowd is a problem," he said.

"I can see that," she snapped.

Nadine knocked on the driver's window. "Little help here! Aiuto!"

Paolo emerged from the second cab with a huge smile and his arms outstretched. Inside the train station, he'd looked like a man, but now under the moonlight and streetlights, John could see that he was about seventeen. He jumped onto the hood of his car and grinned at the crowd. If John could speak Italian, this is what he would have heard:

"Ladies, gentlemen, esteemed pickpockets — I bring you the Indians from across the sea here for you, the people of Rome! They have travelled the world and now they are here for our pleasure! They dance, they sing, they play a drum!" Here he stopped to beat the top of his car. The people cheered. "They will do shows for the entire day tomorrow. Be sure to stop in at the hotel to ask them for times and get your tickets! And your pictures! You can get pictures with the Indians!"

There were more cheers.

"What's he saying?" John asked Nadine.

"Who cares? It's working."

John felt his suitcases ripped out of his hands. Then he watched as two men carried them towards the hotel. Next he felt two burly men wrap their arms around him and propel him towards the hotel.

He craned his neck back and saw his co-Indians being subjected to the same treatment. He realized then that they were being honoured in some way and scraped together a smile.

Once inside, his bearers dropped him. His braids were pulled a few times and then his "helpers" left. John looked around. They were the only guests checking in.

A large man sat at the front desk looking like the second coming of Christ wouldn't impress him. "Indian?"

John, too tired to correct him, nodded.

The door opened with a chime and more Indians were deposited inside.

"Indians," the large man said with calm acceptance.

Paolo entered, his smile as broad as before. "That was the best thing," he announced in accented English. He looked at John. "Nice to meet you. I am Paolo. Like the pope."

"I'm John, this is Lucas."

"You are big, *big* men. You must have killed many white men, taken many scalps."

"I've lost count." John held out his hand for Paolo to shake enthusiastically.

Paolo did a Hollywood Indian–style war whoop.

"We don't actually do that," Nadine said.

"But I do!" Paolo yelled as he ran out the door. "See you tomorrow! Sleep well, Indians!"

The door slammed behind him.

Desiree said, "He's really cute."

NADINE

The tour was almost over and they were in the most romantic city in the world (even though their hotel smelled like dead fish) and she had to make the most of it. "Do or die," she whispered to herself as she stared out the window so tiny that a fish couldn't jump through it. "Do or die." If she leaned far to the left and squinted, she could see a sliver of sunlight bouncing off the water. Why would you put a hotel on the waterfront and then not give the guests a view?

"That's okay, no distractions," Nadine announced, deciding that she would be optimistic. "Do or die."

Before leaving Germany, she'd had some pictures developed. She laid them out in front of her. The majority of them were of Lucas. Lucas standing in front of different things, usually with his back to her as he didn't like his photo being taken but she had to take his photo because she had no one else to photograph. Pictures with no one in them were boring.

She had a picture of Desiree with her aunt; Desiree was smiling, her aunt was staring at the camera like she was trying to bore a hole through it. Nadine had a picture of Lucas standing next to John and then a little further away from them, Shane. She had a picture of herself with their host, Robert Golden-fudgesickle or whatever his name was. She had a picture of her with Edna and she was proud to say that she looked a thousand times better (plus she had smiled and Edna had that sour look on her face. If that sour look meant you were closer to god, then Nadine would take being a happy agnostic any day).

She laid one photo of Lucas next to one of John. They were both handsome men, one a bit older, one a bit broader. Both quiet, noble, intelligent. They both danced. John loved horses. Lucas had a great car. One lived in Canada, one was American, but both were Native American Indian. One she had loved for decades, and the other for less than a week.

Which you think would give her the answer — go with the guy you know best. But she'd spent more one-on-one time with Lucas; they'd slept next to each other on two separate occasions (on planes) and that counted for something. Being next to another person, your breath moving in time with theirs, that was an intimate act. (Which kind of made public travel all that much more creepy when you thought about it.)

"I have to kiss them." She announced this decision to the faded orange flowery wallpaper and the strange-smelling blanket. She as suddenly regretted her volume, remembering the paper-thin walls. For god's sake, she'd heard Edna the nun praying all night.

Do or die. Die or do.

Nadine was not meant to live out her life in spinsterhood; she was a woman of flesh and blood and desire. She loved sex like a man — or more like five men — according to her last boyfriend. How many years ago had that been? It was hard to love, hard to find a good man. Which is why this decision was doubly difficult. In a lifetime, you couldn't expect to meet one special man and right now she had two within her grasp. She had two more days. No time like the present. She got up. At least one of them would be at breakfast.

She wasn't naïve — she knew she was no Sophia Loren. But she was the right age, she had a decent figure, she had a house and a car, she had a business, and she was smart. That was a lot of check marks. Most importantly, she liked them a lot and whichever one she chose would find himself immersed in a tornado of love from which there would be no escape.

~

At breakfast, Desiree made a peculiar announcement. "We have to go to the German consulate. Me and my aunt."

"Why?" John asked.

"We have to," Desiree said through a mouthful of bread.

"You can't do that, we have activities planned," Nadine said.

"I saw the schedule, we're sightseeing, like that fountain of pizza or something — we can skip that. We'll meet you at that place where they sacrificed all the Christians."

"The Coliseum?" Nadine asked.

"Yeah, it's big, should be easy to find."

Nadine glared at her. "We have a performance at two, back here at the hotel. That's early and we shouldn't be splitting up. You saw the crowd last night — what if you got caught in something like that with only your aunt around?"

"I'll go with them," Lucas volunteered.

Nadine looked at him in surprise. So did everyone else. He rarely spoke — it was like seeing a statue come to life.

"If you're going, then I'm going," Nadine said.

"Why?" Desiree asked. "Are you his mother or something?"

"What? How?" Nadine sputtered. "I'm more like his sister — how old do you think I am?"

Desiree shrugged and smiled into her glass of water.

"Honestly, young people! When I was your age, which wasn't that long ago — I did not assume that people were mothers of their contemporaries. That was not done back then —"

"In the thirties?"

"That is very rude, young lady!"

"Okay, okay." John's voice was deep and commanding and brought a bit of calm to the room even though Nadine suspected he was using the same tone he would use on a horse. "If all four of you are going to the German place, then we might as well all go," John said. "Save money on cabs and whatnot. Besides, you see one fountain, you seen them all."

Nadine looked to Edna for support. But she wasn't there.

EDNA

As soon as she got up that morning she had rushed over to her purse. Edna rifled through it again to make sure the package was there. She felt it and was relieved. She'd forgotten about the darn thing until Desiree had reminded her the night before. She'd stuck her head in Edna's room and said, "Hey Auntie, don't we have to deliver that package or something for the National Indian Brotherhood Chief?"

To be honest, she'd been in kind of a fog since they'd gotten into Rome. Knowing how close they were to God — well, it boggled the mind. Less than a few miles away stood the living representative of God on earth. He was probably eating his breakfast as she sat there on her hotel bed. Or maybe he was brushing his teeth. What were his teeth like? Were they marked with holes from growing up as a poor child? Or was his family able to afford a dentist? Were God's holy people allowed to see dentists — even though they'd taken a vow of poverty?

It was a shame that she would never get to ask him such questions. Personal audiences with the pope were saved for kings, queens, and world leaders. Not for a woman from a reserve so small that you could blink and miss driving through it. But she didn't need to talk to him. She only needed to get close enough to brush against his vestments and then . . . she would be healed. Like the sick and the lame with Jesus, one touch and voila! All pain and suffering excised. She could dance, she could ride horses with her niece, she could travel without complaint. She could pray on her knees again. She looked down at her right hand, so twisted. In the beginning it had been one joint and then it grew. And then it left. Then it came back and moved to her knee. Then her hip, then her back and then to her hands, twisting them into useless shapes. Her beautiful hands.

Then it would go away. Sometimes for a few days. Sometimes weeks of hope. She'd learned over the years that it would always return. But now she had a chance to make it go away forever. Or even for a month, a month would be heaven. A year would be divine. But she would take anything she could get.

"Hurry up, Auntie," Desiree yelled from the hallway. "Everyone is waiting for you."

"I'm coming," Edna yelled back.

Desiree bounced into the room, looking like summer itself, cheeks glowing and eyes sparkling. She didn't look the least bit sweaty. How did the young do that?

"What do you want me to carry?" Desiree often carried her purse, her sweater, and whatever outfit they needed that day.

"Uh . . . me?" Edna winced as she got to her feet.

"As if. You're skinny but I ain't that strong." Desiree hesitated. "Do you need me to grab John or one of the guys?"

Edna smiled. "Of course not. Foot fell asleep, I'll be fine in a bit." Edna shook her foot.

Desiree grasped at the answer. "I hate it when that happens to me! Gotta stop sitting cross-legged, Aunt. Can't sit like an Indian no more. Hey, have you looked around this hotel lately? I think it's sinking . . ." she chattered on and the sound of her voice soothed Edna's joints.

Love is a miracle of sorts.

Desiree stopped in the hallway before they reached the others. "Are you ready for today?" she asked, her voice low.

"Do you remember the name of the man we have to meet?" Edna whispered.

Desiree shook her head. "But he'll know us. I mean — look at us — we're not exactly inconspicuous."

"You think this is a good idea? Maybe we'll end up in prison."

"Oh puleeze, we'll tell them we don't know how to read. Everyone thinks Indians are dumb as shit anyway. Might as well use that to our benefit," said Desiree. "Did you hear the things that cab driver was saying last night? He thinks he's John Wayne."

"He helped us out."

"Yeah, well, he's still a bonehead. Handsome though. Does everyone here have eyelashes like that? Like you could trip over them."

~

Paolo the cab driver was downstairs waiting. He'd found a van that would fit all of them. It turned out that he was the nephew of the hotel owner and so was their self-declared tour director. "I hear everyone wants to see the German consulate? I can't understand why you want to see more Germans after leaving them — but your wishes are my command! Indians are such strange people." Here he attempted to grab one of Lucas's braids. Lucas pushed him away with one arm.

Paolo continued: "Has everyone eaten? Has everyone got something to drink? Has everyone gone to the bathroom?!"

On this, John headed for the restroom.

"There's always one," Paolo said and winked at Desiree.

They piled into the van. Nadine grabbed the front seat and turned back to watch everyone else. Edna and Desiree sat at the back. Lucas sat near them and John sat across from him. In her mind, Edna referred to them as the twins; they were so often together.

"How long to the consulate?" Edna asked.

"How far is this thing?" yelled Desiree.

"Five minutes," Paolo yelled back.

"No time to nap," Desiree told her aunt. "Look at all these old buildings and I think the streets are made of rocks. Sharp damned rocks."

"It's only in Rome — san pietrini cobblestone," Paolo proclaimed as he slipped the van into gear. "We are so special that we have our own special stone."

"Look at you, all smart," Desiree called forward. Edna wished Desiree had sat closer to her latest crush.

"I have dream of being . . . a tourism guide. Then everyone will love my city as I do . . ." Paolo looked off dreamily and nearly drove into the side of a building.

Whatever that special stone was made of, it made the streets bumpy. Edna could feel every pebble in her bones. She tried to relax but still tensed every time the vehicle bounced into the air.

She reached the consulate a lot worse for wear. Still, she had a mission and was determined to do her part for the Chiefs who had sent her. She hoped that she wasn't part of some government conspiracy to rob someone of their homes and livelihood. But it was only a package. How much trouble could a small package cause?

The consulate was a three-storey building with ominous-looking pillars out front. A tall, strongly built, blonde man stood out front in a suit. Edna was no expert but even she could see the outline of a gun under his jacket.

"Looks like the right place," John commented. He was calm in new situations. Edna still wasn't sure that he wasn't a dumb man. Only idiots were always calm.

With a cacophony of words, Paolo explained who they were and the guard stepped aside.

"He looks German," Desiree whispered.

"He looks huge," Nadine replied. "Don't piss him off."

"We just came from Germany!" Desiree said. "We couldn't get enough of it," she added with a wink to the guard.

"For shame." Edna pulled on Desiree's arm and glanced at the tall man with surprise; he had not smiled at Desiree.

The tour had done its damage to her ego. She'd never be able to look at white people again without expecting some kind of warm welcome or request to pose for a picture. Europe was sending an uppity group of Indians home to Saskatchewan.

A large black door swung open and they went inside. It was cool and clean, no clutter, organized. Like Germany had been transported to this wild, sweaty country. An efficient-looking woman appeared in front of them. "Who are you here to see?"

Edna admired how tight her hair bun was. "I don't know," Edna said honestly. "Can you say that Edna and Desiree from Canada are here? Sent by the National Indian Brotherhood."

The woman looked confused. "But who should I tell?"

"Whoever is in charge, I guess."

The woman backed away.

"That's it?" Nadine exclaimed. "You weren't expected or anything? And you didn't call ahead? Honestly, you people tramp around like a group of ignorant reserve Indians. In places like this you have to be invited and even then you should call to confirm first. Guess they'll be kicking us out on our asses soon enough!" She sat down with a huff on a leather chair.

"This place is amazing!" proclaimed Paolo as he touched a set of metal armour. "I've never been here before. It's like Nazis in Italy. But this time, we don't have to be scared of them!"

"Weren't you allies?" John asked.

"Well . . . some people were." Paolo smiled. "But my family was part of the resistance. We made life difficult for the Nazis and that fat pig's band of traitors. They called us traitors but we were the true Italians." He puffed out his chest.

"Did you fight too?" Desiree asked.

"Alas, I was just a twinkle in my dad's eye."

The woman returned, this time with an elderly man beside her. The man was bald like an egg. His ramrod posture and mechanical way of walking told Edna he was ex-military. He held out his hand. "Edna Shield. I am Oscar. I have been waiting."

"Of course, you were." Edna wasn't too mature to shoot Nadine an "I told you so" look.

"Come with me." He turned away. As they all followed, he turned back. "These two only," he said, gesturing towards Edna and Desiree. "Greta will bring you some refreshments."

He walked Desiree and Edna to a door. He closed it carefully behind them. "Can I see it?"

"Depends." Edna had seen a version of this play out on *Hawaii Five-o* a few times. "Do you have the money?"

"What were you promised?"

"Five hundred dollars," Edna said boldly.

Oscar shook his head. "We have already paid the Chiefs."

"This is the delivery fee." Edna gave him a look like she had ice in her veins.

He looked unsure but went to his desk.

Desiree shot her an impressed look; Edna waved for her be cool.

He returned with the cash and handed it to her.

"What is this?" Edna asked.

"Lira."

"I can't — don't you have any Canadian?"

Oscar shook his head. Edna let out an exasperated sigh and held the money out to Desiree who looked at it closely. "Pretty."

"And you have it?"

"Yes, yes, cool your heels." Edna reached into her bag and handed him the package.

He put it down and proceeded to open it. He drew out the contents, a black-and-white bone choker. It was old, Edna could see that much. The hide had grown hard and turned a dark brown. Oscar ran his hand over it.

"It's here." His voice had a reverential tone.

Desiree looked at her aunt. "It's a choker," she whispered.

Edna nodded. But it was old. Edna felt a knot in her tummy that she knew could only be guilt. Whose choker was it? She knew she wouldn't like the answer. Edna gave her niece a push. "Okay, we'll be on our way."

But before she could open the door, it burst open and a voice called out like in the movies: "Freeze."

Lucas stood in the doorway with a gun drawn and pointed in their general direction. Edna took a big step out of the gun's direction, pulling Desiree behind her. Oscar put down the choker on the desk and raised his hands. Edna stuffed the cash in her pocket.

"What the hell are you doing?" Edna demanded of Lucas. "Other than scaring the hell out of us? You almost gave me a heart attack!"

"You are under arrest by the power of the United States of America —" Lucas stepped forward and held out a badge.

Edna snatched it out of his hand. It certainly looked like a badge but then she'd never seen one up close before. "FBI, really?"

Lucas snatched it back. "Yes, really."

Oscar came forward. "We have done nothing wrong."

Lucas bent and picked up the choker with a handkerchief. "You are smuggling treasures. Treasures that are not yours to sell."

"Not yours either," Edna said. "And you can't prove that we knew what it was — so there!"

"I need you to tell me who gave you this package."

"Why in God's name would I do that?" Edna asked. "You have a gun in my face and I have no idea who you are. The other Lucas —"

"Shane —" Desiree interjected.

"Was a goddamn hurricane of trouble but at least he never stuck a gun in my face. And me an elder!"

"You're only forty-one," Desiree clarified.

"Thirty-nine! Plus I'm a respectable — Christian — woman!" Edna countered, hitting "Christian" hard.

"Plus you travelled with us all this time — making us think that you were one of our friends," Desiree added. "Guess you were lying to us the whole time. Can't believe I felt bad about Shane knocking you out and stuffing you in that bathroom."

Lucas looked embarrassed. He pulled back his gun. "Sorry." He looked at Oscar. "Who was your contact in the States?"

Oscar shrugged.

"See there, you have nothing," Edna said, stepping closer to Lucas. "Don't move."

"I have to pee —" Edna looked at Oscar. "Where is your bathroom?"

Oscar pointed to the left.

"No one is going anywhere!" Lucas said.

"This is crazy," Desiree said. "Is something bad going to happen to us?" Her face glowed with excitement.

Lucas didn't answer. Which is probably the worst answer that someone can give. For the first time, Edna felt the walls closing in.

"The closet," Edna said quickly.

"What?" Lucas looked at her.

"There's a man hiding in the closet. He heard you coming and jumped in there."

Lucas walked over to the closet. He opened the door cautiously. "You need to come out of there —" He looked deep inside. "There's no one —"

Edna had never considered herself a violent person before this trip. If you kept mostly to yourself and to people you trusted, why would you ever have cause to fight? Even when the cowboys on her ranch acted up, wild on booze, she only had to give them a look and they cooled their heels. As she was not experienced in such matters, she wasn't sure how much force to use on Lucas when she pushed him into the closet. It must have been enough because he went flying into it. It was a deep one, as far as closets go, more like a mini-room actually. He fell ass over teakettle and there was a loud thunk as his long legs hit the back wall. She slammed the closet door and twisted the little lock-thingie.

Oscar and Desiree stared at her open-mouthed.

"I can't be arrested," she said. "I don't have the time."

CHAPTER 12

EDNA

Edna rushed out of the room in such a hurry that she scraped her right hip on the doorframe. She couldn't explain why she ran directly into Paolo and fell on him with a "whoof." She couldn't explain why she grabbed his keys as they fell together into the display of armour and then scrambled to her feet and rushed out the door. Desiree ran behind her, skirting chairs and the fallen Italian with cute eyelashes. She was out the door a foot behind her auntie.

If Desiree had more time she would have said, "My aunt has gone crazy, please help me." Instead all Edna heard behind her was "Crazzzeeee," as she ran out the door of the German consulate. Edna already had the van moving as Desiree jumped inside.

Edna did not expect people to act with a lot of sense in this world. She realized that she was part of a select minority that believed rules were necessary to tamp down on all the nuttiness of the average person. However, she was not prepared for the nonsense that ruled Roman drivers. They seemed to be driving the wrong way most of the time and some were even moving sideways down the street. There was no logic, etiquette, or empathy employed beyond "this is how I get to my destination." And they sure did like their horns.

The night before she had gotten herself a map and studied the location of the pope's home. She traced the streets with her fingers and said their names over and over until they seemed vaguely familiar. And now, with much interference from the other drivers, she endeavoured to follow that path.

"Do you know where you're going?" Desiree was breathless as she clung to the dashboard with one hand and her seat with the other.

Edna nodded as she veered out of the path of a speeding truck.

"Okay then." Desiree's teeth chattered.

NADINE

John seemed the most worried. Paolo seemed caught between bragging about the wildness of Indians and then mourning the loss of his van. Lucas was quiet. Disturbingly quiet. After he'd raced out the door after the two women only to watch them drive away, he had kicked the side of the building so hard that he was limping afterwards.

Nadine had many questions but Lucas didn't seem open to answering at the moment as he limped back and forth, his expression set to scowl. Nadine wanted to tell him to sit down and rest his foot but kept her mouth shut.

She hadn't even seen him this upset when he was locked in that bathroom or in that ignorant RCMP's cell. Now that she thought of it, Lucas sure got himself locked into a lot of places.

She approached John instead. "What's going on here?"

"Far as I can guess, Lucas is a spy or something."

"I am not a spy!" Lucas exclaimed from across the room.

"All right then, who are you working for?"

"Clearly he's CIA," Paolo said, "or 007. Or KGB!"

"007 isn't even real," Nadine replied. "Right?" She looked at John.

"How much gas did you have in your vehicle?" Lucas demanded of Paolo.

"That is a difficult question," Paolo answered. "My mother filled it up last and then she borrowed it this morning. I woke up late because I was with my girlfriend, who is married to a very stupid —"

"Goddammit," Lucas scowled again. "I never should have taken this job, it's been nothing but trouble."

"You are a spy," Nadine said. "You've been one from the beginning. You lied to me."

"I am a dancer," Lucas said. "I went to Canada to dance for the troupe . . . but I also had another job to do."

"Intercepting a package from Edna," said John. "The one she's been hiding in her purse."

"You knew?"

"I was the tour manager. It's my business to know." John sighed. "I didn't think it was anything that would get them in trouble."

Nadine piped up, "Where did you get a gun? And a badge? You had nothing when I picked you up at that gas station."

"I met up with another agent in Stockholm."

"When? I was watching you so closely — I mean, I was with you most of the time."

"You sleep in, I don't," Lucas said.

John chuckled. Then stopped himself. "Those ladies aren't in any trouble, right?"

"They're not in trouble yet," Lucas said. "I prevented the drop. But I need to know who gave it to her."

"They won't be arrested? Or charged with anything?" John asked.

"'Cause I need them for the show!" Nadine pointed out.

"And also because they are two nice ladies who wouldn't hurt anyone for the world," John added with a look at Nadine.

"Plus that young woman is very pretty," Paolo interjected. "Pretty women should never be locked up. That would be the real crime."

John's upbraiding prickled Nadine. As usual, she was the only one worrying about the tour. Goddamn him and his judgemental ways. Mentally she moved Lucas back to the top of her two-person list. She could deal with a spy before someone who made her feel guilty about being professional.

Lucas glared at John. "Do you know where they went?"

"I have an idea," John replied.

"You're obligated to tell me — by order of the U.S. government."

"Of all the governments in the world — that's probably the last one I'd listen to," John answered, a smile growing across his face.

Paolo moved closer. "Is someone going to be scalped? Can you wait for a me to get a camera?"

"Tell him, for god's sake, John," Nadine said. "I need to damn well know or we aren't going to make it to the show."

John stared Lucas down. "Only if he says nothing will happen to them."

Lucas rubbed his head, stamped his foot, and then spit on the ground. Finally, he nodded.

John looked at Paolo. "Can you get us another ride?"

"No problem," Paolo assured him. "No scalping then?"

"No scalping," John said firmly.

JOHN

John found the country so hot that he could barely think. He could only feel the drops of sweat forming on his face and the river that was rolling down his back, creating a sensation that was both refreshing and itchy as hell. He had a headache from dehydration that had started the moment he woke up. His hotel room even smelled damp. He moved at a sloth's pace because his pants were sticking to him and he wished he had scissors so that he could cut his jeans into cut-offs, not caring how that looked at all.

Paolo was chattering in the front seat to the other cab driver. He kept proclaiming the word "Indian" over and over. The other cab driver seemed less interested in Indians than Paolo because he merely nodded and kept his eyes on the road.

John glanced at Lucas. His face was frozen in a frown. John figured he was pissed off about being taken down by a woman, and a tiny, arthritic woman at that. He shouldn't be. She'd attacked a man with a gun once before, and she'd gotten the drop on him after all.

Nothing was going to keep her from her pope, not after all she'd gone through. Not this crazy little Catholic dancer.

"You're sure then?" Nadine asked.

"It's all she talks about. She prays non-stop. And to Catholics, the pope is like their Elvis and the Vatican would be her Graceland."

"I thought you could worship god anywhere," Nadine mused. "He's in the trees and the grass and the lakes — isn't that in a psalm?"

"A miracle," Lucas grunted. "Like Lazarus. He had to see Jesus to be healed."

"Oh," Nadine said. "I guess I didn't realize how bad it was."

John thought about the look on Edna's face after each of her performances. What it must feel like to know your body was crumbling.

"There is a man who can bend spoons, I've seen him on TV!" Paolo said.

"He's a fraud," Lucas said.

"If a man can bend spoons, what else can he do?!"

"Why would you bend spoons in the first place?" John asked. "What would be the point?"

"For the spoon companies — they could sell more!" Paolo pointed out.

"It's not real!" Lucas roared.

Paolo mumbled under his breath. "It is real."

John didn't believe in miracles himself. He'd seen too many things that made him believe that endurance was the only power you had over life. But then his thoughts drifted to a smile that was welcoming. And so brave that it made you feel brave. And what were the chances that John would ever have seen that smile? If his brother had not called, if John had not said yes, if Nadine's crew hadn't gotten sick, if Nadine hadn't planned and fundraised for years . . . Nadine then was the source of his miracle. And the source of that gut-burning he felt every time he thought about leaving it all behind.

I will never see him again. He closed his eyes, wishing for a time machine.

"This isn't time for a nap." Nadine's voice was sharp. She wasn't a fan of weakness.

"It's too damn hot," John said, his eyes still closed.

"Pull over!" Nadine ordered. "This guy needs some water."

"No, we'll lose them!" Lucas rasped (he needed water as well).

The cab pulled over next to a market. Nadine went inside with Paolo.

Lucas looked over at John. "You look like death."

John nodded. "Seems about right."

"We can't lose them."

"We won't. She ain't leaving that place until she sees the King Priest —"

"Pope —"

"Whatever. I feel sorry for the Vatican, they're gonna have a helluva time trying to get rid of her."

Lucas drummed his fingers against the seat.

"What's the big deal with the package?"

"It's valuable."

"Really? I can buy like ten of them chokers at any powwow in Saskatchewan."

"You opened it?"

"'Course I did. I told you I was responsible for these people. I gotta know what these fools are carrying on the plane and whatnot. I opened it while Edna was sleeping, saw the choker, and figured it was a gift for some dignitary. That's what we use them for in Saskatchewan. Even have two myself, from when I was dancing." His grandmother Yellow Belly had made them.

Don't lose them now, they got my fingerprints all over them, she'd warned him. Kokum believed that fingerprints were like tiny parts of the soul.

John went on: "I never worried about it because those things are pretty common all over the west. But I guess this one is special, huh? Y'know, I did notice that it was old. Like my kokum used to use hide to make hers but I saw some sinew on the bindings. Sinew! Nobody's used that in a dog's age. Damned hard to work with, most people don't even have that skill anymore. Which makes me think now, it must have been really old. And old stuff, well, it's probably worth more. Also, why would that Chief think to send it to Germany . . . maybe it belonged to someone that the Germans respected. The Germans are all on the side of the Indians — as you saw from their festival — so then this choker must have belonged to an important Chief."

Lucas turned his head towards the window. "Stop talking."

"I haven't done nothing wrong. I mean, unless it's a crime to wear Chief Crazyhorse's choker."

"You wore it!"

"You wouldn't?" John was enjoying the vein throbbing in Lucas's forehead.

"It's a national treasure. The National Indian Brotherhood had no right to sell it off."

"From what I know about politics, it is a very expensive business. Maybe selling stuff to interested parties is the only way to finance their government . . . I wouldn't do it — mostly because I think politics is a load of bullshit. But I could see other people making that choice."

Lucas glared at John. "I know who your brother is."

"He'll be glad to hear that." John grinned.

EDNA

"Do you believe in miracles?" Edna asked her niece, who was still clinging to surfaces of the van like a spider.

"Like not getting into an accident with you driving like a crazy person? I frickin' hope so."

"They are real. They are all over the Bible. You should know that."

"I've never read the Bible —"

"But I told you to —"

"You tell me a lot of things. I'm not going to read a damn book when it's warm outside. I've told you that a thousand times."

Edna had had her suspicions that Desiree was sneaking out her bedroom window when she was supposed to be doing her homework or her assigned Bible readings. But she could never catch her in the act, sneaky little cat.

"There are many miracles in the Bible, the miracle of the Virgin birth, the miracle of the resurrection —"

"The miracle on 34th street. I know miracles can happen. Like that time that pimple went away right on grad night. I barely even prayed for that. Car!"

Edna steered around the car that had inexplicably stopped right in front of them. "But some things, they take more than prayer . . . they take special places, like the water at Lac Ste. Anne."

"Where you went last summer."

Edna had visited the lake with the other visitors; she'd prayed outside and even watched as others spoke in tongues. She attended twice-daily mass and evening rosary circles. She even helped out as dozens of adults went through their first baptism. On her last night, she waded into the water herself and stood there as two nuns prayed next to her, holding each of her hands. It was the first time she'd allowed a nun to touch her since her school days. Edna returned back to the reserve with a greater love and appreciation for the Church but she also returned with her affliction. In fact, it seemed angered by her efforts to get rid of it; she'd had to use crutches for a few weeks afterwards.

At the dinner table, her brother joked, "Looks like God isn't ready to give you your miracle. Maybe you didn't pray hard enough."

Her sister-in-law added, "It isn't good for people in your condition to be around all that damp."

They were both wrong. The problem was the place. God had wanted her to go further for her miracle so that she would appreciate it all the more. And he had taken her to the city where beauty and faith had become one. Where else should a great miracle take place than where Da Vinci had left his mark, where Michelangelo had contemplated what light best portrayed God's love? The Vatican.

She'd known that she was destined to be in this car the moment that the Chief had mentioned this tour.

"Miracles are destiny," she murmured as she steered around two men pushing a cart of sausage down the middle of the street for some ungodly reason.

"I don't know about that," Desiree said. "'Cause that pimple never would have gone away if I'd kept eating chocolate."

The traffic was lighter now and slower. "Look!" Edna shouted.

Desiree flinched. "Jesus, I'm sitting right next to you."

Edna stared up at the building stretched up in front of them. The building looked about twelve storeys high, way bigger than anything she'd ever seen in the big city. In front of it was a large courtyard filled with chairs in the middle and on the right, with people milling about in a sloppy line towards the entrance, she figured. Dotted around the walls were figures of holy people looking down on everyone. Imagine looking up at those faces every day and seeing all the power there.

"What the hell is this place?" Desiree asked. "It's so damned big."

"It's St. Peter's Basilica. That's where the Pope addresses the people." Edna made the sign of the cross.

Desiree craned her neck to look closer. "Is he there?"

"He's inside. We have to get inside."

~

Edna figured that the pope had a special love for Indians. Who else deserved the love and protection of the Catholic Church more than Indians? They'd endured more than any other group: starvation, war, being thrown off their land, smallpox, and TB — even the church had delivered some kicks. Which brought her to her second point: there were very few Indians wandering around, and she was certain that her novelty would work in her favour. To be sure, before getting out of the car, she took her sweater off, revealing her traditional dress underneath, its fringes flattened by the sweater. She flicked them to perk them up.

"Help me with my hair." Edna handed Desiree a beaded barrette. A moose was beaded into the barrette, reminding her of the swamps back home where the long-legged creatures roamed. Desiree fastened her bangs back.

"Now you." Edna pulled Desiree's fancy dance dress out of her enormous purse.

"Oh god, I don't want to be an Indian around all these people." Desiree gestured at the crowds of tourists milling about.

"Desiree." Edna looked into her niece's eyes. "For me."

Desiree looked back at the crowds and then at her aunt. "All right." She reluctantly put on her regalia but left her hair free. "It's more impressive this way," she explained, already savvy to the way that the world perceived her.

As Edna and Desiree approached the Basilica's entrance, cameras began snapping. The entrance was forty feet high with ornate metal grating on top of it, just in case you might miss its immensity, Edna thought to herself. As she and Desiree strode quickly towards the building, she could feel the people closing in, as they had done the night before. Edna kept the crowd moving closer and closer to the opening. Two guards wearing peppermint-striped pajamas stood on each side. They were hard to miss. She handed Desiree her shawl.

Desiree shook her head but Edna waved it insistently at her. "There's not even any music," Desiree hissed.

"You think that matters? These people will never get another chance to see this."

Desiree glared at her aunt. She unfolded the shawl and moved it into place on her shoulders and tucked beneath her arms. She took a couple graceful hops and then stopped. Edna was about to castigate her again and then stopped. Desiree moved towards a young man with a bongo. She spoke or gestured her way into an agreement. He began to hit his drums.

Desiree gathered up her shawl and began again. The crowd moved away from her to give her room to dance. The crowd built and built — then Edna spotted the guards move towards Desiree as well. She looked up at the sky, clear blue, and prayed, and then she ran.

～

Edna slipped inside the doorway and found herself in a hallway as big as heaven. She looked up at the gold inlaid ceiling that looked like the Pope's hat, and then down at the marble floors, marked with stars. The north star will lead the way, isn't that what they always said? She turned into another hallway that was grander. She felt as though she were staring at the sky. Keep moving, she chided herself, don't stand there with your mouth open like a bush Indian. There had to be private apartments somewhere.

She heard drumming behind her. Not Native drumming. Something faster and not as deep. But Desiree would make something of it. Desiree. She had told her so many lies to get her to this place and still she was out there dancing for her aunt. People brushed past Edna, trying to get back outside to the music. She turned to the right and stopped short. Lit from behind, there was a sculpture of a beautiful woman holding the broken body of her adult son. Edna knelt and bowed her head. She whispered into her hands, "Forgive me. I did what I had to do."

From the corner of her eye, she saw the swish of robes. She found her way to standing, slowly, carefully, and followed the robes. She lifted her skirt to move faster. The robes moved around a corner and she followed.

The hallway was bright, the windows covered with mesh so that the sunlight gave the air a golden glow. She kept moving, seeing this as some sort of sign. She saw a library to her right, a kitchen and a bathroom area. Was she inside someone's private area? The furnishings were nice but not that nice. She stuck her head inside the library. It was smaller than the one she had built at home. But these books were much smaller and older.

She pulled one off the shelf. It was pages bound together with a leather binding, on the cover was "Invictus." She said the word, knowing it was Latin but not understanding it. That was how most church was to her, lots of Latin words that she didn't understand but knew them to be important and holy. "Invictus," she whispered.

"Who are you?"

A man stood in the doorway, silhouetted by the light. His head was bare except for fine baby hairs covering his skull. He was rather thin, in that way that old people get when they can't put on fat anymore.

"I'm Edna. I've come for a miracle."

He looked uncomfortable. "Miracles are all around us, that is what God teaches us."

"But if you need one, specifically health-related, isn't this the place to come?"

"It doesn't work like that, my child."

Edna stared at him for a long moment. "I see."

"Would you like some tea?" he asked gently and Edna lunged at him, her hands outstretched. For a second she was in the air, fully stretched out from fingertip to toes, like a Cree superwoman. She had judged her distance well and ended up landing on the ground in front of him with a fistful of his robes.

"Bless me, oh Lord," she whispered and then passed out.

NADINE

From what she could surmise from the rapid Italian and English flying between Paolo and the man dressed in striped puffy pants, Edna was in some kind of jail within the Vatican. She was supposed to wait there until the Italian police came and got her.

Nadine glanced at Lucas. "Can't you argue some kind of jurisdiction? Like she's your prisoner first or something?"

"I don't want to complicate matters." Lucas seemed much calmer now that they were around other authority figures, despite their colourful get-ups.

Desiree elbowed Nadine. "When is she getting out?"

"Nobody is saying. Maybe never."

"Never!"

"The Vatican has its own laws," said Lucas. "Technically it is its own country and apparently she attacked some high-ranking priest or something. You know why she'd do something like that?"

"Nope," Desiree's head moved from side to side and her earrings jingled, catching the attention of Paolo and the pantaloon guy. Nadine guessed those guards hadn't taken a vow of celibacy like the priests.

Nadine pushed Desiree forward. "You should talk to them."

Desiree bounced into Paolo. "Where's my aunt?" she demanded of the guard.

There was a flurry of Italian.

Paolo turned to her. "The guard says that there is nothing he can do. She is being held until the police come. We can't even see her."

"I need to make sure that she's okay!"

"You can't," Paolo said. "I'm sorry, mio caro."

Nadine looked at her watch. "I hate to be the bitch here . . ."

John looked at her warningly and Nadine glared back. "But we need to get going if we're going to make our first show."

"Are you serious?" Desiree's cheeks were pink. "My aunt could be getting murdered right now!"

"It's a church," John said.

"I don't know. This place is creepy!"

"This place was designed in 1506 and completed in 1615 and it has the actual tomb of St. Peter under the main dome," Paolo said.

"That is creepy," Nadine agreed. She'd always found church stuff kind of scary. Religion reminded her of death.

Paolo added, "Interesting detail, St. Peter was crucified upside down because he didn't think he was good enough to be crucified the same way as Jesus."

Desiree stared at him and then shouted, "I want my aunt now!"

Nadine saw more pantaloons approaching. "Hey," she said. "Better cool it, Desiree."

But Desiree was not in the mood to be obedient (when was she ever?) and ramped it up a notch. "GET MY AUNT NOW!" and stamped her feet for good measure.

Nadine hadn't seen a lot of tantrums in her time but she could sure as shit recognize one. Desiree's hands were balled into fists, her face was beet red, and her voice was as loud as it was shrill. The pantaloons started to run in their direction. Nadine noticed that tourists were now taking pictures with abandon.

Nadine looked over at John and knew they were thinking the same thing — they were all going to be arrested.

Nadine glanced at Paolo; he was weeping into his hands. "The poor Indians," he kept saying over and over again. Nadine supposed that was a type of advocacy.

"John?"

John was rubbing his temple with his hand. "This is . . . a lot."

"Lucas?"

Lucas was backing away from the melee. Nadine started to do the same. The pantaloons had reached Desiree and started grabbing for her limbs. Desiree's rage only increased and Nadine was starting to worry about her sanity when suddenly Desiree's scream changed. "I'm pregnant!"

Paolo wiped his tears with one hand and yelled, "Incinta!" He repeated the word a few times until it echoed around the square.

All hands were dropped. Desiree looked coldly at the men surrounding her. "How dare you touch an Indian woman?" Desiree started to walk forward. Her voice was no longer shrill but rather deep and complicated like a Swedish movie. "I want to see my aunt now."

JOHN

They were moving so fast through the complex that John barely got to see what the place looked like. Lots of stonework, gold glinting in the low light, and so many flickering candles that John wondered how the place wasn't a smoldering pile of ash. John wasn't much of a fan of fire; even as a kid he always stayed away from the wood stove.

They were being escorted — he hoped — to Edna. Paolo, their translator, was still sobbing. Apparently being arrested by guys in colourful pants was a big deal in Italy and the young driver was worried about what his parents would say. For a second, John wondered what his brother would say — another run-in with the law, late for their performance, and now arrested by the pope's army.

They reached a small office of sorts and John could see some bars off to the side. He counted three cells, deep and dark — had anyone ever been forgotten in there? Then he saw a coffee maker on a desk and realized that this was the twentieth century. The office was warm and he could see some comfortable seating inside the cells. Edna at least would be able to rest.

The head fancy guard opened a cell and beckoned for someone to come out. John felt a wave of relief when he saw Edna's short hair emerge. And then he felt another feeling when he saw her smile. Surprise. He'd never seen her smile like a person. She looked like Desiree.

"Sorry for all the trouble," she said to the general audience and looked like she meant it.

"No trouble at all," John said quickly. "We're just glad to see you up and around."

Desiree rushed forward, grabbed both her hands, and examined her aunt from head to foot. "You're okay!"

"I'm okay."

John figured Desiree was a bit overcome with the experience because she began to weep loudly. Edna pulled her close. Desiree's head rested on her shoulder. "I thought you weren't coming back," Desiree sobbed.

"I'm here," Edna whispered.

John turned away and gave them some privacy.

Much to his chagrin, *someone* chose this moment to clear her throat loudly and expressively. "You know, I hate to do this but we really have to go."

"Yes, we must go!" Paolo said. "But first there is the matter of the fine."

Everyone visibly flinched, except Edna, who as it turned out was carrying a fair bit of cash.

John shook his head. *Damn Indians, always holding out.*

C H A P T E R   1 3

NADINE

Nadine glanced out at the crowd from the side of the stage. It was huge and boisterous with people yelling and whistling.

Missing the first show had only increased the audience's anticipation — she'd have to remember that trick.

Nadine glanced at the dancers lining up on stage. They all looked tired but during the pep talk she reminded them that this was their second-last dance and that they ought to make the most of it. *You'll never be here again,* she told them, *so make it memorable.* They had stared back at her with no expression on their damned faces (honestly, Indians really were good at that stoic thing) but she knew they got the message.

Behind her she heard the drum start up. Lucas was doing the honours on a hand-drum. He kept a good beat and Nadine added that her to column of pros. She hadn't made her final decision but Lucas was definitely pulling ahead in the personality department. Especially since John had been so crotchety with her lately. She'd always thought they saw eye to eye on most things but she could see now that he was way more permissive with Desiree than she ever would be. That wouldn't work when they had kids! He practically coddled that little Desiree whereas Nadine would have taken her aside and smacked her for making such a scene at the Vatican. At the Vatican! Nadine wasn't even religious and even she was offended.

Would she ever have kids? She was getting up there. Everyone else her age was practically a grandma. How had she let this happen?

How had she wasted so much time? Her eyes spotted the tall man on stage, dancing the hell out of the sneak up dance and remembered. John. For John she had waited, across the way, for him to walk through the yard, down the road, and turn into her approach. How many nights had she sat on her porch waiting to see his front door open and then take her in his arms? Too many nights. It had always been John she loved. He was her first choice forever and she couldn't wait a second longer.

"I'm losing my mind," she whispered to herself.

"We know," Desiree said, standing behind her waiting for her turn to go on.

"I was talking to myself," Nadine said.

"Yeah, like crazy people do."

"Have you told your aunt that you're pregnant?"

"Nope." Desiree flipped her hair and Nadine wondered why it wasn't braided. Kids — you had to be on them all the time.

"Don't you think you should?"

"No." Desiree moved up to the side of the stage, as she heard the drum song change. "'Cause I'm not." Then she grinned, lifted her arms, shook out her fringes, and ran onstage.

John came through the curtain, breathing heavily.

"You know she's not pregnant!" Nadine proclaimed.

"One less reason for her dad to kill me." John wiped his face with a towel.

"You should be upset. She lied to us."

"She lied to the fancy police. Those guys weren't okay talking about female stuff and she knew it. You gotta give her more credit. She's not a kid."

This was the longest amount of time that she and John had ever spoken and it emboldened her. "Do you want kids?"

John couldn't have looked more shocked if she had kicked him in the ball sack.

She repeated her question: "Kids — don't you want them?"

"Never thought about it."

278

He was lying; she knew this as sure she knew the number of dance moves that each of her dancers had screwed up in the past thirty minutes. But for some reason this lie struck something inside of Nadine and she felt all the gears and wheels move in her brain and then suddenly lock in place as they reached their destination. "John — are you a homosexual?" She felt like all the letters in that word were getting caught up in her tongue.

"What?"

He was staring right through her and Nadine suddenly regretted ever opening her mouth. She wished she was Superman and could fly around the world and reverse time. She rushed her next words trying to make it okay. "It's okay, John. I won't think less of you. But I need to know . . ." Nadine's throat was dry and the rest of the sentence crumbled in her mouth.

She heard the drum beating fast. Right at this moment, the dancer would be moving into a spin that would awe the audience. The applause would pick up as Desiree moved from the turn into a high-kneed run across the stage. But Nadine wasn't paying attention to that right now; she was noticing how John's dark skin was draining of colour and his eyes had grown cold. "I wouldn't judge you." Why was she doing this? Pursuing this conversation down this dangerous path? Prodding a man she loved and accusing him of the one thing that would most definitely bar him from her life? *Stop it,* she commanded herself, *stop.* But she couldn't. "I know lots of gay people, lots of dancers, they call themselves two-spirited."

John's face was turning to stone and the way his mouth was set, it looked like he had never spoken a word in his life and never would.

"I love you." She knew it in her heart to be true. She reached for his hand and he moved it away from her. He walked away. Not quickly but the same slow, assured pace he always used.

She knew then that he would never cross the grass, would never end up at her door, knocking once before walking in. She'd never be picked up in his arms, never kissed, never whispered to. *God, I'm a fool.* She sucked in a breath that felt wet and realized that she was crying. She wiped her face quickly and pinched the back of her right hand with her left. *No crying.*

A few feet away, the crowd clapped wildly and stamped their feet as the dancer spun and spun, her fringes standing straight out, looking for all the world like a porcupine caught in tornado.

Nadine used to dance like that, before she took up the slower dances. Because that's what women were supposed to do when they reached a certain age. Nadine bit her lip so hard that her mouth filled with blood.

She was a jingle dancer now. That was the healing dance. A stray tear made its way down her cheek. She wiped it aside. The music changed and Nadine heard her cue.

JOHN

John watched Lucas on the drum. He had one more song before John took over and played an Honour song that he remembered the old men playing when he was a child. He knew another Honour song; it had played the day they put his mushum Long Guns into the ground. That song, however, was family and he held it close to him. It would be played when his brother died and the spirits willing, when he died too. If anyone remembered. That was always the problem: would the children learn and would there be someone to teach them? When Yellow Belly was alive, people brought their children from all over to learn from her and she taught only the ones she felt would keep the songs sacred.

John had heard of elders dying with their songs and ceremonies because they could not find the right person to share their knowledge. So many sick people. John knew that was the problem. His reserve had them too. Shacked up in their homes of unhappiness. Sick children, sick animals, sick men, sick wives, sick lives. He did not blame them. He visited with them and drank their tea or sometimes sipped from a short-necked brown bottle and listened to them tell stories from when they were young. But stories that only told half the truth. John knew that that was their medicine, those happy times plucked from the sea of unhappy memories. John had gone to school with them and his luck had won out (except for a few painful beatings) and theirs had not held.

He knew what white people saw when they looked at his people at the powwows, their bright shiny eyes sparkling when they laughed, their braids askew as they ran. Where is their Honour song for surviving?

"You must have children," Yellow Belly said to him when he was only five. She touched his heart and then hers and then pointed at the sun. "Children come from the sky and they connect us with the spirit world. You must have children."

I'm sorry, Kokum.

If she had lived longer, would she have made such a request? If she'd been there when he started to realize that he would not be able to choose a wife. Would her love have still flowed over him like a warm rain?

John closed his mind to that thought. He looked over at the drum; Lucas's eyes were closed as he finished the last few beats of the song. The man had a voice, that's for sure.

She knows. They all know. Well, maybe not Edna — she wasn't the most worldly person on the planet, clinging stubbornly to her Jesus. He admired that love; she'd found it early and now it kept her strong.

Where is my love?

The horses, his dog, the drum, the dance . . .

Enough to nurture his heart to the end, if he hadn't stepped onto that plane.

John thought love was supposed to free you — didn't people say that? Then he remembered every single country song he'd ever heard and realized those country singers weren't joking around. One night of love, a thousand hours of heartbreak. *My heart is broken* — he had not realized that until now. He'd started to believe that feeling like shit was how he had always felt.

Lucas handed the hand-drum to him and John took it with both hands. He raised it to his lips and kissed it before he began his song.

EDNA

Edna leaned against the other side of the stage. Her regalia still on but askew. She might dance; she might not. She thought back to those last few moments in that big dark church.

He was a strange man, that priest. Close up he smelled like cinnamon. He must like it in his tea, she figured. His robes were made of a thick cotton that must have been hot under the Roman sun. Then again, she had felt some skinny ankles under there. Then she hit the floor, which was softer than you would think. Back in the olden days, they knew how to build things.

He had let out a scream when she lunged at him and tried to toddle backwards away from her but she was too quick. After she hit the ground, he pulled her up and set her on a couch. That's how she woke up, with him staring at her.

He handed her tea and again she smelled cinnamon.

She wanted to tell him about her quest for a miracle, the years that she had spent praying and the visions that she had leading her to this place. But she could see from the way his eyes examined her swollen hands that he understood.

Once in the cell, she wasn't sure that he had understood after all. But the guards had been polite. One of them even helped her to sit down. Once they left, she pressed her hand against the stone wall, wanting to feel the history there. Who else had shared this cell? Crooked bishops? Confused priests? Corrupt popes? Each of them greater than any person she'd ever met. She kept her mind on these histories and did not let herself think of the question burning in her soul. But still it broke through: Did she get a miracle? Was she healed?

When she was a young girl, she had stopped thinking of Christmas as a special time. She spent it in residential school back then because parents weren't allowed to visit and children were never good enough to get to go home. Christmas then was in bed by seven after a barely edible meal and an orange. Edna didn't even like oranges. But you had to be grateful because other kids didn't even have that. But it was hard to feel grateful when they remembered Christmas in their tiny log homes surrounded by relatives who laughed with mouths wide open, fiddle music playing, and kids being handed from auntie to auntie to kokum and back again. She'd taught herself to never get excited about that day again. Besides, she convinced herself, this day is for Jesus and Jesus alone.

A guard left her alone in her cell. Her ears picked up the sound of heavy steps in the hallway, and she wondered if they had sent the army to collect her. She got up from the bed and went to the bars of the cell. She could see across the small office to the door leading to the hallway. It was wooden with a small plate of glass in the centre of it. She saw a face looking in at her, dark eyes, intelligent but tired from a lifetime of reading. She stared back. The eyes twinkled back.

Nobody had to tell her; she knew.

"You up for this?" Nadine asked, breaking her reverie.

Edna was tying on her buckskin leggings. They tended to fall down on her because her calves were thin so she always made sure they were extra tight. Edna nodded.

"You sure? You don't have to if you don't feel up to it?" Nadine thought she was being kind but her kindness always had a distrustful flavour to it.

"I can do it," Edna said. "You tell me when."

"You're up right after Lucas."

Edna started on her second legging. She was humming as she worked it up her leg. What is that song? She stopped. It was "Ave Maria," a hymn she'd memorized after years of singing it in morning mass. It was always her favourite.

The music changed and Edna walked out on stage. There were lots of faces in the audience but she made herself focus on the sky above them. Edna bent her knees with the drum, rising on the beat.

When the honour beats came and she raised her eagle feather, she raised it in memory of herself.

Day 14

Homebound

EDNA

Rome was our favourite stop on the tour. During our stay, we managed to fit in a last-minute visit with the Vatican, a personal dream of mine. After our last shows, our hosts, the owner of the hotel, Louis and his grandson Paolo, who is named after the current pope, extended an invitation to the Prairie Chicken Dance Troupe to perform next year. The young man Paolo asked many questions about the tour but the one that stands out is, "What is the Prairie Chicken? Is it a very graceful bird?" I told him that it had the power and grace of an eagle and the colourful beauty of a peacock. That is a joke. But maybe prairie chickens are graceful to other chickens.

I will begin practising another dance for that trip, perhaps jingle dress which is a dance for healing prayers. Paolo and his friends gave us a ride to the airport and would not take money no matter how much we offered them payment. Which was good, because we didn't have much money when we actually sat down and counted it.

"Give it to me straight," Nadine said as they stood at the check-in counter for Air Canada, although she was already cringing in a way that suggested she could not handle it.

"We are short," John said.

"That can't be. Count it again," Nadine commanded.

John pushed the pile of money across the counter to her.

She began to count.

The flight attendant, resplendent in orange-coloured hair, glared down at Nadine's fingers, moving slowly through the money.

"Look, let's take my word for it," John said to the attendant. "How far can that get us?"

The attendant looked down at her screen. She spoke without looking up. "I can get all of you to Toronto by eleven tonight. Or, I can get three of you to Saskatoon by noon tomorrow."

"There's four of us." This Nadine knew off the top of her head. Lucas's bosses had wired him money for a ticket.

"That's all you can afford."

"But how are we supposed to get from Toronto to home?" Nadine looked genuinely perplexed.

John glanced at the group. He wondered if he could bop Lucas over the head and steal his ticket and let Lucas's government buy another one for him. John dismissed this thought — the poor guy had been bonked on the head enough. He sighed. "I could stay behind and wait for my brother to wire more money." Amos sure would be pissed.

"Nobody is getting left behind," Nadine growled.

"Toronto or Saskatoon?" The attendant was looking past them at the line forming.

Nadine sighed. John could tell she was tempted to take the Saskatoon fare. Since the last show, she had been fired up to get home.

"Whatever you decide is fine with me," John said. "But I don't think these ladies are ready to start a new life in Toronto." He gestured at Desiree and Edna.

"I'll move to Toronto!" Desiree offered.

Everyone ignored her.

Nadine chewed on her fingernails, something she rarely did. "Toronto," she said finally and the attendant's fingers flew, excited to have them away from her.

"What do we do once we get to Toronto?" John asked.

"We call in some favours," Nadine said. "Starting with that Chief shithead who got Edna to carry illegal cargo over the border."

John had to agree, that was a good place to start.

NADINE

She had never been so tired in her life. It seemed as if all the stress from the past two weeks had come crashing down on her in the same night. The plane was quiet but Nadine's head shouted at her about all the mistakes she made: starting with the Chinese food celebration on half-off Tuesday and finishing with bleeding money all the way from Germany to Italy. In addition to the contract mistakes with Hans and the fee to get Edna out of Holy prison — Nadine figured Edna could attend mass for free for the next ten years after paying that fine.

She'd also learned that the Karl May Festival had also withheld some pay — "as per standard contract procedure . . ." and promised that it would arrive six weeks after they got back to Canada. Which wasn't helpful at the moment. Nadine gritted her teeth and muttered under her breath: "This is because I'm a woman. No man would have been treated to so many broken contracts."

"There were the treaties," John murmured from the seat next to her.

"Then it's an Indian thing?" Nadine asked. John didn't reply; he had fallen back asleep. She watched him for a bit as he slept. He looked older than her. Grey was taking over his braids and she saw lines at the corner of his eyes. He never mentioned or acknowledged their conversation but she noticed that he seemed to be flirting with women in front of her. *Was it me?* She wondered for the thousandth time. Then she pushed her self-doubt away. A spade was a spade, no matter how much you might wish for a hoe. Although, technically, they were both used for digging.

She strained to see the top of Lucas's head, seats in front of her. His noggin was listing to the right, he was likely asleep, content that he would accomplish his mission once they reached Toronto. But no matter, Nadine had stuff to say. She unleashed herself and got up on unsteady legs.

She negotiated her way through sleeping bodies until she found herself next to his seat. "Lucas," she whispered. He didn't answer. She leaned closer. "Lucas?"

He started. "What the —" Then, recognizing Nadine, he fell back with relief. Then annoyance: "What's wrong now?"

"Nothing. I wanted to talk to you before we landed."

Nadine's mind went blank: why was she here? "Uh . . . I was wondering if you were wanting to get back to North Dakota or if you'd be flying to Saskatoon . . . that is if we get the money . . ."

Lucas looked thoughtful. "I'm hoping they found my car . . . so I would like to stop in Saskatoon and check in with the police . . . and hopefully not get arrested."

"But you're a cop?"

"That's true. And I'm not undercover anymore."

"I'll help you anyway I can." Nadine rested her hand on his leg.

"I can't wait to get back."

"To your family?"

"Yes, I miss my son. Been calling him but it's not the same. I want to be able to kiss his head before he goes to sleep. Funny how you miss things as simple as that."

"How's he been?"

"Getting spoiled by his grandparents." Lucas yawned and then looked at her. "You happy to get home?"

Nadine sighed. "It seems like we'll never get there." She was thinking of all the phone calls she'd have to make once they reached

Toronto. Everyone else could nap but she had to hit the ground running: track down the needed money, purchase the tickets, and find accommodations before they headed to Saskatoon.

"Tell you what, I'll find a place for us in Toronto," Lucas offered. "One less thing for you to think about."

"How are you going to do that?"

"I have friends."

Nadine waited for more explanation. Lucas closed his eyes instead of offering one. She stared at his head and wondered what his hair would feel like. Much like her own, the practical side of her brain told her. But the other, romantic side said that it would be like patting the nose of a horse, warm and soft at the same time. She held her hand at her side; her bravery was spent.

Sleep came easier after that.

EDNA

The flight over the Atlantic Ocean was long and Edna sat next to a middle-aged woman with bad hair and bad breath who complained about the food, the slowness of the stewardesses, the cologne on the man in the seat in front of them, the lack of legroom, the pilot's strange accent, and on and on. She completed her complaints with: "Not since the *Titanic* has such a terrible trip been taken."

"Seems okay to me." Edna shrugged. "At least no one was taken hostage."

The woman gave her a strange look.

In the airport, Edna could feel that they were back in Canada. Canadian people were slightly less blonde than Swedes though much less brunette than Italians and certainly not as forceful as Germans. Canadians tended to have soft, stupid looks on their faces that she had missed very much. She had even missed that look of guarded contempt when she opened her mouth and her rez accent popped out. You could trust Canadian prejudice; it was as predictable as rain in the spring. Those European whites were so damned confusing, what with the Swedes' total ignorance, the Germans' desire to imitate, and the Romans' love that seemed to be stuck in the 1800s.

The tour gathered their things together in the airport and then went through their wallets again looking for cab fare. They were a sorry sight, no doubt, a bunch of Indians pooling their cash together to get from point A to point B.

"I can call my dad," Desiree offered. "He'd send cash right away."

"No, no!" Nadine and John were quick to jump in. "We're getting money."

And how were they going to accomplish that? Edna wondered. They were both being rather closemouthed. She decided not to worry about it.

She worried a little bit when they pulled up at their hotel. It had the squalid look of a hotel bar in a Saskatchewan small-town. The entire hotel was dirty, as if someone had wiped their muddy boots on it and it made you wonder — how did other buildings stay so clean? The garbage cans were right next to the front door and fat, happy flies buzzed nearby.

"Gross," Desiree muttered, her hand over her mouth and nose.

Edna looked at Nadine.

"Don't look at me," Nadine said. "We got these rooms through Lucas."

Lucas checked them into their rooms. He looked apologetic. "There's a disco on top of the building," he offered.

Desiree visibly lightened. "Really? We should go!" She punched John in the shoulder. "You want to dance, right?"

"I've done enough dancing for a lifetime, I think," John said.

"Oh, c'mon. It'll be fun. It's our last night."

Edna had heard those words often enough. "It's our last night, our last day, our last hour, etc." It was meant to spur you onto behaviour that you normally wouldn't bother with because you were running out of time — like a fifty-percent sale on time.

"Sure, let's check it out," Edna said.

Desiree turned and looked at her, wide-eyed. Lucas laughed and John actually gasped.

"What? I never said I was against dancing. Jes not a fan of all of your Indian dancing." Edna pushed through the doors.

They were inside the elevators when Lucas turned to Nadine. "Can you come to my room in ten minutes?"

Everyone in the elevator went silent. They passed two more floors before Desiree finally giggled. Edna elbowed her. If that nervous woman was finally getting some attention, then Edna didn't want anyone standing in her way.

NADINE

She could feel her heart beating as she stood in front of his door. She raised her fist and then let it fall to her side. She turned from the door and walked down the hallway. Maybe she should have called first? *But he asked me to come to his room — there's no misunderstanding that!*

She turned back. But couldn't move forward.

Maybe she should get him to come to her room, that way she'd be in the power position. But then this would all take longer — the night wasn't young and neither was she — and what if he didn't come? What if he was kidnapped on the way to her room (he was susceptible to being locked up after all).

And she hadn't been having the best luck this trip. And what did he want? He seemed like a noble guy so he wasn't only after sex, was he? Considering the size of his arms and chest, Nadine might be open to negotiating the terms of their agreement.

She turned and padded to his room on green and white carpet festooned with splatters of mud, or what appeared to be mud anyway. Each step felt like she was walking to her death. Under her breath, she sang: *Swing low, sweet chariot* — was a slave song really appropriate? Maybe. She was a slave to her hormones after all.

291

Lucas opened the door after one knock, showing her that he'd been waiting for her. *He did want her!* Then he grabbed her arm and yanked her in the room.

"What the hell!" she sputtered.

He pulled her close and whispered into her face: "Did you contact him?"

"Who?"

"Ernest Standing Bull, the Chief of the National Indian Brotherhood."

"Oh yeah, he's going to meet us at the disco tonight." Nadine had a sinking feeling. "Are you going to arrest him?"

Lucas said nothing.

"Lucas! You can't arrest him. He's supposed to give us money for the trip home."

"He stole a valuable Indian artifact and then attempted to sell it."

"Nobody's perfect. Besides you have the artifact, if I'm not mistaken, right?"

Lucas nodded.

"Then that's that. Leave him alone. Do you even know what the Americans would do to him?"

"He'd go to prison."

"There you go. There's enough brown people in prison already. Personally I think it's great that we have a Chief with some get-up-and-go."

"You admire him then, a thief?"

"I don't even know Ernest. But I know how hard it is to get something off the ground, nurture it and see it grow. This Brotherhood might be the first chance us Indians have had to be heard. If you arrest this Chief, then it'll tar us all. You know how it is — one of us does wrong, we all do wrong." How was he not seeing this? Sometimes these "noble" guys were a pain in the ass.

"I have to arrest him. It's my job."

Nadine plopped down on his bed in exasperation. "Can you at least wait until I get some cash from him?"

"Maybe."

There was a knock on the door.

"Who is it?" Lucas asked.

"John."

He opened the door and John walked in and closed the door behind him.

"You can't arrest Chief Ernest," John said.

John was a quick one after all, Nadine thought with some pride. "I told him that. He's not going to."

"Good to hear." John sat on the bed next to her. He sunk in quite a bit and had to fight to regain his balance. He stood back up.

"I didn't say that," Lucas protested.

"Well, he won't until I get some cash out of him," Nadine explained.

Both men frowned at her.

"I'm getting pretty sick of everyone judging me — for being practical."

"Is this about having to come home with the case solved?" John asked.

Lucas side-eyed him. "It's about doing the job I was sent to do. Find Chief Crazyhorse's choker, return it to the Museum of North Dakota, and arrest the thief."

"You don't know if Chief Ernest is the one who stole it and I guarantee you he ain't gonna tell you. You need to relax on that part," John suggested.

"He'll tell me."

"He won't," John said agreeably. "He will literally make a federal case out of it. Make youse look bad. And again, at the end of the day, you won't have an answer. It seems to me that the best way to solve this case is to explain that the thief got away. As thieves do sometimes."

"I see," said Lucas.

Nadine smiled. "They sure do. And then go on to do good things with their lives. Damn good things."

"Weren't you an old thief?" John poked her in the side. "I forgot about that. Nadine and her wild days."

Lucas kept his lips firm. But Nadine could tell they were having an influence.

She took a deep breath. "John, can you come back later? I need to talk to Lucas about something . . . private."

John's eyes went wide and he struggled to get up in a hurry.

Lucas blocked him before John could get to the door. "What . . . private?"

Nadine took a deep breath and said: "I love you." Shit, she rushed it. And, worse, in front of John.

Lucas looked at her in bewilderment. "But I'm gay."

Nadine's mouth fell open. Then she closed it. Opened it again. She didn't seem to be getting any air so John reached over and slapped her on the back. She let out a squeak.

"I thought I told you," Lucas said.

"You most certainly did not —" she sputtered.

"But I was with Rolf when we were in Stockholm — remember?"

Nadine did have a memory of both of them in robes in the dining room but she thought they had woken at the same time. The matching robes had been weird.

"It wasn't clear," Nadine said.

"I'm sorry, Nadine. You're a great person, the strongest woman I've ever met. And you'd be a great partner for any man, but not me."

"How is it that you're gay and John's gay — is everyone gay?"

"I'm not . . ." But John's voice was so soft, it would have taken a hearing aid turned up high to pick up his whisper.

"When you asked me here, I thought — hoped — it's the last night so . . ." Nadine put her head into the mantle. "I'm so embarrassed," she muttered into the white wood. "Having the shits for five days straight was better than this."

"Sorry. I didn't mean to lead you on." Lucas patted her on the shoulder as Nadine let go of ten years of hope, daydreams, and fantasies of holding hands with a tall strong Native man on one side and a tiny trusting hand on the other side.

She'd never been a crybaby her entire life but at this moment she sobbed like she believed these tears held the cure to cancer or something.

JOHN

John's legs were unsteady, so he leaned against the dresser as Nadine made strangled noises. John wished that he could leap the few feet through the door and be outside this room in one bound. *And then I'll never go into another person's room for as long as I live.* He wanted to run but knew this would draw more attention to himself so he willed himself to be still.

Nadine began to sob heavier.

Lucas tried again. "You'll meet someone, Nadine."

The volcano erupted. "I WASTED MY LIFE WAITING FOR HIM!" Nadine pointed at John and he felt like he'd been hit by a torpedo. For the second time this week, John made a quick decision — he would never leave his reserve for the rest of his life. He'd get his brother to bring groceries to him; Amos certainly owed him that.

"Oh," Lucas said stupidly.

"Yes, oh! Oh! That's all you have to say. Oh! What about you?" Nadine turned on John. "You don't remember dancing with me? You don't remember holding me close and telling me to wait?"

John shook his head. "Maybe you mistook me for my brother Amos?"

"Did John actually tell you to wait — or did you think that he meant that?"

Nadine pursed her lips. "I guess I should have gotten it in writing." She wiped her eyes, glared at John and stalked to the door. Before leaving she turned and looked at John. "I would have given you strong sons." The door slammed behind her. Dust filled the air.

Lucas and John both exhaled.

"That pony sure knows where to kick," Lucas said.

John nodded. He'd always wanted a son.

"It's a bad deal, isn't it?" Lucas said.

John stared at him.

"You're not ready to talk about it. I dig it. Took me a long time too."

But you're younger than me . . .

"If you keep waiting for the right moment, it'll never come."

"I'm not that way," John said.

"I used to tell myself that too. I like men, sometimes." Lucas laughed. "Then it turned out that I liked them often."

"It's nobody's business."

"You're right. World ain't gonna stop turning because you decide not to jump on."

In the hallway, John looked for exits, deciding that it was a good time to run ten kilometres screaming at the top of his lungs.

Instead he took the stairs to the ground floor and found his way to a liquor store.

CHAPTER 15

EDNA

The music was too loud. Desiree kept leaning in to yell something in her ear and Edna would stupidly reply, "What?" Edna could tell that the young woman was having a good time, with her sparkly eyes and perma-grin. Edna wasn't feeling too shabby herself. She'd borrowed a skirt from her niece and it was the shortest thing she'd worn since she was fifteen years old. It hit right at her knee and she felt like she was naked. But it made sense because it was godawful hot in the place.

Edna had never seen so many different colours of people, dancing, all smushed together on the dance floor. Desiree handed her a drink. "Cool you off. Your face is red."

Edna took a sip. She tasted some type of alcohol but the ice was too tempting to resist.

Desiree elbowed her and pointed to the left. John was stumbling towards them.

"Hello there," he drawled, with a goofy grin and he patted Desiree on the head.

Desiree laughed. "Wow, you're hammered."

"Not at all," John said. "Not at all."

He looked at Edna. "You're so short. And your hair is short. You can't dance with short hair."

Edna shrugged. "Well, I did."

"You sure did." He patted her on the head too. "You're a good lady."

"I'm a grouch."

"You're a grouch, but you're a good lady. Never had to worry about you."

"Well, I'm glad."

Desiree was heading to the dance floor with a young black guy. Edna had never talked to a black person in her life. She'd seen them, in the city, but never had a reason to talk to one. She'd always been curious though. Maybe the tour could take them to more places like that next time.

"Would you judge me?" John asked.

"For what?" Edna asked.

"For being different. Doesn't your God say something about that? Like thou shalt not be different."

Edna laughed. He really was drunk. "Never read that part."

"It's in there."

"You're not supposed to read it literally. You're supposed to read it for guidance. God speaks to you through the Bible, you only have to listen." And sometimes he speaks to you through a child's smile, a sunrise, music, or a glance, she wanted to add but knew it would be lost on him in this state. "Maybe you should go to church sometime."

John waved her off. "You like me, right?"

Edna nodded, bracing herself for an awkward moment. He wasn't her type but she supposed some women might find him attractive. And she'd never been attracted to men with alcohol on their breath.

"Okay, that's good." John stumbled away.

Edna had to smile. Across the dance floor, she spotted Nadine leaning against the bar, looking irritated. She always looked irritated but Edna figured she'd be more relaxed now that the tour was over (sort of, they still had to find their way home. Not that Edna was that concerned; her brother, Devon, would buy them tickets the second Desiree asked).

Nadine was talking to someone, rather heatedly from what Edna could see. It was that big handsome Chief — what was his name again? Oh yes, Ernest Standing Bull. She spotted Lucas heading towards them, all in a hurry. (Honestly, didn't these people know how to relax?)

A good song came on then and Edna headed to the dance floor. A time to praise, a time to sing, a time to dance. That was in the Bible too.

NADINE

"Then they wouldn't pay us on time because they claimed that we committed to ten shows and I did not commit to that many — I mean maybe if they had asked months ago, then I would have built it into the tour but they didn't, and to ask at the last minute?! It threw everything off. Then they wouldn't pay. If that little girl hadn't been good at trick-riding —"

"Trick-riding?" Ernest looked bewildered.

"Horse tricks, on-off, handstands, that sort of thing, well, they paid her good for that and that helped but then we lost a day — oh and that's where we lost that young guy — Shane. Nobody told me but he stayed there because he has a criminal record here so maybe that was for the best, technically he was an extra dancer —"

"Criminal record?"

"Nothing serious, a few assaults. He's a young guy, needs to grow up is all. I didn't mind him honestly. A lot of my dancers come to me when they're a little rough around the edges —"

Ernest held up his hand. "It sounds like you did a good job."

Nadine stared at him. "I guess I did. Except that we went over budget. And I lost one Indian."

"I've seen Chiefs conferences where we lost half the Chiefs in two days. And staying on budget?" He laughed. "This is a huge success in my estimation." He smiled broadly.

Nadine didn't know where to look. She wanted to stare at his lips where all these good words were coming from, these words that made her glow. But she couldn't because she suddenly felt like a fish on a hook, all wriggly and slippery and scared as hell.

"Drink?"

"Orange juice." Her voice was squeaky. "Thank you," she added with a bit more bass.

Ernest turned towards the bar. At that moment, Lucas grabbed his arms from behind. "You're under arrest for the theft —"

"Oh, for fuck sakes, Lucas!" Nadine karate-chopped Lucas's arms. He dropped Ernest's, probably from surprise. "We talked about this."

Lucas glared at her. "Law's the law. You can't interfere with the law."

"Depends on what law you're talking about. Myself, I follow the law of the Nehewin." Ernest had turned around. "Who are you?"

"I work for the FBI. I'm their Native American Indian consultant."

"You're not even a real cop?" Nadine asked.

"I've got authority." He showed his badge.

"But no gun?" Ernest asked.

"I've got a gun. I don't need it, right now."

"So do half the yahoos in Alabama, that don't mean they can bring them to Canada and throw their weight around," Ernest replied. He handed an orange juice to Nadine, then took a sip of his own drink.

"Where'd you get it anyway?" Lucas asked. "It was stolen from the Museum of North Dakota."

Ernest looked Lucas up and down. "I bet you could have found the answer to that better in North Dakota. It was given to me when I was down at the Gathering of Nations in Albuquerque. Bunch of Chiefs got together and they asked me to pass it on to the buyer. If I'd known it was illegal . . . I'd probably still have agreed to do it. Who do you think Crazyhorse would rather see benefit — his own people or some white museum?"

"That's not the point — what if you were some opportunist, a thief?"

"Crazyhorse fought against the people taking his land, murdering his people and destroying their way of life — for some reason those aren't considered crimes in the white world. What the hell do I care if you think I'm a thief." Ernest sighed. "We have so much to do, the money that this would have brought us, only a drop in the bucket."

Nadine looked at Lucas. She didn't know him well (had certainly missed a huge part of his character!) but she did know when he was embarrassed. She tried to catch his eye. "Lucas, why don't you go check on the others? I've got to talk to Chief Ernest about some last-minute details."

Lucas looked grateful and nodded. Giant that he was, he still looked forlorn as he walked away.

"Strange how they turn our best ones against us," Ernest said.

Nadine nodded. "They never stop taking."

"You happy to be heading home?"

Nadine smiled. "I've been enjoying the trip. Will be tough to get used to the old routine."

"No moss growing on you." Ernest gave a half-smile and a dimple slipped through.

Nadine felt that fish-feeling coming on again, her bones felt all floaty and she leaned on the bar for support. It was going to be tough to discuss business with this one.

JOHN

John knew he was less than an hour from the spins, which would be quickly followed by a trip to the toilet to make an offering to the drunk gods and then he'd probably pass out. Hopefully in his bed, but he didn't know if he'd be able to make it (even though it was just an elevator ride). Smart of Lucas to put them in a hotel with a bar in it. John made a mental note to always stay in hotels with bars in them.

A young woman sidled up next to him so close John could feel her body heat. He turned slowly and looked at her: she was thin like a ballet dancer and had her hair piled up high on top of her head, making her look even more like an off-duty ballerina.

"Hey Chief," she said in a husky voice.

He said nothing, mostly because he wasn't sure of what would come out of his mouth at this point.

"Me and my boyfriend have been watching you all night." She gestured at a tall, slim, Asian guy a few feet away.

The Asian guy nodded at John and smiled. He had a beautiful smile.

John looked back at the girl.

"If you're up for it — we could all hang out."

Like go for coffee? Hit an all-night diner? Normally John could eat at any time but his stomach wouldn't tolerate anything like that right now.

He shook his head.

She moved closer and put her hand on his back. "Wow, you're so muscular. I've never been with an Indian before, like an Indian in the movies Indian. Kinda been a dream of mine."

Her hand was moving across his back and then to his front getting kind of close to — John jumped to the right. He grabbed her hand and because disappointment was all over her pretty face, he blurted out: "I can't. I'm in love with someone."

The words were out of his mouth before he knew he was saying them.

She looked confused. "Oh."

John looked at her hand and then brought it up to his lips. "You look like a dancer out of Swan Lake." This was a ballet he'd taken his mom to in Regina a couple years before. Stopped her from nagging him about never going anywhere. Sitting next to his mom in the Centre of the Arts, John felt something inside of him leaping like those dancers.

She smiled shyly.

"I gotta go. Or I'm gonna puke all over myself."

He grabbed his beer and drank the rest of it down (no sense in wasting). Lucas walked by, looking all kinds of pissed off, and John grabbed his arm and steered him in the direction of the ballerina and her handsome boyfriend. Holding in the slurs as best he could, he said: "Hey there, Luke, got a couple of people for you to meet."

John didn't have to turn around to see the girl's eyes light up.

Day 15

Saskatoon, Saskatchewan

EDNA

We flew out of Toronto at one in the afternoon, which was perfect because most of us had had a long night. We said goodbye to NIB *Chief Ernest Standing Bull who had followed us to the airport. Such a nice man, he gave each of us an eagle feather. He said it represented our role as messengers for the Nehewin culture, and the Hunkpapa, I added, as I remembered that Lucas Pretends Eagle is from the Dakotas. On our flight to Saskatoon, I thought about how important that was. We brought our culture across the ocean. If not for us, many people might think Indians are all dead, killed by that monias John Wayne.*

At the Saskatoon Airport, our families greeted us. It was wonderful to see them but also sad to say goodbye to our troupe members. We said goodbye to Nadine Redcloud who was already organizing the next tour of the Prairie Chicken Dance Troupe. She hopes that her other dancers will be raring to start rehearsing and get on the road now that powwow season is in full swing. It seems like the ideal way to keep young people busy. Our American member, Lucas Pretends Eagle, was happy to see his car in the airport parking lot. It had been stolen by the other Lucas Pretends Eagle (long story). As my grandfather used to say, the things we love always find their way home. Mr. Pretends Eagle was planning to drive Nadine home; he says that he wants to see her dance troupe.

John Greyeyes said a quick goodbye as he headed off to check on his horses and dog. He told me that this was his first trip ever using a passport. He seems to have been bitten by the travel bug though because before he left the airport, he asked about the price of a trip to Sweden. Desiree and I were greeted at the airport by my brother, Chief Devon Shield. We had a nice trip to the Kentucky Fried Chicken village to celebrate our return. But I can see another goodbye coming in my future. Desiree said that she will be leaving home to start university in the fall. She said she learned a lot from this trip. Like that she wants a good job so that she'll never be stuck at an airport turning her pockets inside out to get home.

I'm glad that we got home in time to see the rest of the summer. The saskatoons are all gone but I'll be heading to the bush to catch the last of the chokecherries.

Acknowledgements

I have never written any acknowledgements for my previous three books. I felt like it was something that real writers did and I was not quite that. Or that it made me seem like I thought so much of myself that I expected the reader to stick around past the last page. But in truth, there is a lot of help that goes into writing a book and it is important to acknowledge the village. I want to thank my editor, Debbie Willis, for her patience, kindness, and understanding. It's amazing how much of a connection you can build with a person you have never met in person. I want to thank my agent, Stephanie Sinclair, for taking a chance on me. I want to thank Alicia Elliott for her generosity — I asked her for a reference to her agent and she introduced me the same day.

I want to thank the real Lucas Pretends Eagle for lending me his wonderful name. Yet another person I have never met in person but who has supported me over the years.

When I was a little girl dreaming of my goals, my great uncle Ed used to listen to me and he would always say, "Go on, go on." The last few years have been difficult ones but I kept going with the love and support of an amazing group of people: Mary, Kalina, Denise, Eleanore, Alicia, Bradlee, Kelly, Kristin and Kelley Jo — thank you for listening and pulling me through.

And of course, thank you to Vincent for giving mommy ten minutes every day of writing time and for giving me the sweetest smiles to look up at when writing time was done.

Dawn Dumont is from the Okanese Cree Nation, located in southern Saskatchewan. She is the award-winning writer of *Nobody Cries at Bingo, Rose's Run* and *Glass Beads*. Dawn is a keynote speaker, comedian and humourist for *Eaglefeather News* and the *Saskatoon StarPhoenix*.